THE
CONFECTIONER'S
GUILD

D1416919

CLAIRE LUANA

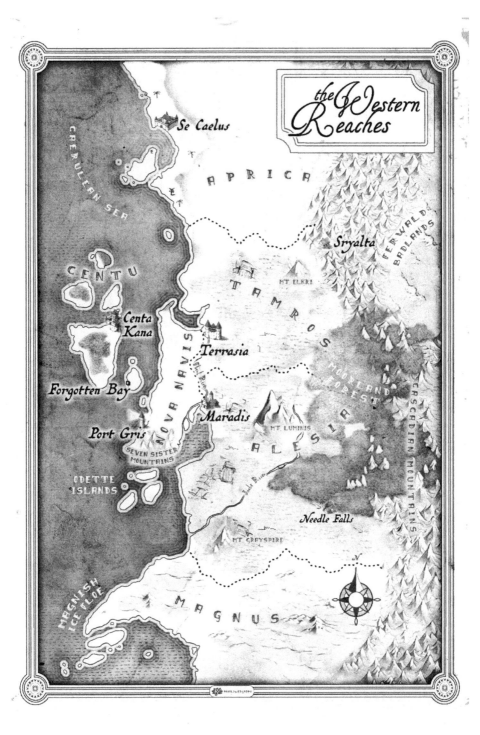

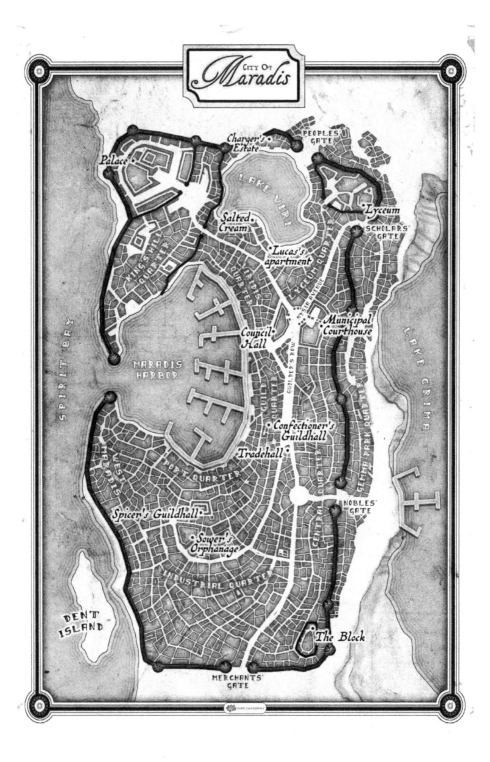

CHAPTER 1

Wren had learned early on that trouble comes in all sorts of packages. Even vanilla ones with rose petal frosting.

"Tell me about these cupcakes," a cold voice demanded from the storefront.

Wren froze on her stool, her ears perked to listen, the cocoa bean she held in her hand forgotten.

"What would you like to know?" asked Master Oldrick, his tone light but wary.

"Everything."

Wren set down her husking knife on the worktable with the rest of the cracked beans, wiping her hands on her streaked apron. She wanted a look at this customer. She crept across the worn tiles of the kitchen and slowly slid open one of the doors leading to the display case in the front room of Master Oldrick's confectionery shop. A wave of cold air hit her, the ice that lined the case chilling her face as well as the chocolates. It was a blessed respite from the stickiness of the kitchen, where the air hung limp in August's hot breath.

Master Oldrick was babbling about the cupcakes now, clearly unsure of the nature of the man's interest. "True, cupcakes are the territory of the Baker's Guild, but I've some friends in that guild, and they don't mind us having a little fun with the cupcakes. It's the frosting that sets ours apart. Pure confectional art. The frosting on this one's so like a rose that you can practically smell its perfume. The ladies love them—they fly off the shelves."

The customer was a stranger, but the cupcake in his hand was not. It was one of Wren's. Only she could pipe the frosting just right, each petal like a rosy-hued sunset. Master Oldrick's arthritis was far too bad for him to perform such delicate work, and the other apprentices, Tate and Hazel, were all right for rolling truffle balls and stirring caramel, but they lacked her steady hand with a piping bag, despite being a few months younger than her sixteen years. Each of those cupcakes had taken her ten minutes to decorate, ten minutes scrunched over the countertop as beads of sweat dribbled down her knees and elbows.

Master Oldrick was continuing his detailed exposition of the cupcakes' finer features, discussing the third-generation ownership of the mill they purchased flour from, the fine sugar imported from Aprica, the fresh cream skimmed off the milk of dairy cows who enjoyed only the finest pastureland below the foothills of Mount Luminis.

The customer held up a hand and Master Oldrick fell silent. Wren narrowed her eyes. Who was this man, and what was his interest in the cupcakes?

"Who made the cupcakes?" the man demanded.

"Ahh," Master Oldrick said nervously. "My apprentice Wren," he said, rubbing his neck with a gnarled hand. His gaze flicked to the far display case, where Wren peeked out between the rows of caramels and chocolate chews.

The man turned and his eyes, steely blue above the high collar of his navy coat, met hers. "I'll speak with this Wren."

"I'll fetch her," Master Oldrick said with a bob of his head.

Wren stood and slammed the door shut, her mind whirring. Despite the oppressive heat of the late afternoon, her body had gone cold.

Master Oldrick's hands were shaking as he came into the kitchen.

"What does he want?" she hissed. "Who is he?"

"I don't know," Master Oldrick said. "But he has a stern way about him. Was there something wrong with the cupcakes? Could the ingredients have spoiled?"

"No!" she said, affronted. Master Oldrick knew the quality of her work was her only currency in this world. "I would never let such a thing happen."

"I know." He sighed. "You're the best apprentice I've ever had, woman or no."

She rolled her eyes. It wasn't the first time she'd heard such antiquated views from Oldrick. She found it best to ignore them.

"I'll stand by your work," he continued. "Now don't keep the man waiting."

Wren straightened her stained apron and attempted to smooth the frizzy auburn halo that wreathed her head in this humidity. She marched into the front of the shop, back straight, head high.

"You asked for me, sir?" she said, getting her first proper look at the customer. He was a tall, thin man with a horsey face topped with thick, dark brows that threatened to join as one. He had an impressive shock of black hair brushed to one side in a fashion that managed to look both windswept and carefully manicured. His slender fingers held her exquisite cupcake before her, as if he were offering her a rose.

His examination of her was as obvious as her scrutiny of him no doubt had been. What did he see? Milky pale skin, elfin features, a small mouth puckered in nervousness? From the slight sneer of his lip, it appeared he found her wanting.

"Did you make this cupcake?" That cold voice again.

She shivered involuntarily. "Yes. Why?"

He ignored her question. "I need you to come with me."

"What? Where?" Wren took a step back.

He put the cupcake back in its tasteful pink-and-white-striped box before deftly retying the white ribbon in a perfect bow. And then, task complete, he came around the counter in two strides, grasping her elbow.

"Master Oldrick!" Wren cried. She struggled against his iron grip, panic rising through her like a pot left to boil.

Master Oldrick bustled through the swinging doors. "What's this? No customers behind the counter."

"He's trying to take me somewhere," Wren explained, trying to draw her master's attention to the more pressing issue at hand.

"Now, sir, what's this all about?" asked Oldrick.

"Guild business," the man said.

"I'm her master; she's got no business with the Guild that doesn't concern me. Is she in some kind of trouble?" Master Oldrick asked. "I'm sure whatever it is, we can come to terms."

The man readjusted his fingers on Wren's arm, tightening his clammy grip. With his other hand, he pulled a card from his pocket. "I am Grandmaster Callidus of the Confectioner's Guild. I set the terms. And this girl is coming with me."

Wren glowered at the grandmaster from across the jostling coach, trying to keep the embers of fear tamped down with the weight of her anger. It was a losing battle. She rubbed her damp palms on her dress, curling her fingers into the thin fabric to still her shaking hands. Whatever was going on, it couldn't be good.

"Where are we going?" she asked for the third time.

For the third time, he looked at her with a contemptuous flick of his gaze before his icy stare returned to the window.

Despite her unanswered questions, Wren had been keeping a close eye past the lace curtains of the carriage and had a strong suspicion of their destination. As they turned off the packed dirt road onto the smooth granite stones of the Maradis town's center, her prediction was confirmed: The Confectioner's Guildhall. Just visible in the distance, nine guildhalls sat like petulant children at the knee of their mother, the gray behemoth Tradehouse where the guilds did business with each other and the rest of the city. The Confectioner's Guildhall was a massive marble monolith resting in the place of honor at the Tradehouse's right hand and was arguably the most magnificent structure of the impressive specimens that lined Guilder's Row.

The carriage came to a stop in front of the steps of the Guildhall and the coachman opened the door. Callidus swept out before her and quickly resumed his position as her captor, grasping her arm as soon as she cleared the steps. It was clear he didn't intend to let her escape. Wren's stomach flipped. What was there to escape from?

Wren struggled up the towering steps of the Guildhall, scraping her shins as Callidus pulled her up. Five steps for the five levels of the Guild: apprentice, journeyman, artisan, master, and grandmaster. Some designer had been so intent on his symbolism that he had thrown practicality straight out the window.

As servants in the Guild's brown and gold livery opened the wide wooden doors before them, Wren found herself pulled through the antechamber of the Guildhall for the second time in her life. And for the second time, she found herself wishing she had something better to wear.

Her first glimpse of the Guildhall had been four years ago. That time, it had been Master Oldrick's fat fingers gripping the flesh of her arm. She'd been a grimy orphan, fresh off the streets of Maradis.

It had started innocently enough. She had been rifling through the trash in the alley behind his shop and had found a worn piping bag, mostly empty save for a dollop of shimmering green frosting. Any other street kid would have squirted the whole bag of sugar into their mouth, but the frosting had called to her. She knew such an act would be a waste, a sacrilege. Crouched under the eaves of the building to keep warm, she had grasped the smooth parchment paper of the bag and decorated the hard shell of the snowbank with a pattern of ivy leaves. The leaves had sparkled against the snow in the low light of the alley, mesmerizing her, pulling her into a daydream where she was surrounded by lush green foliage rather than frozen garbage.

Master Oldrick had woken her with a kick in the dim gray morning, but as she'd scrambled away down the alley, he'd called to her. "Stop!"

She'd kept running.

"I'll feed you!" he'd called.

She had frozen, looking over one shoulder, her gnawing stomach compelling her to turn around. He had fed her half a loaf of warm bread smeared with butter and jam, along with a glass of sweet milk. Once she had eaten, he'd made her scrub her hands in scalding water until they'd turned pink and had given her an audition. Wren had swirled ganache, puffed powdered sugar, drizzled white chocolate and piped more frosting. When she had tried to sneak a taste of the ganache, Master Oldrick had whacked her hand so hard with a wooden spoon that she'd felt the vibrations in her teeth.

"Never. Ever. Eat. The. Confections," he'd said.

But despite her faux pas, she had passed his test. Because that afternoon, he had marched her, dressed in a tattered woolen smock, into the marble cavern of the Confectioner's Guildhall. And she had become his apprentice.

The interior of the Guildhall looked exactly the same as it had four years ago, but for the exchange of one sour-faced captor for another. The walls were made of creamy veined marble, and the tall pillars around the circular antechamber rose to form a massive dome coated in gold filigree. A magnificent crystal chandelier hung from the dome, dusting the room with sparkles of sugary light.

Wren eyed Callidus sideways as she struggled to match his pace. Guildmembers seemed to part before him as he walked, nodding deferentially and sidestepping out of his way. He didn't acknowledge any of them with so much as a smile or nod in return. So he *was* someone important. And, Wren decided, he was most definitely an ass.

They ascended a twisting staircase at the far end of the antechamber, heading towards the upper floors. Where were they going? She could ask Callidus, but she didn't want to give him the satisfaction of knowing that his silent treatment was flustering her. He probably wouldn't tell her, anyway.

They continued up two more levels until they reached a floor that was hushed and empty. Two guards in brown and gold flanked the top of the stair, their golden spears resting on the polished parquet floor. Their uniforms bore the Guild's symbol on the breast, a golden whisk and spoon crossed like the letter "X."

Wren's heart hammered in her chest as they came to a halt before a carved mahogany door. Why had she been summoned here? Was she being kicked out of the Guild? Had there been something wrong with the cupcakes? They were so deep in the Guildhall, if she screamed now, would anyone hear her?

Callidus released her arm and rapped on the door three times with his pale knuckles.

CHAPTER 2

The door swung open and Wren almost laughed in relief at the sight. A short ruddy man with a rotund belly and a thick head of snowy white hair stood before her. He reminded her of nothing so much as one of her cupcakes, the red velvet kind sprinkled with coconut shavings.

"Come in, come in," he said, waving them into the room enthusiastically. He wore a crisp shirt with the sleeves rolled up, revealing substantial forearms covered with downy white hair. As she passed him, she caught a whiff of butterscotch.

"Have a seat, my dear. Have a seat," he repeated, motioning to one of the two studded leather chairs that sat before his huge desk. Not at all the dungeon she had expected—the room was bright and cheerful, with tall windows letting in streams of sluggish summer sun.

Wren sat, smoothing her faded cotton dress over her knees.

"Callidus, feel free to sit," the man said, motioning to the other chair.

She shied away from it involuntarily.

"I'll stand," Callidus replied, leaning against a bookshelf by the door.

"Of course you will." The man paused for a moment. "I hope Callidus didn't scare you too terribly. He lacks something of a bedside manner."

Wren laughed, a forced bark that belied her nervousness. "He was… mysterious," she admitted, thinking it best not to antagonize him.

"Well, let's put the mystery to an end. I am Guildmaster Kasper, Head of the Confectioner's Guild. And you are?"

"Wren," she said. "Wren Confectioner," she added, in the Alesian style. In the country of Alesia, a guildmember who didn't wish to keep their father's surname, or who didn't know their father's name, could take the name of their craft as their surname.

"It's a delight to meet you, Wren," Kasper said. "Did Callidus explain why we summoned you?"

"No."

"Of course not." He pursed his lips. "You're no doubt wondering why you're here. Callidus, where are those cupcakes?"

Callidus dropped the box on the desk between them before resuming his statue-like pose against the bookcase.

"Excellent," Kasper said, opening the box. He removed one of the cupcakes and turned it before him, admiring it from various angles. "These are magnificent, my dear. I've known masters who couldn't make such masterpieces. You're what, an artisan?"

"Apprentice, guildmaster."

"Apprentice!" his brown eyes flew open. "For how long?"

"Four years, guildmaster."

"Four years!" He harrumphed. "Outrageous. You could cook circles around some of my best guildmembers. Your master will be hearing from me."

"Thank you, guildmaster," she said, keeping the vindicated smile from her face. She knew Master Oldrick had been lying about her not being ready for a promotion within the Guild, she just hadn't figured out what to do about it. Oldrick wasn't a bad man—only greedy. And promoting her meant paying her higher wages.

"I can tell you have a gift for confections. Such gifts are rare, even within the Guild," Kasper said. His eyes gleamed in the sunlight as he studied her, setting the cupcake before her. "You've sampled your confections, haven't you?"

She shook her head. "Master Oldrick forbids it." More for the customers. And the cash register.

Guildmaster Kasper sputtered, slapping his hand on the desk. "This Oldrick fellow, I like him less and less! How do you make chocolate if you don't taste it?"

"I follow the recipe. And get it right the first time." No need to mention that she had stolen a taste or two when Oldrick wasn't looking.

"Quite right, quite right. I suppose that explains how skinny you are. No respectable confectioner should be skinny!" He slapped the girth of his stomach and laughed, a warm husky sound. "Confections are what make the world go 'round, don't you agree?"

Wren cracked a smile despite herself. His enthusiasm was infectious. "The world would be a happier place if that were true."

"But it *is* true," he said, as if he had a secret he couldn't wait to share. Kasper reached in the breast pocket of his shirt and pulled out a heavy gold coin. It was an Alesian gold crown, more money than Wren made in a year. He handed it to her.

Wren cradled it reverently. "What's this for?"

"Flip it," he said. "If you get heads, you can keep it."

Sending a prayer up to the gods, she flipped and caught it, slapping it on the back of her other hand. The stately profile of Mount Luminis gleamed on the surface. Tails. Trying to still her disappointment, she put the crown back on the desk.

"Bad luck," he said, the corners of his eyes crinkling in a smile. "Eat the cupcake. You'll feel better. In fact, I think I'll have one myself."

She looked at him, unsure of his game. But the cupcake did look good, and she had missed lunch today, what with the bustle of the shop. He was already unwrapping his own, taking a monstrous bite that enveloped half the cupcake in one go. She shrugged and retrieved hers, unwrapping the lace around its base.

The first bite was the best. The sweet vanilla flavor of the fluffy cupcake mingled with the silky sugar of the frosting, hitting her taste buds like a cotton candy cloud. She closed her eyes as she chewed, trying to commit the pleasure of the moment to memory. She opened her eyes and found Kasper watching her with an amused expression on his face.

"Ehts gud," she admitted around the bite of cupcake. Her body buzzed pleasantly as she swallowed.

"Yes, it is," he said, licking frosting off his fingers.

She set the rest of the cupcake on its wrapper on the desk. "It seems a shame to eat it," she said. "It's so pretty. I love making those."

"And your love comes through in every bite," Kasper said. He tossed the coin back to her. "Fancy another go?"

She shrugged and flipped the coin, thinking that this was very unlike how she imagined this meeting would go. When she turned the coin over she laughed with delight. The face of the former King Leon shined up at her. "Heads!"

"I guess your luck has changed," Kasper said, as pleased as she.

Callidus made an exasperated noise against the wall.

"Best two out of three?" Kasper asked.

"No, thank you," she said, clutching the coin in her sweaty palm, dreaming about what she could do with the money. A new dress that wasn't three inches too short. An oil lamp for her room, rather than the stubby candles she had been using. A new palette knife without the wobbly handle of her current model.

"Go ahead," said Kasper. "You can keep the crown even if you lose. Humor me."

Wondering if it was a trap, Wren nevertheless did as she was told, flipping the coin once again.

"Heads!" she said.

"Try again."

Another toss.

"Heads!"

"One more time."

She tossed again.

"Heads," she said, shaking her head in amazement.

"What if I asked you to throw tails," he said.

Getting into it now, she tossed the coin again and hit tails. Not once, but three more times.

"I think you get the point," he said.

She looked at him in amazement. "Is the coin… enchanted?"

"No, my dear. *You* are enchanted."

"What?" She shook her head, confused. "Trust me, I'm about the least lucky person in the city of Maradis."

"You *were* the least lucky person."

"Get to the point, man. I've got places to be," Callidus growled from his place at the bookshelf.

"Don't begrudge me a bit of theatrics," Kasper said. "It's not every day I get to reveal one of our biggest secrets to a new initiate."

Callidus huffed, and Wren looked back and forth between them. She was completely lost now.

Kasper stood and came around the desk, picking up the cupcake and sitting against the desk.

"This cupcake is magic," he said. "It imparts luck upon whoever consumes it."

An incredulous laugh escaped her throat. The man had to be mad. It was the only explanation.

"I assure you, it's no laughing matter. Such an item, in the wrong hands, could change the tide of nations. Wars. Destinies."

"I don't understand," she said. She was overcome with the urge to take her gold crown and get the hell out of this man's office.

"The guilds regulate the practice of their craft within Alesia. But do you truly think that a bunch of chocolatiers or bakers or winemakers warrant this kind of influence?" He waved his hand at the office, at the decadent guildhall around them. "No. This is the secret behind Alesia's political and economic success. The secret behind the royal family. A very special few individuals have an ability. An ability to imbue food with magic. You are one such individual. When you lovingly crafted this cupcake, frosting each rose petal, you filled it with magic. With luck. So that whoever ate it—their life would be forever changed."

Wren's mouth fell open as she looked from the cupcake to Kasper's face. Could it be true? It was insanity. Magic. True, there were tales of magic. Witches and sorcerers and genies in bottles. But they were children's tales. There was no true magic in the world. Just the grim reality of working hard until your body broke down and they laid you in the ground. If there had been anything special or magical about her, her life would have gone very differently up to this point. But she looked down at the golden coin, sitting so mundanely in her hand. She couldn't deny that something strange had happened to that coin.

"It is much to take in at first, I know." Kasper set down the cupcake. "But I assure you, it's all true. And now you understand why we can't have products like this, made by a person like yourself, out in the world."

Wren stilled, her body growing as taut as a wire. Here it was, what some part of her had been expecting all along. Girls like her didn't happen upon magic cupcakes and a fortune in gold. "What do you mean to do with me?" Wren asked, grasping the supple leather arms of her chair. She glanced at Callidus, leaning by the door. Is this why he had stayed? To intercept her when she tried to make a run for it?

"My, you are a skittish thing! I'm sorry, my dear. I didn't mean for that to sound so ominous," Kasper said. "We want to train you. You have a rare gift, and it is valuable to this Guild and the king. Only the highest levels within the Guild know of this secret—the grandmasters of the Guild, like Callidus and myself. You will become one of us."

Words fled as a sliver of hope surfaced within her. She looked around at the room they sat in, at the casual luxuries that she had never dreamed of having. Could he be serious?

"I assure you it will be quite a pleasant life," Kasper said. "We're not all so serious as Callidus. There will be other students for you to learn with, friends to make. Of course, you cannot share the true nature of this secret with them, but that won't be too difficult. What do you say?"

Wren looked between Kasper and Callidus, her thoughts spinning. Though she didn't generally trust people, she had found over the last few years that she had a knack for reading them. Despite Kasper's seemingly calm exterior, lines around his kind eyes betrayed his tension. "I don't have a choice in this, do I?" she asked, realizing the true nature of this summons.

"I'm afraid not, my dear, but it is truly an honor we are bestowing on you. Besides," he said, leaning forward. "Do you have somewhere better to be?"

She thought of the streets of Maradis, the other grubby orphans who had been her family but were now scattered, no doubt dead or selling themselves as whores or mercenaries. She thought of Master Oldrick, refusing to make her a journeyman for four years despite the fact that her skill had surpassed his long ago. It was her turn to sigh. "No," she said. "I don't."

"Excellent!" Kasper clapped his hands and stood, turning to the wooden credenza lining the wall behind his desk. "A toast is in order."

He poured three glasses of what looked like a sweet rosé wine from a crystal decanter. He offered one to Callidus, who declined with a curt shake of his head.

"More for me," Kasper grumbled, handing another glass to Wren. Wren wished she could decline, too, but feared offending the guildmaster. "Stand up, stand up," Kasper said, and she obliged, feeling a sudden poignancy to the moment.

"Now, before we toast to our newest future grandmaster, I need a promise from you. Do you solemnly swear that you will not speak of the truth of your magic, of our magic, to anyone save Callidus, myself, and the others we say are safe?"

"I do," she agreed. She wasn't sure she even believed what he was saying, so there seemed to be little danger in making such a promise.

"Excellent! Cheers!" He clinked his glass to hers and took a healthy swallow. She took a nervous sip of the wine, letting the effervescent flavors of peach and grass swirl across her tongue. She had sampled wine a few times before but hadn't yet developed a palate for it. Watching her father drink himself to death had been enough to quell any burgeoning interest in alcohol.

The instant she swallowed, the wine's sweet finish changed, turning hot and bitter on her tongue.

Callidus strode forward and grabbed the glass from her hand before she could drop it.

Her tongue burned, and when she went to open her mouth, she found she couldn't. It was glued shut. She backed up in panic, knocking into the leather chair, looking from one man to another with wide eyes. She clutched at her throat, grasping fingers leaving red trails down her skin. Had they poisoned her? What was the point of all this show if they were just going to kill her?

"Easy now," Kasper said. "It will pass in a moment, my dear."

He was right. Already the burning sensation was dying, leaving only the tingling aftereffects of the wine and the thudding of her heartbeat in her ears. She opened her mouth wide, gasping in air. "What... What did you do to me?" Her eyes were rimmed with salty tears.

"Standard procedure, my dear. We've found it's best to do it quickly, like pulling out a splinter."

"Do what quickly?"

"You are bound to your oath now. You are physically unable to break your word, to tell our secret. Your secret."

"How?" she croaked, her hands still at her throat, working her jaw as if she could stop it from sealing shut once again. The memory clung to her like taffy.

"Our Guild isn't the only guild with true magic. Vintner's Guild," he said, holding the decanter up to the light. "The magic of truth and lies. Secrets and whispers. Very helpful stuff. In the right hands."

Kasper's pleasant demeanor hadn't changed, but Wren shuddered, eyeing him warily.

Guildmaster Kasper came around the desk and put his arm around her, leading her towards the door. Wren shrank away from his touch, but he didn't seem to notice. "It is a lot to take in, but I promise you will be safe here. A world of wonder is now open to you. Learn. Discover. Explore. And make more cupcakes." He squeezed her shoulder and released her into Callidus's care. "Callidus will see you to Guildmistress Greer, who will take care of getting you situated. I'll come see how you are acclimating tomorrow."

"Thank you," she said haltingly. She felt faint from the whirlwind of the last few minutes and was content to follow Callidus's grim visage into the hallway like an obedient puppy. Kasper said she would be safe here. Dare she believe him? She had learned through trial and painful error what it took to be safe in this world. Blend in. Work hard and don't cause trouble. These things had kept her safe at Master Oldrick's. Would it be enough here?

Callidus towed her back down the corridor towards the staircase. As they reached the landing, a muffled crash sounded behind them, emanating from Guildmaster Kasper's office.

Callidus whirled and darted back down the hallway with startling speed, bursting into the office. The two guards looked at each other and followed suit, spears held before them, surcoats billowing behind.

Unsure of what to do, Wren drifted back down the corridor towards the office, not wanting to intrude but overcome with curiosity. When she reached the open door, she gasped.

Kasper was on the floor, his face an unnatural shade of purple. Foam bubbled from his mouth. His body shook and convulsed as Callidus and the guards tried to hold him down, shouting at each other for antidotes and doctors.

But it was over before it began. Kasper gave a final gurgling breath, convulsed once more, and fell still.

Wren's hands flew to her mouth as bile rose in her throat. Kasper's brown eyes, eyes that had sparkled with life just moments before, now bulged out in a blank stare that transfixed her own.

"He's dead," Callidus said, still on his knees, his head hanging in disbelief.

"Poison," one of the guards announced, standing and wiping his mouth with a shaky hand. "Nasty one." He pointed at the cupcake wrapper forgotten on the desk. "Where did that come from? It didn't pass the security screening."

"I brought it up… But the girl…" Callidus said, his voice ghostly. Then his head whipped around, his eyes locking on Wren with such force that she stumbled back.

"It was her confection," he said, pointing a spindly finger at her. "She must have poisoned it. Arrest her."

CHAPTER 3

Wren sat on a pillowy damask sofa, her hands twisted painfully behind her by a set of heavy iron manacles. A pair of guild guards flanked each set of doors while Callidus stood guarding the bank of floor-to-ceiling windows, as if to prevent her from slithering through the narrow opening between the leaden panes and dashing herself on the cobbles below.

She surveyed him through wide eyes. He couldn't honestly think she had murdered the head of the Guild, could he? She hadn't even known the man's name a few hours ago.

The enameled double doors flew open across the room, startling her and setting her heart pounding. Two men strode in.

"Callidus," the first said, his voice nasal. His copper hair flashed in the shaft of sunlight illuminating the room. His impeccably-tailored emerald suit stood in strange contrast to his pockmarked cheeks and crooked teeth. Someone who had risen high quickly, then.

"Steward Willings," Callidus said, meeting the other with a handshake. "Good to see you again. I wish it were under happier circumstances."

"Indeed. Dark day, this is."

"How is it you're here? I sent word to the Grand Inspector to send someone from his office."

"That's where I come in, sir. Lucas Imbris, inspector." The other man stepped forward, shaking Callidus's hand. This fellow was tall and broad-shouldered, with dark hair flecked with the beginnings of gray.

"Lucas Imbris." Callidus raised an eyebrow, though Wren was unsure why. Certainly, the king hailed from clan Imbris, but so did thousands of other Alesian citizens. And the clans hadn't truly mattered for hundreds of years, since the first king—Leon Imbris—had united them and formed the country of Alesia.

"I'm here on behalf of the crown to observe the investigation," Steward Willings said. "The murder of a guild head is very troubling to the king."

"Of course," Callidus said.

The Steward's words rang hollow to Wren. People turned up murdered all the time in Maradis, if the bodies were found at all. There was no disease deadlier to poor and rich alike than the king's displeasure. Well, beside the Red Plague. But that hadn't been seen in Alesia for two years now.

"Where is the murderer?" Steward Willings asked, looking about as if Wren were a piece of furniture, rather than sitting on one.

The word sent tendrils of fear skittering down her spine. She had spent years running from that word. Some small part of her had expected the name to catch up with her someday. But even her darkest thoughts couldn't have predicted this.

"Alleged murderer," the inspector said, examining her with a thoughtful look.

She was surprised to see that he was much younger than his salt-and-pepper hair belied, perhaps only a few years older than her.

"That's her," Callidus said. Steward Willings's eyes found Wren and narrowed.

She shrank back into the sofa under the weight of his scrutiny. The set of heavy keys that jangled on Steward Willings's belt was the telltale symbol of his position. He was *the* king's steward, right hand to the crown. Though she knew little of politics, she knew enough to know that the king and his court were not renowned for their magnanimity. If King Imbris's reign were a recipe, it would call for healthy scoops of fear and intimidation whisked with a dash of cruelty and a pinch of excess. If his steward was here, she was in deep trouble indeed.

The inspector sat on the sofa across from her, resting his forearms on his lanky knees. He pulled a black leather notebook and a pen from his jacket pocket. The buttonhole of his tailored black jacket held a sprig of rosemary. Its scent soothed her, as did his light gray eyes, which were filled with something that looked like sympathy.

"Grandmaster, would you have the guards uncuff her?" the man asked.

Callidus grumbled to one of the guards, who obliged.

When the irons came off, Wren sighed with relief and rubbed her darkened wrists. She would have bruises for days. If she lived for days, her cynical side warned.

"What is your name?" the inspector asked.

"Wren Confectioner." The words felt strange in her mouth. Hours ago, she had known what that meant, to be Wren Confectioner. Now, she was in uncharted waters.

"Wren, it's nice to meet you. You may call me Lucas," he said. "I'll be investigating Guildmaster Kasper's murder." Lucas had a square face with serious brows and a slightly-too-large-nose, but the overall effect was rather arresting. "Why don't you tell me what happened, in your own words?"

Wren recited her tale, beginning with Callidus showing up at Master Oldrick's shop and unceremoniously turning her life upside down. Her throat began to burn as her story traversed too close to the topic of magic, the binding magic of the wine rudely reminding her that some subjects were now, and forevermore, forbidden.

"Why did Callidus bring you to the Guildhall in the first place?" Lucas asked, his nimble pen flying across the notepad.

Wren's heart hiccupped. She considered herself a good liar, thanks to her father's worldly teaching and her subsequent time on the streets, but to be forced to lie so publicly, with Callidus watching over her, knowing the truth of her lies...

Callidus came to her rescue. "One of Wren's confections caught the notice of a great lady. She notified Guildmaster Kasper of her admiration, and Kasper wanted to evaluate her talents to see if she should be invited to train with a grandmaster."

She looked at him in gratitude and was met by a glare. Did his brow ever cramp from all the scrunching?

"How did he find you?" Lucas asked.

"He invited me to live here," Wren replied, struggling to stay calm. This was all a horrible misunderstanding. Surely, they would see that.

"And look at what he got for his trouble!" said Callidus. "Murdered."

"I didn't murder him," Wren shot back. Guilt coiled in her stomach. Kasper, at least, she didn't murder. "I had barely heard of him before this afternoon. Why would I want to kill him?"

"I'm conducting this investigation, Grandmaster," Lucas said, smooth and polite. "Tell me what happened next."

Wren finished explaining the afternoon's events, leaving out the revelation of her magical ability. She watched Lucas as he wrote, the curve of his long torso over the notepad, the encouraging grunts he gave as she talked, urging her to continue.

She fell silent at the end, and Lucas did too, looking up to study her. His silence unnerved her, demanded something of her, and so she spoke, cursing herself as she did it, knowing that only fools spoke with nothing to say, while those who listened stayed alive. "Am I going to prison?"

Lucas unfolded himself from the sofa and stood. "Grandmaster, do you agree with Ms. Confectioner's version of events?"

A curt nod.

"No, Wren," said Lucas, "you're not going to prison."

"What?" Both Steward Willings and Callidus exploded.

"She is guilty of a most heinous crime," Callidus cried.

"All she appears guilty of is being in the wrong place at the wrong time."

"It was her cupcake that killed the man," Steward Willings said, a corner of his lip curling up in an inadvertent snarl. "What more do you need?"

"Why didn't she die too?" Lucas asked.

The two men paused.

"She must have ingested some sort of antidote," Willings said triumphantly. "Before she ate it."

"Quite a feat when Callidus surprised her at her place of employment, seized her that moment, and took her immediately to the Guildmaster's office. She did not know of the meeting in advance, and Grandmaster Callidus did not see her ingest any substance. Did you?" Lucas asked.

"No," Callidus admitted petulantly.

Wren watched the exchange as if she were a spectator at a palm match, watching the white ball fly back and forth. Silently, she cheered her champion, daring to hope that she might escape this disaster alive.

"The king has the right to have his Grand Inquisitor question her. Before you officially clear her as a suspect." Willings crossed his arms.

"The Grand Inquisitor?" Lucas's eyes widened. "Surely, Killian's tactics aren't necessary for this scrap of a girl."

Lucas shot her an apologetic look, which wasn't strictly necessary. He could call her a loaf of burnt bread if it kept her away from the Grand Inquisitor. Wren had heard that the inquisitor had once served a man a plate of ladyfingers in an effort to break him. And not the spongy biscuit kind. The kind that came from the man's own wife.

"She should be properly questioned," Callidus said. "We must do everything we can to bring Kasper's killer to justice. I insist."

"He insists," Willings said.

Wren glared.

"Killian is with the King in Tamros, negotiating with the Apricans." Lucas shook his head. "It could be a month before they return."

"Then she'll have to be held until he returns."

Lucas strode to meet Willings, drawing him towards the window to converse out of Wren's hearing.

Little did he know, Wren had excellent hearing.

"You and I both know she won't last two hours in the Block," Lucas hissed. "Why are you doing this?"

The Block, Maradis's prison, had a reputation as black as tar. Filled with cutthroats and thieves, rapists and murderers, Wren had no delusions that the quick wits that had saved her as a young orphan would be enough on the inside.

"If one worthless confectioner must be sacrificed to get to the truth of this, it is a price I am willing to pay ten times over," Willings said, his crooked teeth bared in a scowl.

Lucas ran his hands through his hair, turning from Willings with a frustrated hiss. His eyes met Wren's, and she held them in her own, her gaze full of pleading and hope. *Don't abandon me,* she wanted to beg.

I won't, his eyes seemed to say back. *Though I'm not sure why I'm going to such lengths to help you.*

She could live with that.

"Very well," Lucas announced, turning back to her two detractors. "She will be questioned by the Grand Inquisitor when he returns. If we haven't found the real culprit by then."

"I will send for the gaoler from the Block," Willings said, striding towards the door.

Wren whimpered despite herself, his comment setting her heart racing like a predator nipping at her heels.

"That won't be necessary," Lucas said.

"She's a murder suspect," Willings said, turning. "She can't go free."

"I will vouch for her," Lucas said.

The room went silent.

What did he mean, vouch for her? Wren had never heard of such a thing. Perhaps an archaic legal concept? Curiosity bloomed in her—a single flower bright against the dark winds of fear buffeting her.

"Surely not," Callidus said. "Why would you do such a thing?"

"My reasons are my own," Lucas said. "Callidus, she is a member of your guild, and by law she is entitled to lodging and protection here. She may be treated no differently than your other guild members."

"I won't have her under this roof after what she did. It's too dangerous. What if she kills again?"

"What she has done has yet to be determined," Lucas said, his voice like steel. "And I have vouched for her. By law, it is enough. Or shall I summon a magister to remind you of your obligations under crown law?"

"Very well," Callidus said, his thick brows merging as he glowered at Lucas. "What if she runs?"

"She won't run, will she?" Lucas said, turning to Wren. "Innocent people don't run."

She shook her head woodenly. Her thoughts hadn't even caught up enough to think about running.

"I must continue my investigation," Lucas said. "Gentlemen. My lady." He pulled on a black hat and tipped the brow to her before striding out of the room, three sets of wide eyes following in his wake.

Wren found herself alone in the sitting room, summarily abandoned by the men who had been so keenly interested in her fate just moments before. She watched their retreating forms before sinking into the plush sofa with a shaky breath, her knees going weak.

Wren weighed her options. Run. Or stay. She had the gold crown, but how long would that last her? Would it be enough to buy her way out of Maradis, past the borders of Alesia? Perhaps she could go north, into Tamros… or find a vessel to take her Centu. But then what? Even if she could find work as a confectioner, it would make her too easy to find. The king's eyes saw far, even into the countries bordering Alesia. With no way to earn a living… she had begged and stolen for scraps for two years before starting her apprenticeship. She never wanted to go back to that life. She couldn't.

And then there was her promise to the inspector that she wouldn't run. She felt a strange obligation to honor it, after what he had done for her. *Innocent people don't run,* he had said. She didn't want him to think he had misjudged her. Her mind lingered on the memory of Lucas Imbris—his keen gray eyes, his pen scratching across the page. The fact that he had had shown up with a soft spot where the other two had a crusty black desire to see a young girl tortured and maimed… her eyes widened. It had been quite a turn of luck. She pulled the gold crown out of her pocket, worrying the kingly profile with her thumb. Was the magic of the cupcake still working? It must have been. How long before it wore off?

She sighed, putting it back in her pocket. "Better take advantage before it does," she muttered, getting to her feet. Gods help her, she was going to stay. The Guildhall may be an unknown commodity, but it still felt safer than the unknown beyond this city. She had run once before, and it had taken her years to find a semblance of safety.

She peeked her head into the empty corridor outside the room. It was deserted. Wren was no stranger to being alone. She preferred solitude. No one to stab you in the back or rob you if there was no one there.

But now, staring down the cavernous hallway in this strange place, her isolation began to taunt her, as the reality of staying set in. She knew no one but Callidus, who was worse than no one. She knew nothing of this world, how to navigate its treacherous waters safely. She didn't understand what had happened back in that room, why Callidus and Willings seemed bent on her destruction, why Lucas had vouched for her. What did that even mean? Was it her future to wander these corridors alone, hungry and unable to find a washroom in the labyrinthine hallways?

She looked to the left, then the right, chewing her lip in indecision. Finally, letting the luck of the cupcake take hold of her, she spun in a circle until dizzy, coming to a stop facing to the left. Left it was.

CHAPTER 4

Wren turned the corner into a wide open room. It was a conservatory. Walls of diamond-shaped leaded-glass windows looked out over a garden to her left, and an arched ceiling of paned glass yawned above. She walked down the aisle between neat rows filled with plants—tidy herb beds, fragrant flowers, towering tropical palms. She recognized a date tree and a lime tree as she passed, her mouth watering at the thought of fresh fruit.

Wren was so engrossed on the verdure around her that she jumped a foot when she bumped into another, living, moving thing.

The living, moving thing squealed.

Wren whirled, sighing with relief as she saw a plump girl about her own age.

"You gave me a fright, miss!" the girl said, her hand to her chest. She had a sweet face, cherubic with dimples that revealed themselves when she smiled.

"I'm sorry," Wren said shakily. "I wasn't looking where I was going.

This is all quite lovely."

"Yes," the girl said, her golden curls bouncing in agreement. "Though they are a son of a spicer to water." She hefted a shiny red watering can before her with a rueful grin.

"I can imagine," Wren said, a smile tugging at the corner of her own mouth. "Do you need some help?"

"Oh, no." The girl's blue eyes widened in alarm. "I appreciate the offer, of course. But it's my job. I couldn't take help from a... guest... of the Guild?" She said the word like a question.

Wren didn't blame her. She was unsure of her status as well.

"I suppose I'm a guest," she said. "I met Grandmaster Callidus today. I'm... to be living here. I'm an apprentice."

"Welcome!" The girl's grin returned. "It's exciting to have another girl around! Most of the apprentices and journeymen live with their masters—only a few live here. You'll be the only other girl, except for Marina, but she's so horrible, she hardly counts."

"Are you an apprentice?"

"No, I live here with my grandaunt and granduncle. I help around the Guildhall in exchange for my room and board. My grandaunt is the Guildmistress. She's training me to take over for her someday."

"Wonderful," Wren said, trying to put some enthusiasm into the word. Kasper had mentioned Guildmistress Greer before... Wren's mind stumbled over the thought. *Before he died,* she forced herself to think. She would need to be able to face the facts.

"I'm Olivia," the girl said, extending her hand.

"Wren."

"Oh!" Olivia said, her mouth forming a rosy 'o.' "Did Callidus just abandon you? Is that why you're wandering the Guildhall? The man is notorious for such things. My grandaunt has scolded him for it a hundred times."

Wren nodded, her cheeks reddening. She thought she'd like to meet this grandaunt, if she was truly in a position to scold black-hearted Callidus.

"I can take you to her to find you a room," Olivia said, setting her watering can down and weaving her arm through Wren's.

"Actually..." Wren's cheeks reddened further. "I really need a washroom."

"Ock!" Olivia *tsked*, towing Wren towards the far end of the room. "That man! Can't gain respect, so he has to rule by fear. Now Guildmaster Kasper, he's so very different. You've met him, have you?"

Wren nodded mutely, her rising spirits suddenly sinking like a weight. Poor Olivia didn't yet know of the guildmaster's death. When she found out, she would hate Wren as much as Callidus did. Everyone in the Guild would. How could Wren ever survive here, let alone make this her home?

Despite the bleak outlook, Wren brightened considerably when Olivia found her a washroom.

Olivia was waiting for her in the hallway when Wren finished, toying with a thread on her linen apron. She threaded her arm back into the crook of Wren's elbow and continued forward.

Wren's stomach rumbled. Her body seemed determined to assert itself, despite this uncertain new landscape.

"When's the last time you ate?" Olivia asked, alarmed by the sound.

"Breakfast?" Wren offered. She didn't think she should count the bite of magical cupcake or sip of binding wine that had tried to close her throat up.

"Breakfast!" Olivia squealed in outrage. "I have half a mind to thump Callidus myself. No wonder you're such a skinny thing!"

Wren had been called a skinny thing all her life, as well as some less flattering turns of phrase, but it was the first time she had heard someone say it with a tone of wistfulness. She eyed Olivia sideways.

"I'll take you to the kitchens before we go to see my grandaunt."

"Olivia!" a voice called from behind them.

The girls whirled.

"Come with me." A stately older woman stood at the end of the hallway, her hands twisting in the fabric of her sleek navy dress. Her strawberry-blonde hair was pulled into an elegant bun on top of her head, several wisps artfully framing her face. This must be Guildmistress Greer, Olivia's grandaunt.

"Grandaunt, this is a new apprentice, Wren," Olivia said, approaching.

Wren dragged her feet, resisting Olivia's pull.

The Guildmistress's blue eyes were red-rimmed, and the look she leveled at Wren was far from friendly. Greer wiped her face hastily with a shaky hand, her fingers stained blue with some sort of dye. She quickly buried her hands in the folds of her skirt. "Leave her," the Guildmistress said. "I must speak to you. Something has happened."

Olivia looked between them, suddenly unsure.

Wren withdrew her arm. "Go ahead. I'll be fine."

"Turn right at the end of this hallway. Pass the classroom kitchens—the real kitchens are at the far end. The cooks will be able to find you something," Olivia said, following her grandaunt, who had already turned on her heel. "I'll come find you when I'm done!" She waved.

No you won't, Wren thought with a twinge of sorrow. Wren watched the swishing skirts of the two women until they disappeared around the corner. She had known Olivia for all of four minutes, but somehow Wren's plight felt even darker now than before her sudden appearance. She had represented the promise of a friend, an ally in this strange place. But Olivia wouldn't want anything to do with her once she found out about the guildmaster.

Wren sighed and headed down the hallway in the direction Olivia had pointed her. Alone once again. It was probably for the best. Wren had never enjoyed good luck when it came to her friendships. If no one was close to you, there was no one to betray you. She pushed the thoughts aside and set her mind to the manageable task of navigating towards the kitchen. But as she rounded the corner into the next hallway, an open doorway called to her like a siren, seeming to glow with light. Wren poked her head inside and her brown eyes went as round as saucers.

It might have been the loveliest thing she had ever seen. The large, rectangular room was lined with long, butcher block countertops illuminated from above by a central skylight that displayed a stamp of blue sky. A tidy white tile backsplash guarded majestic iron stoves. Shiny copper pots hung from hooks on the ceiling. A squat candy stove sat tucked in the corner. And in the center of it all was an island of warm wood, its swirling surface calling to be covered in flour and chocolate. She ran her fingers along the grain, letting its simple beauty soothe her soul. It was a kitchen called forth from a confectioner's dream.

Her knees grew weak and Wren found her way onto a stool at the end of the island. She rested her cheek on the smooth surface of the wood, letting the surroundings calm her racing thoughts and jangling nerves. This was a place she understood. More her home than anywhere else.

"Miss?" a deep voice said. "Are you all right?"

Wren shot bolt upright to meet the intruder, shoving a curtain of auburn locks back from her face. "Of course," she said.

A man stood in the doorway, framing it with his height and broad torso. She had never seen a man so tall or muscular. He looked like a god from the priests' stories, the golden Sower himself fresh from harvesting the seasons. "Are you Wren?"

"Yes," she admitted.

"Great. Stay right there." He disappeared, leaving Wren perched on the stool, her mouth gaping like a fish.

Wren stood, hastily combing her hair with her fingers, straightening her thin dress on her thin frame. She stifled a sigh and sat back down. What did it matter how she looked?

No sooner had she sat than a raven-haired woman strode into the room, her crimson skirts swishing with purpose. Her foot tapped on the white marble tiles of the floor while she inspected Wren. "This is her?"

"Yep," the man said, reappearing behind the woman.

"She doesn't look like much, does she?"

"Only the wise man sees the treasure that hides in plain sight," the tall man said appraisingly.

The woman looked back, arching one fine, ebony eyebrow. "When did you get so philosophical?"

"I learn from the best." The man grinned, a broad arc of mirth and white teeth that made Wren glad she was already sitting down.

"That you do." The woman retrieved another stool from beneath the island and perched upon it. The man stayed standing, leaning against the countertop, crossing muscled arms before him.

"Don't mind Hale," the woman said. "He likes to position himself in the best light."

Hale chuckled. "Everywhere is my best light."

Wren was loath to admit it, but she tended to agree with him. From his bronze skin to his honey-blonde locks pulled back into a knot to the fine brows and high cheekbones that framed his aquamarine eyes, the man was the most beautiful thing she had ever seen.

She ripped her eyes from him and turned to the woman. She was watching Wren with an amused expression on her face. "I'm

Grandmaster Sable," she said. "And you've already met my Hale, my artisan."

"You're a grandmaster?" Wren couldn't help herself. The woman looked so young, her olive skin smooth and supple, her dark eyes framed by a fringe of black-feathered lashes.

"I get that a lot," Sable said. "Youngest in a century. Though Hale is on his way to beating my record."

"If you don't hold me back out of spite," Hale said, a dimple appearing around his arresting grin.

Wren was staring again! She turned back to Sable, keeping her eyes firmly fixed on the woman. She wore a beautiful choker made of tiny beads, a riot of color swirling about her throat. *Just look at the necklace, Wren,* she told herself. Not at the living god standing behind her.

"Callidus told me you were here," Sable said.

"Callidus?" Wren swallowed.

"I see his name strikes fear into your heart already. He would be pleased. He aspires to new heights of wretchedness."

"Did he tell you…" Wren trailed off. *That I'm a suspected murderer?* Surely, this woman wouldn't be talking to her if she knew of the afternoon's events.

"Yes." Sable stilled for a moment, rubbing the space between her arching brows. "He filled me in on his conspiracy theory. Not his best work. But the fact that Callidus seeks to pin poor Kasper's murder on you is reason enough for me to take up your cause."

"Nothing brings Sable pleasure like confounding Callidus," Hale quipped, though his bright smile had faltered at the mention of their guildmaster's death.

Sable glanced at him in annoyance but then dismissed it with a shrug. "That's true."

"Take up my cause," Wren asked. "How do you mean?"

"Kasper told me he had discovered another Gifted confectioner. You will need to be trained. Taught the ways of the guilds, the court, the political arena."

"I've been trained for four years," Wren said, her pride chaffing at Sable's words. "I'm an excellent confectioner."

"I'm sure you are. But I didn't mean that you were a gifted confectioner, I meant Gifted." Sable emphasized the last word with a knowing look.

"Gifted," Wren said. The burning in her throat and tongue that had been present before when she'd gotten too close to her new secret was absent.

"That's right. You can talk about it with us. Hale and I are Gifted as well. We're in the know."

"You make… magic confections as well?" she asked, still disbelieving this was all really happening.

"Indeed. It's the three of us and Callidus. And since Callidus is inclined to leave you drifting in the wind, I will claim you for our side. With Kasper gone, we need all the allies we can get."

"Allies? I'm sorry, are you at war?" Wren said the word like a joke, but the expression on Sable's face was deadly serious.

"We're always at war. With those who seek the power of the Guild from the outside and in. The thing about power like ours is that there is always someone waiting to take it from you."

A bubble of fear surfaced in Wren's mind. She had done everything she could in the last four years to stay as far away as she could from danger. Yet it had found her again. "It sounds very tiring," she managed.

Sable let out a bitter laugh. "It can be. But it's the way of this world, and the world does not see fit to be changed by mortals like us. But know this. We are your family now, Hale and I. Your tribe. I am your chieftain, and Hale is your brother. I have already transferred your apprenticeship from that half-wit Master Oldrick. You are promoted immediately to journeyman status, and if you are as good as Oldrick says you are, I may make you an artisan soon enough."

"Thank you," Wren said, surprised by the sudden kindness. So, Sable was her family and Hale was her brother. She'd had a brother once. Three lives ago. Before he had died. Hugo… To her horror, she found tears welling in her eyes. She tried to shove the thought of him away, cursing herself for still getting emotional when thinking of him, despite the passage of so many years. Like Sable said—it was the way of the world—those with power taking what they wished.

"Don't cry. I don't tolerate criers. Hale cried for days when he arrived, and I had to beat it out of him."

A great booming laugh exploded from Hale, nearly startling Wren from her stool. She couldn't tell if Sable was joking. She bit her inner cheek, letting the sharp pain stun the tears into oblivion.

"Yes, Grandmaster."

"Hale will be seeing to most of your lessons because frankly, I don't have the time. I'll stop by from time to time. But all that comes second to your chief task."

"Which is?"

"We must uncover the identity of Kasper's killer before the king returns from Tamros with the Grand Inquisitor. You'll be of no use to our cause if the inquisitor gets his hands on you and tortures you into a quivering mess."

Wren paled, gripping the countertop to steady herself.

"Make no mistake. We cannot let it come to pass, or you are lost to me. Lost to yourself. I don't know why Steward Willings took such a dislike to you, but even I cannot keep you from the inquisitor's knives once the King's steward has called for an inquiry. At least you somehow convinced that inspector to vouch for you, which shows you have some wits at your disposal. He has secured you the opportunity to save yourself."

"I don't know where to start," Wren lamented. "I know nothing about this place... who would want to kill Kasper."

Sable rolled her dark eyes. "I don't take apprentices only to abandon them. I will seek to put together the political pieces, if there is something there. You and Hale must discover what lurks in the hidden corners of this place, the things that the walls and servants know but keep from grandmasters like me."

"All right," Wren said softly, cold doubt gnawing at her insides. This task felt too big, too wide and foreign.

"Believe me," Sable said. "Someone knows who did this deed. All you have to do is find out who."

CHAPTER 5

Wren tossed and turned that night. Though her body felt leaden, her mind whirred and skipped over the day's events. The bed she lay in felt strange—too large, too soft, the goose-down comforter too cloud-like against her skin. She thought with longing of the hard narrow bed in her postage stamp room above Master Oldrick's shop. It was a miserly offering, in keeping with Master Oldrick's cheap nature, but it had a door that locked, and it had been the first place she had ever laid her head that felt safe. This room wasn't safe, no matter how tasteful the furnishings. She had no compunctions about thinking so. She felt a sting of resentment towards her Gift. It felt more like a curse, landing her in this strange bed with a murder charge hanging over her head.

Hale had shown her to her room after Sable had unceremoniously swept from the teaching kitchen to gods-knew-where. He had beamed down on her with such genuine good humor that Wren felt her tension melting, despite her best efforts to remain cool and aloof. She had found herself offering back a shy smile, much to her horror. Did none of her natural defenses work against this man?

"The Guildhall is not a bad place to live," he said as they walked. "Everyone is quite nice. Well, except Callidus. A person has everything they need. A roof over their head, access to the most powerful and interesting people in Maradis, and the best food you've ever eaten. Plus, there's chocolate in every room." He'd snagged one from a bowl sitting in the hallway and tossed it to her. She had startled like a deer as the foil-wrapped chocolate flew over her hands. She'd retrieved it and jogged to keep up with Hale's impossibly long strides.

"I wouldn't mind living here, I suppose," she'd said softly, finding her voice embarrassingly scratchy in his presence. She'd cleared it. "But I don't know how I'm supposed to discover who killed Kasper. I don't know why anyone would want him dead."

"Well, that's easy," Hale had said. "Callidus and Kasper have been at each other for years. It's gotten much worse as of late, though no one really understands why. Plus, Callidus is in line to take Kasper's job."

"Callidus will become guildmaster?" Wren had asked, horrified to think of the sour man taking charge of their lives and futures. In particular, her life. In Maradis, all unmarried women had an appointed male guardian. Whether father or brother or sponsor or husband, Alesian women were beholden to men in almost every aspect of life. A guardian could emancipate his ward, which wasn't unheard of, but it wasn't exactly common, either. And though she hadn't had time to discuss it with him, she had assumed Kasper would take over the role from Oldrick upon her joining the guild. She didn't relish the thought of Callidus having the job.

"He, Sable, and Beckett are the only other grandmasters of note. Not to mention"—he'd leaned towards her conspiratorially in a way that had set her heart racing—"Callidus and Sable are the only other Gifted guildmembers besides us. The Head is always Gifted."

"Why can't Sable take over?"

Hale's gaze had grown distant for a moment, his face softening. "She's younger than Callidus, and ten times as smart, but she doesn't have the political backing. She was trying to position herself to challenge Callidus for the position, but this all happened too soon."

"So Callidus knew that if Kasper didn't pass away for years more, he would have a challenger for the head seat, and perhaps even lose it?"

"Good to see you're not just a pretty face." Hale had winked at her.

Her heart fluttered, and she squashed it ruthlessly. *Steady, Wren,* she'd cautioned herself. *Focus.*

"Callidus was the one who suggested the guards arrest me. He was angry when the inspector wanted to let me go. And he's the only reason I was in Kasper's office this afternoon." Wren's blood had begun to boil as the pieces fell into place.

"Truly?"

"So Callidus... tried to frame me? Kill the guildmaster and blame it on some nobody who wouldn't be missed? That... blooming bastard!" She'd exploded.

Hale had let out a boom of laughter and put his arm around Wren's shoulders, pulling her sideways into his body with a squeeze. "I'm glad you're here, Wren. Things have been far too dull for far too long."

Her traitorous body had shifted from anger to something low and tingly in a second, responding to his warmth and scent of orange and spice. She'd shrugged his arm off her, not trusting herself to remain in her right mind if he continued the contact.

They had arrived at the bedchamber Sable had secured for Wren, and Hale had swept through the door, ducking his head slightly to enter.

The room was larger than Master Oldrick's whole shop and was adorned with handsome wooden furniture with wrought-iron legs. Green succulent plants curled in containers on the desk and wardrobe, and gauzy white curtains covered the window panes.

"It's not much, but it'll do," Hale had said, looking around, opening the wardrobe to reveal its empty shelves.

It had been difficult for Wren to take in her surroundings, so attune had been her awareness to the fact that this godlike man stood in her bedroom. It was frustrating, really, how her thoughts seemed to addle when he was near.

He'd continued his exploration, crossing to the other side of the room to the bookshelf, where a few volumes sat lonely and unused.

"See," he'd said. "Chocolate everywhere."

He'd tossed another chocolate to her from the bowl on the shelf, which had promptly sailed over her shoulder before she'd gotten her startled hands up to intercept it.

"Will you stop that?" she'd asked.

He'd cackled and crossed to the bed, giving it a few bounces as he sat. The bed was covered in a cloud of white pillows and comforters, but nothing was so dreamlike as him sitting on it.

He'd grinned roguishly at her wide-eyed expression, and realization had dawned on her. *He's doing this on purpose!* He knew his impact on women and he was exploiting it for his own merrymaking.

Wren's eyes had narrowed. "Thank you for showing me to my room. Now if you don't mind, I've had a trying day and should get some sleep."

"Want me to tuck you in?" He'd leaned back on his elbows, the collar of his striped button-down shirt opening slightly to reveal a V of tanned flesh.

"No, thank you."

He had stood in a flash. "Good girl. I'll see you in the morning for your first lesson."

Wren's mind replayed the scene in a loop, her face flushed in memory. Wren's position here was precarious, to put it kindly. The last thing she needed was to muddy her thinking with some school-girl crush. Especially on a man who must have had women throwing themselves at him on an hourly basis. She'd only embarrass herself.

She wasn't bad-looking, she supposed; her thick, auburn curls had drawn compliments in the past from customers, and her face was petite with tilted eyes and elfin features. But that was where the good ended. Her skin was pale, and her frame was thin, lacking any semblance of feminine curve. No doubt Hale had sampled choicer morsels than she. Not that she even wanted to be sampled, she reminded herself. No attachments was her rule. That included romantic ones.

She finally threw the covers back, huffing. Though the light of the August sun barely cleared the horizon, she could tell there would be no more sleep this morning.

As she filled the copper bathtub with hot water from the tap, she pondered the mystery of Kasper's death. She was sorry he was gone. He had been kind to her. In the few minutes she had known him, he had struck her as a warm soul with infectious enthusiasm for life and his craft. Wren had always felt a bit sorry for those types of people, as in her estimate, such optimism could only be a byproduct of naïveté about the cruel nature of the world. Though it didn't seem to be so with Kasper… He had been savvy enough to rise to the top of this complex world.

Master Oldrick's apprentice Hazel was the bubbly type, hailing from a big family full of warmth and love and bedtime stories full of hope. Wren had been sure that some twist of fate would open Hazel's eyes to their harsh reality sooner or later and had been ready to commiserate about dashed dreams and unscrupulous men. She felt a sudden twinge of fondness, though she had never been fond of Hazel before. Would she ever see her again?

Wren stepped into the heat of the water, shuddering with pleasure. Master Oldrick's shop had been too small for a proper bath; she had washed at the public bathhouse once a week. Bathing alone in this giant tub of water was an unprecedented luxury.

Wren drifted for a time in a warm haze, the tension in her body uncurling until her muscles felt as soft as taffy.

Her mind was buzzing with pleasant nothingness when the door to her bedroom opened. Wren sat up in the tub, sloshing water onto the slate tile floor. "Don't come in!" she shrieked.

"Wren?" a feminine voice called, unsure.

Wren peeked around the end of the tub and sighed with relief. "Olivia, thank the Beekeeper. I thought you were Hale."

Olivia approached, standing just shy of the bathroom doorway. A sly smile crossed her face, the gossip clearly too juicy to pass up, even if it concerned an accused murderer. "Why would you think I was Hale? Did something happen between the two of you?"

"No!" Wren said, her ears burning. "He showed me to my room last night, that's all."

"Uh-huh," Olivia said with a giggle.

"Hand me that towel?" Wren asked, pointing to the fluffy, white monstrosity hanging on the iron rod.

Olivia obliged and then turned her back, giving Wren privacy.

Wren dried herself and grabbed her faded dress, pulling it on.

"All done," Wren said. "What are you doing here?"

"I brought you breakfast," Olivia said, crossing to the desk and pulling the silver cover off a tray of biscuits, jam, and coffee.

"Thank you," Wren said, sitting down and slathering the first biscuit with thick clotted cream. She didn't care if she was being rude. She hadn't eaten in a day, as her neglected stomach reminded her. "I have to say, though, I wasn't sure I'd see you again."

Olivia looked out the window, wiping an invisible smudge off one of the diamond panes. "I'm sorry I had to leave so suddenly yesterday."

"This is amazing," Wren said, staring in shock at the biscuit in her hand.

Olivia giggled, swiping a dollop of cream from the ramekin and popping it in her mouth. "All our food comes from the other guildhouses. Best you'll ever eat."

Wren finished the biscuit and began slathering another. "I'm so very sorry about the guildmaster. Your grandaunt must have been very upset. Did they know each other a long time?"

A sad smile flitted across Olivia's pretty face. "You could say that. Kasper was my granduncle. My grandaunt's twin brother."

Wren's hand flew to her mouth in horror. "I didn't know. How awful."

"How could you?" she said, her rosy lips puckered in a frown. "It's all right. I don't believe what they are saying for a minute. That you poisoned him. What a terrible thing to suggest."

"You... believe I didn't do it?"

"Of course! You jump at your own shadow—how could you be a murderer! And why? You'd never even met him. It's a big misunderstanding."

"That means more than you know," Wren said, though guilt snaked through her. That word again. Murderer. If Olivia knew of Wren's past, she might not be so quick to dismiss Wren as a suspect. But Wren *hadn't* murdered Kasper, despite what else she might have done. So she'd accept Olivia's goodwill. She had never cared about having friends, but somehow, she wanted this girl to like her. Needed her to. Olivia could be an anchor against the swirling tides of this place.

"Now, it may take Grandaunt a bit longer to reach the right conclusion. She's distraught at Kasper's death, and Callidus was telling her all manner of horrible things about you last night. But Grandmaster Sable has sponsored you, and that will count for something. Grandaunt will come around, don't you worry."

Wren nodded, washing down the last of her biscuits with the heavenly black coffee.

"Hungry, were you?" Olivia retrieved a crumb from the silver tray and ate it.

"I didn't end up getting dinner last night," Wren said.

"That's embarrassing. We're normally excellent hosts here." Olivia frowned. "Why are you wearing the same dress?"

"I only have the one," Wren mumbled. "Callidus grabbed me so quickly yesterday, I didn't have time to bring anything."

"Honestly, is everyone in this place totally incompetent?" Olivia threw up her hands. "We're going shopping today."

"I'm supposed to have a lesson with Hale," Wren said. She didn't feel like mentioning that she also had very little money. She did have the gold crown she had won off Kasper, but somehow, she didn't want to spend that. It was all she had to remember the little man by.

"You can't need the whole day for your lesson," Olivia said, pulling Wren to her feet. "And I need the distraction. Let's go find him."

CHAPTER 6

Olivia gave Wren a tour of the entire Guildhall in their search for Hale. It was three sprawling stories—ballroom, dining hall, conservatory, kitchens and pantries, and servants's quarters on the bottom floor; living quarters for guildmembers and guests, classrooms, and the library on the second floor; with offices, meeting rooms, and the guildmaster's suite on the third.

The icing on the white marble cake was the rooftop deck. Wren gasped as the nondescript door at the end of a lonely corridor opened to reveal a stunning vista of sugary morning light.

"Beautiful," Wren breathed, her spirit lifting as if ready to take flight. The Cerulean Bay sparkled in the light of the morning sun, which hung heavily over the unfurled carpet of stone that made up Guilder's Row. Raised beds brimmed with fresh herbs and vegetables, filling the air with the fragrance of warm cherry tomatoes, flowering summer squash, and sweet snap peas. There was even a beehive in the far corner of the terrace, its inhabitants buzzing purposefully from plant to plant.

"I come up here when I need to be alone," Olivia said, basking in the tangerine sun with an upturned face and closed eyes. "Some of the servants come out here to tend the garden, but it's usually deserted. I figured you could use a place like this. Especially if Hale is going to barge into your room unannounced."

"I'm not sure if I'll need to worry about that. Apparently, the man has disappeared," Wren said. They hadn't been able to locate him despite venturing into every nook and cranny of the Guildhall.

"I had hoped he'd be up, but he's probably sleeping in," Olivia said. "He's often out late—partying with the other guildmembers at the bars on Nysia Avenue. Let's return the favor and barge in on him!"

"That's a bad idea," Wren said, but Olivia was already pulling her back inside.

Wren found herself shoved in front of a rough wooden door on the second floor. They had ended up where they'd started, just three doors down from her own. It made her stomach flip, thinking of Hale so close.

Olivia stood behind her, practically bouncing with impatience.

Wren rapped lightly on the door.

Nothing.

"He's not here." Wren turned, but Olivia spun her back around. "Nice try."

Wren took a deep breath and rapped harder. "Hale?"

Muffled sounds and curses emanated through the thick door.

She took a step back.

The door flew open to reveal Hale wearing nothing but a pair of low-slung pajama pants.

"New girl," he said, squinting and rubbing his hands through his golden hair. It was out of its tie from yesterday and hung in tousled waves over his shoulders.

Olivia let out a soft peep behind her, and when Wren glanced back, she saw Olivia's wide eyes transfixed by Hale's bronzed chest and ripping stomach.

Wren's face burned and she looked down, trying to regain some semblance of composure. If she didn't look directly at the man, she could just free her tongue from the knots it seemed tied in.

"Olivia and I would like to go into town to run an errand," Wren blurted out. "Can we push our lesson to this afternoon?"

"Yah," Hale said in a sleepy voice. "I never start lessons until after noon, anyway."

A thump sounded inside his room, followed by a feminine exclamation.

Wren looked up into his face, growing cold. "Is there someone in your room?"

A leisurely grin spread across Hale's face. "See you this afternoon, chickadee."

The door closed, and Wren turned woodenly. "There was someone in there!"

"Who cares?" Olivia squealed, linking her arm through Wren's and towing her down the hallway. "Did you see his stomach? I so hoped we'd get to see his stomach."

"You hoped…" Wren said. "You little traitor! You planned this."

Olivia let out her infectious giggle. "And you fell for it. I'm so glad you're here. We're going to have so much fun."

"If I don't get tortured and executed as a murderer," Wren grumbled.

"Yes, that." Olivia frowned, a flicker of melancholy flashing across her face. "Shopping first, then we'll work on solving the murder."

"I think you have your priorities out of line," Wren said, but she relented, allowing Olivia to pull her downstairs. She was content, for now, to let Olivia lead until she got her bearings in this place. Besides, Wren suspected that Olivia needed this trip as much, if not more, than she did.

They stopped in the Guild Controller's office on the first floor, where Olivia explained that Wren needed an advance on her monthly stipend.

"Stipend?" Wren whispered, as the praying mantis of a man uncurled himself from his ledger to head to the safe.

"Of course! Grandmistress Sable didn't tell you? You're a journeyman now; you're entitled to wages. Sable is quite generous."

"Wages?" Wren's eyes grew wide.

"Your former master never gave you a wage? All of them are supposed to, even if it's small. How did you buy clothes? Pay if you went out to eat?"

"I didn't do any of those things," Wren mumbled, thinking of how she had hoarded the precious tips customers had slipped her, sneaking out to buy a new dress to replace the one that had gone up over her knees after her growth spurt two years before.

Olivia's eyes were wide. "What did you do with yourself? Didn't you have any fun? Friends?"

"I worked a lot," Wren said. Work was safe. Work didn't get you into trouble, or break your heart, or try to take advantage of you. "I'm a very good confectioner."

"There is more to life than work," Olivia said, which drew a snort from the controller as he returned, dropping two gold crowns into Wren's hand.

"This is my… monthly stipend?" Wren whispered in awe.

"Like I said," Olivia beamed. "Quite generous."

As the girls walked into the antechamber of the Guildhall, Olivia faltered. "Brace yourself," she whispered. "You're about to meet Marina."

A stately brunette approached from the dining hall, towing a young man in her wake. "Olivia," the girl said. She was lovely, her grass-green eyes set off by the emerald of her well-tailored dress, her ample bosom set off by its tight embroidered corset. Somehow, Wren admitted, to her annoyance, the horn-rimmed glasses the girl wore seemed to compliment her effortless beauty, rather than stifle it.

"Marina," Olivia said coolly. "You're looking well this morning."

"I am, aren't I? And I see you've made a new friend. Forced to choose from the murderers and thieves now, are you?"

"Alleged murderer," Wren said more calmly than she felt, the word stabbing at her gut, years-old guilt and shame threatening to bubble forth. She shoved it back down, focusing on the enemy at hand. She had dealt with this type before, leaders of orphan gangs who ruled by fear and cruelty. To not be inside was to be outside, and to be outside was to be a target.

"I've heard that the poison was in your cupcake," Marina said. "I've never made a confection so bad it killed someone, but I suppose it's possible."

The lanky, black-haired boy behind Marina looked away, as if made uncomfortable by Marina's words. Perhaps he had been fond of the guildmaster.

Wren swallowed an angry retort, instead taking Olivia's hand in her own and pulling her towards the front door. She didn't need to draw this girl's ire more than she apparently already had. Callidus and Willings were enemies enough. *Keep your head down. Don't draw attention.*

"They'll string you up before the month is out," Marina announced behind her.

"Oh, Marina." Olivia turned back. "There was a visitor in Hale's room this morning. I thought it might be you, but... alas, it looks like he has truly moved on."

Marina's eyes narrowed as Wren and Olivia turned and swept through the front door, Wren struggling to keep the smile off her face.

Olivia leaped down the giant steps of the Guildhall, turning right towards the fashion district of the Guilder's Quarter. Wren hadn't spent much time in this part of Maradis, but she had a general sense of the layout. Most of the business and commerce occurred in this quarter. Maradis itself was sandwiched between the Cerulean Bay on the west and Lake Crima on the east. It was a lovely city, bordered by blue water, green trees, and white-tipped mountains. It was no wonder the Imbris clan had chosen it as their capital when they had officially crushed the other clans and driven them east, over the mountains.

"Were Hale and Marina really involved?" Wren asked as they wove through the shoppers on the busy avenue. She couldn't help but be curious about Hale. She had never met anyone like him—so... exuberant. Bold? She wasn't sure how to categorize him. The man unapologetically took up the space of two people in the world. While she took up less than one.

"Briefly," Olivia said. "She's desperately in love with him still."

"Why did they separate?"

"Hale will bed anything that moves. I don't think it was ever more than a fling to him."

Wren processed this information, placing it on a prominent pedestal in the front of her mind. *Do not fall for him!* she chided herself.

"Have you and Hale ever...?" Wren asked.

"No!" Olivia squealed. "Grandaunt would kill me. It'd almost be worth it..." She trailed off, her eyes turning dreamy for a moment.

"Who was that other boy with Marina?"

"Lennon," Olivia said. "Poor guy has to suffer her reign."

"Do they both live at the Guildhall?"

"Yes. They are both sponsored by Grandmaster Beckett, who's the guild's ambassador to the Tradehouse. The guildmaster represents the Guild on the Guilder's Council, but the ambassador does much of the real political work. Policymaking, securing alliances and such. Since he lives at the hall, they live at the hall."

"The Guilder's Council reports to the king, right?" Wren asked. She had dropped out of school when she'd been only eight, and so her understanding of the Alesian political system was sketchy at best.

"Right. The Nobles' Council and the Guilder's Council are the two legislative branches. They make and oversee the laws. All the guilds have a representative on the council, but the ten aperitive guilds make up the Inner Council. They have the most power."

"The aperitive guilds. Those are the ones who… make food, yes? And the Confectioner's is one of those, yes?"

"Yes, and drink. I'm not actually sure why those have more influence than the other guilds, like the Solicitor's or Seamstress's Guild. But that's how it's always been."

Wren thought she did, in fact, know why the aperitive guilds held more power than the rest, thanks to her revealing conversation with Kasper yesterday. But she could never tell Olivia. Or anyone else, for that matter.

"Here we are!" Olivia said, stopping in front of a shop with a stylized needle and thread on the front window.

A cheerful bell trilled as they opened the shop door.

The seamstress, an elegant woman, glided to the front of the shop to meet them. "Olivia, my buttercup," Elda said, kissing the girl on both cheeks. "I'm so, so sorry to hear about your granduncle."

"Thank you, Elda." Olivia dimmed for a moment.

"You let me know if there is anything I can do for you or Iris," Elda said, taking Olivia's hands in hers and squeezing.

"I will. You could help my friend. She needs a full wardrobe," Olivia remarked, seeming to brighten at the thought of shopping.

Wren felt a pang of sympathy for Olivia. She knew what it was to try to shove aside your sorrow, to pretend that everything was fine and normal. The grief would catch up with Olivia sooner or later. But, she supposed, Wren could help distract her today.

With a businesslike nod, Elda led Olivia to a plush velvet divan, retrieving a cold glass of ginger soda for the girl.

Wren, on the other hand, was unceremoniously shooed onto a raised pedestal, where Elda began measuring, poking, and prodding with disapproving clucks and sighs.

"Just a few things," Wren protested, "a dress or two."

Elda and Olivia exchanged a knowing glance and proceeded to ignore Wren completely, spinning through yards of fabric, spindles of ribbon, and piles of accessories. Wren didn't really mind. She knew little about dresses and fashion; it was a relief to not have to try to muddle her way through on her own.

"Seamstress Elda and my grandaunt are old friends," Olivia explained from her perch, trying on a burgundy hat she had pulled off a nearby stand.

"Well, yes and no. You should have seen her back then," Elda said as she measured Wren's foot for a pair of shoes. "Iris was the most beautiful rose in a field of poppies. Lovely, gregarious, funny. All the eligible men sought to win her hand. When Carter Greer, the king's up-and-coming finance minister, caught her eye, it was the talk of the town."

Wren declined to say that she rather liked poppies, thinking their understated beauty far more interesting than the cloying scent of roses.

Elda continued. "I was a young artisan seamstress, just out of my master's shop. I had few clients, barely enough money to buy fabric to make my samples. Until Iris saw one of my designs in the window, a daring floral beaded corset with sheer sleeves, and a full velvet skirt…" Elda's eyes grew misty. "Every woman in Maradis wanted my designs after Iris wore that dress to her wedding. I was set, and Iris and I have made striking gowns together ever since. I suppose you could say she is my muse."

Wren murmured platitudes, wondering what it would be like to know and trust someone for decades. She looked over at Olivia, who was pawing through a pile of jeweled brooches. She couldn't help but smile. If Iris Greer had any of Olivia's infectious enthusiasm in her youth, Wren could see why men had lined up to court her.

"How did your grandaunt end up at the guild?" Wren asked.

Olivia grimaced, putting a brooch back in the pile. "Her husband died very young. He fell off a horse. Grandaunt was with child, but she lost the baby. Her husband's family was unkind to her, and she came to live with her brother, Kasper, at the guild while she recovered."

"Those curs threw her out when she needed them most," Elda said, curling her fist around a pair of scissors. "I hope they're going hungry in hell."

Wren and Olivia looked at each other with eyes wide, and Olivia covered her mouth to keep from giggling. "Elda! Language."

"Well, it's true, my little bluebell," Elda said, picking up four jeweled headbands and holding one after another up to Wren's auburn locks.

"What happened to them?" Wren asked, curiosity overcoming her.

"Bad meat. Apparently, their head cuisiner was buying cheap goods from non-guild members, skimming off the top. The whole Greer clan was taken with an awful stomach ailment at a feast. I hear it was a messy way to go."

Wren wrinkled her nose, shuddering slightly. In her experience, those who deserved punishment didn't often get it. Perhaps justice had been done, after a fashion, on this occasion.

"Anyway," Olivia said brightly, "Grandaunt stayed with the Guild to help Kasper rise to the top. She has an excellent nose for politics."

"That she does," Elda said with a proud nod. "And she can run a household better than anyone. Your Guild is purring like a prize tomcat. It's a shame she never married again, or had children. She still comes in every month for a new dress, though, whatever I design. It's our little tradition."

A dress a month! Wren had never dreamed of such excess. Wren's eyes wandered as she imagined such a life, staring out the window onto the sunny street as the two women continued to sing and chirp about her like nesting robins.

A man strode by the front window, tall and lean, with a sprinkle of white in his dark hair. It was Lucas! The inspector who had vouched for her yesterday. Before she knew what she was doing, Wren launched herself from the platform, twirling to unroll herself from a draping of polka dot lace.

CHAPTER 7

Wren raced into the street, pulling the jeweled headband from her tresses. "Mr. Imbris! Lucas!"

He turned, his eyes widening when he saw her.

She stilled. He looked a different man off the job—hair tousled rather than slicked down, a tweed waistcoat hanging unbuttoned down his front, white shirtsleeves rolled up to reveal strong forearms. Yes, despite the flecks of gray in his hair, he definitely wasn't old. Twenty, maybe?

"Hello, Wren," he said, taking in the headband in her hand and the shopfront from which she had emerged. "Shopping, are we?"

Her face flushed. What was she thinking, wasting time at Mistress Elda's store instead of spending every moment trying to find the real murderer? "I... only have one dress," she stammered lamely.

"I'm not judging," he said soothingly. "You're entitled to a bit of merriment after yesterday's events. How are you holding up?"

"Decently, I suppose. Grandmaster Sable has sponsored me, so I'm not a total orphan. Well, I am an orphan, but not at the guild." Sweet mercy, she was babbling. "What I mean is, she and her other sponsored artisan have promised to help me uncover the truth." She breathed in the faint smell of rosemary wafting from the sprig in the buttonhole of his waistcoat, trying to calm her galloping nerves.

"That's excellent," Lucas said. "Though I can't condone anyone interfering with the official investigation."

"Of course not," Wren said. "We'll just help where we can."

"Good," Lucas said.

A pause. Wren worried the headband with her hand, watching it glitter in the light. "I… didn't get to thank you."

She looked up, meeting his gaze. His eyes were smoky gray quartz. Mesmerizing. "For believing me. For vouching for me. I'll repay you, I swear." She wasn't used to being in a person's debt, besides Master Oldrick's perhaps. It wasn't entirely comfortable.

"You're welcome. But you don't owe me anything. It's my job to protect the vulnerable in Maradis."

"Your job," Wren said. Of course, he was doing his job. What he did for her, he would have done for anyone in need. But still, in her experience, nothing came for free.

"Wren," Olivia said, peeking her head out the door.

"A moment," Wren said over her shoulder before turning back. "Well, thank you again. Please let me know if I can help with your investigation."

A shadow passed across Lucas's handsome face. "There is… something I'd like to discuss with you. Could you meet me in an hour?"

"Of course," Wren said.

"Do you know of the Bitterbird Cafe on Third Avenue?"

"No, but I'm sure Olivia can help me find it."

He pulled a silver pocket watch from his waistcoat, checking it. "Meet me at 12:30, and if it's not too difficult, come alone. My news is for your ears alone."

Wren fidgeted through the remainder of her fitting, unable to focus on the chattering around her. When Elda finally finished the ordering, Wren numbly handed over two of her precious gold crowns, getting a handful of silver and copper in return. It was more money than she had ever had in her life, let alone parted with in one sitting. But Olivia assured her that she was getting an assortment of dresses for casual and dress wear, stockings, shoes, undergarments, and even jewelry and accessories to match. If she was going to live longer than a month, she *would* need something to wear.

"We'll take that burgundy hat, too," Wren said, coming out of her reverie, pointing to the one Olivia had been eying wistfully.

"Oh no," Olivia said. "You needn't!"

"It's the least I can do to thank you for your kindness," Wren said, finding she meant it deeply. She had already grown to depend on Olivia. She cautioned herself. Depending on anyone else was a sure path to ruin.

"Thank you, thank you," Olivia squealed, hugging Wren. "I have the perfect dress to wear it with!"

Wren and Olivia left with one package wrapped in white paper and twine tucked under Wren's arm. A sky blue dress that Elda had sewn for another customer before the order had been canceled. It would be enough to get Wren through until the rest of her order was ready.

"Olivia," Wren said, "do you know of the Bitterbird Cafe?"

"Of course. It's at the intersection where Nysia Avenue meets Third."

"Can I ask you to take me there and then head back to the Guildhall?"'

"Why?"

"I'm to meet Lucas, er, Mr. Imbris, the inspector. He said he has something to tell just me."

"How mysterious," Olivia said with delight. "Let's go."

Olivia deposited Wren on the doorstep of the Bitterbird Cafe five minutes early. Wren pulled open the red front door and entered, taking in the warm exposed brick, the curving wooden tables, the inviting worn leather chairs. The pungent smell of roasting coffee beans swirled about the cafe's patrons—Maradis's upper class, rich nobles and scholars who had the luxury of leisure.

Wren shyly ordered herself a coffee, black, and after retrieving the earthen mug with its warm inky brew from the bar, tucked herself into a small corner facing the street. She looked out the window with wide eyes, watching the world go by. It seemed the whole of the Western Reaches had been brought together on Nysia Avenue—from aristocratic Apricans swathed in silk and leather to a dark-haired Centu clansman heading to his ship nestled in the Port Quarter to grubby Tamrosis in their flowing patchwork cloaks, refugees from the Red Plague or Aprican occupation. She even saw two Magnish children, their dark skin and inky hair decrying their heritage even more than their matching starched uniforms. Sable's exotic coloring and beaded choker suggested she was from the conquered land of Magnus in the far south. Could she have been one of the unfortunate children plucked from the fur and ice of their homes to be educated and "civilized" in Maradis?

"Hello," a deep voice said.

She looked up from the street to see Lucas standing above her, his hands in his pockets. She hastily stood and gestured to the chair opposite her. "Please."

"See something interesting?" He motioned with his head to the street.

"All of it," she said wistfully. "I've never been somewhere like this before."

"A coffee shop?" he asked, bemused.

"I've been to coffee shops before—to drop off confections, mostly. Hardly ever as a patron. Do none of these people work for a living?" she whispered. Wren could hardly remember a day that wasn't filled with eye-twisting work.

Lucas laughed, his smile spilling across his face like a sunbeam. "Not in the way you think, I suspect. Some are writers or artists, some are businesspeople here for meetings, like me," he said. "And you. But yes, some of them don't have to work."

Wren shook her head, unable to comprehend such a life. Living on the street, she'd aspired to having a steady paycheck and a roof over her head. To think that there would ever be more than that... It had been unthinkable.

"You're not like other guildmembers I've met," Lucas said, tilting his head appraisingly.

Wren gripped her hands together to keep from smoothing her dress under his gaze. "Is that why you... vouched for me?" Her eyes met his.

"Yes, I suppose," he said. "I don't know what you did to get Grandmaster Callidus and Steward Willings so out of sorts, but I couldn't stand by while you were blamed for something you didn't do. It would be a miscarriage of justice."

Wren didn't think much of Alesian justice, but she supposed Lucas must believe in the concept to have entered the field he had.

He continued. "The guilds are full of wolves waiting to pounce and spiders weaving their webs. No offense. Not just your guild—all of them."

Wren waved the comment away. She agreed.

"Anyway, it's plain to see you are neither a wolf nor a spider."

"Oh?" She arched a curious eyebrow. "What am I then?"

"I don't know…" He looked at the bricked ceiling, his handsome face twisted in thought. "A sparrow, perhaps."

"A sparrow?" She found a smile forming and struggled to restrain it. "Five points for not saying a wren, but minus three for sticking in the small bird category. Lacking in creativity."

"I'll leave the creativity to the artists and confectioners. I deal in facts. I'll take the two points." He pretended to catch them in the air and pocket them.

"And you? What are you in this zoological metaphor?"

He laughed. He drummed his elegant fingers on his knee, just once. "A wolf. But a wolf trying to find a new way."

A wolf? Was that a warning somehow? "I would have thought you would have said a falcon." The falcon was the Imbris clan crest, blazoned across Alesia's flag and carved into its buildings.

He shook his head vehemently. "Definitely not. I try to keep as far away from… my clan as I can."

That was interesting. She filed the information away. "So a wolf then. Choosing your own destiny. But wolves aren't meant to be solitary creatures," she said.

"No," he agreed.

They looked at each other over the table, the bustling world orbiting around the frozen moment. She felt herself teetering on the edge of something as she pondered his words, trying to ignore how his presence alone steadied and soothed her. And then she pulled back from the edge and looked away, grabbing her forgotten and cooling coffee from the table and taking a gulp. The bitter flavor of the brew brought her back to herself. Affection was a distraction she could ill afford. She did better alone. It had always seen her through. Besides, she didn't know this man.

Wolf or falcon, it didn't matter. Either could take down a wren.

"So," she said. "You said you had news. Have you discovered something?"

"Yes." He leaned forward. "We discovered what type of poison was used." Lucas looked around and leaned closer. He smelled fresh like mint and rosemary. "It's a poison known as Gemini. It's extremely rare and extremely expensive. As far as I know, one needs contacts in the Spicer's Guild to get it, as it comes from beyond Ferwich territory in the east."

"So someone like me would never have had access to something like that," Wren said. That was promising.

"No, you'd need to have a benefactor or be working for someone with connections. But that's not the most interesting thing. Gemini is effective because it's a two-part poison. One part can be hidden in something like your cupcake, while the other part is hidden in another edible. Only individuals who ingest both elements of the poison will die. Either half of the poison, on its own, is harmless."

"Which is why I didn't get sick when I also ate the cupcake?" Wren asked, piecing it together.

"Exactly."

"But... that looks bad for me, doesn't it. I could have poisoned the cupcake safely, knowing I could eat it and be fine." Disappointment pooled heavy in her chest.

Lucas nodded with a grimace. "Discovery that it was Gemini doesn't clear you, not by a long shot. But if we can discover where the second poison was hidden, if it was something you never had access to..."

"Then it couldn't be me."

"That's the hope."

"Where do we even start? If it was something Kasper ate, it could be long gone by now."

"That's a real possibility. But maybe we'll get lucky."

Luck, Wren thought, thinking of the Alesian gold coin hitting heads four times in a row. How long did her cupcake luck last? She needed to talk to Hale about her Gift—and soon.

"What do you want me to do?"

"Nothing, for now. Just keep your ears open. I'm headed back to the Guildhall to go over the scene again and interview some of the servants and kitchen staff. We'll get to the bottom of this mystery."

CHAPTER 8

Wren and Lucas walked back to the Guildhall under the sharp August sun. Their conversation was light. They spoke of the hot summer weather, Lucas's flat above a bookstore across the street from Lake Viri, Wren's history as a confectioner. If he picked up her grimace and change of subject when he asked her about her life before Master Oldrick's shop, he was tactful enough to move on without question.

As she hopped up the stone steps to the Guildhall, she found herself sorry that the walk was ending. They came to a stop in the antechamber of the Guildhall before the yawning mouth of the staircase leading to the second floor. Wren stared at her sandaled feet, feeling strangely tongue-tied.

"Thank—" Wren said, while Lucas said, "Wren—"

They laughed nervously. "Go ahead," she said.

"Wren!" a booming voice called from above. Hale closed the distance from the balcony in two strides and slid, literally slid down the staircase bannister before hopping off next to Wren.

"There's my little robin! Trying to get out of your lesson?" Hale teased, putting his arm around her and pulling her against his body in a side-embrace.

Lucas's eyes narrowed ever so slightly as he took in Hale's virile form. Lucas was tall, but Hale stood a head above him and was much broader in stature. He was muscled where Lucas was lean, bright and obvious where Lucas was dark and subtle.

Wren was the first to recover from her surprise, shrugging her shoulder in an attempt to dislodge Hale's meaty arm. "Hale, this is—"

"Inspector Imbris." Lucas offered his hand. "I'm in charge of the investigation into Guildmaster Kasper's murder."

Hale unwound his arm from Wren's slender shoulders and shook Lucas's hand, pumping it several times. Wren could see the whitening of the men's knuckles as the handshake lasted longer than was strictly necessary.

"Aren't you a little young to be investigating such an important murder?"

"The office of the crown didn't think so," Lucas said with a grim smile.

"You Imbrises do all stick together."

"Hale," Wren said, astounded at his sudden rudeness. "Lucas is helping me clear my name." She looked at Hale pointedly. *We need him.*

"Lucas, is it?" Hale said, raising a golden eyebrow to Wren. "Well, it's nice to meet you. Anyone who's looking out for our girl is all right by me."

"I'm happy to hear I meet with your approval," Lucas said dryly.

"Now we must be off to the teaching kitchens," Hale said.

"Of course," Lucas said. "Wren, I'll be in touch." He turned up the stairs, missing the "I'm sorry" she mouthed at him.

Hale slung his arm around Wren's shoulders once more and led her to the left into the hallway with the teaching kitchens.

"Why were you so...?" Wren couldn't articulate Hale's behavior. "Rude," she finished, knowing that wasn't quite right.

"Naw," Hale said. "I was perfectly polite."

"We need him. He wants to help me figure out who really killed Kasper."

"He's useful, but don't put too much faith in him." Hale turned into one of the kitchens and turned up the lights on the gas chandelier. He shut the door behind him, leaving them alone in the room.

"What do you mean? Why shouldn't I trust Lucas?"

"Inspector Imbris," he said, speaking the name with a mocking undertone, "works for the office of the crown, first and foremost. His loyalties lie with the crown. He will seek to secure their best interest, not ours."

"I don't understand," Wren said.

"The king and the guilds tolerate each other, but each fear the other growing too powerful. Power can't coexist with power. Not peacefully. Not for long."

Wren shook her head. "I thought the guilds worked for the king?"

"We work for ourselves," Hale said. "We do favors for the king because it suits us."

"So we can't trust the crown. Who can we trust? The other guilds?"

Hale laughed. "No! The guilds are constantly vying for power, for a greater share of the market, for control of the council. I wouldn't be surprised if one of the other guildheads was guilty of Kasper's murder. If it wasn't Callidus, that is. My money's still on him."

Wren rubbed her temples. "So we can't trust the crown. We can't trust the other guilds. And we can't trust those within our Guild who may be loyal to Callidus. Who *can* we trust?"

"You can trust me and Sable. That's it. And this." He motioned to the kitchen in a grand gesture. "Our Gifts will never betray us."

Wren chewed the inside of her cheek in thought. Hale's words were a good reminder. Distrust everyone. This had been the unofficial motto she'd lived by, after she had learned the hard way that humanity's capacity for cruelty was only surpassed by the ease of its betrayal. She had grown too comfortable with Lucas too quickly when she didn't truly know anything about him. Perhaps his decision to vouch for her was intended to gain her trust in some way, to use her for some purpose she was too ignorant to conceive of. So she would trust nobody but Sable and Hale. She looked at Hale, leaning against the countertop with an easy arrogance. Her new "family" could have ulterior motives for helping her as well. She would trust nobody, she amended.

"You're right," she said sweetly to Hale. "I'm lucky to have you and

Sable. There's so much I don't understand about this place."

"That's all right," Hale said, brightening and pulling two stools up to the counter. "We're here to teach you."

Wren sat, donning the guise of a wide-eyed and pliable pupil. But as Hale began to talk, she found herself growing into her charade, fascinated by what he told her.

"Our understanding of the Gifted is limited because each guild is extremely secretive about their own power. Kasper made you drink the binding wine, yes?"

Wren touched her lips, shivering with the memory of her mouth and throat sealing shut. She nodded.

"So you understand how closely this secret is guarded. It's why the king tolerates the guilds having such power. Because he needs us. Our Gifts. This secret, these Gifts, are what made Alesia what it is today."

"I don't understand," Wren admitted.

"How much history do you know?"

"Not much," she admitted.

"But you know that Alesia was not always united, that in the past the clans each held their own territory and warred between one another?"

"Yes, until the Imbris clan conquered the others, claimed the territory of Alesia, and set up Maradis as its capital. The other clans were driven east over the Cascadian mountains into Ferwald."

"Precisely. But do you know how King Leon Imbris, the father of Alesia, rose and conquered the other clans after centuries of petty wars?"

"No."

"Few know the real reason. He discovered the first Gifted. It was said he was Gifted himself."

Wren's eyebrows raised. "He used Gifted guildmembers to win battles? Surely, it couldn't have such an impact."

"What magic does your Gift generate, if you know?"

"Luck," she said.

"What type?"

"Good luck."

"We're a pair, aren't we! I'm good luck too," Hale said. "But only when it comes to betting. Games."

Wren's eyes were wide.

"Can you see how a little luck might change the course of a battle? Make a man his fortune? An arrow missing its mark, a gambler hitting the right number and making his fortune. Small things change the course of history."

She nodded. "So the king uses the Gifted to maintain his throne?"

"Yes," Hale said. "The deal is simple. The Gifted supply their wares to the king for his use and discretion, and they keep the secret of the king's power. In return, the king leaves the guilds alone, allows us to do what we please—set our own rates, collect our own tariffs and dues. We renegotiate the terms of the Accord between the king and the guilds every twenty-five years, but it's mostly symbolic. The terms haven't changed in centuries. Actually, it's up for negotiation this fall."

"I understand why you distrust the crown," Wren said. "But what do all these Gifts do? Surely, they don't all have to do with luck."

"You are correct, my bright pupil. Kasper and the prior guildheads have spent decades uncovering the power of the other guilds. We know generally what magic most of their Gifts create. We don't, however, know the identities of the Gifted in other guilds, or the specifics of their Gifts. With the exception of a few."

"Why don't the guilds work together? Share information to become more powerful?"

"There's a history of distrust between us, which Sable suspects the king encourages. And revealing you are Gifted makes you a target. Kidnapping, murder, extortion. All are risks. No one is willing to be the first to bare themselves."

His words chilled her. Kidnapping? Extortion? Someone would go to such lengths to get their hands on a Gifted... She thought of Kasper, convulsing on the floor, his mouth foaming. Yes... she supposed he spoke the truth. She wasn't sure she wanted any part of this.

"You said you know the general nature of the other Guilds' magic. What is it?"

"The ten aperitive guilds are divided into the three orders. The Leavening Guilds—that is, us, the Baker's Guild, and the Cheesemonger's Guild. Our powers deal with luck and fortune. The Cheesemonger's Guild's magic deals with intelligence and learning. Imagine being able to learn a new skill overnight. It would come in handy, would it not?"

"I wouldn't mind getting my hands on that," she admitted, thinking of all the learning she had missed through her childhood. She wouldn't even be able to read if it hadn't been for her brother.

"You and me both."

"What's next? The Infusing Guilds?"

"Precisely. The Piscator's, Butcher's, and Cuisinier's Guilds. Their magic is a bit more foreign to us since they don't make something from scratch, like we do. But best as we figure it, the Butcher's Guild's magic gives strength and prowess in battle, and the Cuisinier's Guild has the power of healing and health."

"Healing?" Wren's eyes widened.

He nodded. "You can see how those would all be important on the battlefield. The last Order are the Fermenting Guilds—the Vintner's, Distiller's, and Brewer's Guilds. The Vintner's Guild magic deals with secrets and lies. We're not sure about all the rest."

"Secrets and lies..." she said. "The wine I drank."

"Oh, yes," Hale said. "All the guilds know of the Vintner's Guild's magic, thanks to the binding wine. It's part of the Accord, that we will bind all Gifted with it."

"That's only nine guilds." Wren said, ticking them off on her fingers. "The last is the Spicer's Guild? What power do they have?"

"The magic of death."

"Death?" Wren asked. "As in, their spices kill people?"

"Is it so hard to believe? Food gives life... or it can bring death. Steal years from a life, bring on wasting sickness."

"Do you think they had anything to do with Kasper's death?" Wren asked. "Would another guild oppose ours in that way?"

Hale frowned, an expression that still managed to look alluring on his handsome face. "The guilds tend to prefer political maneuvering and dirty looks over the council table, but it's possible. The head of the Spicer's Guild is a devil of a man named Pike. He'd poison his own sister if it put a few crowns in his pocket. Sable seems to adore him; the gods only know why. I'll ask her about him, though."

"Ask me about who?"

Hale and Wren both jumped, as if they had been caught with their hands in the candy jar.

Sable stood at the door, looking effortlessly beautiful in an olive gown with a mustard-gold bodice. One dark eyebrow was arched in a question.

"Grandmaster." Hale straightened, inclining his head. "Wren and I were discussing our theories about potential suspects."

Sable pulled Hale's stool out from behind him and sat on it, motioning Wren to sit as well. Hale leaned against the wooden countertops, at ease despite Sable's slight. So far, Sable seemed to be the only woman Hale didn't turn his charms on. He was strangely deferential around her. *Perhaps she's immune,* Wren thought, with more than a little jealousy. If her stupid stomach would quit performing somersaults in Hale's presence, it would simplify things considerably.

"Tell me your theories," Sable said.

"Well," Wren stuttered, caught off guard. It had been less than a day since Kasper had been declared dead. Was she already expected to have theories? "Callidus."

"No," Sable said, shaking her head curtly. "What else?"

"But... He stands to be the next guildmaster. And he had access to the cupcake. He was alone with it. He knew I would be there, and he literally pointed the finger at me. He's the obvious suspect."

"It was not Callidus. Do not focus your energy there."

Wren looked at Hale for support. His eyes were sympathetic, but his face remained stony.

"How do you know?"

"I know, girl," Sable said. "Callidus is miserable and spiteful and unfeeling, but he is not a murderer. He certainly wouldn't have harmed Kasper in particular."

Wren opened her mouth to protest again, but the intensity of Sable's expression made her think the better of it.

"Got it," Wren said. "Not Callidus."

"Who else?"

Hale chimed in. "Wren had the good instincts that it might be one of the other guildmasters. Moving in on our territory, seeking to consolidate power."

"Perhaps," Sable said, pondering. "The Distiller's Guild and the Confectioner's have always vied for position at the head of the table, so to speak. Guildmaster Chandler seems innocuous enough, but that could be a façade. I will think on it."

Wren let out a breath, dismayed to find how much this woman's approval mattered to her. But as Sable had said last night, she and Hale were her family now. They were the only guild members besides Olivia who had shown any interest in helping or protecting her. If she was going to find Kasper's killer, she couldn't do it alone. She needed to be in Sable's good graces.

"Have you learned anything else?" Sable asked. "You spoke to the Inspector today, yes?"

"Yes," Wren said, glancing sidelong at Hale. How had Sable known? Hale hadn't left her side. "The poison that killed Kasper is called Gemini."

Sable's eyes widened.

"You've heard of it?" asked Wren.

"Yes. Very hard to come by. Very hard indeed. And expensive. This will narrow our pool of suspects considerably. I will speak to Guildmaster Pike to see what he knows."

"Luc—Inspector Imbris still doesn't know how the second poison was delivered," Wren admitted. "It's possible we'll never know."

"Then I suggest you focus on what we do know."

A pause.

"The cupcake," Sable said, exasperated. "We know the cupcake was poisoned."

"Right, which Callidus had," Wren countered, wishing the woman would reconsider her position on the man.

"The cupcake didn't spring into existence fully formed in Callidus's hand."

"No…" Wren admitted.

"Presumably your Master sold it to someone, someone who had knowledge of its unusual properties ate it, and somehow Kasper learned of it. There shouldn't be a long list of individuals who meet those criteria."

"Does Callidus know who the original purchaser was?" Wren asked. "Did he retrieve it?"

Sable shook her head. "I asked him. Kasper was the one who learned of your Gift and acquired the cupcakes. Callidus is unaware of how."

So he says, Wren wanted to scream. Callidus may have Sable convinced, but Wren wouldn't be fooled so easily.

"I could ask Master Oldrick whom he sold the cupcakes to," suggested Wren. "He may still have a record."

"Excellent," Sable said. "The Masters will be convening in two days' time to vote on a new guildmaster. You can ask him then." Sable rose with a swish of silk and chiffon. "Hale, I have need of you. You can resume your lessons tomorrow."

She nodded to Wren and swept from the room, Hale trailing like an eager puppy.

Wren sat on the stool for a moment, dumbfounded. Sable was like a looming thunderstorm, full of barely contained power and force.

She looked about the kitchen, biting her lip. Did she have the rest of the afternoon to herself? She needed to discover who'd killed Kasper, that much was perfectly clear. The cupcake, the secret of the second part of the poison, these were both possibilities to explore. But where should she start? Indecision gnawed at her.

Lucas should still be upstairs investigating Kasper's rooms, she realized, her feet propelling her before her conscious mind made the decision. Maybe he'd found something.

CHAPTER 9

Wren met no resistance until she rounded the hallway and found an ebony-haired guardsman with a mustache standing sentry before Kasper's door. "No one allowed inside, miss," he said with more than a little hostility. "'Specially you."

"I'm assisting Inspector Imbris with the investigation," Wren said, sticking her chin out haughtily. "He asked for me."

The man looked at her, his bushy eyebrows furrowed.

"Ask him yourself," she said, praying that Lucas would corroborate her story.

The guard slipped through the door with a grumble, closing it in her face. Muffled voices sounded inside.

He reappeared and opened the door for her, clearly not happy about it. "You leave when the Inspector leaves," he said. "And I supervise. It's the scene of a crime."

"Fine," she said, stepping inside, the guard following close on her heels. The man positioned himself against the bookshelf where Callidus himself had been leaning just the day before.

"Hello," Wren said, crossing to where Lucas was pawing through a pile of papers on Kasper's desk.

"I asked for you, did I?" Lucas said in a low voice.

A guilty smile flitted across her face. "Thanks for going with it," she whispered.

"That Hale fellow bored with you already?" he asked, not looking at her.

Wren crossed her arms. "No. Sable had need of him. Our lesson was short today."

Lucas snorted. "I'll offer another lesson then, free of charge. That artisan has been under the skirts of half of Maradis. Watch yourself with him."

"You presume that I'm foolish enough to need that type of lesson?" she snapped. "Give me a little credit."

He held his hands up in surrender. "Forgive me for questioning your wisdom, my lady. Surely, you don't have time for such distractions anyway."

"I don't," she said, as much to herself as to him. "As you said, the king and his inquisitor return in less than a month."

"Is that why you're here? To keep away from... distractions?" His eyes met hers and warmth blazed through her.

"Yes. I thought I could help you do... whatever you're doing. It *is* my neck on the line." Her eyes drifted to the dark spot on the patterned Ferwich rug where Kasper's blood and foam had mingled as he'd died. Why did the man have to die? It might not have been so bad—to be sleeping in her huge feather bed, taking lessons from Hale, shopping with Olivia—if there wasn't a murder charge hanging over her head. Why could things not have gone her way, just once?

Lucas straightened, considering her appraisingly. He softened. "There's a lot to go through... But no."

"No?" Wren said, dismayed at the waver in her voice.

"I'll find whoever did this. But I can't have your help," he said softly, his eyes flicking to where the guard stood, watching them. "It's bad enough that I vouched for you. I'm lucky they didn't take me off the case."

Her throat constricted as she tried to suppress her disappointment.

"There must be something," she said. "I can't... I can't just do nothing."

He sighed, looking about the room. "Just—sit over there." Lucas pointed to the couch. "I can't have you touching anything, but you can observe.

"Thank you!" she said, following instructions. At least she could be the first to learn of anything he learned.

"You there," Lucas said to the mustached guard. "What's your name?"

"Pimm," the man said.

"Would you mind helping if you're going to be in here?"

The man's mustache twitched with distaste, but he nodded, leaning his spear against the bookshelf.

"Take everything you find that you can eat or drink and pile it in that corner," Lucas said to the guard. He crossed to a table near where Wren sat, riffling through some papers, speaking low. "I procured a bit of Gemini poison that was forgotten in the evidence vault. If one of these items reacts..."

"Then we know it's filled with Gemini's other half."

"Precisely."

Wren watched as the guard piled bottles of wine and brandy, boxes of chocolates, and even a wedge of hard cheese. "This man had quite an appetite," Wren commented as she surveyed the growing pile.

Lucas stood from the desk where he had resumed leafing through letters and knelt by the pile, pulling a small indigo vial out of his vest pocket.

Wren held her breath, watching like a hawk as Lucas removed the stopper and began administering a tiny drop in each of the bottles and delectables Kasper had in his office.

"That's the last I could find," Pimm said, depositing a bottle of bourbon-infused maple syrup on the floor next to the others. "What're you looking for?" the guard asked, his role in the investigation apparently sparking his curiosity.

"I'm not sure," Lucas said. "But I feel like there should be something out of the ordinary... I'm basically going on instinct here."

Wren knew that feeling.

As Lucas put the last drop on the wedge of what looked and smelled like gruyere cheese, she deflated slightly. None of the edibles had reacted.

They exchanged a disappointed look.

"I was so sure…" Lucas said. He shook his head. "It's fine. We'll find it."

Wren looked about the room, a niggling feeling biting at her. She had been so sure he would find it here too.

"Is there anywhere you didn't look?" she asked.

"No. Well—" he amended. "The bottom desk drawer is locked, but I haven't found the keys. It's pretty solid. I'll have to come back with one of our locksmiths."

"There are a spare set of keys to everything in the guardsmen's office," Pimm suggested. "It might have a key to the desk."

"Would you run and grab them?" Lucas asked. "We can check."

"Sure," the man said, turning and jogging out the door, apparently forgetting he had angrily sworn to supervise her.

Wren grinned, suddenly thankful she had aid to offer, no matter how illicit. One didn't spend two years on the streets of Maradis without picking up a few tricks. She was terrible at fighting, but she had quick fingers. The same gifts that made her an excellent confectioner made her handy at picking a lock. "No need to wait and see," she said, standing and striding to the desk.

Wren knelt down, eyeing the lock. She rummaged around the desk for something long and thin. The lock was large, the kind that would turn with an ornate key. Her eyes lit up as they fell upon a thin letter opener, and a twisted clip of metal holding the pages of a ledger together. "This'll do."

"Wren…" Lucas said with warning in his tone.

Wren shushed him. "I'll be done before he even gets back."

She jimmied the makeshift instruments into the lock, feeling around for the tumblers. She was rusty at this. She hadn't picked a lock since before Master Oldrick had found her. But her hands fell into their old rhythm easily, and in another minute, the lock turned with a satisfying click.

Lucas offered her a hand to help her up, his thick eyebrows raised. "The king's inspector is going to pretend he didn't see that."

"I think that's wise." With a deep breath, Wren opened the drawer. Her senses were tingling. There was something here, she knew it.

"Well done," Lucas breathed, lifting out a bottle of amber liquid. Wren peered at the bottom of the empty drawer for a moment. It looked strange to her, smaller than she would have expected from the exterior. She poked at the bottom, experimentally. Yes, there was something odd about it.

He opened the stopper and whiffed, rearing back slightly. "Whiskey."

She abandoned the drawer and looked at the label, a plain parchment affair with two words inked across it. "Destrier's Reserve," Wren read.

"It looks like a private label," Lucas remarked. He took the stopper off the tiny vial of poison and let a single drop fall into the neck of the whiskey bottle. The instant it hit the liquid, the amber turned milky, foam covering the surface.

"We found it." She squealed in relief, hugging Lucas before she thought better of it.

He didn't seem to mind, and after a moment of stiffness wrapped his long arms around her, burying his nose in her hair.

"What in the Beekeeper's name is going on in here?" a stern voice barked from the doorway.

Lucas and Wren flew apart like oil and water.

Callidus stood at the door, his expression thunderous under his swooping black hair.

Pimm stood behind him with a ring of keys.

"Your investigation methods are quite irregular, Imbris," Callidus snarled. "What am I to think other than she's corrupted you too, and now you're aiding her cause? Perhaps I should have you replaced as inspector."

Wren trembled with anger and regret. Lucas had told her she shouldn't be here, yet she had insisted. Had she jeopardized the whole investigation? No other inspector would believe her like Lucas. Though she had only met him yesterday, she somehow trusted him to find the real killer, at least more so than anyone else. He had believed her. Vouched for her. If he was removed from the investigation... the thought struck terror in her heart.

"You don't have the authority," Lucas growled, taking a step towards Callidus. "Besides, Wren and I were just celebrating the discovery of a key piece of evidence. She sat on the couch the entire time and didn't touch a single piece of evidence. She was supervised the entire time by both myself and Mr. Pimm here, isn't that right?"

"Yes," Pimm admitted, his face darkening with embarrassment. "I wouldn't let her in without watching her like a hawk, Grandmaster."

"Supervised. Is that what you call it?" Callidus's piercing blue eyes flicked between Wren and Lucas with a look of disdain.

"We're done here," Lucas said, tidying the papers on the desk, pocketing the little flask, and grabbing the bottle by its neck. "If you're done with your insults, I'll be going." He walked towards the door and Wren followed involuntarily, towed along behind him like a moon orbiting its planet. She didn't want to be alone in this room with Callidus.

"Imbris," Callidus said, stopping him with a hand on his chest. "The girl is not allowed back in this room. Am I understood?"

Lucas nodded curtly.

Wren's blood boiled over. To talk about her as if she weren't even in the room! Like she didn't have a name, an identity. She suddenly hated herself for staying small and meek and quiet, a little wren as light as air, a flitting shadow barely there. "What's the matter, Grandmaster?" she said quietly, her normal reserve overcome by a sudden recklessness. "Worried this girl will discover who the real killer is? That you have a traitor in your hall?" She met his gaze, the challenge written on her face. *I know it's you,* she thought. *And I'm going to prove it.*

"Come on, Wren," Lucas said, taking her gently by the arm. "I agree to your terms, Grandmaster." Lucas pulled Wren out the door.

They strode down the two sets of stairs, not looking back. Lucas's warm fingers still rested on her arm, heating her skin. His face was stormy.

Her roiling anger gave way as they left Callidus behind them, leaving guilt in its wake. "I'm sorry. Have I jeopardized the investigation? Will you be taken off it?"

"It's all right. The Grand Inspector trusts me. He wouldn't take me off the case, especially…"

"Especially why?"

"Nothing," he said. "Because I've already begun to know the case."

"Good."

They stopped near the front door to the Guildhall, under the hanging gas chandelier of iron and glowing bulbs. "I'd like to continue to help, if I can," Wren said. "I'll keep my ears open here, like you asked."

"That will be valuable, thank you."

"How will I contact you if I find something? I don't want to just walk into the inspector's office."

He considered this, scrunching his lips in thought. The gesture pulled at a string in her chest. She had a sudden urge to run her fingers across the right angle of his jaw and clutched her hands behind her to still them.

"My brother is a priest at the Temple of the Sower. It's not far from here, across the plaza from the end of Guilder's Row. To the south. We could meet there to exchange information."

"The Temple of the Sower?" She blanched. She had sworn she would never reenter a temple, never trust the Sower or its priests. Not... Not after what had happened.

Lucas cocked his head, watching her. Those gray falcon eyes missed little. "Will you be struck down if you enter?" he joked.

She shook her head and forced a laugh, struggling to ignore the crawling feeling that itched across her skin. "I just..." She couldn't explain, and so she settled on a joke. "I have a hard time trusting authority figures..."

"Who doesn't?" He shrugged. "I can try to find somewhere else..."

"Your brother is a priest? Is he... trustworthy?"

"He's my brother," Lucas said. "Well, yes, he's one of the trustworthy brothers."

"How many brothers do you have?"

"Six."

"Six?" She raised an eyebrow.

"And a sister."

"My, your parents must have been busy. And your poor sister, to be terrorized by seven brothers!"

"Feel sympathy for us! She's the headstrong terror." Lucas joked, his hands on his heart.

Wren smiled. "I only have to deal with your brother? No other priests?"

"I'll make sure of it," he said.

She nodded her assent. "When should we meet?"

"We need some sort of signal…" He drummed his slender fingers on the bottle tucked under his arm. Then he pulled something out of his pocket and flipped it to her.

It slipped through her fingers, but she retrieved it from the ground with a grunt of annoyance. It was a silver button—the outline of a bird etched into its surface. Wren saw that it matched the buttons on his waistcoat. The bottom button was missing, the thread hanging.

"In the front vestibule of the temple, there's a statue of the Sower. People leave offerings, coins. Leave that in his outstretched hand. I'll check it daily, and you do the same. If it's there by six, we meet at ten that night. My brother's name is Virgil."

She looked at the button in her hand. "You need one too," she protested, holding it out.

"I have four more," he grinned, tapping his chest. "We have both the poisons now. I should be able to discover how Kasper acquired this one. It was locked away, which means the true killer is unlikely to be a servant."

But also unlikely to be Callidus, she thought. Unless he had a key or had picked the lock. She shook her head to clear it. She would think on it.

Lucas watched her with obvious amusement. "It will all be fine, Wren. I'll see you soon," he said, his voice thick with promise.

CHAPTER 10

Wren fell into a deep and soundless sleep that night, exhausted from the revelations of the day. When morning came, bright and strong, she rose and splashed water on her face, examining how her alabaster skin glowed in the illuminated light pooling through the window, how the sun's rays highlighted the flecks of gold in her eyes. She brushed her auburn hair until it cascaded about her shoulders in thick, shining waves before dressing in the cornflower blue dress she had taken from the seamstress's shop. The dress was lovely, its neat white stitching and marching row of buttons accenting its simple tailoring. She smoothed her hands down the soft fabric. It was finer than anything she had ever owned.

Despite the murder charge hanging over her head, Wren felt like a new woman in this place. She had to stay. She couldn't go back to the dingy room above Master Oldrick's shop. She had been standing still for far too long, unwilling to leave the safe monotony of life as an apprentice. She had told herself she was being cautious, biding her time, but the truth whispered in the corners of her soul. She'd been afraid.

Afraid to reopen old wounds, unwilling to risk old vulnerabilities. But she was older now, shrewder, wiser. And for whatever it was worth, she was enchanted. Valuable. Perhaps she was readier to meet this world than she realized.

Wren descended the stairs and found her way to the dining hall. The simple wooden tables and benches were sparsely attended, with only a half-dozen guildmembers and guards sitting down to breakfast. The dining hall was large enough to house all of the guildmembers en masse, which was clearly not a daily occurrence.

Wren retrieved a plate from the front of the room, where the food was laid out buffet style. She grabbed two of the amazing biscuits and the loganberry jam she had devoured the day before and added a poached egg and a cluster of grapes. Finally, balancing a steaming cup of coffee in the other hand, she turned. Marina and her artisan colleague, Lennon, stood behind her, toothy wolves waiting for a sheep.

Wren's face paled, her newfound confidence leaving her with a rush of breath.

"Are you still here?" Marina sneered. She wore a pale lavender dress today, cut low to reveal her swan's neck and generous bosom. "Haven't you been hanged yet?"

"The king doesn't hang murderers," Wren said coolly. "He beheads them." Hardly the most comforting of retorts, but it seemed to give Marina pause.

Wren seized the opportunity and stepped past them. A heel-clad foot shot out and tripped her, sending her sprawling on the floor in a splatter of jam and coffee.

Laughter rang out behind her as Wren gathered herself and got to her feet. She surveyed her dress in dismay. It was ruined—scarlet jam and egg yolk smeared down the bodice, coffee soaking through the skirt. Her face burned in anger and embarrassment.

Wren was overcome with an urge to pummel the girl, to hear her fist connect with Marina's nose in a satisfying crunch. It was a fleeting fantasy. She'd just as likely break her hand. And so she stood, her cheeks on fire, glaring into Marina's haughty face. Even when she had lived on the street, where casual violence was a currency much respected and often traded between street gangs, she'd been no good at fighting. Ansel, the head of the orphan gang she had run with, the Red Wraiths, had tried to teach her to fight for weeks before declaring the cause hopeless and teaching her to pick locks instead.

"What in the heavens?" Guildmistress Greer said from across the room, swooping towards them. "Wren, what happened?" She surveyed the broken dishes on the floor. She lifted the hem of her damask skirt away from the mess, her lip curling in distaste.

Marina closed her mouth and donned an innocent expression as the Guildmistress turned the full weight of her withering glare on the girl. Lennon looked away, guilt playing across his features like sunlight on a lake.

"Marina, you wretched girl, this has your handwriting all over it," the Guildmistress thundered, gesturing across the room to a serving girl in a "get-over-here-and-clean-this-up" motion.

"But, Guildmistress—" Marina said, her green eyes wide and wounded behind her thick frames.

"Don't you 'but, Guildmistress' me," Greer said. "I see you. This isn't the schoolyard anymore. This is your Guild, your place of business, and Wren is your business partner. Act like it, or your father will hear of it. And I suspect, he won't be as forgiving as I."

A grim smile grew on Wren's face as Marina blanched at the dressing down. Guildmistress Greer was not whom Wren had expected based on their previous frosty interaction.

"Come with me, Wren." The Guildmistress motioned with a curt nod of her head. "We'll see what we can do about getting those stains out before they set."

Greer led Wren down a back hallway.

"Marigold, follow us, please," Greer said to a mousy brunette hurrying past.

"Me?" The girl squeaked and turned as Greer continued down the hallway.

"Is there another Marigold I could be talking to?" Greer said over her shoulder, and Wren suppressed a smile. She suddenly understood why the guild members snapped to attention when Greer was nearby.

After a few more twists and turns, Greer led Wren and Marigold into a bright sundrenched sitting room. The room was furnished in white and gray, accented with gold. A pair of cushy armchairs flanked the marble fireplace, and the white rug on the floor before them looked plush enough to bury her toes into. Blooming bouquets of huge-headed dahlias burst in vibrant explosions of color on every flat surface.

"Are these your chambers?" Wren asked, her eyes wide. She had never seen something quite so beautiful, so tastefully manicured. They made her own wide chambers look downright shabby.

"Yes, I've been here for almost twenty years," Greer said, retrieving a basket from the washroom. "Since before Kasper became a grandmaster." When she said his name, she paused for a moment before shaking her head, as if clearing a memory. "Come on, off with it."

"What?"

"Your dress! Take it off. Marigold can't very well clean it with you still in it."

Wren exchanged a look with Marigold, who hovered awkwardly by the door. Marigold's look seemed to say, *there's no resisting, so you better get on with it.*

The last thing Wren wanted was to undress in front of these two strangers, but she pushed aside her anxiety and unzipped her dress, stepping out of it so she stood only in her thin slip.

"Don't drop it on the rug," Greer said, holding the basket out.

Wren deposited the garment into the basket. Marigold darted forward and grabbed it, practically fleeing the room.

Goosebumps pebbled Wren's skin as the door swung shut, leaving the two of them alone. She couldn't decide where to put her hands, and so they twitched aimlessly about her, clasping and unclasping. She itched for pockets to thrust them into.

Greer seemed to be studying her, her stately form still and poised.

"I'm so sorry about your brother," Wren said when the silence stretched too thin. "I… didn't kill him." Best to just get it out there.

"I know, dear. I know," Greer said, her sudden kindness reminding Wren of Kasper. A small smile appeared on her creaseless face. "I'm sorry about the other day. My rudeness. I was in shock."

"I understand," Wren said. "It's awful what happened."

"Yes, it is. Kasper was a good man, and a good head of this Guild. He was so excited to have found another Gifted, you know. Excited about you."

Wren's eyes widened. "You… know… about that?" Her throat didn't burn, so clearly Greer was on the approved list.

"Come with me," Greer said, motioning with an outstretched hand, her nails carefully painted a red as bright as her dahlias. "Let's find you something to wear while I tell you the tale."

Greer led Wren through a bedroom filled with a mountain of a snowy comforter surrounded by another field of dahlias into a closet the size of the cabin Wren had grown up in as a child.

"Any of my things will be swimming on you, you're so thin," Greer said, tiptoeing her fingers across one of the wall-length racks of dresses, "but a belt can work wonders. Let me see…"

Greer pawed through her domain while Wren turned in a circle, gaping at what she saw. Racks of dresses; shelves of shoes; hooks full of glittering necklaces, scarves, and hats. A gold-trimmed vanity table sat against the far wall, its surface practically buried beneath a rainbow of bottles, perfumes, and powders.

"I've always loved fine things," Greer said, only a hint of contrition in her voice. "Ever since Carter started courting me in my teens. He spoiled me," she said, her eyes faraway for a moment. "But we weren't speaking of me. We were speaking of you, and the Gifted. Kasper and I were twins, you know. Born three minutes apart. He was the older, and he never let me forget it. That was the only formative moment of his life that I missed."

"His birth?" Wren asked. "You can't hardly be blamed for that."

"I think I was supposed to be born first. I always told Kasper as much. Ah!" Greer said, triumphantly pulling a teal dress with tiny red and white dots from the rack. "This one was a gift and is much too small for me. Try it on."

Wren stepped into the dress as Greer continued.

"Kasper and I did everything together as children. We were much closer than we were with our younger sister, Olivia's grandmother. She was ten years younger than us, a surprise addition. I was there when Kasper first discovered his Gift. I ate most of his early work, which caught up with me." She patted her bottom with a grimace.

The dress was loose on Wren, but Greer cinched it with a wide leather belt, and the look wasn't half-bad.

Greer continued her tale. "We explored his Gift together, discovered what it meant. After Kasper became guildmaster, we uncovered that other guilds had similar Gifted, but with different talents. We still don't know who all the Gifted are, or what they can do. The guilds guard their secrets jealously."

"Did you and Kasper discover why the Gifting occurs?" *Why me?* she thought. *Why am I different?*

"No. We've never discovered why a particular person is Gifted while another is not," she said sharply. "It frustrated Kasper to no end. He was even talking about trying to work together with other guilds, pool knowledge and resources." She shook her head.

"You don't think that was a good idea?"

"Kasper was always too trusting," Greer said. "If there are two constants in this life, it's men and their power. If they don't have it, they want it; if they have it, they want more of it. Like roosters in the henyard. I didn't think it was safe to trust anyone. And though it gives me no comfort to say it, perhaps I was right. Because now he's dead."

Wren had to agree with the Guildmistress. But it was an interesting piece of information, if Kasper was indeed trying to cooperate with another guild. Perhaps his efforts to band together had gotten him killed. "What guild was Kasper cooperating with?"

Guildmistress Greer looked at her shrewdly, and Wren realized she had gone too far.

"Don't you worry about that," Greer said, suddenly shepherding her towards the door. "The king's inspectors will uncover who was to blame for this horrible crime. No need to worry about things you don't fully understand."

Wren chaffed at the dismissal but knew not to push the Guildmistress's affability. "Thank you for your assistance with my dress. And Marina," she added.

"It was my pleasure. The girl's only here because Grandmaster Beckett is her father. She misses no chance to make Olivia's life miserable, so I don't miss an opportunity to return the favor." Greer grinned a wolfish smile, and Wren found herself smiling back.

CHAPTER 11

Wren tugged at the borrowed dress as she made her way to the teaching kitchen. Her stomach growled. She hadn't been able to eat any of her breakfast, thanks to Marina's cruelty.

She found Hale already waiting when she entered the kitchen.

"There's my little hummingbird!" Hale exclaimed when she entered, clapping his hands. "I hear you, Marina, and your breakfast had a disagreement this morning."

Wren's face reddened. "She did most of the disagreeing."

"Don't let her bother you," Hale said. "She's jealous."

"Jealous? Of a suspected murderer?"

"She wanted Sable to sponsor her, get her away from dear old daddy. He's strict—and a bit of a self-righteous ass," Hale said.

"But… he's her father," Wren said. To have a father who cared… even if he was strict… Marina was luckier than many.

"Right. Sable didn't want any part of that family drama."

Wren shook her head. "I won't let her pull me in. I don't know what you saw in her." Wren tossed this last bit out like a fishing line, hoping Hale would take the bait. Was there anything still between him and Marina? Her interest was purely academic, of course.

"It was a fleeting madness," he said. "There was a lot of eyelash-batting and hair-flipping. In the end, she wasn't really my type."

"Your type?" Wren scoffed. "You mean female?"

"Ouch, this bird has talons," he said, pressing a hand to his broad chest in mock affront. He drew closer to her with a mischievous grin, threatening to overwhelm her with his size, his bright smile, his sculpture-fine features. "It's all right, Wren. I like it when they bite." He feinted towards her with fingers crooked like claws, quickly, playfully.

Her heart skittered in her chest, and she drew in a breath, shying away from him. *Steady, Wren.* The man was incorrigible. He was flirting with her just because he could. Because he enjoyed the effect he had on women. "Are we going to cook today, or are you going to waste the whole morning with sad attempts to stroke your male ego?"

"Oh, that's not the part I'm attempting to get stroked—"

"Hale!" she shrieked, punching him in the shoulder with all her might. "Enough!"

He rocked back on his stool and guffawed with great booming laughs.

Wren tried to hold the disapproving mask on her features, but it slipped with a twitch of her lips. She started laughing too, surprised at how good it felt.

After a minute, Hale settled down, wiping a tear from the corner of his eye. "You're too easy to mess with."

"And do you mess with Sable like that?"

"Sable…" He rubbed his jaw, seeming to be momentarily lost for words. He shook his head. "All right, Wren. You win. We cook."

And with that flipped switch, Hale began teaching her how to use her Gift.

"Lesson number one. It's a matter of intuition," he said. "Which you know, because you already used your Gift without meaning to. But it's important to learn what it feels like when you infuse a batch with magic. As far as we can tell, our Gifts are innate, and we can't change them. Meaning, if your Gift is producing good luck, that's pretty much it. You can learn to control the dose, the strength, how long the luck lasts, but you can't create a confection that heals wounds or helps a man lift a cart with his bare hands."

"Makes sense," Wren said, though she wasn't sure if it did.

"That brings us to lesson number two. Magic comes with a price. When you infuse a confection with luck, that luck has to come from somewhere. It comes from you. Your natural store of magic is depleted, transmuted into the food."

Wren's mouth dropped open as her mind reeled. "So… if I've been infusing things without knowing it, I've been wasting my luck?"

"Wasting it, gifting it, it's a matter of interpretation. Who's to say if it's a waste?"

"I am! Trust me, whoever ate those confections, I needed that luck more than they did." The tenor of her life came into sudden focus. Escaping one cruel captor only to find another. Her father's drunken rages. Losing Hugo. Brother Brax at the Sower's orphanage. Life on the street—finding Ansel and his unruly gang of orphans, only to feel the sting of his betrayal. Mistreatment, misfortune, misery. Every skinned knuckle, every rent seam, every cup of coffee spilled onto herself. They shone in stark relief. "Son of a spicer," she cursed. "Everything makes so much sense."

Hale tried to hide the smile creeping onto his face.

"You think this is funny?" Wren said. "My whole life has been a nightmare because I've been giving away my luck to gods-know-who!"

Hale shook his head. "Best we can tell, the Gifting starts in puberty. Whatever woes you suffered before then, you can blame on the gods. Or your parents. Or whomever."

Wren calmed down slightly. That's true. She hadn't been Infusing things before she joined Master Oldrick, had she. So, she wouldn't have been wasting magic back then. Another thought struck her with horror. "Will I run out? Have I wasted it all?"

"No," Hale said. "As far as we figure it, the depletion is temporary. But if you make an especially strong batch, it will take a bit longer for it to build back up."

The breath left her in a woosh, and she slumped back. So as long as she started hoarding her luck, things would look up. That was promising.

"What's Sable's Gift?" she asked, watching Hale for a reaction to her mention of their sponsor. She couldn't quite get the measure of Hale's relationship with Sable, and it was bothering her.

"Bad luck," Hale said, his expression neutral. "She cooks a lot. Likes to get rid of it."

"That could be helpful. Can we give some to Willings? Or Callidus?" Wren said, only half joking.

"Guildmembers are forbidden from imbibing infused food or drink without the king's permission. It's part of the Accord the guilds and the crown reached long ago. But that doesn't stop us from sneaking a bite now and then." He winked.

"So we're supposed to hand all this power over to the king? Trust he'll use it wisely, for the good of Alesia?"

"Yes." Hale shrugged. "Isn't that what being governed is? Giving power and trusting that it will be used for the good of the people?"

Wren crossed her arms. "You don't really believe that, do you?"

Hale mirrored her posture. "Enlighten me, my wise owl."

Wren rolled her eyes, but memories flared to life and refused to be silent. "I grew up in a logging town in the Cascadian foothills. The forest belonged to the king. The town stores belonged to the king. The blooming shack we lived in belonged to the king. He paid a copper crown for a week of work, and our rent was more than that. We were supposed to pay for wood to heat our hearth. Wood! It was all around us, more wood than a thousand kings could ever need. We had to pay for everything on credit and every month we sank deeper into debt. My father. My brother... It was slavery. It was worse than slavery. At least as a slave, you don't pay to work. So tell me, Hale, how that served the good of the people?"

His features were kind, his eyes soft like warm honey. He reached out to take her hand in his own and she yanked hers back, standing and spinning away from him, fighting the sudden sting of tears. *Stupid, stupid, Wren.* Why had she shared that? Why had she felt compelled? The past was best kept in the past, that girl kept locked away. Her father had deserved everything he had gotten, and more beyond. Visions of blood and violence swam up to meet her, and she shoved them back down, tamped down earth and night and iron over those memories.

"Wren." Her name was soft on Hale's lips, and she gave herself one final shake before stilling her face and turning.

"Sorry. I don't usually don't dwell on the past."

"I'm sorry your family went through that. I know the system's not perfect…"

"Forget it," she said. "Let's just talk confections. Agreed?"

"Agreed," Hale said, with more than a little hesitation. "I thought we could make caramels today."

"Caramels?" Wren asked.

"You're familiar with them, I presume?"

"Of course," she said. "It's been a while, but I know how to make them."

"They're simple. I thought they would be a good confection to start with."

Wren and Hale gathered the ingredients from the icebox and the cupboards. They laid out the tools they would need—a heavy-bottomed steel pot, a large square baking tray, the confection thermometer, measuring cups, parchment paper, and the guitar cutter that would slice the caramel into perfectly even squares.

Hale rolled up the sleeves of his shirt and tossed Wren a thick linen apron, donning one himself.

Hale worked as the master confectioner with Wren as his assistant, directing her to measure the ingredients they needed: sugar, water, heavy cream, butter. So simple.

"The magic, as best we figure it, is a combination of mind and body. It comes from your movements—the stirring, the pouring, the cutting or drizzling. But the movements themselves aren't enough. It's almost like meditation. You've felt it before, I'm sure, when you get in the zone of work. Your mind and body are humming together, your hands working as if they need no direction from your mind. It's a place of feeling, of instinct and intuition, of transcendence."

Wren nodded, understanding his words exactly despite the vagueness of them. She had felt it, those moments where her talent took over and she was one with her confections. She measured and added while Hale spoke. The butter and cream, melted together and set aside. The sugar and water, turned on high to begin caramelizing.

"It's easiest to use your Gift when you're alone, and when you're in a familiar kitchen. It's innate in you, but the more you consciously practice, the more quickly you'll learn how to slip into the mindset, the better you'll get at summoning it by will. Make sense?"

"It does," she said, looking at Hale with a new respect. He was more than muscled forearms and a trim waist in his apron. From the tenderness in his words... she could see that he loved confections as much as she did, felt this in his blood. She was unprepared for the sudden fondness that swept over her, awakened by her recognition of his kindred spirit.

"I'm going to leave you now," he said. "To let you finish. I wish you good luck in discovering your Gift."

Wren watched the caramel bubble as the thermometer crept higher, entranced by the luscious golden color that deepened and browned. The smell of toasting sugar frosted the air, swirling about her senses. Her soul felt at rest for the first time since Callidus had seized her arm in Master Oldrick's shop. Her vision—her very consciousness—narrowed to the spinning sugar, the chemical reactions, the flickering blue flame of the gas burner beneath the pot. As she added the cream and butter, whisking the swirls of golden brown and milky white, she felt the power of creation within her, the giving of her life to create this joyful sustenance for others. She felt a trickle of self winding into the bubbling pot, infusing and binding until the caramel became something more than mere sugar and cream. She had felt this before and had thought it love and care and pride in her work. Now, she saw it for something more.

Once the creamy caramel reached the right temperature, she seized the pot and heaved it, deftly pouring the contents out onto the waiting parchment-covered tray. She shook the tray gently until the candy settled to the bottom, as soft as silk and as smooth as glass. She sank onto the waiting stool before her creation.

She had done it. Magic.

CHAPTER 12

Wren's elation over her success was short-lived. While cleaning up the kitchen, she managed to whack her kneecap on the kitchen island, close her fingertips in a cabinet door, and trip over the stool, which seemed to manifest out of nowhere directly between her feet. Wren had been lanky and uncoordinated all her life, but had usually managed to keep it together in the kitchen. But now that she knew how cooking spent her magic, it seemed her luck had run out on that front as well.

Wren left her confections to cool, and found herself in the hallway with an entirely unknown commodity on her hands: free time. Her growling stomach informed her of her first order of business, and since it was well past lunch time, she made her way to the real kitchens, where she managed to beg a bowl of cool cucumber gazpacho soup with a dollop of minted cream and triangles of buttered toast. She wolfed it down, the crisp tastes of the cucumber and mint silky on her tongue. Returning the licked-clean bowl with a murmur of thanks, Wren headed for the Guildhall's library. It seemed as good a place as any to solve a mystery.

Wren hadn't been in many libraries, but she imagined this library was unique. First was the fact that it was brimming with cookbooks—some published, some hand-lettered in cramped scrawls and butter smears. It was evident that the collection was the result of years of study and collection by the guild members. Books on other subjects seemed an afterthought, relegated to a lone set of shelves in the far corner of the room. Second was the fact that it was really more kitchen than library. Bright and airy, rather than dark and forbidding, full of white and gray-veined tile rather than dark wood panels, this alternate rendition suited Wren just fine. Rather than a fireplace, a kitchen stove stood sentinel in the room, and coffee and delectables were laid out for the taking along the long countertop. Third were the mismatched sofas and armchairs that dotted the room like they had blown in from a squall. Cracking studded leather couches, velvety divans, and brocade wingbacks sat about the room in a potpourri of furnishings. The library felt worn and real, like catching a glimpse of the guild waking up in the morning before it had washed and put its face on. She loved it at once.

Wren had the library to herself, and she set to work putting a kettle on the stove, filling the glass press with fragrant coffee grounds. She explored the room while she waited, peering at a fox and geese board left abandoned on one of the tables, its carved white geese and red foxes frozen in form. On a threadbare marigold armchair sat the front page of the day's *Maradis Morning,* the city's newspaper. She snagged it and returned to the stove, where the kettle was cheerfully boiling. Coffee in hand, she settled into an enveloping gray-blue sofa facing the far window. She closed her eyes and blew out a breath. Her days at the Guildhall had thus far been filled with people, navigating the treacherous water of human interaction. It was a far cry from her days with Master Oldrick, where the only conversation she might have had in a day had been with an unruly batch of nougat.

She tried to categorize what she had learned so far but found her thoughts drifting to Hale and Lucas. Both had gone out of their way to help her. But why? For what purpose?

Footsteps sounded down the hall and Callidus swept into the library, one of Marina's lackeys in orbit behind him. What was the black-haired boy's name? Lennon.

Wren scooted down on the couch so her head wasn't visible over its back, peering around the edge to watch the two men.

"If you sponsored me, I could be useful to you. Assist with your duties, look out for your interests among the guild. I'm a trained journeyman; you wouldn't even have to take much time to finish my education."

Callidus, in a gray velvet jacket that had all the summer cheer of a funeral, was rooting around the library while the boy made his case, lifting up cushions and searching under chairs.

"If you told me what you were looking for," Lennon said, " I could help you find it. See how helpful it would be to have a sponsored?"

Callidus scoffed, his black hair shaking above his brow. "I'm looking for my damnable notebook," he said. "It's a black moleskin."

Wren's eyes widened as she spotted the notebook on the far cushion. *Fool!* She had been on the same couch as all of Callidus's secret thoughts and she hadn't even seen it!

Callidus's search grew closer and her heart fluttered into her chest. If he found her here, he would never believe that she hadn't been reading it. She grabbed the notebook, snuck another peek around the corner of the sofa, and slid it across the tiled floor in one silent movement.

"Here it is!" Lennon said, retrieving it with a victory cry. "You have to sponsor me now." The boy wore a sheepish grin as Callidus snatched the notebook from him.

"Thank you," Callidus said. "I would have found it myself in a moment."

Wren rolled her eyes. It must have been a physical impossibility for Callidus to be nice to another human being.

"I'm not sponsoring anyone. I work better alone, and I don't need to draw Grandmaster Beckett's ire by stealing away his journeyman. Why do you want to move?"

Lennon looked anywhere but Callidus's eye. "I just… I can't be there anymore. I need a change. I admire your skills as a confectioner, and you aren't sponsoring anyone. I'd stay out of your hair…"

"Like you're doing right now?" Callidus arched an impressive eyebrow.

"Please, sir. If you're going to be guildmaster, you'll need someone to help you, an ally…"

Guildmaster? Wren thought, her blood chilling in her veins. So it was true what Hale had said. Callidus would likely be leading the guild, and her life would be that much more difficult.

"We all have burdens to bear," Callidus said, his dark eyes shrewd. "Now I have errands to run and a meeting with the Grand Inspector. Make yourself scarce."

"Yes, sir," Lennon said glumly.

Wren let out a whooshing breath as Callidus left the room, leaving a conspicuous vacuum in his absence. How had she missed the notebook? She'd had a critical piece of evidence within inches of her, and she'd completely missed it. *Stupid, stupid.* She would never prove her innocence with that kind of crack detective work. She bit her lip. Why was Callidus going to see the Grand Inspector? What "errands" was he running? She had missed one chance to learn more about Callidus; she wouldn't miss another.

She sprang to her feet, her decision made. She grabbed the newspaper in case she needed cover for her spying and hurried through the hallways of the Guildhall. She caught a glimpse of Callidus's bleak gray coat in the distance, passing through the front doors out into the bright afternoon.

A smile ghosted across her face when she saw that Callidus was walking, not taking a carriage or horse. She slipped into the crowd after him.

As it turned out, Wren rather enjoyed tailing a suspect. Her palms were sweaty and her heart galloped in her chest, but she hadn't felt so alive… well, since she had roamed the streets as a member of Ansel's gang of orphans. She stiffened when she passed a pair of puffed-chest Guards in their ruddy-brown uniforms—Cedars, as the population called them—but they just nodded to her, one even flashing an appraising smile. Back then, she had to be invisible to the world, sink beneath the notice of marks, rival gangs, and Cedars alike. Now, there was only one set of eyes she had to avoid.

After an hour of following Callidus, her enthusiasm faltered. So far he had visited a barbershop (no doubt to pick up more of whatever magical concoction kept his hair so well-coiffed) and a music shop with a fiddle on its sign. A music shop? Perhaps he was really just… running errands.

She found herself a park bench while he went in the shop and sat under the shade of a magnolia tree, reading the paper. The front page story told of a fire that had enveloped a building on the edge of the Guild and Central Quarters. The building had been a specialty foods market owned by the Spicer's Guild. The fire appeared to be arson, but there were no suspects. She scrunched her lips, pondering. From what Hale had said, anything involving the Spicer's Guild was suspect. But she didn't have the foggiest idea what it could mean, or if it had any connection to Kasper's killing.

As she turned the page, keeping a keen eye for Callidus exiting the music shop, she grew still. The next article told of King Imbris's efforts in Tamros, their neighbor to the north, to arrange peace terms with the Apricans. Wren remembered the precise moment Master Oldrick had shared that Aprica had invaded Tamros—his solemn face, his hands covered in powdered sugar. There was no question that Aprica's superior resources and army would crush the Tamrosi, especially when the Tamrosi royal family and ruling class had been decimated by the Red Plague. There was only the lingering question of whether the Aprican king would be satisfied with Tamros or set his sights on more juicy prey to the south. Alesia. As it turned out, the Aprican king had paused, content to enjoy his spoils for a few years. But no one in Alesia was comfortable having the might of Aprica's army next door, especially with the "border exercises" the army had been performing as of late. It was all troubling and worrisome. But that wasn't what set Wren's teeth on edge. It was the final line of the article. The king's delegation had completed the current phase of negotiations and was returning. In two weeks' time.

Wren let the newspaper fall, the breath stolen from her lungs. She had only two weeks, if that. She had thought she had a month. A month at least, to feel the sunshine on her face, savor loganberry jam on her biscuits, and enjoy laughter with Olivia and Hale. Did she truly believe she could solve this mystery—understand this spiderweb of guilds and royal interests—in less than fourteen days? She felt tears of panic sting her eyes and blinked them away. There was no way.

Callidus chose that moment to exit the store, a storm cloud of gray and black amongst the bright colors of the passersby. She struggled to her feet and followed on numb legs, feeling the weight of this new information settle upon her.

She navigated the crowds in a daze, only coming back to herself when she realized Callidus had stopped, and she had practically run into the back of him. She spun in a desperate circle and slipped behind a stand of flowers, peeking through peonies and primroses. The scene before her swam into sudden focus. Callidus stood before the charred remains of a building, the massive blackened skeleton that had once been the Spicer's Guild market.

"You're acting very suspicious, miss," said a wizened voice behind her. She whirled to find the proprietor of the flower stand, a wrinkled man with a dandelion puff of downy hair. "Perhaps I should call the Grand Inspector over?"

Wren looked back and realized that Callidus was now shaking hands with a tall, vigorous man in a rust-brown uniform.

Her mind whirled for an excuse as she turned back to the man. "You've caught me," she said. "I'm... following that fellow. I'm... in love with him... and I was hoping to gain some insight that will help me win his heart." She smiled weakly, trying not to retch at the thought of being in love with Callidus.

The man softened. "I imagine a lovely young lady like yourself only need tell the fellow. No need for all this cloak and dagger."

"You're right, of course. But I'm... shy," she said lamely, her mind struggling for an excuse. "I need to do things in my own way. I don't suppose, for the price of... one of these bouquets of peonies, you'd let me stand here and read my newspaper for a few minutes?"

A crinkled smile touched the man's blue eyes. "I suppose that won't hurt anyone."

Wren paid the man as he wrapped up her flowers in brown paper and twine, and she turned her newspaper over, all the while keeping a keen eye on Callidus and the inspector. She couldn't hear what they were talking about, but there was no way she could get closer, as she would be completely exposed in the streets surrounding the charred block of building. She sighed, watching Callidus gesticulate towards the building. What could he be saying?

An image on the back page of the newspaper caught her eye, a fine portrait of a handsome young man and woman in old-fashioned clothing. When she saw the headline, the ground tilted. It was Kasper's obituary. The caption on the portrait read *Francis and Iris Kasper*. Her heart twisted at the sight of them, so young and full to the brim with dreams. Had Kasper gotten to live the life he had hoped for? Had anyone?

"Wren," a voice hissed.

She started.

Lucas loomed before her, standing tall in a chestnut houndstooth suit. "What're you doing here?" he asked, his voice low.

"Buying flowers," Wren said lamely, retrieving the bouquet of pink blooms from the little man, who was looking from her to Lucas with more than a little suspicion.

Lucas looked over his shoulder and took her arm, gently but firmly steering her into the shadow of an alley.

Wren stilled herself, ignoring the way her skin warmed beneath his touch.

He turned to face her. "You can't be here, Wren. Callidus is already trying to get me thrown off your case. He's telling the inspector I'm too involved." He made air quotes around the last word.

"Is that what they're talking about?" She peered around the corner, fear rising within her.

"Yes, and the fire. But you really can't take these risks. Let me do my job."

Wren bristled and brandished the newspaper at him like a weapon. "Two weeks, Lucas. The king will be back in two weeks. I know you vouched for me, but I don't even know you! Not really. I can't just sit back and do nothing."

He grimaced and took one of her hands in his own. His was warm, calloused. It was hard to focus on his words, with his touch filling her senses. "Trust me. I will do everything in my power to find Kasper's killer. As if... my own life depended on it. And I'm not asking you to do nothing. Just don't take stupid risks. Callidus could have turned around at any moment and spotted you."

"I know," she said, suitably chastised. "There was this notebook..." She sighed. Though a voice in her head still cried that she couldn't trust him, it was growing softer. She found she wanted to trust Lucas. Being able to count on him... truly... it would go far to calm the ever-present sense of dread that coiled within her. She searched his slate-gray eyes for any hint of guile and found none. But what if he betrayed her? Ansel had. Brax. Her father. *But what if he doesn't,* the other part of her whispered. "I'll be more careful," she managed.

"That's all I ask. Have you learned anything at the guild?"

"Not really," she admitted. "My sponsor, Sable, doesn't think it's Callidus. Though I'm not convinced. Obviously."

Lucas frowned, his wide mouth turning down in thought. "Did she say why?"

"She's more the 'sweep in, make a broad pronouncement, sweep out' type of person. Light on the explanation."

"Helpful. Did she have any alternate theories?"

"Other guildheads? It looks like something might be going on with the Spicer's Guild?" Wren motioned to the burnt wreckage of the building.

"The timing is suspicious, but I haven't seen any other links between the arson and Kasper's killing." Lucas glanced over his shoulder and saw that Callidus and the Grand Inspector had parted. "I have to go. Don't hang around here. Please. You remember the signal, if you have something to tell me?"

"I remember."

"That's my girl."

And then he was gone, leaving her alone with an armful of flowers and a stomach full of butterflies.

CHAPTER 13

The Grand Assembly of the Confectioner's Guild took place the next day.

Even before dawn, when Wren found herself inexplicably wide-eyed and awake, the Guildhall was buzzing like a beehive, filled to bursting with drones flitting every which way. She managed to navigate through the busy halls to the library to make herself a cup of coffee before retreating back up the stairs.

She found herself ducking through the little door out onto the roof, entering that lovely land of vegetables and rooftops and solitude. The thin fabric of her cornflower blue dress, which had been delivered last night washed and pressed, did little to ward against the crisp chill of morning. Her skin pebbled against the cold, and she gripped the warmth of her coffee mug tightly, letting its fragrance wash over her.

She found a bench to sit on in the far corner of the rooftop, smiling shyly at two servants who were hard at work harvesting zucchinis and kale for the guild. She closed her eyes as dawn's first rays broke over the horizon, turning the inside of her eyelids sherbet orange. She sighed. She needed this moment. To regroup. To prepare herself for the madness of the day. And—she opened her eyes, letting them fall on the newspaper she'd brought, safely tucked under her arm—to say goodbye to Kasper.

She had only known him for an hour—less in fact. But somehow she felt she had seen inside him, and what she had seen was good. Most men she had known were rotten at the core, if you peeled the layers far enough, you got to some hard pit filled with hubris and self-loathing, violence and desire, all grown together in a tight little ball. But not Kasper. He had a caramel center. Sweet and soft and golden. He hadn't deserved to die.

She sighed. It was never those who deserve to die who found such a fate. Her brother's face swam to view in her mind's eye, shaggy brown hair that he refused to cut falling over his eyes, dimpled smile with a faint scar on his upper lip from when he had fallen out of the big cottonwood tree. That same youthful face, bloodied and battered, screaming at her to hide. She scrunched her eyes closed, as if it could shut off the images too. It was the curse of her memories of Hugo. She couldn't think of him without thinking of all the rest. And she did everything in her power not to think of all the rest.

Wren found that her hands were shaking and set her coffee cup down, afraid to spill on her dress again. She wasn't sure Greer's matronly generosity extended to a second spill a second day. She shook her hands out and shook Hugo from her mind. With a deep breath, she turned to Kasper's obituary.

It told a tale of chubby twins growing up on the windswept peninsula of Nova Navis. A young boy making saltwater taffy at the local mercantile. A prodigy found by a master and brought to Maradis to learn the art of confectionery. A sister following, and the star-touched siblings that had captivated the aristocracy with laughter and chocolate.

It detailed Kasper's meteoric rise to the head of the guild, his tireless negotiations on behalf of the guild, days filled with trade and tariffs and taxes. Tragedy, with the loss of Iris Greer's husband, and the deaths of Carter Greer's family following close behind. Finally, philanthropy, efforts to improve conditions for Maradis's poor and downtrodden, hospitals for victims of the Red Plague, public health, education, work release programs for the debtors' prison. Tears stung Wren's eyes. This man had not only been good, he had done good. What had she done with her own miserable sixteen years that was worth one fraction of this man's value?

"Wren!" Olivia was making her way through the rows of green, her blonde hair dazzling in the morning sun, a flattering blush-hued dress hugging her curves.

Wren brushed the tears from her cheeks, feeling foolish. Here she was crying over Olivia's granduncle, and she hadn't even known the man. Not truly.

"Are you all right?" Olivia asked, concern written across her cherubic face.

"Fine!" Wren managed with unconvincing brightness. "It's bright up here this morning."

"It is," Olivia said with a hint of disbelief.

"What are you doing up here?"

"Grabbing some chives for the eggs," Olivia said. "Grandaunt sent me. It's madness down there already. The hall is bursting at the seams. All our guest rooms were full last night, and we had to put people up at the inn down the street. The whole Guild is here."

"To vote on the new guildmaster, right?" Wren asked.

"Many of them," she said. "The new leader will set the tone for the Guild for years to come. Everyone wants to get in the good graces of whoever it will be. But they've also come for the Appointment Gala."

"Appointment Gala?"

"Tomorrow night. You've not been to one? For one of the other guilds?"

"We didn't get out much," Wren said. *Too busy working and making Master Oldrick money,* she thought. "How did they manage to pick a name that sounds so grand and boring in one breath?"

Olivia let out a quiet laugh. "I'm not sure who came up with the name. But after a new guildmaster is appointed, the Tradehouse hosts a gala with the other guild leaders and some of the king's family and cabinet. A gala is the event of the season. They don't happen every year, of course. Only when…" She trailed off.

"When a guildmaster dies." Wren grimaced.

A dark shadow passed over Olivia's face at the mention of Kasper, but she recovered quickly. "That's why I had you order that dress! With the gold and blue flowers."

Wren wracked her brain. She had tried on so many things on their whirlwind shopping trip, she was only half-sure which garment Olivia referred to.

"I remember. I'm looking forward to it." Wren smiled weakly. She wasn't sure she could get through the bustle of this day, let alone a gala with the other guilds and nobles and royals. It sounded terrifying.

"You'll be fine," Olivia said, seeming to see the weariness in Wren's face.

A servant hurried up behind Olivia, a look of near panic on her face. "Olivia, miss. Cuisinier Brandywine says he can't find any more bacon in the larder. Half the guests haven't eaten yet."

Olivia groaned. "There should be at least five more pounds in there." She turned to Wren. "I need to go. If the cuisinier can't find the rest, we'll have a riot on our hands."

"By all means," Wren said. "Attend to your bacon emergency. I should come down anyway." She tucked the newspaper behind her back and followed Olivia and the servant as they hurried back down the stairs. She paused on the landing as she took in the milling crowd. She really needed to get some breakfast, but she wasn't particularly inclined to face the crowd.

"Wren!" a voice called from below. It was Hazel, one of Master Oldrick's apprentices, waving enthusiastically over the crowd.

Wren wove through the bustle of bodies into Hazel's enthusiastic hug, surprised to find herself genuinely pleased to see her. Hazel's dirty blonde hair was pulled into a tidy braid over her shoulder, and her dress looked almost new. Master Oldrick must have been pulling out all the stops for the assembly.

Tate, the gangly other apprentice, hung back, shuffling. "Hey, Wren," he said, and she found herself pulling him into an embrace as well. Their familiar faces were a balm to her chaffed soul in this strange place.

"Hey, Tate," she said.

"Is it true that you killed the head of the guild?" he asked. "Talk's all over town."

"*Tate,*" Hazel chastised, cuffing his ear lightly. "You know those are foul lies. Aren't they, Wren?" Her words held an inquisitive tone.

"Yes," Wren said. "I've been accused of it, but I didn't do it. I was in the wrong place at the wrong time."

"Wren's confections only bring joy and happiness," a gruff voice said behind her. "Not sorrow."

She turned to find Master Oldrick, as ruddy and round as ever. She hugged him, feeling strangely sentimental, despite spending nights and weeks and months dreaming of being free of him.

"Miss you, Wren," he said. "Shop ain't the same without you."

"You mean your profits aren't the same without me," she said, crossing her arms.

"Aye. Same thing. Tate and Hazel don't have half your talent between the two of them."

"*Oldrick!*" she said, looking apologetically at the other apprentices.

They seemed unperturbed. "'It's true," Tate said. "You always did have a gift."

His words sank within her. It was true. How had she never seen it for what it was? Something different than what other people had? Something more than a deft hand or a good nose for flavor?

"I miss you all too. But I think… I will like it here. Once the murder investigation is over."

"Don't let that Grand Inquisitor lay his hands on you. Whatever happens. If the worst should come, end it," Master Oldrick said. "I hear his ways are twisted. He takes pleasure in it. Finds your weaknesses and your fears. Exploits them."

Wren's stomach turned and the blood drained from her face as Master Oldrick went on. "I knew a man who had the misfortune of crossing the royals. Fell in love with one of the royal ladies, and she loved him too. Killian took the man apart, piece by piece, in front of her."

All the saliva had left Wren's mouth. She tried to swallow, but her throat felt as sticky as glue.

"What a cheerful fellow you are." Hale came to her rescue, banishing the dark spell that had fallen over them with his brash golden aura. He slung one arm around Wren's shoulder and squeezed her arm while offering his other hand to Master Oldrick. "Master Oldrick, I imagine. Hale Firena, of Aprica. Artisan of the Guild."

Hazel's mouth dropped open as she stared at the vision before her.

Wren pasted on a smile, grateful for the change of subject, though not entirely soothed. Oldrick's words rung in her ears. *Twisted. Took the man apart piece by piece.*

Master Oldrick shook his hand, staring up at Hale with more than a bit of surprise. "Pleasure," he managed.

Hale turned to her. "Wren, my dear, the Assembly is starting. We should take our seats."

"Of course," Wren said, ready to be away from Oldrick's dark tale. "Master Oldrick, can I speak with you after the assembly? I have a question I must ask you."

"Of course," Master Oldrick said. "We're staying through tomorrow."

As Wren let Hale steer her away from her former life with a commanding arm, she heard Hazel whisper to Tate behind her. "I see why she likes it here."

CHAPTER 14

Rows of chairs sat neatly in the ballroom, leading to a low wooden platform erected for the assembly. Hale's arm was still wrapped protectively around Wren's shoulder, and the guild members melted away as they cut a path to their seats. She should have shrugged it off, she thought, prove to herself she wasn't being sucked into Hale's orbit, lulled by warm skin and flashing white teeth. But it was a comfort amongst these unfamiliar faces and questioning eyes. So she let it stay.

Three chairs sat empty atop the platform, facing the crowd. "Callidus and Sable—and who is the third candidate?" Wren asked Hale.

"Grandmaster Beckett," Hale explained. "There are two other Grandmasters in the guild, Legox and Swift, but Legox is off negotiating a trade deal with the Centu Clans in the islands, and Swift is as old as death itself."

"How does one become a grandmaster?" She realized that while she knew the procession through the first four steps of the guild, the final title was a mystery to her.

"It's a combination of exceptional skill and service to the Guild. The

head of the Guild makes the nomination, but it requires a vote of two-thirds of the masters to make the next level. To become a grandmaster, you need to be well-connected and have allies within the Guild. The idea is that the voting requirement ensures that the next level of guild leadership will take the diverse interests of the guild into account."

Wren considered this. "In other words, it becomes a campaign of favors, deals, and political machinations?"

Hale chuckled, ushering her to a seat near the front. "You are wise for one so young, my blue jay. Yes and no. Sable had to make a lot of promises to achieve her rank so young, especially because she was female. But she figured by the time she was guildmaster, most of those people would be dead. Kasper seemed to do what he wanted."

A bell sounded in the back of the room, and guildmembers streamed in to take their places, the room humming with conversation. There had to be almost one hundred masters in the room.

"I almost forgot," Wren whispered to Hale. "I brought you something."

"A present? For me?" His turquoise eyes sparkled, and she was suddenly very aware of how close they were.

She tried to cover the hitch in her breath with a roll of her eyes. "Don't get too excited. It's nothing." She pulled two caramels out of the pocket of her dress and handed one to him. After the previous day's failed attempt at spying on Callidus, she had returned to the teaching kitchen to cut and wrap her cooled caramels. She hadn't tried one yet.

A mischievous grin transformed Hale's face, his dimples flashing. "This is not nothing, my sly little raven. This is precious as gold."

"Just proving to my teacher that I'm an apt pupil," she said.

"Bottoms up," he said, unwrapping his caramel and popping it in his mouth.

She did the same, glancing furtively at the chatting guildmembers around her. Hale had said all infused products were supposed to go to the king, but how would she know if she had been successful if she couldn't try a thing or two?

Hale nodded approvingly as he chewed the caramel. "Delicious. You *are* an apt pupil."

The hair on her arms stood up as the tingle of the magic swept through her like a ray of sunshine bursting through the clouds. How had

she never noticed this for what it was? Something special? Magic.

A wizened old man taking the stage distracted her from her thoughts. He ascended to the platform with laborious steps and a wobbly hand on his cane.

"Grandmaster Swift," Hale whispered. "You can see where he gets his name."

"Guildmembers," the old man called, quieting the crowd. His voice was strong and clear, incongruous coming out of the withered body. "We gathered here twenty-four years ago to select our last guildmaster. Francis Kasper was a diplomat, a scholar, a friend. His loss is felt keenly by our Guild and its members. Especially as he was taken from us too soon."

Wren's stomach flipped nervously at his words. Hushed whispers fluttered around her.

"Let us have a moment of silence in his memory."

Wren bowed her head, the thudding of her heart seeming to fill the silence. Fear curled through her, banishing the warm tingles from the magic. Lucas had said that the Guild had a legal obligation to protect her until the investigation had been completed—his vouching for her had made certain of that. But what did that really mean? People could turn to cruelty in a heartbeat, especially when together in large groups. Maybe she shouldn't be here.

"Thank you," Swift said, rapping his cane once to summon the crowd's attention. "The task falls on us, those who remain behind, to elect new leadership. This is a task we must go about thoughtfully, and with great care. The choice we make today will set the direction our ship will sail for the next decade or two or three."

Grandmaster Swift called the three candidates up on stage, and they were met with applause and the occasional cheer. Sable looked stunning in a dress of royal blue embroidered with a rainbow of colors at the hem, cuffs, and scooping neckline. She wore the elaborate beaded necklace that was her signature, and her gleaming midnight hair was swept back and curled around her shoulders.

Callidus looked as unpleasant as ever, his pale face twisted, as if he had just caught a whiff of curdled milk. He wore a fine black suit and charcoal gray waistcoat, modeling his styling after an undertaker. A black journal was tucked under his arm. That damn journal, taunting her. So close, yet infinitely out of reach.

The last man, Beckett, was fair-skinned and fair-haired with watery blue eyes, a plump mid-section, and clammy-looking sausage fingers. This was Marina's father? She looked nothing like him. It was a mystery how he had snared a woman beautiful enough to produce an offspring as lovely as Marina.

"Quiet, quiet," ancient Grandmaster Swift called, shushing the audience with his hands. "Each of the candidates will have five minutes to speak to you. Give them your utmost attention."

Sable went first, her words velvety and eloquent. She complimented the Guild, the wisdom and talent its members had shown over the years. She looked each member in the eye with a smile and a challenge to usher the guild into a new era of prosperity and cooperation with the other guilds. Hale sat next to her in rapt silence, and around the room Wren saw heads nodding. The applause was thunderous when Sable was done.

Beckett went next, talking in length about his experience as an ambassador with the Tradehouse and other guilds. He promised "lower tariffs, lower taxes, and greater profit," and the crowd seemed impressed with his rhetoric.

Last but not least, Callidus stood, walking slowly to center stage. He glared at the members with startling blue eyes. The audience quieted until an uneasy silence hung over the room.

"These are not easy times for the guilds, for our city, or for Alesia," Callidus began, his voice strong and powerful. "Strikes and union uprisings throughout the city are growing in numbers and frequency. There are riots in the Central Quarter over the conditions of the poor and working class. On our northern border, our friend and ally Tamros has been aggressively occupied by the Apricans."

Wren glanced at Hale, whose golden coloring was so common in Aprica. She hadn't thought about why he was here, living in the Guild under Sable's sponsorship. Was he originally from Aprica? If so, had the war in his home country driven him from it?

Callidus continued. "While the Aprican king speaks of peace, the marshaling of his forces suggest he would push on into fertile Alesia itself. The Ferwich clans harry us on the east, and the Centu—growing ever bolder in the Cerulean sea—seek to renegotiate our trade deals, refusing to transport our exports on their ships without a heavy toll. Rest assured," Callidus said. "It will not be an easy road ahead."

Wren blew out a breath. By the Beekeeper! She had heard rumbles of unrest in Maradis, of the burdensome impact the king's domestic policy was having on the lower class of the city, but to be surrounded by enemies on every side… She didn't envy the next guildmaster their role.

"Pretty words or pie-in-the-sky promises will not be enough to navigate our ship, as Grandmaster Swift so aptly put it, through the treacherous waters ahead. We need clear-headed and shrewd leadership. We need willingness to sacrifice, to make difficult decisions, to protect the safety and security of our guild from any threat, even a threat from the inside."

Callidus looked directly at Wren; his powerful gaze pinning her to her seat like an arrow.

"I am that leader. I am the only one who seems to remember why we are even here today. Our guildmaster was murdered. I watched Kasper die. Watched the light leave his eyes. Someone killed him. Someone who may very well be sitting in this room."

Whispers snaked throughout the crowd and Wren felt the blood drain from her, leaving her an empty shell. Faces turned her direction, pointing eyes and mouths and fingers.

"That's enough, Callidus," Sable thundered, standing, her chair rocking back behind her.

Wren tensed to flee, her breath coming in quick gasps. The murmuring of the crowd pressed upon her, a living angry thing, bringing flashes of memories to the front of her mind. The feeling of being cornered, of being small and powerless, swept over her. She hated that feeling, had forgotten it for a time in the relative peace of her apprenticeship under Oldrick. But who was she kidding? It had never really gone. Magic or no, she would always be weak and alone.

Callidus continued, assuring the Guild that he was the only one to take the threat seriously, who had the cunning and will to do what needed to be done.

Panic thrummed through her, and her muscles tensed to run. She needed to get out of here, be away from these people and their accusing eyes. As she started to rise, Hale grasped her hand in his own, his grip painful. "Sit," he hissed in her ear. "If you move, you're the target."

"I'm already the target," Wren hissed back.

"The focus is still on him," Hale retorted.

Wren saw he was right. Callidus was coming to the final crescendo of his tirade. But the urge to flee was powerful—she felt like a flighty deer in a den of wolves.

"Stay. I won't let anything happen to you," Hale whispered. His hand was warm and firm, and it made the difference. In that moment, he reminded her so powerfully of Hugo that the pain of her brother's memory took her breath away. A long time ago, she *had* felt safe. Hugo had been that shelter from the uncertainty of the world, from her father's drunken rages. To have found that again… she didn't dare hope.

Callidus finally finished and the audience erupted, applause and voices filling the space.

"Settle down, settle down!" Using Beckett's shoulders as a railing, Swift stood on Callidus's chair, shouting over the din. The crowd quieted, stunned at the sight of the frail man teetering over them. "It is time to vote. Ballots have been handed out to the masters. Mark your vote and drop them in the box at the back. Then, join me in the dining hall for a meal!"

With Sable's help this time, Swift made it to the ground, where he retrieved his cane. He began the slow walk to the back of the room while the other guild members began marking paper ballots.

Wren let out a breath. Hale loosened his death grip on her fingers. "Are you sure you made those caramels right?"

A shaky laugh escaped Wren, but it died on her lips as her eyes met Callidus's. He was staring right at her, a silent herald of doom amongst the buzz of voices.

"We wait until everyone is gone," Hale said. "And we'll sneak out the back."

CHAPTER 15

Hale shouldered into the conservatory, his hand wrapped around hers. As they drew deeper into the shadows of the foliage, Wren felt the tension in her body begin to uncoil.

"Fool!" Hale exploded, knocking a potted herb onto the ground with a powerful strike.

Wren jumped away from him with wide eyes, backing against a workbench draped with ferns, rattling them with her body.

Hale turned and took in her wide eyes and white face. "I'm sorry, Wren—not you. Callidus." He advanced and enveloped her in his arms, pulling her tightly against his chest. She stiffened, but the solid comfort of his arms soothed the alarm ringing in her senses, and she leaned into him. For once, his nearness—the leather and musk scent of him—didn't send all reason fleeing from her mind. Yes, Hale was the most handsome man she had ever seen. But she wanted more from him than a fling—or even a romance. She wanted something that she hadn't had in a long time. A friend.

Voices sounded outside the door, and he pulled her farther into the conservatory, to a vine-draped corner illuminated by rays of sunlight pooling through the glass walls.

"Sit," he said, gesturing to the little table and chairs, and she obliged, her knees shaky. "I can't believe he pointed the finger at you in front of the whole guild," Hale said. "He really doesn't like you, does he?"

"I have that effect on people," Wren joked, her voice hoarse. A feeling of wretchedness washed over her. Why *did* he hate her so much?

"Nonsense," he said. "You're perfectly lovely."

She found a smile crossing her face. "Do you think Sable will win?"

"I don't know," he said. "Sable is the newest grandmaster. We knew Callidus's chances were stronger to start. It depends on whether his fearmongering resonates with people."

It resonated with me, Wren thought. "I didn't realize things were so bad. I had heard about the war in Tamros... Do you really think Aprica will attack?"

Hale nodded grimly. "That bastard on the throne is hungry. Nothing will ever be enough for him. Could be a month, could be a year. He'll come." Hale's eyes flashed, the thick muscles of his jaw stiff with anger. "But don't worry about that right now. Our one and only job is to figure out who killed Kasper."

Wren's emotions roiled, circling down into despair. "We're no closer to discovering anything. We know about the whiskey... maybe Lucas has discovered something." *Since yesterday?* Her skepticism harried her.

"Don't pin your hopes on him." Hale shook his head. "The inspector's office has their own agenda."

Wren groaned. "Does anyone not have an agenda?"

"Welcome to the world of the guilds, my swan," Hale said. "I'll tell you what. I'll go steal us some food from the kitchen. We can hide in here and have a little picnic. The votes won't be counted until tonight, and I don't think you should be in the dining room today."

"Okay."

With a nod, Hale was gone, leaving her alone with motes of dust dancing in the sunlight and the fragrance of green for company.

Wren closed her eyes, trying to summon her courage, whatever toughness she had developed in her time on the street. They felt weak and atrophied from years of labor under Master Oldrick's direction. It had been a simple life, exhausting and monotonous, but she'd known where her next meal was coming from, and had slept hard and deep behind a locked door. The comfort had been hard-won and its loss now petrified her. She had hardened in her two years with Ansel's Red Wraith gang, or had seemed to, anyway. If she was being honest with herself, her hardness in those years had never been hers—it had belonged to the Wraiths. It had been easy to be brave and bold with allies at her side, friends to watch her back. Beneath them, the ever-present fear had remained, leaving her thin and brittle. And when it had all gone to hell and Ansel had betrayed her… she had shattered. No, she had never been brave. Not really.

Movement flickered at the other end of the conservatory and Wren ducked down, peering through the foliage. It wasn't Hale.

"We need to call in extra staff for the gala tomorrow." It was Olivia's voice. Wren relaxed. Thank the Beekeeper.

"There's no one else I trust." The other figure was Guildmistress Greer, her curving form backlit against the open doorway. "We don't even know that all of our staff is trustworthy—we can't be bringing in strangers from other guilds. It's bad enough that the catering staff, valets, and footmen are unknown."

"You can't believe there's still a threat to members of the Guild, do you?" Olivia sounded stricken.

"Until Kasper's killer is brought to justice, I can't afford to think otherwise. Now, are preparations made for tomorrow? Everyone knows their places and tasks?"

"Yes, I believe so," Olivia said. "I'll go over the schedule with the maidservants before breakfast tomorrow. I've drawn a map of the decor and table settings; they'll get to it as soon as dawn breaks. I'll be picking up the flowers from the market with Trina, and we'll spend the afternoon arranging. Caterers from the other guilds arrive at two P.M. to start cooking, musicians and other vendors at six."

"The fermenting guilds will have all the alcohol delivered before four, as I asked?"

"Yes, Grandaunt, for the third time." Wren could practically hear Olivia roll her eyes. "The only thing I can't figure out is when I'm going to get into Guildmaster Kasper's office to clean it out. Can you believe Callidus is insisting on moving in the day after tomorrow, should he win the vote? We'll all be dead on our feet from pulling off the gala of the decade, and all he can worry about is getting his dusty books on the shelf."

Dismay filled Wren. Was Callidus so sure of his victory he was already moving in?

Greer harrumphed. "Forget him. If he wants to move in so soon, he can move himself. Leave Kasper's office alone."

"Music to my ears," Olivia said.

"What in the name of a spicer—?" Greer said. "Hale? What do you think you're doing?"

"Ladies, good morning," he said, his deep voice syrupy sweet. "Let's see. I'm slipping into an abandoned room with a plate of fruit and cheeses and a bottle of sparkling wine. What do you think I'm doing?"

"You have no shame," Olivia said, sounding much less scandalized than her words implied.

He moved into the room. "Now if you could find another dark corner, I'd be much obliged. I've claimed this one."

"Hale, one of these days, that beautiful face of yours is going to get you into trouble." Greer *tsked*.

"I'm counting on it," he said.

Wren rolled her eyes. She could practically see his wink as he leaned in towards the ladies conspiratorially.

"Until later," Olivia said, a wistful sigh in her voice.

In a blink, Hale deposited his treasure on the table with a victorious air.

"Now they're going to think you and I are… up to something," Wren said, her arms folded.

"They don't know it's you," he said, unscrewing the wire cage atop the wine cork. "At least I presume, as you remained sitting silently as a field mouse."

"Running out of bird metaphors?"

"I'm regrouping. Don't think you're off the hook."

"I wouldn't dream of it," Wren said. "Isn't it a little early for wine?" From the two glasses he had set down, he intended her to have some too.

"Not so, my little whip-poor-will. We're making mimosas." Hale flourished a bow before pulling three oranges out of his back pocket.

He tossed them to Wren, one-two-three in quick succession, and with flailing hands, she managed to drop all of them.

Hale let out a golden peal of laughter at Wren's cross look, leaning over her to pick them up off the floor. He deposited them gently in her hands. "You really do have no hand-eye coordination."

"Only when it comes to most everything but confectionery." She squashed a creeping flush of embarrassment. A lack of coordination was the least of her worries.

"I would say that more than makes up for your other deficiencies."

"I'm glad you think so," Wren said, setting the oranges down and slicing herself a chunk of creamy white cheese. She smeared it on a cracker and popped it in her mouth. The tangy herb-infused flavor of the cheese exploded on her tongue, silky and creamy as the finest ganache. "Dis is uh-maz-ng," she said around a mouthful of cracker. "What is it?"

"Herbed goat cheese," Hale said, twisting the cork out of the wine with a satisfying pop. "From the Cheesemonger's Guild."

"I love it," she said. "I am in love."

"That's enough to make a fellow jealous of the cheese," he said, pouring wine into a slender flute.

"I would marry this cheese," she said, slathering another cracker.

Hale sliced the oranges and squeezed the juice into their glasses, little concerned by the sticky juice dribbling down his muscular forearm.

He handed her the glass, licking the juice off his fingers. He held his glass aloft. "To supporting, or confounding, the next Head of the Confectioner's Guild."

"Here, here," she said, clinking her glass with his own. She didn't want to drink much, but his kindness in trying to distract her was touching. So she took a small cautious sip of the concoction, letting its sweet flavor wash over her taste buds. The bubbles tickled her nose, but the flavor was outstanding, as fresh and cheerful as a summer morning.

"Thank you, Hale," she said earnestly, looking him in the eyes. "For your kindness. It has been… an unexpected bright spot."

He cleared his throat, looking away. Too earnest, it seemed. "So, eavesdrop on anything good?" he asked.

"I wasn't eavesdropping," she protested. "I didn't want to bother them."

"Of course." That devilish wink. "Did you hear anything good while you weren't eavesdropping?"

"No," Wren said, taking a more generous sip. She liked this stuff. "They were going over plans for tomorrow. Oh, you wouldn't believe Callidus. He's so sure of his victory that he's already demanding to move into Kasper's office."

"Ass," Hale said.

Wren chuckled, raising her glass to her lips for another sip. She froze.

"What is it?"

"If Callidus moves in, Lucas won't be able to do any further investigation. The scene will be compromised. What if there are more clues?"

"The inspector isn't done?" Hale asked, his voice neutral.

"I don't know," she said, gnawing at a fingernail absentmindedly. "There were letters to go through, files... I don't know if he made it through them all. And in the desk drawer where we found the wine..."

"What?" Hale asked.

"It's probably nothing, but it seemed like there might have been a panel in the drawer... a false bottom."

Hale leaned forward. "Did you find anything in it?"

"No, we didn't get a chance to look. Callidus came in."

"There could be something in there. Something important."

"I'm sure I'm imagining it," Wren said, taking another sip before stealing a cluster of grapes from the plate. The drawer swam into her mind as she popped one of the cool grapes into her mouth. The way the whiskey bottle had been laid down... the drawer should have been deep enough to stand the bottle on its end.

Hale speared a wedge of cheese with a hard cracker and chomped it down before tossing back the rest of his mimosa. "Let's check it out."

"What?" Wren said. "No! I was forbidden from entering the office."

"Do you always do as you're told?" Hale asked.

"No," Wren said, bristling. *Yes,* the little voice in her head corrected. "I don't want to jeopardize the investigation. And how would we get in, anyway? There's a guard in the hallway."

Hale considered this. "The secret passage doesn't extend to the third floor, unfortunately..."

"The secret passage?" Wren asked, incredulous.

"Oh, Wren," Hale said. "You have so much to learn."

Wren considered. It would be good to get back in the office one more time before it officially transferred to enemy territory. Of course, if Sable won the position of guildmaster, it wouldn't be necessary. But if she didn't...

"We *did* eat your caramels," Hale said. "And everyone is busy downstairs. There's no time like the present."

Wren's heart thudded. She only had two weeks left until the king and his inquisitor returned. She couldn't let any opportunity pass her by. She thought of Callidus's journal, once so tantalizingly close, now so far out of reach. An unexplained courage raced through her veins. "Olivia showed me a way onto the roof. Do you think we could get in through his window?"

"I think there's only one way to find out," Hale said, his dimples flashing.

CHAPTER 16

Wren and Hale hurried past the din of the dining hall, taking the stairs two by two. The antechamber of the hall was empty.

Wren's heart pounded in her throat as they made their way onto the rooftop. Maradis was awash with light, stone and granite buildings carved like fondant, the sea a glittering sapphire in the distance.

"I miss Aprica sometimes," Hale said. "Especially when the rain and gray come in the winter. But Maradis sure knows how to impress."

So he was from Aprica. "Why did you leave?" Wren asked as they walked across the flat rooftop.

"We fled when King Evander, the current ruler, came to power. My father was a cabinet minister under the former king. He was killed when the crown changed hands. My mother, brother, and I fled. We were aiming for Tamros at first, but… things got complicated, and I thought Maradis would be safer." His words grew hard. "Perhaps nowhere will be far enough."

"Where's your family now?"

"My brother was killed by bandits soon after leaving Aprica. My mother died in the Red Plague two years ago. Sable took me in."

"I'm sorry," Wren murmured, stopping at the roof's fenced edge, which came up to her waist. Perhaps that explained why Hale treated Sable differently from anyone else. In a way, she had rescued him. "My parents are dead too," Wren said.

"How did they die? If you don't mind me asking?"

Wren hesitated. She did mind. The question cut to the core of her, the place where sorrow and fear and anger had swirled together so long that she didn't think she knew how to separate them anymore. But Hale had been kind to her, and she didn't want to alienate him. "My mother died in childbirth. With me. My father was a logger in the Ferwich mountains. We lived out in the foothills. His foot was mangled in a logging accident a few years later, and... I think the pain bothered him a lot. So he drank to numb the pain. I hardly remember a time growing up when he wasn't at work or drunk. My older brother basically raised me."

"You have a brother?"

"*Had* a brother," Wren said, more harshly than she meant to. "Hugo... Hugo and I were doing okay, the two of us. My father got violent when he drank, but Hugo was always there to protect me, to take the worst of it. We planned to leave and come to Maradis as soon as Hugo turned eighteen and could become my guardian. But my father was getting worse, and we needed money, so Hugo started working. He was a big kid. Like you were, I bet," Wren said, her eyes wistful. "Big enough for the logging crews. Big enough to be crushed to death when a limb of a falling tree struck a snag and landed on him."

Hale placed a comforting hand on her shoulder, but Wren hardly felt it. The bright August day was replaced in her mind's eye with towering cedar trees, misty gray rain, and a red flannel shirt bundled in the foreman's hands, offered to her father at the door with condolences and a tipped hat. As if anything, let alone such meager offerings, could make up for the loss of her entire world.

"I'm so sorry, Wren."

She shook her head to clear the memory, banishing it back to the corner of herself where she kept it tucked away. "My father died the same day. So I came to Maradis."

"What? How?"

How. Such an innocuous question. She may have been beginning to trust Hale, but she doubted she would ever trust him enough to share the truth. A half-truth, then. "He... got raging drunk. Picked a fight. He was killed." The word tasted like salt and blood on her tongue.

"That's awful," he said. "How old were you?"

"Ten."

"Gods. What did you do?"

"I stayed in one of the Sower's orphanages for a few months. But... then I had to leave."

"Why?"

She shook her head, closing her eyes to the horror of the memories that threatened to bubble forth. "I think that's enough for one day. We should keep on task here."

Hale nodded, understanding and sympathy in his eyes. "Like Sable said. We're family now," Hale said softly.

Family. As Wren looked at the shadow of his profile, the dimples that pricked his cheeks, she realized she wanted that more than anything. But in the past, such things had been too good to be true. Was she a fool if she thought it could be real this time? She cleared her throat. "Lead the way."

"His office should be under here," Hale said, advancing to the edge and peering over.

Wren followed suit. "So... we drop down to that balcony?" The effervescent excitement she had felt minutes earlier as they dashed up the stairs was dimming, replaced by her usual hesitation and reserve. Were they really going to break into Kasper's office? The balcony seemed farther down than she had expected.

Hale saw her hesitation and flashed his dazzling grin. "Nothing ventured, nothing gained."

She took a deep breath and blew it out. This would be her only chance to discover what was in that drawer. Hale was right. She climbed over the edge, wishing she had chosen pants that day. She clung to the wrought-iron fence as she lowered her body down towards the balcony.

"Steady," Hale said as she extended her arms to dangle over the edge. The iron railing groaned and shifted, unsettling her. With a cry of surprise, she dropped to the hard stones of the balcony.

Hale vaulted over the edge and dropped besides her, as nimble as a deer. "Are you all right?" he asked, brushing her hair back and pulling her to her feet. "Anything hurt?"

"Just my pride," she said, dusting off her dress.

Hale peered through the glass squares of the double doors into Kasper's dark office. "It's empty. Let's just hope it's unlocked." He turned the handle, and the door swung inward on silent hinges.

"We're in luck." She smiled.

He gestured through the door. "Ladies first."

She padded into the room, her eyes adjusting to the darkness. They needed to be careful not to disturb anything.

"Light a candle," she said. "Let's try the drawer first."

Hale obliged and brought the candle over to the desk. They knelt, opening the bottom drawer where Lucas and Wren has discovered the bottle. Her heart twanged when she thought of Lucas. How was his investigation progressing? Had he discovered anything?

Hale held the candle over the drawer while Wren poked and prodded. She felt the outside of the drawer and then the inside, measuring its size. The inside was definitely smaller. The edge of the bottom seemed worn where it met the front of the drawer as well, like someone had been chipping at it.

She looked on the desk for something she could pry it open with. "Grab me that letter opener." She pointed.

Hale obliged, handing her the implement like a diligent sous-chef.

Wren inserted the knife, and with a deft flick of her wrists, popped the bottom out.

Hale whistled. "You were right," he said.

A letter rested at the bottom of the drawer, a nondescript piece of vellum folded in thirds. The rest of the secret compartment was empty.

Wren lifted it out, and Hale lifted the candle.

She unfolded the letter. It was written in a wide, looping cursive.

Guildmaster,

It is out of my respect for you that I write this plea. Your recent actions have convinced me of its necessity. You reach too high, you reach too far.

For no good reason that I can see, you threaten to unravel all the work we have done, to reveal the secrets that are our truest currency. It cannot be. It will not stand. I entreat you once more to turn from this foolish path and back to the course decided by our forefathers. This is not your choice. You are but one man. And man is fallible. It pains me dearly to remind you of such, but let me be clear. The guilds are far more important than any one man. They came before him, and they will continue after him, perhaps sooner, rather than later. Do not force my hand.

Your brother, C.

Wren and Hale looked at each other over the flame of the candle, eyes wide.

"This is from Callidus," Wren whispered excitedly. "He threatened Kasper. This is what I need. This could prove me innocent!"

Hale looked unconvinced. "Are you sure it's a threat? It's a bit vague."

"Well, he's not very well going to write: I will murder you. Of course it's a bit vague. But look at this! *The guild is far more important than any one man. It came before him, and it will continue after him? Perhaps sooner? Do not force my hand?* That's a threat if I've ever seen one!"

Hale nodded. "What does he mean, our truest currency? Is this about the Gifted? Would Kasper really reveal that? For what end?"

"I don't know," Wren said. "Perhaps Sable can help us puzzle it out."

Wren took the letter, folded it, and tucked it in the bodice of her dress.

Hale raised a roguish eyebrow. "Lucky letter," he joked.

Wren snorted, opening her mouth to retort, when she heard the jingle of keys in the door.

Wren and Hale looked at each other in panic, looking back towards the balcony. It was across the room. They'd never make it in time.

The door was already opening. Light streamed through.

"Forgive me," Hale said. Then kissed her.

Hale surrounded her, filling her senses to the brim. His lips were soft but firm, parting her own in skilled rhythm. His muscled arms wrapped around her, pulling the length of her body against his, backing her against the desk. He smelled musky and sweet, like leather and toffee, the sugary taste of wine and oranges still on his tongue.

Surprise warred with outrage for a moment until she realized what he was doing. Giving them an excuse for being here.

"Blooming hell!" an accented voice called in surprise as the door opened fully.

Hale pulled back, still pinning her hips to the desk, leaning one arm down to brace himself as he looked at the unwelcome intruder.

"Can't a man get a little privacy?" Hale asked with a growl.

"Hale? You scared the sugar outta me."

Hale pulled Wren to her feet, turning to the guard at the door. He

kept his hand firmly around Wren's waist, which was just i
because she feared that without it, her knees would give wa
Hale's kiss, but from fear. If Callidus found out she was in l
was declared grandmaster... she didn't want to think of wha
do to her.

"Sorry, friend," Hale said, his incorrigible demeanor resumed once
again. "Can't find much privacy today; the Guild filled to the brim as it
is. Thought we'd be left alone in here."

"Have a little decency, man. Getting your kicks with the old
guildmaster still warm in his grave?" The guard's shoulders had relaxed
as soon as he recognized Hale, the two men seemed to know each other.

"It's not like he's in here with us," Hale retorted.

His tone grated on her, reminding him of who he was pretending to
be. No, who he *was*. Who was she to say that the kindness he had shown
her wasn't the act? She didn't like that anyone might think Hale's over-
the-top flirtation had actually worked on her.

She straightened and squirmed, trying to move away.

His hand tightened on her waist in warning.

She stilled.

"I'm not one to spoil anyone's fun, but the Guildmaster was explicit.
No one is to come in or out of this room. I only came in when I heard
voices."

"Guildmaster?" Hale's voice was low.

"Aye, they just announced it. Callidus is the new Head of the
Confectioner's Guild."

Wren's heart sank, and she felt Hale's body deflate next to her. They
knew it had been a long shot for Sable to win, but the reality of the
alternative still stung.

"Very well," Hale said, pulling Wren with him. "I'd be much obliged
if you don't mention this to our new guildmaster. Or Grandmaster
Sable, for that matter. I'll make sure to snag you some of that fresh-
hopped ale you like the next time the Distiller's Guild delivers some to
make it worth your while."

"No problem, Hale," the guard said, giving the man a little mock
salute. Hale clapped him on the shoulder as they breezed through the
door and down the hallway.

Wren let Hale lead her down the stairs, only letting go of her when were safely down to the second level.

"Callidus is Guildmaster," Hale said. "Flame it."

Wren felt the crinkle of paper against the skin between her breasts and pulled out a corner of the letter. "Maybe not for long," she said.

"I need to find Sable," Hale said. "She'll be into her wine by now. I can't let her say something she'll regret. She still needs to work with these people."

Wren thought the comment an odd one but let it go. "I'll contact Lucas," she offered. "Show him the letter."

With that, Hale was gone, eating up the stairs two-by-two with his long strides.

Wren stood for a moment, dumbfounded, the memory of Hale's kiss lingering on her lips. Deep within her, relief welled to the surface. Because while being wrapped in Hale's arms was objectively pleasant, the kiss hadn't stirred her soul, hadn't lit her afire from the inside. Thank the Beekeeper. She wasn't falling for Hale. Her fondness for him was… sisterly. She let out a little relieved laugh as she headed down the stairs. This was no time for romance. A pair of flashing gray eyes flickered in her mind's eye, and her stomach twisted. She banished the thought. *This was no time for romance.*

CHAPTER 17

Wren slipped out the front door of the Guildhall, leaping down the huge stairs. The afternoon was warm and Guilder's Row was filled with the hum of voices and the clop of carriage-horse hooves. A flock of messenger boys flew from the Guildhall behind her, carrying news of the new Head of the Confectioner's Guild and invitations to tomorrow night's gala.

Callidus. Callidus sitting in Kasper's chair, a hard nib of cocoa replacing Kasper's marshmallow. Callidus, able to bring the full power of the Guild to bear on his singular mission: framing her. Wren sighed. She shouldn't have let herself dare hope that Sable could win. Despite Wren's Gift, perhaps *because* of her Gift, it seemed that every turn of fortune was bad. One would think that someone who could spin good luck from sugar should be able to secure a bit more of it for herself.

She pressed her hand to the bodice of her dress, feeling the reassuring texture of the paper against her skin. It was more precious than gold now. Her only evidence connecting Callidus to the crime. Besides the cupcake that was, which also connected her.

At the end of Guilder's Row, she paused to get her bearings. An ochre building stood across the square, topped by a red tile roof and fronted by three huge arched doorways. The carriage doors adorning each curving arch were made of warm wood with twisting iron hinges, lovely in their function. The Temple of the Sower whispered of silky ears of golden grain and abundant autumn harvests, but to her, that whisper chilled her soul.

A cold sweat pricked across Wren's skin despite the heat of the afternoon sun. *This is not the orphanage,* she told herself. *Lucas's brother Virgil is not Brother Brax.*

In the end, it was practicality that propelled her feet forward. She worried the letter's ink might smudge in the slick humidity of her bodice. She needed to find Lucas.

The inside of the temple was brightly lit with gas chandeliers. Soaring pillars of ochre stone met above her head amongst colorful frescoes depicting scenes of the gods and their home of Mount Luminis. The Sower, first among the gods, plowing fields to provide for humanity, and his wife, the Beekeeper, the goddess worshiped by her guild, collecting nectar and pollen from the flowering things of the earth. The Carpenter and the Seamstress, providing shelter and clothing for humanity, and the Midwife and the Brewer, presiding over swelling life and birth and celebration. And then there were the panels with the gods who presided over death—the Piscator and the Huntress with her hellhounds, keeping balance in the world, pulling those who did wrong into the furnace of hell. At least the Huntress was truthful about the death and destruction she brought. It seemed a more honest thing.

The neat rows of pews stood empty. Wren's sandals were quiet on the tiled floor, formed of a swirling mosaic of undulating waves of grain. As she walked up the temple's expanse, she couldn't help but feel the pantheon of gods watching her from above. At the foot of the stairs to the dais were two long tables set with votive candles. Flickering wishes fervently prayed. Wren resisted an urge to blow them all out. She had learned a long time ago not to waste any energy on belief.

Between the tables was the statue Lucas had referred to: the Sower in all his bronze glory. He was depicted as a broad man holding a wooden plow over one shoulder. His other hand was outstretched with a little pile of seed in it. His face looked hard, his eyes vacant. Perhaps the artisan had shared her opinions of theology.

She pulled Lucas's silver button from the pocket of her dress, worrying it with her thumb absentmindedly. The Sower stood at least eight feet tall. But she thought if she stood on her tiptoes, she could likely deposit the button in his outstretched hand.

Wren sighed. Better not stand around here like an imbecile. Better to be done with it. She hitched her dress and jumped, trying to release the button at the right moment. It tumbled through the Sower's fingers, clattering onto the tiles.

"A valiant effort."

Wren whirled. Behind her stood Lucas. But... not Lucas. She cocked her head in fascination. Not Lucas was a few inches shorter, perhaps, less lean muscle and more densely made. His face was a bit squarer and his eyebrows were a bit bushier... but besides that it was Lucas, the broad smile, the easy air of confidence, the long nose and salt-and-pepper hair. It was uncanny.

"Virgil." Not-Lucas held out his hand to shake her own. "You must be Wren."

"You look so much like him," she said dumbly.

"We get that a lot. The four of us are like peas in a pod. Luckily, our sister, Ellarose, diverged a bit for the better. Can you imagine a lady with this nose?"

Wren laughed, finding herself relaxing. Virgil wore the sienna robes of the brothers of the Sower, but his similarity to Lucas was comforting.

"I thought there were some ridiculous number of brothers? Seven?"

"True, true. I see Lucas has divulged all our secrets."

"Hardly."

"The oldest four brothers were by my father's first wife, Queen Clemente."

"Queen?" Wren's brow furrowed.

"Yes, the king's wife is typically referred to as a queen," Virgil quipped.

"King?" She felt faint, her thoughts like a puff of powdered sugar.

Virgil rubbed his jaw as he realized his mistake. "I see Lucas has not divulged all of our secrets."

"Is your father King Imbris?" Her voice sounded distant.

"Yes."

"And Lucas's..." This could not be. Lucas. Her Lucas... who had been a balm to her fears, who had made her feel like perhaps there were good men in this world. He was spawn of that king?

"Yes."

She whirled away from him, pacing up the row of flickering wishes and prayers, her heart in her throat. How many of those problems could the king solve if he turned his attention from padding his pockets to improving the lives of his people? She suddenly felt the eyes of the Sower and the king upon her in this place, men and gods with too much power, too much control over her life. Men and gods who could end her, destroy her in an instant, leaving not even a remnant of her life upon this earth.

"I should go," Wren said, her feet itching to flee the suffocating eyes on her.

"Wren, please," Virgil said, his hands outstretched. "Lucas will never forgive me if I let you leave like this."

"You can't make me stay." Her hands came up before her in an unconscious gesture.

Virgil recoiled. "Of course not. I'm asking you to stay."

"I'm sorry…" She backed away, down the aisle. "I shouldn't have come."

Wren broke into a run, throwing her body against the massive wooden door, pushing it open. Just as someone moved to open it from the outside. She fell through the opening, bowling into another, the force of her flight bearing them both to the cobblestones.

Wren's fall was broken by a warm body and a pair of strong arms. "Oof!" The man grunted.

Wren squirmed to her feet, pushing off the interloper. She grew cold when she saw Lucas's handsome face beneath her, his brow furrowed crossly.

"You don't know your own strength," he jested.

She stoked the fire of her anger with her new knowledge of his parentage. She gave a mocking half-bow. "I apologize, Prince Imbris. You may have me whipped for my impertinence."

A storm cloud passed across his face, and he stood, brushing himself off. "Oh. You…"

"I know your little secret. Virgil told me." She softened a bit. "Don't be mad at him. He didn't mean to. Now I will be going." The letter in her bodice was forgotten. She needed to be away from him, from his lies, from the Imbris clan with their cruelty and spite.

"Wren!" He grabbed her wrist as she tried to walk away.

"Don't touch me." She practically spit the words.

He released her like she was the handle of a scalding pot. "Please let me explain."

She stormed away.

He called after her. "Do you want to be known for everything your father did? Are you that same person?"

She stopped in her tracks, his words cutting her to the quick. No. She was not her father. She had spent her life trying to put as much distance as she could between that man and his memory.

He approached behind her. "I'm the sixth of seven sons and will never be king. I distance myself as much as I can from my family, from the court and the politics and the intrigue. To make what small difference I can for the good of this city. I'm not like him."

She turned, taking in his wide pleading eyes, his outstretched hands. "You should have told me."

"So you could react like this?" A crooked grin.

She started to turn away.

"I know, I know. I didn't tell you because that's not who I am. Prince Imbris. I'm just a man. Or I'm trying to be. I don't want to conquer or lead armies or live in the palace. I'm an inspector. I like to help people. Put bad men in prison, even if they're on my father's payroll. *Especially* if they're on my father's payroll. I like to go for morning runs around Lake Viri without a contingent of guards flanking me. I like to eat ice cream at Salted Cream and then sit on Nysia Avenue watching people go by. I can't change who my parents are. I can only control the life I live. That's the real me. That's the person I wanted you to know."

She turned back, his words sending warm tendrils into the icy anger that had flooded her. Gods, the pleading in his eyes. The earnestness and hope and apology. How could Lucas be from the same stock as King Hadrian Imbris?

"I learned a long time ago that when people meet 'Prince Imbris' first, they never see the real me."

"You still shouldn't have lied."

"Technically, I didn't lie…"

She huffed.

"I shouldn't have lied."

She heaved a sigh and closed her eyes for a minute. As angry as she was at Lucas's omission... she found herself wanting to forgive him. She didn't want to walk away from him. True, he had broken her trust, but his was a betrayal she understood. Trying to escape his past, to be a different person. Wasn't she guilty of the same thing? Plus, she needed him. *Less than two weeks,* the little voice inside her whispered. *Can you do this without him?* "All right." She heaved a sigh. "You're forgiven."

"Thank you!" He took her hands and kissed them. His sudden gesture seemed to have surprised him as much as her, and he dropped her hands quickly, shoving his hands in his pocket. The gesture tugged at her heart, and warning bells sounded within her. *Not a time for romance,* she reminded herself sternly.

"So... you met Virgil."

"Apologize to him for me, will you? He surprised me, that's all."

"Do you want to go back in?"

Wren shook her head. "I do have something to tell you, though. Can we sit?"

They settled onto a bench nestled in the shade of the temple.

"Before I tell you, I need a promise," Wren said, a sudden urge coming over her. Now was not a time for romance... but maybe someday.

"Anything," he said eagerly.

"We have to go to Salted Cream when all this is done. I've never been and Master Oldrick's apprentice Hazel raved about it on a near daily-basis. Their strawberry rhubarb ice cream was apparently 'worth killing for.'"

"It's true. I'll have to put her on the inspector's ice cream watch list," Lucas said, a smile tugging at the corner of his lips.

"You didn't hear it from me," Wren said.

"It's a deal. When we clear your name, we will celebrate with ice cream. Now, what do you have for me?"

"I snuck back into Kasper's room..."

"Wren!" Lucas chided. "You shouldn't have done that. If someone had found you..."

"It's fine," she said, shoving down her guilt. Hopefully, the guard wouldn't say anything. "I had to. Callidus is the new guildmaster. He'll be moving into the office tomorrow. I knew we'd never get in there again once that happened."

"Damn," Lucas said. "Callidus will pursue you relentlessly as guildmaster. That's not a good development."

"Tell me about it," Wren said. "But I discovered something!" She pulled the crumpled letter out of the bodice of her dress.

Lucas raised an eyebrow and a grin flickered across his face. "Lucky letter."

Wren shook her head in exasperation. "Why does everyone say that?"

"Who else is saying… Never mind that. Give it here."

Lucas quickly scanned the note while Wren watched his expression like a hawk.

"This is interesting," he said. "It seems like a threat. It could be from the real killer."

Wren nodded enthusiastically. "That's what I thought! And did you see the signature? It's from someone who calls themselves 'C.' I think we both know who that is."

"Callidus?" Lucas stroked his chin while he considered. Wren found herself watching as he ran his fingers along the rough stubble at his jaw. "But why would Callidus write a letter? They're in the same guild, together all the time. Why put a threat in writing when you could say it directly and leave no evidence?"

"Maybe… he's cowardly," Wren suggested. "Or he was out of town and wrote the letter."

"Not beyond the realm of possibility, but it still doesn't quite fit. What we need to do is to compare this to Callidus's handwriting to see if they match."

"I can do that," Wren said. "I'm sure I could sneak into Callidus's office and snag some unimportant paper."

"Bad idea," Lucas said. "I don't want you to get caught. Callidus can't know we're trying to build a case against him. You can't take on a guildhead unless your case is airtight. But maybe you can find his handwriting somewhere else around the Guild. Approving the budget or some other sort of bureaucratic nonsense."

"I'll see what I can find," she said.

"The other piece we need to understand is what this threat is about. What does he mean by 'revealing the secret of our truest currency?' What secret?"

Wren carefully ordered her features into blankness. "I'm not sure," she said, though she was fairly certain she did know what secret Callidus spoke of. Her throat began to burn even with the thought of voicing it to Lucas. The question in her mind was why? Was Kasper planning to reveal the existence of their Gifts? But to who? And for what purpose?

Lucas watched her, examining the emotions play across her face. "Are you sure you don't know what he's talking about?"

Wren cleared her throat. "I haven't been at the guild very long. There's a lot I don't understand yet. I'll talk to Sable. Maybe she has insight into this."

Lucas nodded slowly, still watching her. "Very well," he said. "We'll drop it." His unspoken words sounded like an echo. *For now.*

CHAPTER 18

Olivia flew into Wren's bedroom the next morning, throwing open the door with a crash. She bounced on Wren's bed as Wren groaned, pulling a pillow back over her head. The sky outside the window was pale and watery with dawn's first light. "What time is it?" Wren asked, when Olivia continued her bouncing.

"5:30," Olivia said. "Lots to do today to get ready for Callidus's appointment gala. But I wanted to tell you that your dresses came!"

Wren sat up, suddenly alert. "Really? I thought they weren't going to be ready until next week?"

"Elda is a miracle worker. I told her how you needed a dress for the gala and how you'd have to borrow something and it would be so horrible and she got all of them done early just to be rid of me."

Wren laughed, throwing off the covers. She could see the older woman working through the night to appease Olivia's insistent enthusiasm.

"I'd be lost without you, Olivia," Wren said. "Now if I'm executed,

I'll have peace of mind knowing I experienced my first gala," she joked.

"None of that doom and gloom talk," Olivia said. "You still have weeks to discover who the real killer is before the king and the inquisitor return. We'll focus on that tomorrow. Today, we look beautiful."

Wren opened her mouth to tell Olivia that weeks were really just days, but the words left her as Olivia shook out Wren's dress for the gala.

The cut was simple, a floor-length A-line gown dipping low in front. But the fabric. Wren reached out and touched it reverentially, stroking its velvety length. The dress was rich in texture and dimension, with abstract flowers of velvet pressed into the gold thread.

"Isn't it amazing?" Olivia said. "I love the jewel tones of the flowers… the burgundy and teal and gold will look so nice with your auburn hair…"

Wren pulled back, suddenly raw with emotion. Tears threatened in the corner of her eyes. What was it about this place? She hadn't cried in years before she had come to the Guildhall. Crying was for the weak, for those who expected sunshine and jelly beans from life. And then she realized what it was. Kindness. She was unaccustomed to such human kindness.

"Do you not like it?" Olivia asked, unsure.

Wren shook her head, trying to gather herself enough to speak. "I think this is the nicest thing anyone has ever done for me," she said softly.

Olivia threw her arms around Wren in a hug. "I'm glad you like it."

"I love it."

The Guildhall buzzed with activity as preparations were made for Callidus's appointment gala. The gala itself was to be held at the massive Tradehouse next door, but guild servants, staff, and vendors swarmed between the two buildings.

After bathing and dressing in another of her new dresses, a simple cut with an overlay of green leafy lace, she set off to find breakfast and Master Oldrick. In the excitement of breaking into Kasper's office and finding the note, she had completely forgotten that she had asked Oldrick to meet her after yesterday's voting. She was grateful he hadn't returned to his shop.

He was staying in the guest wing on the second floor. He answered the door in a rumpled shirt, his hair wild around his temples. A surge of nostalgia washed over Wren, surprising her with its ferocity. While her life under Master Oldrick had been sparse and simple, it had been satisfying as well, each day focused on making beautiful confections.

"Have a seat," he said, gesturing to a shabby velvet divan in the sitting room. "How're they treating you, my Wren?"

"Well, Master Oldrick. They have made me a journeyman, and Grandmaster Sable said artisan will not be far after." The comment was pointed.

Master Oldrick had the decency to look embarrassed. "Ah. I always knew you were too fine a flower to bloom in my garden for long. Your confections... are a thing of wonder. I wanted to keep you to myself as long as possible."

Wren softened. "I bear you no ill will, Master Oldrick. In truth, if you hadn't taken me in, I don't know where I'd be right now. Certainly not in this Guildhall."

"You never needed me, Wren. There's hardly a thing I taught you that your hands didn't already know. All you needed was a chance."

"Don't discount the importance of a chance," she said.

"Be careful, my dear. This place... it takes the love of the thing we do and replaces it with a love of power. It pains me to see they're already using you as a piece in their little game, what with this accusation of murder. It's preposterous, and all know it. But they don't care. They don't see the people. Just pawns."

Wren bristled. "That may be true of Callidus, but not of Sable and Hale. They've been kind to me."

Master Oldrick shook his head. "Just because they're kind doesn't mean they're not using you. I'm not saying it's malicious—it's just how they think. Be careful. Trust no one but yourself."

She sighed. "I know you're right. But it seems like the makings of a lonely life." She had been berating herself every day to stay on her guard, to look at everything offered with a discerning gaze. But part of her yearned to throw that caution aside, to embrace the friendships offered. Was it so impossible to think Hale and Olivia just wanted... to be her friends?

"You're living your own life now—I respect that. Perhaps you can make a happy life here, and if that's so, I'll eat my words quicker than one of your buttercreams. But mark my words, after a year or two here, you may find yourself craving a quiet little shop with a front window full of chocolates."

"Like yours?" She chuckled.

"I won't be around forever. I'll need someone to take over with more brains than Tate and more commitment than Hazel. You and I both know she'll be married with three babes before the brittle sets."

"I'll keep that in mind," she said. "Backup plan." *If I live that long.*

"Now, Wren, I know you didn't come here for advice. So how can I help you? I'll do whatever I can."

"I need to know who purchased the rose cupcakes. The kind that Grandmaster Callidus brought to the shop the day he brought me here. They… they were poisoned. I need to know who might have had the opportunity to slip in the poison."

Master Oldrick shook his head. "Poisoned! It's a travesty to pervert such a wonderful confection. I don't know if I kept the records… Tate has been terrible about the bookkeeping. But I'll look when I get back to my shop tomorrow."

"Thank you," she said, rising. "You'll be at the gala?"

"Yes. I was going to head back, but Hazel damn near blew her head off at the suggestion. We'll stay and leave tomorrow."

Wren smiled, imagining the fit the girl must have thrown. "I'll see you all there then."

Master Oldrick clasped her hands as she neared the door, his gnarled grip surprisingly strong.

"You be careful now," he said. "If someone's mad enough to kill the head of the Guild, they're mad enough to kill anyone who gets too close. Keep your eyes open."

Wren nodded in thanks and slipped through the door, Master Oldrick's words of warning ringing in her ears.

A surprise was waiting for Wren when she entered the teaching kitchen for her afternoon lesson with Hale. Sable was perched on a stool wearing an azure dress and an annoyed expression.

"You're late," she said.

"I'm sorry. Hale never set a fixed time…" Wren trailed off.

"Hale isn't teaching your lesson today. I am," Sable said. "And when I'm teaching, you're on time."

Wren nodded, biting back a sarcastic comment about how she would have known to be on time if Sable had given her some warning.

"Hale told me you made caramels in your first lesson?"

Wren nodded again.

"That's about as easy as it gets. We'll make something a bit more difficult this time." Sable lofted a bundle of fresh mint leaves with a flourish.

Wren's mind danced over the various choices of what they could be making.

Sable answered the silent question. "Mint truffles."

"Great," Wren said. Truffles were one of her favorite things to eat, although they were a bit boring to make. She could go for a truffle.

"Did Hale explain how you can vary the level of infusion in your confections?"

"Yes, though we didn't get to the lesson where he told me how."

"Our Gifts work through a combination of three forces. Our minds, our actions, and the ingredients."

"Hale explained the mindset to me. That it's focus, plus… movement."

"More or less. The mindset, I call it 'flow.' The state where you are completely engrossed in your work, your mind clear of all else. The deeper in this state you are, the stronger the confection. But that's not all. Our actions imbue magic as well. The more complex the movement, the stronger the infusion."

Wren thought about the poisoned cupcake, its intricately crafted petals. The cupcakes were about the most labor-intensive sweet she made. No wonder she'd felt wrung out and empty after completing a batch.

"These two factors are like levers you can push to vary the outcome. What little control we have over our Gifts comes from the application of these principles."

"You said there was a third factor. The ingredients?"

"We don't fully understand this piece yet. Perhaps if the guilds could work together to puzzle through it… but that was Kasper's foolish dream. What we know is that sometimes the infusion doesn't take. Everything else could be the same, the flow, the movements. But the confection is as ordinary as a gumdrop. We only know the ingredients matter because of the fact that the magic doesn't always work."

Wren picked up the mint, examining it, its crisp fragrance washing over her. How could an innocuous plant have a role to play in the rising and falling tides of countries and kings?

"Before you get started, have you and Hale discovered anything new regarding Kasper's death?"

Wren's thoughts flew to the note discovered in the secret compartment. But Sable was convinced it wasn't Callidus. Wren didn't think she would be convinced with only a letter. Once she had the handwriting match, she would share her discovery. "The king returns in two weeks," she said haltingly.

"Yes, I can read the newspaper, thank you for that insightful update. What else?"

Wren's face burned. "I talked to Master Oldrick this morning. He's going to search his records to find out where the cupcake went."

"That's something, I suppose. You'll have to do better than that, Wren, if you want to keep your head."

Anger flared in her. "What have you discovered? You said you'd help me, and so far only Hale seems to give a damn! How am I supposed to discover a killer in this political maze if you can't and you've been doing this for years?"

Sable's dark eyes gleamed. "How indeed. I said I'd protect you, but I never said I'd coddle you. I'm not your mother or your nursemaid or your friend. I am your sponsor and grandmaster. You don't need to like me, but you do need to trust me. I have been a part of this tangled messy web for years, and I didn't become the youngest grandmaster in history by bumbling about. I am looking for clues in my own way, and my way is subtle. I get results precisely because no one is the wiser. We both need to do our part if we are to outsmart a murderer."

Sable's rebuke stung like a slap. Wren had assumed Sable wasn't helping, because she hadn't seen or heard anything. But what did she know about the world of political machinations? Could it be possible that Sable was trying to solve the mystery her own way?

Her doubt must have been written across her face because Sable let out a breath, the hard set of her jaw softening. "Why don't you come with me tomorrow to the meeting of the Guilder's Council? Then you'll see the board where I play my game of fox and geese."

Wren nodded woodenly, not sure she wanted to spend another minute in the woman's company, but knowing she couldn't say *no*.

"Now get to work on these truffles," Sable said, rising gracefully, sweeping her curtain of black hair over her shoulder. "I've been craving them for a few days."

It took Wren an hour, much longer than it should have, to find her flow. Her thoughts spun with Master Oldrick's warning, Sable's rebuke, and Lucas's—Prince Imbris's—pleading words. And always, stirred throughout it all like a ribbon of color in a batch of frosting, Callidus and Kasper. Kasper and Callidus. What had gone wrong? Why had Callidus murdered his own guildmaster? And how would she ever prove it?

CHAPTER 19

"Wren, there you are!" Olivia said brightly, rounding the corner. "I've been looking everywhere for you!"

"Why?" Wren asked. She had just finished pouring the ganache for the truffles into a square confectionery frame and was setting a sheet of parchment paper over the top. It would need to crystallize overnight before she could cut and dip the truffles in dark chocolate.

"Grandaunt said we can use her makeup and jewelry." Olivia's eyes were shining with excitement. "We need to get ready!"

Wren peered out the door of the kitchen to the bright light of the conservatory. "It's still the afternoon, isn't it?"

"It takes time to get ready," Olivia said, as if it were the most obvious thing in the world.

Wren stifled a chuckle and stood. "Lead the way."

The girls retrieved their dresses and darted through the crowds of harried servants to Greer's chambers.

"I don't know anything about makeup, or doing my hair…" Wren admitted.

"Don't worry," Olivia said, "I'm an expert."

"An expert?" Wren raised an eyebrow.

"Well, no, but things get pretty boring around here sometimes. Grandaunt lets me experiment. And she's an expert."

They entered Greer's chambers. The sun-speckled room was as pristine as the first time Wren had glimpsed it, though the riot of dahlias had been replaced with vases of vibrant sunflowers. Their cheerful upturned faces brought a smile to Wren's. Where had Greer gotten them all?

"Grandaunt has an admirer in the Florist's Guild," Olivia explained, pulling Wren into the massive closet and pushing her down into the chair before the vanity table. "We'll do you first."

A charcoal sketch of a young man framed in silver and glass caught her eye. Wren lifted and examined it. He was very handsome, even rendered in pencil—his dark eyes smoldering, his mouth crooked with a roguish smile.

"Grandaunt's husband," Olivia said, selecting a gold-lettered glass pot from the forest of products on the vanity top. "He died tragically when they were young."

"He was handsome," Wren admitted, remembering the story Elda had told.

"Grandaunt was one of the most fashionable ladies in Maradis when she married Carter Greer," Olivia said. "She's going to help me find a husband as fine as he was. Now close your eyes."

Wren complied, putting the picture back. Olivia began painting some sort of powder across her skin. The touch of the brush was as light as a butterfly's wings. It wasn't an altogether unpleasant experience.

"Are you sure you want her to find you a husband?" Wren asked, opening her eyes. "Aren't you happy at the Guild?"

Olivia had retrieved a pot as black as night and a tiny brush. "Close your eyes again. And don't move. I'm going to line your eyes."

"That sounds dangerous," Wren said.

"Yes, I'd like to find a husband," Olivia said. "Grandaunt talks so fondly about her time as a lady—hosting elaborate dinner parties, touring Lake Crima on the king's yacht. They even had a summer house in the Odette Isles. It sounds so glamorous."

"And that's… what you'd like to do? Host parties? Be… someone's wealthy wife?"

"If I can swing it!" Olivia laughed. "Don't sound so shocked, Wren. We don't all want to spend our lives hunched over a countertop. I like working at the guild, but if I had my choice? Yes. I'd choose a handsome man who curls my toes, children to chase through the garden, friends to laugh with. Leisure. Those things all sound quite wonderful. Now open," Olivia said, retrieving another silver pot and unscrewing its lid. "Pout with your lips," she said, before continuing. "It's not like I'm totally heartless. You can do a lot of good if you have money. You can help people."

"That's wonderful," Wren said halfheartedly.

"What about you, Wren?" Olivia eyed her appraisingly. "Don't you want to get married? Have a family?"

"I don't think I'll ever marry," Wren said as Olivia came at her with another brush.

"What? Why?"

Wren chose her words carefully. "I've never had the best… luck with family. The family I wanted… my mother and brother… I lost them. And the family I had left… I was better off without them. I guess I can't imagine being happy with someone."

"You'll change your mind when you meet the right person," Olivia said confidently.

Wren didn't think so. She thought she had met someone who'd cared for her when Ansel had taken her in—the brash, swaggering orphan king with fiery red hair and a chipped front tooth. But he had traded her. Betrayed her. If she had misjudged him so completely, what hope did she have with other men? Her thoughts drifted to Lucas, his rosemary scent and easy manner. He had deceived her, too, in his own way. And though she found herself drawn to him, was it enough? Was she fooling herself to think she could ever really trust him—or be with him? The son of the king?

Olivia seemed content to let Wren ruminate as she finished her makeup and pinned locks of Wren's auburn hair back into a shining waterfall that cascaded down her back.

"I hardly recognize myself," Wren said with an amazed laugh when

Olivia stepped back. Her eyes were lined with onyx, her lashes long and wide. Her pale skin was flawless and her angular face was softened by rosy cheeks that looked flushed, as if by a brisk winter's day. Wren pressed her painted lips together. They reminded her of a ripe plum ready to be plucked.

"You're a miracle worker," Wren said, standing and giving Olivia the chair.

With a proud smile, Olivia went to quick work on herself, expertly painting on the colors, while Wren roamed about the room, flipping through beaded dresses and silky scarves, examining towering shoes with fascination.

"I wonder what Hale will say when he sees you," Olivia said, watching Wren slyly in the mirror.

Wren reddened, shaking her head. Had Olivia heard about the kiss? Gods, she hoped not. "I'm sure he'll say something charming and perfect, like he says to all the girls."

"You say that like it's a bad thing," Olivia said with a giggle.

"I am not interested in Hale like that," Wren said, glad at her certainty that the words were true. "Trust me. He's like… a brother."

"Well, he's not my brother," Olivia said. "So I'll admire all I want."

Wren let out a little laugh, unscrewing a deep purple bottle of perfume and taking a whiff of its saccharine sweetness. "Smell this," she said. "What a strange scent."

"Don't touch that," Greer said, choosing that moment to sweep through the room.

Wren jumped and screwed the top back on hastily, putting it back. "I'm sorry," she said, her face scarlet. "Olivia said…"

Greer crossed to the desk and patted her arm. "I shouldn't have startled you. It's quite expensive. It was a gift from a Centu trader. I save it for special occasions."

"Of course," Wren said.

"You look lovely, Wren," Greer said.

"Olivia did it all," Wren said.

"I learned from the best," Olivia said, standing and kissing her grandaunt on the cheek. She curtsied. "What do you think?"

Greer examined Olivia like a surgeon dissecting a patient. "A bit light on the eyeshadow," she murmured, "and I do wish you'd lose a few pounds"—she pinched Olivia's plump chin in her fingers—"but overall, you are quite the beauty. Your mother would be proud."

"Thank you, Grandaunt," Olivia said mechanically, her sparkle dulled by Greer's criticism.

Wren stilled her face to keep a scowl from it. She thought Olivia looked absolutely perfect, her cascading blonde curls and tasteful makeup setting off her sweet features.

"Now go put your dresses on," Greer said. "It's almost time to head to the Tradehouse, and I want to see the full effect before I have to get back to work."

"You're not coming?" Wren asked.

"I'll be there in the background, making sure the caterers don't fall over themselves. Duty calls." Greer let out a heavy sigh as she glanced back to the army of fancy dresses in the closet.

Wren and Olivia slipped into the washroom to put their dresses on, and when they turned to survey each other, their mouths dropped.

"Your dress is marvelous," Wren said. Olivia looked like a glittering jewel in a gown of rose gold. Its lace bodice tapered at her waist, and then flared into a pleated chiffon skirt that dropped gracefully to the floor.

"So is yours!" Olivia's eyes were shining.

Wren looked down with more than a little awe at the drape of the velvet over her body. A field of teal and ruby flowers undulated over the golden field of the fabric, soft and mesmerizing. "I feel half-naked."

"You look stunning. Hale will be speechless."

"I bet that's a first," Wren joked, ignoring the mention of Hale. She would convince Olivia that she didn't have her sights on Hale sooner or later.

They emerged from the washroom and Greer clasped her hands to her bosom in delight. "You both look so lovely!"

She embraced them both, and Wren's heartstrings twanged painfully. This must have been what it felt like to have a mother. It was a nice feeling.

"One last thing before you go," Greer said, opening a drawer in her vanity and rummaging through it. "Ah!"

She deposited a pair of earrings into each of their outstretched hands, golden blossoms for Olivia, and teardrops of ruby glass for Wren.

"I can't—" Wren began, but Greer shushed her. "They do no good collecting dust in the drawer. They'll look perfect on you."

Olivia locked arms with Wren as they swept out the door and down the hallway towards the antechamber. Wren's heart thudded with excitement. She couldn't wait to see what the night had in store.

CHAPTER 20

The night was warm, but a cool breeze tousled Wren's hair. She shivered in her thin dress as she and Olivia walked the short distance to the Tradehouse arm in arm, navigating through the crowd of carriages waiting to be opened by liveried footmen. Once inside the stained-glass front doors, Wren's mouth dropped open. Sets of open doors led to the ballroom, where four impossibly large chandeliers hung from the vaulted ceiling, casting refracting light over hundreds of colorfully-clad partygoers. The rectangular room was lined with four long tables, paralleling a wide expanse of floor for dancing. The tables were covered in glittering cutlery and green and white centerpieces of fragrant blossoms.

A Vintner's Guild servant with a silver tray approached and handed them each a tapered flute of sparkling rose wine.

Olivia giggled, taking a sip. "Let's go."

They wove through the crowd, wide eyes taking in the handsome faces, fine clothes, and jewels bedecking the crowd. Olivia pointed out the people she recognized—guildmasters, nobles, members of the royal court. The names and titles washed over Wren like rain until one grabbed her to attention.

"That's Guildmaster Chandler, of the Distiller's Guild," Olivia was saying.

The Distiller's Guild. Wren examined the man from across the room. Did this Chandler know who had given Kasper the poisoned whiskey? He was plump with drooping jowls and a lined face, but his features were friendly, his expression warm. His wife was quite lovely with white at her temples and fine lines around her mouth and eyes that spoke of a lifetime of laughter. Should she go talk to them? Wren chewed her lip in indecision. What would she say? *"Do you know who happened to gift my guildmaster a poisoned bottle of spirits?"* She dismissed the idea. She would bungle it. Perhaps Sable or Hale could help her lure the information out of him with their honeyed words and smiles.

Her ruminations were cut short as another figure caught her eye. "Who is that?" Wren asked, pointing to an ebony-haired man with tawny skin. He wore knee-high black boots, a long burgundy coat, and a predatory expression that made Wren shiver.

"Don't look at him," Olivia said, whirling Wren around as her eyes caught the man's. "He's the guildmaster of the Spicer's Guild. He was a pirate in the Centu Isles before he took over the guild. They say he once dug a man's eyes out with a fork for looking at him the wrong way."

Wren wrinkled her nose. "I hope that's an exaggeration."

"Oh, no. Kasper told me at the last gala."

"When was that?" Wren asked. It sounded like Kasper had been pulling the girl's leg, but Wren kept her thoughts to herself.

"I was twelve the last time they held one," Olivia said. "Greer didn't let me stay past nine and I couldn't even have a drink of wine."

"I think you'll have much more fun tonight," Wren said, spotting a tall copper-haired young man in a navy suit taking in Olivia with an appreciative expression. "Eleven o'clock," she whispered, nodding to the man.

The man began making his way through the crowd as his eyes met Olivia's, but he faltered halfway to the approach.

Wren felt a prickle on the back of her neck and turned.

"Wren Confectioner," Steward Willings said, his pockmarked face twisted into a grimace. "We're now allowing murderers to dance the waltz, rather than hang from the gallows, are we?"

"I'm not a murderer," Wren said, squaring her shoulders. "I will be proven innocent." *Murderer. Murderer.* How she hated that word. Her conscience whispered it to her in her dreams.

He snorted. "I know what you are. And I know exactly how a woman like you convinced a weak man like Imbris to vouch for you." He looked her up and down with a sneer that made her skin crawl and made her wish her dress covered much more than it did.

She clutched the fabric, stilling her hands at her sides, lest they betray her discomfort. "Inspector Imbris vouched for me because he cares about the truth." Her voice was as strong as steel. "Whereas you apparently don't mind letting a real killer go free." Her breath caught as a piece fit into place. Why *would* Willings be unconcerned with letting the true killer stay undiscovered? Unless… he had some role in the plot? Could Callidus and Willings be in on it together?

Willings grabbed her arm suddenly, drawing her near to him, digging his nails into her flesh. "Listen here, you little harlot…"

Wren reeled at the sour smell of his breath, the cold of his skin on hers.

"Steward Willings," a stern voice said. "Surely, you can take a break from terrorizing young ladies for one night. In the name of guild-crown relations."

Willings's eyes widened and he released her, stepping back inadvertently.

When Wren turned to her rescuer, she couldn't hide her shock. It was the dark Head of the Spicer's Guild.

The man took her hand and bowed, marking it with a soft kiss. "Guildmaster Pike, at your service."

"Pretending like you don't know each other, eh?" Willings said. "I'm sure she got the poison from you."

"Poison?" Pike raised a dark eyebrow, his handsome face dangerous. "You must misunderstand. We humble guildmembers supply spices. Surely, the king wouldn't want to be without his saffron and salt."

Willings snorted. "Don't you threaten me. We'll prove this girl's connection, and yours, just as soon as the Grand Inquisitor returns. Enjoy the party," he said to Wren, a twisted smile flitting across his face. "I'll be seeing you very soon."

He turned and stalked into the crowd.

Wren blew out a shaky breath, rubbing her arms vigorously to banish the chill that had swept through her. "Thank you, sir, for your assistance."

Olivia had stood mutely through the whole thing, frozen to the spot.

"I'm afraid my aid may have only cast a deeper suspicion upon you." Pike exuded a casual malice that kept her heart rapidly beating as he watched Willings go with sharp eyes. This was not a man to cross. Yet he *had* come to her aid.

"He's already convinced of my guilt and determined to see me tortured and hanged," Wren said. "He made up his mind long before you arrived."

"It would pain me to see a young lady of such beauty and gifts suffer such a fate," he said, taking one of her hands in his own and running his thumb over the back. The hairs on the back of her arm raised. The way he said "gifts" was knowing, and his eyes said the rest. He knew she was Gifted. Which meant he knew of the Gifts. Was he Gifted himself? She supposed most guildheads must be. Did this make him an ally—or an enemy? Did he wish to protect her—or use her?

"I appreciate your concern," she said, retrieving her hand from his grasp as politely as possible. "Truly. We are working on discovering the truth of what happened."

"If you need my assistance," he said, "you need only ask. Tell my men you seek the marlin's blade." He winked.

Marlin's blade? Wren wondered.

"What makes you think she needs your assistance when she has mine?" Sable asked, breaking into the group. "Moving in on my journeyman?"

A wide grin split Pike's face, and he lifted Sable off the ground in a crushing embrace. "I live and breathe. You get more beautiful each passing day." He pulled back to take in Sable's sleek black dress with admiration, keeping one hand firmly affixed to her waist.

"And you get bolder," she joked.

"Can't blame a man for trying. I would trade all the spices in my warehouse for a night with you."

Wren and Olivia looked at each other, scandalized, but Sable laughed. "Just your warehouse?"

"All my guild's warehouses?"

"Get me a drink and we'll negotiate."

With a nod to the girls, Pike led Sable away towards the bar.

Wren deflated slightly and drained her flute. Forget her aversion to alcohol. She'd need it if she was going to get through tonight. "I think that's about enough excitement for one night," Wren said. "Let's find that fellow who was admiring you."

"Are you all right?" Olivia asked as they began to walk.

"I will be," Wren said, half to convince herself. She looked over her shoulder at where Willings stood amidst a cluster of nobles. His eyes were locked on her. She whipped her head back around with a rush of breath.

"I hate him," Olivia said with a hiss.

"Willings?" Wren raised an eyebrow. She hadn't ever heard Olivia say a negative word about anyone.

"The man is devious and self-serving," Olivia said. A storm cloud seemed to pass over the golden sun that usually lit her countenance. "Did you know my parents died in the Red Plague?"

"I didn't. I'm so sorry." A flicker of guilt passed through her. She had been so concerned with her own situation, she hadn't made much of an effort to get to know Olivia, to ask her about her past. Wren chided herself. She hadn't had a friend in so long, she had forgotten how to be one.

"The crown summoned most of the Physician's Guild into the palace and then sealed the gates. It was Willings who gave the order. No one in the palace died. They say..." She lowered her voice. "They say there was a cure. But the king and his staff kept it for themselves."

Wren's eyes widened, shocked. "How could that be true? Thousands died. If they could have stopped it..." She faltered. Of course it could be true. The king hadn't given a damn about the people in the town where she'd grown up... Why would he care about his subjects here?

"If not for that man, my parents might still be alive," Olivia said.

"Oh, Olivia..." Wren said, her heart twisting.

A bell clanged, reverberating through the ballroom. "Dinner time." Olivia brightened, seeming to leave the past behind in a blink. Wren envied her that skill. "Let's find seats."

Wren and Olivia found a row of empty chairs at one of the long tables. The handsome copper-haired man who had been making eyes at Olivia claimed the spot next to her, and Olivia turned to Wren with shining eyes, once again effervescent and full of life.

"Can I sit here?" a male voice asked, and Wren turned to find Lennon hovering uncertainly to her left.

"I suppose," Wren said, looking around. "You're not sitting with Marina and Grandmaster Beckett?"

Lennon sank into the chair. "There wasn't room."

Servants all around the ballroom brought the first course, a chilled gazpacho soup with truffle oil and shaved parmesan cheese. Another filled her wineglass.

"I've heard the food at these things is the best you'll ever eat," Lennon said. "All the guilds are trying to show each other up and put out the best course."

"I'd happily judge that competition," Wren said.

"Me too." Lennon smiled shyly.

"Maybe they'll need two judges," Wren offered.

"Wren… I'm sorry about what Marina did to you in the dining hall," Lennon said, the words coming in a rush. "And I'm sorry… that I didn't step in. Marina's like a force of nature when she has something on her mind. It's usually easier to let her have her way. But… it was wrong."

"Why is she like that?" Wren asked, surprised at his candor.

"She's not always that bad. She really doesn't like you for some reason."

"Great." Wren rolled her eyes.

"I think… she's threatened by you?" Lennon ventured a guess. "She and her father don't get along. She's been vying to be sponsored by Sable for years now, plus she half-loves, half-hates Hale, and then you breeze in and take everything she's ever wanted."

Wren let out a laugh of disbelief. "Yes, my glamorous life as an accused murderer. She can have it."

"I'm not saying she's right, but that's what seems to be going on."

"Do you mind being sponsored by Beckett?" Wren didn't want to tell him she had overheard him pleading with Callidus to take on his sponsorship. She didn't think eavesdropping would help the truce they seemed to be developing.

"He's a good confectioner and a good diplomat, and I've learned a lot from him, but…" Lennon looked up and down the table to make sure the man wasn't near. "He's kind of an ass."

Wren laughed.

"He goes to the temple every day and forces us to come with him. I think religion is fine if you're into that sort of thing, but neither Marina nor I are. It's always temperance this, discipline that. He's constantly judging everyone for their behavior, holding us up to impossible standards. I've pieced together that Marina had an older sister who fell in love with a man Beckett thought was too low-born for her, and it basically tore the family apart. I don't think Marina's ever forgiven her father for driving her sister away."

Wren put her spoon down, her appetite temporarily gone. She knew a thing or two about horrible fathers, and Beckett sounded awful. She felt a pang of sympathy for Marina.

"This got a little heavy for the soup course." Lennon forced a laugh. "Sorry."

"It's all right," Wren said. "It helps me understand. The guild is a complicated place for a newcomer."

"You'll get the hang of it." He popped a flake of parmesan cheese into his mouth. Wren considered Lennon—his round face, his upturned nose with a sprinkle of freckles, his obliviousness to the cuff of his jacket trailing in the soup. He had a naive sincerity about him. How had he once seemed threatening? He looked at her with a spoonful of soup halfway to his mouth and paused. "What?"

"I'm glad you sat next to me."

"Me too."

CHAPTER 21

A nd so it was that Wren settled in for the finest meal of her life. Course after course emerged, each new dish a culinary delight. Fresh briny oysters from the Piscator's Guild, thick knotty challah bread from the Baker's, seared pork belly glazed with fig sauce from the Butcher's. Wren shared squeals and groans of delight with Lennon, Olivia, and Olivia's new friend, Reed, as they sampled each new dish, relaxing until she found herself laughing into her wine, fully at ease.

Dessert was courtesy of the Confectioner's Guild—personal chocolate tarts filled with molten raspberry filling that spilled out in a dreamy puddle of fuchsia when sliced into. When Wren took her first bite she closed her eyes, savoring the tangy bite of the dark chocolate mingling with the buoyancy of the raspberry. It was perfect. A work of art. She glanced in amazement down the row of tables, wondering who had made all of the tarts. Guildmistress Greer must have enlisted an army!

"I think my dress is going to burst at the seams," Olivia said, leaning back in her chair. Lennon had excused himself, joking that he was headed back to the guild for a bigger pair of pants.

"I know the feeling." Wren chuckled, breathing out heavily. She stood, stretching her too-full stomach.

"Doesn't he look like a sculpture by a master?" Olivia whispered conspiratorially as she nodded across the room. Hale was approaching them.

To say Hale looked handsome would be to call the ocean a wishing well. His bronze hair, normally pulled into a bun on the top of his head, was down around his shoulders, brushed to a sheen. He wore a black suit with a subtle check, a violet waistcoat and thin tie, and black wingtip shoes polished to a shine. Half the room (the female half) seemed to rotate, following his progress towards them.

"Ladies," Hale said, giving a bow of his head as he approached. "I've not seen such a lovely sight in all my days."

"You probably say that to all the girls," Wren said wryly.

"But I only meant it with you." He winked.

"Reed Montagne." Reed shoved out one hand while the other snaked around Olivia's waist, seeming to convey that he had seen this one first.

"Hale Firena." Hale shook Reed's hand, and for once, he seemed to have left his territorial nonsense at home. "Any friend of Olivia's is a friend of mine."

Reed inclined his head, before turning. "Olivia, would you like to dance?"

"I'd love to," she said, her cheeks dimpling in pleasure.

"Please excuse us," Reed said, and Wren gave Olivia an encouraging grin as they vanished into the crowd with Reed at her side.

"Hale," Wren said with feigned surprise. "That was downright civilized."

"I have to keep you guessing," he said, flashing his cheeky grin. "But on to the more important business." He took her hand and turned her about in a twirl. "You, Wren, look good enough to eat."

She groaned, letting out a little laugh. "Not the bad sexual puns again!"

He guffawed. "Force of habit. I'll work on it. What did you think of that chocolate tart? One of Callidus's recipes. The man can't dress, but I guess he can cook."

She nodded, grateful for the change of subject. "It was divine. Everything was amazing. I've never eaten so well."

"One of the perks of the job." He took her arm and tucked it into the crook of his elbow, leading her towards the dance floor. "Have you been enjoying yourself? Besides fending off what I imagine are dozens of slobbering suitors?"

"No slobbering suitors," she said. She grimaced with remembrance. "Willings did slime his way over to me at one point."

Hale stiffened next to her. "What did he say?"

"I'm a guilty murderer who will get her comeuppance. Torture and execution, etcetera." She kept her tone light, though her stomach flipped. A feeling of nausea washed over her. A week had already passed. The return of the Grand Inquisitor was closer than ever, and she couldn't yet pin Callidus to the crime. Suddenly, it felt silly to be here, eating and making merry, while the sands of time slipped through her fingers.

Hale seemed to sense her change of mood, turning to her. "Don't worry. We'll figure it out. The Guild has power. We won't let anything happen to you."

"I might have believed that before Callidus was guildmaster. But would Sable openly defy him? The king? I can't ask that of her. Or you."

"We're not defeated yet. We found the letter," he said quietly. "We're closer than ever. We'll figure it out."

"Thank you," she said. "I feel slightly better."

"Only slightly?" he said. "I can do better. Dance with me."

Wren didn't protest. She wasn't much of a dancer, but he pulled her amidst the other couples, cinching his arm around her waist. The song was languid, and though Hale could have simply swayed to the music like many other couples, he pulled her around the floor, twirling and spinning her in graceful arcs. *Of course he's a good dancer,* she thought with a wry smile.

"Crown for your thoughts," he said, pulling her close once again.

"Are my thoughts worth so much?" she joked.

"They are to me," he said.

She looked up into his eyes and saw that they were vibrant, his words serious. "I guess I'm thinking that even though it might not be for good, I'm glad to be here. To have met you and Olivia and Sable."

Hale nodded. "You're not going anywhere, Wren—"

"There she is," a biting voice said. "The girl who has condemned my brother. Is this how you repay him?"

Wren's eyes flew open as she turned to the interloper.

A willowy dark-haired girl stood before her, her hands on her hips, her chin upraised in defiance. Her emerald dress was exquisite silk and embroidery, and she wore a thin circlet on her brow. Beside her, a young man stood with an apologetic look on his face, lean and tall, with similar black hair. He looked strangely familiar.

"I'm sorry," Wren said. "You must have me confused with someone else."

"Do I?" the girl asked. "You are Wren of the Confectioner's Guild, are you not? Kasper's murderer?"

Hale growled at her side, and Wren put a hand on his arm. "I am Wren. But I did not kill Kasper. And who, I pray, are you? Who is this brother of yours?"

"Lucas." She spat the word. "My brother is Lucas. Do you even remember him? The man who put everything on the line for you while you're apparently whoring through your guild with the time he's given you?"

"Listen here, girl—" Hale began.

"Listen here, *princess*," the girl said, cutting Hale off. "You will address me with the respect I am due."

Wren was torn between anger and bewilderment.

"I know Lucas. But I don't understand," she said. "What do you think I've done to him? He's helping with the investigation. To clear my name."

The boy broke in, trying to soothe the girl. "Ella—"

"No, Trick." She whirled, her black curls flying. "I will say my piece. I don't care if Lucas is fooled by this girl. I see who she is."

"Who I am?" Wren said. "What in the Sower's name are you talking about?"

She turned back. "My brother Lucas. He vouched for you." She spit the word *vouched* with more venom than Wren thought possible.

"So? That was only to give me time to clear my name, so I wouldn't have to sit in jail."

The girl let out an angry huff. "He didn't tell you, did he? How like Lucas. How perfectly gallant. You don't even know what you've done to him."

"What do you mean? What have I done to him?"

"He vouched for you. That means if you're found guilty, he's found guilty. If you die... he dies."

A chill fell over Wren, stilling her to her very core. Her knees went weak. "That can't be true."

"It is true." The girl shrieked, her voice drawing the attention of other partygoers. "That's why no one vouches for anyone. It's suicide."

Wren's hand flew to her mouth as the horror of the princess's words washed over her. Lucas had put his own life on the line for her. A girl he had never met. He had risked everything. And had said nothing to her, never urged her on, told her the true importance of what they did. That it wasn't just some nameless guild orphan who would be lost. That it was his life, too. The life of a prince of Alesia.

Wren opened her mouth to speak, but the girl, who could only be Princess Ellarose, the darling youngest daughter of King Hadrian Imbris, beat her to it. "I wish I could see you hang for what you've done to my brother," she hissed, an angry tear falling down the perfect porcelain of her cheek. "If it didn't mean he would hang too."

With that, she whirled, pushing through the crowd. The boy turned to go too, but Wren caught his arm.

"Wait, please," she said. "Is what she said true?"

He nodded sadly. She realized now who the lad reminded her of. Lucas. "He's your brother too, isn't he?"

"Yes," he said. "I'm Patrick Imbris. Journeyman of the Vintner's Guild."

"I..." She could barely form words. "I won't let him die for me." Her fingers tightened on his arm. "I promise."

He nodded. "I'm sorry about my sister." He slipped from her grasp and was gone.

She turned to Hale, horror in her eyes. Willings's threats, Oldrick's words about the inquisitor... they flew through her head like debris in a gale, slicing her with sharp edges and points.

"How... could he do that?" she asked. "Put himself at such risk... for a stranger?"

"You didn't know?" Hale asked.

She examined his face. No surprise showed there. "You did?" She shrank from him.

"Of course. That's what vouching means. I thought you understood."

"They don't teach the ins and outs of the Alesian judicial system on the street," she retorted. "The lessons pretty much start with 'don't get caught' and end with 'don't get killed.'"

"I'm sorry," Hale said. "But this doesn't change anything. We'll still find who the killer is. You and Lucas will be fine."

"It changes everything," Wren breathed. "I can't ask him to die for me. Before it was my life on the line. But now... he has to take it back. He'll un-vouch for me and I'll go to jail."

"It doesn't work that way," Hale said. "Besides, then you'd be in jail and have no chance of proving who the real killer is."

"Then I'll... I'll confess," she said. "Tell them it was me."

"No good." Hale shook his head. "If you confess, you and Lucas both hang."

The room around her suddenly felt loud and overwhelming. The people and the sounds pressed against her with stifling weight.

"I need to get out of here." Her hands flitted uselessly, tearing at her hair, her gown. This stupid dress! What did she think she was playing at, eating and dancing while Lucas was dying for her?

"Okay," Hale said, putting his arm around her shoulder and steering her towards the door. "We'll get you back to the Guild."

"No," she said, shrugging his arm off of her. His presence, which had felt so warm and comforting before, now threatened to choke her, drown her. "I need some time. Alone. Please. Leave me alone," she said, and she tore out the front of the Tradehouse, down the stairs into the indifferent night.

CHAPTER 22

Wren sat with a thunk on one of the massive steps of her Guildhall, gasping for breath. Angry tears flowed freely as the enormity of Lucas's sacrifice washed over her. He had no guarantee that they would ever find the killer. Or that she wasn't, in fact, the killer! He had known her for all of five minutes when he had vouched for her. How could he do something like that? Put himself in harm's way—for her?

She couldn't get over what he had done for her; her thoughts circled back to it time and time again. What kind of man did a thing like that? Her heart twisted painfully at the thought of his graphite eyes and rosemary scent and lean saunter.

How much time she'd wasted, playing with Olivia, stirring caramel, dancing and eating and sleeping. Chances she had squandered, playing at this thing like it was a game, unwilling to face the reality of her situation. She had distracted herself, enjoyed the perks of this new life, because the truth waiting for her at the end of these few blessed weeks of freedom had been too horrible to confront. Torture and death. A sacrifice for someone's political gain, a discarded piece in a game she didn't understand. At her core, she had never believed she would prove Callidus's guilt. Who was she to go against the Head of the Guild? A man who would kill his own mentor to gain power and take his position for his own?

Wren wiped her tears with the heel of her hand, taking a deep shuddering breath. She didn't have the luxury of time or apathy anymore. It wasn't only her life at stake, but Lucas's. It was time to act.

But what could she do? What next?

She looked across the dark street to the bright entrance to the Tradehouse. Music and laughter floated on the air, signs that the party was still in full swing.

She turned behind her to the dim light of the Guildhall. The building was practically empty right now. Callidus was gone, distracted at the gala. It would be a perfect time to sneak into his chambers and find a sample of his handwriting to match with the letter. And anything else she might find. That ebony notebook.

Wren stood, spirits buoyed now that she had a plan in hand. They had ten days left. Perhaps they could pull this one out of the fire yet.

Wren hiked up her dress and flew up the stairs of the Guild, pulling the door open. The normal guards were gone. As she entered the antechamber, she realized that she wasn't certain where Callidus's chambers were. She thought back to Olivia's tour that first day and recalled that the guildmaster's chambers were on the third floor, with his office. If Callidus was in such a hurry to move into the guildmaster's office, he'd probably moved chambers as well.

Wren flew up the two flights of stairs, the long skirt of her dress clutched in her hands. She turned left and strode to the doorway, swiftly pulling two of the pins out of her hair. She bent over the lock, making quick work of it. These types of door locks were simple, so it took a matter of seconds.

When the lock made a telltale click, she squeezed through the door and locked it behind her. The room was dark but for the lamplight that streamed through the window outside.

She didn't dare light a candle, so she let her eyes adjust while she moved to the desk. She rifled through papers in a drawer, looking for one with his signature that she could take. It was difficult to find. Most of the letters in the desk were to Callidus, not from him. At least she knew that she had come to the right room.

She hissed in frustration, trying another drawer. Here, her luck held. A to-do list on stationery bearing his name. Of course Callidus was the type of man to have monogrammed stationery. He had probably dreamed about it as a wretched boy while other youths had been playing ball and catching fish. She couldn't make out the items on the list in the light, but she could imagine what it said. "Poison clueless guildmaster and take his rightful place." "Ruin young stranger's life by pinning crime on her." "Buy pomade."

Wren looked at the list and frowned. The handwriting seemed different than the writing she had remembered from the letter. But without it to compare to side by side, she couldn't be sure. She folded the paper and tucked it in the bosom of her dress, wishing, not for the first time, that the gown had pockets. That would be priority number one in dress-buying from now on. Pockets.

As she closed the desk drawer, the knob on the door rattled. A clink of keys. Someone was coming in!

Wren launched herself into action, flying through the door into the bedchamber. Under the bed. She would hide under the bed.

She dropped to the floor and swore. The bed sat on the ground, its monster frame looming two feet tall. She jumped to her feet and spun in a panicked circle, looking for the next best place to hide. The wardrobe? No, if he opened it, she'd be a sitting duck. The curtains dropped to the floor. But her form might show…

The door opened, and Callidus's unpleasant voice drifted in from the next room. The curtains it was. She moved silently behind them, swathing her body in the thick velvet drapes. She tried to make herself as small as possible, willing her body to shrink into itself until she was nothing. Why couldn't her magic be something really useful? Like flight or invisibility.

A lamp came on in the bedroom, and Wren stifled the hitch in her breathing. Her heart thudded in her ears and her body had broken out in a cold sweat. If he caught her, she was done for. And so was Lucas.

Callidus was alone, but he was muttering to himself angrily. "Blooming servants, can't do a thing right, two left feet…" He trailed off.

Wren peeked around the corner the tiniest amount so she could see a sliver of what was going on. Callidus was at his desk, wiping at his little notebook with a handkerchief. His jacket was off and a wine stain as red as blood blossomed across his chest. A small smile of satisfaction crept onto Wren's face. Served him right, getting spilled on at his own party.

He finished dabbing at the pages and left the notebook open on the table, undoubtedly to dry.

Callidus unbuttoned his shirt and retrieved another from the wardrobe. Wren's face flamed and she pulled back a touch as he took his shirt off to switch to the clean one, revealing pale skin and wiry muscles.

He put the new one on but didn't button it, sinking instead against the bed, his head in his hands. She felt like an interloper in this surprisingly intimate scene, taken aback by how vulnerable and human Callidus had become without the armor of his scowl and starched suit.

"Oh, Francis," he said. "Why'd you go and leave such a mess? I told you I never wanted any of this. I don't think I can do it alone…"

Wren's heart skipped a beat. Francis. Francis Kasper. He was lamenting Kasper leaving him? Of all the things she might have eavesdropped on in this room, this was the last thing she'd expected.

Callidus stood and crossed to the corner of the room, an arm's reach from her. She froze, going as still as the grave, fearing Callidus would hear the drumbeat of her heart.

He didn't. He retrieved an instrument from a stand, a lovely little mandolin, all playful scrolls and warm wood. He sunk back down on the bed and began picking a tune on the eight strings. It was the most haunting melody Wren had ever heard, a mournful song full of yearning and loss. His long, thin fingers danced over the strings, transforming from crafty spider-like digits to instruments of wonder.

Too soon, the song stopped, and it was as if the very air mourned its absence. She felt wrung out, raw, as he placed the instrument back on its stand, buttoned his shirt, grabbed his jacket, and walked from the room.

She heard the lock click as Callidus left his chambers, but she didn't move. She stood behind the curtain for a long time, astounded at the certainty washing over her. She had seen a man's soul tonight, and it wasn't the soul of a murderer. It was that of a sad lonely man missing his mentor. And friend.

As her toes began to go numb in her heeled shoes, Wren finally emerged from behind the curtain, moving to the desk where the precious journal sat, pages drying in the dark air. Her enthusiasm at reading it had withered completely. She wasn't sure what she would find within, but she no longer thought it was the plan for Kasper's murder. She flipped through the pages under the low light of the single oil lamp Callidus had left on. She looked at it nervously. Perhaps he intended to return quickly. She needed to get out of here.

On each page of the journal was a name. Notes were scribbled beneath them in a cramped, sloping handwriting. Some she recognized. Pike. Sable. Beckett. Some she didn't. Hythia. Nix. Castlerock. The pages seemed endless, containing every person Callidus had ever met. As she scanned the writing, she realized what this was. Not every person Callidus had ever met. Every person Kasper had known. Callidus's investigation into Kasper's murder. Each page contained his notes about the person's whereabouts, motives, connections to Kasper. Her eyes widened as she flipped through more pages, feeling foolish. Her own "investigation" was a raindrop compared to this ocean of connections and knowledge. He had everyone in here! Even Olivia and Greer… the maids, the guild controller. She hissed in a breath when she came to her page.

Her name had been circled, and then crossed out. What did that mean? Did he mean to be rid of her? But as she read down, squinting in the low light at his handwriting, she came to understand. He had ruled her out as a suspect. The notes were simple enough. "No connections to Kasper." "No connections to other guilds." "No motive." "No means of obtaining poison." "Unaware of Gift."

So… he believed her? Wren let out a little laugh of disbelief. Then why in the Beekeeper's name was he still singling her out? Why had he all but pointed his finger at her at yesterday's assembly? Did he just… hate her?

She turned back to the journal, wanting to shake it for answers that weren't forthcoming. She set it back down, a feeling of helplessness washing over her. She wanted to stay here with this journal forever, analyzing the secrets within its pages. But she knew she had already pushed her luck. So Wren set the journal down, and with one final longing glance at the mysteries contained in its wine-soaked pages, she left.

CHAPTER 23

The moon was high in the sky, its cheerful face incongruous with the turmoil within her. Wren needed to talk to Lucas. Now. She still had the note with Callidus's handwriting hidden within her dress, though she suspected glumly that it would not contain the answer she had once hoped for.

Where could she find him? She didn't know where he lived. But she knew someone who did.

The Temple of the Sower looked as it had two days prior. Soaring ceilings, intricate paintings, flickering candles, and the ever-present feeling of her skin crawling that came upon her in the presence of the Sower or one of his priests.

"Virgil?" she called, her voice echoing throughout the temple and earning her dirty looks from the two devout worshippers who sat in the pews. She didn't care. She didn't have the patience to leave the button and wait for him to find her the next day. She needed to talk to him now. Besides, anyone who might take interest in her meeting with Lucas was likely at the Appointment Gala.

"Virgil!" she called again, louder this time, trying to keep the edge of hysteria from her voice.

"Wren?" He appeared at the front of the temple, his visage so much like Lucas's that her heart twisted painfully.

He hurried to her side, shepherding her towards the back of the temple. "What is it? What's wrong?"

"I met your sister today. And your brother Patrick. She told me what Lucas did for me. What it means that he vouched for me."

His face softened. "You didn't know?"

"Why does everyone assume that I did? Is it such a common occurrence, someone dooming themselves for another?"

"No, of course not. We were trained at the palace in every conceivable facet of Alesian life; we forget sometimes that not everyone has the benefit of such an education."

"Why would he do that?" Wren asked. She couldn't shake the thought from her head. Why had he done it? Was Lucas truly that selfless a man, or was it something more? Something personal?

"Only Lucas can answer that," Virgil said.

"I need to talk to him," Wren said. "Can you tell me where he lives?"

Virgil raised an eyebrow. "At this hour?"

"Please. It can't wait."

"Very well," he said. "Give me a moment. I'll write down the directions."

Virgil returned in a moment with a scrap of paper, and Wren's lip quivered. She felt as if she was coming apart at the seams. She looked at Virgil's kind eyes and concerned expression. She thought she could see the truth of him, that he was holding himself open to her as a peace offering, and what she saw was that he was cut from the same selfless cloth as his brother. He was nothing like Brother Brax or the other priests at the orphanage. "I think I owe you an apology," she said. "We started off on the wrong foot. And now… now I've taken your brother from you."

He shook his head, a kind smile crossing his face, so alike Lucas's that it took her breath away. "No apology needed. And at the risk of delving too deep, I suspect that I owe you an apology."

"Why?"

"On behalf of my order. And my god. For whoever wrong deeply."

She stiffened, drawing back, fighting her natural urge to flee, her mind's ringing warning of *too close, too close.*

He held up his hands to her, as if comforting a skittish horse. "If you ever wish to talk, it would be a great honor. If you never wish to talk, I understand. We each must own our story and live with it how we see fit. But as for my brother, do not underestimate him. He is not lost to us yet, not by a long shot. And neither are you. Don't give up hope."

Don't give up hope. Those words took root in her frayed soul, buoying her. She nodded and squeezed his hand once before slipping out the door into the night.

Lucas lived in a flat over a bookshop on the edge of the Lyceum Quarter. After ten minutes of running, Wren slowed to a walk to catch her breath. She smoothed her hair, wiping the sweat from her brow. Her stomach flipped nervously at the thought of seeing him, and she found she didn't want to look a total fright when she arrived.

Wren let herself into the front door of the building, turning the lock on the gated entry easily. Her hairpins had been busy tonight. She climbed the three flights and found herself standing before the door to number 303. She blew out a breath, finding her nerves jittery. She tried to calm herself. She was here to discuss the case. His vouching. Her heart was hammering from her run, that was all.

She rapped firmly on the door, trying to look composed.

The peephole went dark for a moment, as if someone was looking through the other side.

Lucas opened the door, standing in a pair of half-buttoned trousers, holding a lamp in his hand. His hair was mussed, and the lamplight cast golden shadows on the muscles of his chest.

Her breath stilled for a moment.

"Wren," he said. "What are you doing here?"

"I… I need to talk to you. It's urgent. May I come in?"

He opened the door wider to let her pass. "Let me get a shirt," he said, disappearing into the other room.

Lucas's flat was tidy and sparse. A gray sofa, a table and chairs, a

tchen with a two-burner stove and a small icebox. The
spoke of Lucas was a bookshelf lined with books and the
ames that sat on the side table, the kitchen counter, the
door.

turned, fully clothed, to Wren's slight disappointment. He lit
another lamp and bid her to sit on the couch. He didn't sit beside her,
instead pulling one of the dining room chairs out and swiveling it
around.

"You look... fancy," he said carefully. "Did you come from the
gala?"

She smoothed her dress, suddenly feeling foolish and tongue-tied.
Part of her had wanted Lucas to see her in this dress, to see her at her
most beautiful. What was she playing at? Lives were at stake. This wasn't
the time for crushes or romance. A fancy gown wouldn't save her from
the gallows.

"I met your sister at the gala," she said, meeting his gaze. "And your
brother Patrick."

He stiffened, his face growing wary. "Did you?"

"She was... not kind in her assessment of me. She was quite
distraught at the thought that you might die for my crime."

He looked away, running his hand over his hair.

"Tell me it isn't true, Lucas." Her voice was harder than she'd
intended it to be. "Tell me she misunderstood. That it doesn't work that
way. I never would have asked you to put your own life in danger. It's
not right."

He looked at her, his expression soft. "It wasn't right what they were
doing to you. Willings and Callidus. I had a way to delay it, to give you
a chance. So I did. It was my choice, Wren. You have nothing to feel
sorry for."

"But you barely knew me. You barely know me now. What if I really
did murder Kasper?"

"I'm an excellent judge of character," Lucas said. "I was confident
you were innocent."

"An excellent judge of character?" She let out a huff. "That's
madness. You're a prince! You're worth ten of me. How could you risk
yourself?"

"Wren, I'm not the saint you make me out to be. Yes, it was a risk, but a calculated one. It is *because* I'm a prince that I could vouch for you. I knew, however right or wrong, that my father would think twice before he executes me. The case will get the consideration it might not have warranted if it was only a guild apprentice's life on the line. No offense…"

"It's fine. I'm no stranger to how the world works." She stood, pacing across the room, unable to look at him for fear the warmth filling her heart might spill out.

"It's not fine," Lucas said, standing too, laying his hands on her shoulders, and turning her around gently to face him.

His touch sent a rush of heat through her, and she tried to focus on the words he spoke, not the fine stubble at his jaw, the stretch of exposed skin showing through his haphazardly buttoned shirt.

"I became an inspector because I wanted to help people. Growing up around my father, I realized that Alesian justice was a malleable concept; it depended entirely on whether you had money or connections. It infuriated me. I wanted to have some small role in setting that right, even if it was one case at a time, one person at a time. I had never seen Willings go for someone with the vengeance that he went for you. It wasn't fair. So yes, I had an opportunity to use my position to help you when you needed it, and I took it. I won't apologize for what I did, and I don't regret it."

A knot grew in Wren's throat. There had been so few moments of true kindness in her life. Selfless sacrifice, white knights in shining armor—those were stories meant to distract from the cruelty of reality.

But here one was. A man of myth.

"Don't worry," he said. He reached out and touched her cheek, tracing the line of her jaw with the rough skin of his thumb. "It'll be fine. We'll both be fine."

Words were lost to her, unsatisfactory vessels to convey the depth of what his gesture had meant to her. What he meant to her.

So she kissed him. She wrapped her arms around him and pressed her lips to his, desperate to say what she didn't know how.

He tangled his fingers in her hair and pulled her body flush against his, parting her lips with his tongue and the heat of his breath. The muscles of his body were hard against her, and excitement trilled inside of her at the knowledge that he wanted her too.

But then his kiss was gone, empty space left between them. He pulled back with a shuddering breath, pushing her shoulders from him, his head down with a curse. "Wren." He growled the word. "You don't… owe me anything." He met her eyes, his own smoldering in the lamplight. "I made my choice freely. Don't do this because you feel you have some debt to repay."

She blinked in surprise, embarrassment and shame flooding through her like a bite of a hot pepper. He thought she had kissed him to pay a debt? That her only currency was her body? That there could never be anything real between them?

She stepped back, pulling away. "I'm not a whore, Lucas. I don't pay people with…" She gestured to herself. "This. That you would think that of me shows that you don't know me at all." She turned towards the door, wanting to flee. Of course, even in his rejection of her, he'd be noble. It had been a mistake to come here. A mistake to kiss him.

"Wren." His voice was tender. "Forgive me. That's not what I meant. The fact is, I'm terrible at interpreting the language of women, and so I've always found it better to be clear upfront. I wanted to make sure this was what you wanted. That you wanted… me."

"Do you have so many women kiss you out of obligation that you've had to establish a protocol?" Wren pointed out. But his expression when she turned around was so miserable that she softened, her anger cooling.

"No, of course not." He ran his fingers through his hair in frustration. "That's not what I meant."

"Well, thank you for clarifying. I do owe you much, Lucas Imbris," Wren said. "But I kissed you because that's what *I* wanted, not just because it's what I thought you wanted."

"Want*ed?*" His eyes were pleading, and he took her hands. "Don't tell me I ruined this, Wren. Let's start again. The last thirty seconds never happened. Where were we…? Yes. I was telling you not to worry…" He stroked her cheek with his thumb once again. "Which doesn't seem right at all since now you seem like you'd rather pummel me than worry." A smile tugged at the corner of his mouth.

She pursed her lips to stop the grin from spreading across her face. "I wanted to pummel you then, too," she said. "For selflessly risking your life for mine."

"The truth is, I vouched for you for selfish reasons," he murmured, taking her face in his hands. "Not for justice, or because I'm a champion for the disenfranchised. It's because you were the fiercest and loveliest thing I had ever seen, sitting on that couch without a trace of fear, and I couldn't imagine a world where I didn't get to know you."

His words broke through the last of her anger and hurt, and she kissed him again, soft and sweet this time. She wanted to be that version of herself, the version Lucas had glimpsed. The version without fear. She had lived half a life, letting fear rob her of the rest. She wouldn't let it rob her of this, too.

They explored the taste and the feel of each other with gentle lips. Lucas pulled back, drinking in the sight of her, brushing a loose curl off her forehead. "So glad I didn't screw that up."

"There's still time," she retorted, and he let out a bark of laughter, wrapping his arms around her, crushing his lips to hers.

Then there was no holding back. They were a tangle of tongues and hands and skin. His mouth traced a line of fire down her neck while his hands glided across the skin of her back, leaving sparks in their wake. He was everywhere, and she found herself falling into a universe that was only the feel and the smell of him—like fresh laundry dried in sunshine and spring breezes. He lifted her off her feet, spinning her and setting her down on the dining room table. The table rocked beneath them, and Lucas reached out to steady them.

A bottle fell and shattered on the floor.

They broke apart and Wren let out a careless laugh. Until she saw the label of the bottle. Destrier's Reserve. The bottle from Kasper's office. They had just destroyed the evidence.

CHAPTER 24

L ucas and Wren stared at each other in horror.

"Is that...?" she asked.

He nodded, misery painted across his face. "Flame it," he swore. "I knew I should have taken it to the station!"

"Why didn't you?" Wren demanded.

"I was worried there was someone on the inside, who might... tamper with the evidence. I've never seen Willings so rabid about a case and I didn't want to risk it."

"That risk is looking pretty good right about now," she said.

He ran his hands through his hair. "Damn, damn, damn."

Wren retrieved two towels and a bowl from the kitchen.

Lucas broke from his daze and went into the other room. He returned with a stoppered flask and an eye dropper. "We can at least get some of the whiskey. It should be enough."

He proceeded to suck up several ounces of liquid while Wren carefully picked up the glass shards.

"I have so much to tell you," she said. "Much has happened since we last spoke."

"Oh?" he asked, holding up the flask. It was mostly full now. He stoppered it and set it carefully on the table.

Wren picked up the neck of the bottle, with half of the bottle, including the label, still connected. She set it in the bowl.

"I got a sample of Callidus's handwriting to compare to the note."

"Are you serious?" Lucas asked, wiping up the whiskey with the towel. Its pungent smell burned her nostrils.

"Yes," Wren said. "But… I'm not sure it's Callidus anymore."

"Why not?" Lucas asked, taking the wet towels and depositing them in the sink.

She stood and stretched her knees, setting the bowl on the table. She thought they had gotten it all.

"After the gala… I went to Callidus's room."

"Wren!" Lucas chided. "Do you know how dangerous that was? What if he had returned?"

"Well," she said, turning from his intense gaze. "He did. But he didn't find me!" she continued quickly.

"You know how lucky you were?" he said, blowing out a breath.

"Yes, yes. But I overheard him talking to himself. He was lamenting Kasper's death. Missing him. And he's investigating Kasper's death himself."

"That could be for show," Lucas said. "To make it seem like he cared about finding the killer."

"Perhaps. But it didn't seem like it. And if it's for show, why is he doing it in secret?"

"I can't answer that. Who was he investigating?"

"Everyone. Everyone in our guild, and the heads of the other guilds. The Spicer's. The Distiller's Guild. Names I don't recognize as well."

Lucas frowned, considering. "Grandmaster Pike is odd enough. No one knows all the plots he has in play. But Grandmaster Chandler? He seems so… grandfatherly."

"Maybe it's an act?" Wren asked. "Someone gave Kasper this whiskey and wouldn't the head of the guild know what was going on under his own roof?"

"True," Lucas said. "But he's such a humanitarian. He spends half his time campaigning for better hospitals in the city. He had a granddaughter die in the Red Plague, and it has been his cause ever since. It's hard for me to imagine him as a cold-blooded murderer."

"I don't know," Wren admitted.

"I was so sure it was Callidus," Lucas said. "He had the character, the motive, the means. My focus has been on him. Perhaps I've missed something if he's innocent."

"We can find out," Wren said, reaching into her dress to pull out the list she had swiped from Callidus's room.

Lucas raised an eyebrow. "Do you keep everything in there?"

"No pockets." She rolled her eyes, moving the bowl with the broken bottle and smoothing the list down on the table. "Do you have the letter we found? We can compare the handwriting."

Lucas disappeared into the bedroom and returned bearing the letter they had discovered in the secret compartment in Kasper's desk.

He set it down next to the list.

Right away, Wren could see the differences. It was as she suspected when she had first glanced at the list. She was no expert, but it seemed impossible that they were written by the same hand. Callidus's list had been written in that same cramped hand she had seen in the journal, miserly and enigmatic as he was. There was no flair, no passion in that hand.

The letter, on the other hand, was written in a flowing cursive, a script that sprawled across the page with flourishes and curls.

"These aren't the same person," Lucas said. "Look at the tail on the letter 'C' at the end of the threat. It's not the same as this 'C' at all."

"It's not Callidus," Wren said, the certainty sinking into her and settling in her bones. She had wanted it to be Callidus. Had wanted to unmask the wretched man's crimes, to show the world that he was terrible. But mostly, she'd wanted it to be him because then it would all be over. And if it wasn't, it meant their search was only just beginning. "Sable was convinced all along that it wasn't Callidus. We can't make a square peg fit in a round hole."

Lucas groaned, slamming a hand on the table, hanging his head. "I feel like I'm failing you."

Wren jumped slightly at the noise but reached out a hand to Lucas.

She laid it on his shoulder, trying to communicate her gratitude with her touch.

He stiffened under her. "Wren," he said.

"I'm sorry," she said, the rebuke biting.

"No, Wren, look." He was staring with wide eyes at the bowl of glass shards. He reached out and picked up the neck of the broken whiskey bottle, turning it so the inside of the label was revealed.

Something was written there.

"What... What is that?" Wren asked, breathless with excitement.

"It's a message. One you can only see once you drink the contents."

Wren peered closer, turning the bottle in Lucas's hand. "*Charger's Estate. Hermitage. New moon. Midnight.* This bottle was in Kasper's office. It must have been a message intended for Kasper alone?"

"Not just a message. A meeting," Lucas said. "And that's not all. Look at the 'C' in 'Charger.'"

"The flourish!" Wren's eyes opened wide as she grabbed the letter and held it beside the broken bottle. "The handwriting is the same."

"And the message is *inside* the bottle. Meaning whoever left it *made* the whiskey or at least bottled it. They didn't just buy it."

"So we find who made the whiskey, we know who wrote the letter."

"And we find who wrote the letter, we find the killer."

"Exactly."

Lucas sank onto the couch. "Thank the gods we have somewhere to start. We're still missing something, though. The letter references Kasper revealing a secret. Their truest currency. We still don't know what the letter-writer meant."

Wren stilled. She knew the Guild's deepest secret. A secret worth killing over. The Gifted. What she didn't know was why Kasper would threaten to reveal it. For what end?

Lucas was examining her with his discerning gaze. "You know, don't you? The secret. What is it?"

Wren stepped back involuntarily, shaking her head. "I don't know what the letter is talking about."

He crossed his arms over his chest. "You're a terrible liar."

"I'm not lying," she said.

"You can't even effectively lie about being a liar," he said. "What's the secret, Wren?" He took one of her hands in his own, drawing her close, looking up at her expectantly. "You can trust me. I won't tell anyone. But I need to know if I'm going to solve this crime."

She shook her head, her lips pressed together in a hard line. She wanted to tell him more than anything. To share this revelation, this burden, with someone else. To share how she wasn't only a girl from the street, she was unique, special—magic.

Even as the thoughts surfaced, her throat burned like fire, her tongue grew large in her mouth and her lips felt like they were covered in glue. That damn wine!

She jerked her hands from his, turning from him, focusing her mind on other things. The crack in the plaster snaking down from the corner of the living room. The painting of Mount Luminis in twilight, its snowcapped peak shining in the last glimmers of sun.

She took a shuddering breath, opening her mouth once again.

She turned back. "Can I have some water?" she croaked.

He eyed her strangely but complied, filling up a mason jar with water from a pitcher.

She drank it greedily, watching him watch her, two animals facing off warily.

"Wren—" he began.

"I can't." She shook her head, her throat burning even at the thought of explaining the wine. She couldn't even say why she couldn't say! "I can't, I can't. Don't ask it of me."

"All right," he said, taking the glass from her and rubbing her arms. "It's all right. I won't ask." From the twist of his brow, he didn't seem happy about it.

She relaxed under his touch, his hands heating her skin and more besides. She stepped into him and let him wrap her in an embrace, laying her head against his chest. Suddenly, she felt very weary.

"You should get some sleep," he said. "It's late. We can talk things through in the morning."

The thought of walking back through the dark streets to the Guildhall overwhelmed her. But she didn't want to ask to stay here. She looked at him and nodded.

"Stay here," he said in a rush. "I mean, I'll sleep on the couch. You take the bed. It's too late to walk back."

She nodded. "I'm happy to take the couch."

"My mother didn't raise me to let a lady sleep on the couch."

"Do they even have couches in the palace?" she retorted.

"You know what I mean. Please."

"Fine," she relented, and he led her into the bedroom.

The white sheets and gray-striped comforter were thrown back, no doubt tossed aside as he came to the door at her pounding.

The room was sparse but homey, an earthenware pot full of nestled succulents on the desk, a wardrobe with hanging shirts and suits, iron hooks on the wall hung with hats and a scarf. This room felt like Lucas, and the intimate glimpse made her want very badly to belong here, to fit into this space and this life as naturally as the books on the bedside table.

He pulled some pajamas out of the wardrobe. "You're welcome to wear these if you want," he said, setting them on the bed.

She turned to him, every fiber of her singing with awareness of his nearness, his fresh scent, his capable hands searching nervously for somewhere to rest. How easy it would be to pull him to her, to fall back onto the bed and forget about murder and politics and guilds.

"Sweet dreams," he said, leaning to kiss her on the forehead, and then taking a large step back, as if to remove himself from temptation.

"You too."

He stepped towards the door.

"Lucas," she said, not wanting him to go. *Invite him to stay.* Just to sleep beside her… nothing more. Warmth and comfort.

He turned.

Her courage left her. "The meeting," she said. "We need to go. The new moon…"

"It's three nights from now," he said.

"We need to find the Charger's Estate hermitage and be there at the meeting. It's the only way to know for sure."

"It's too dangerous," he said, shaking his head. "We don't know what we'll find there. It could be an army waiting to take Kasper."

"Why set up a meeting if you're planning on killing someone before it takes place?" she asked. "Maybe there will be no one there, but… I have to know. It may be our only way of discovering what was between Kasper and Chandler. We'll sneak in. Surveillance only."

He sighed. "You don't take *no* for an answer, do you?"

"No." She smiled.

"We'll look into it," he said. "That's all I can promise. It won't help either of us to clear your name if we walk into a death trap."

"Thank you, Lucas," she said.

He leaned against the doorjamb for a moment, his gray eyes seeming to spark in the dim as they met hers. He heaved a heavy breath. "Now good night." He closed the door, leaving Wren in darkness.

Wren stood for a long while, staring at the door as if she could see through it, wishing that he would open it again, stride across the room, and take her in his arms. Somehow, she knew that he was standing on the other side, wishing he could do the same thing.

CHAPTER 25

Despite her exhaustion, it took Wren an hour to drift off to sleep. Her hyperawareness of Lucas's presence in the next room was like a bolt of energy zinging through her body. It was worse that he was all around her, his smell in the pajamas she wore, the pillow she rested her head on, his kiss in her memories. *Foolish girl,* she chided herself. If she didn't stay focused, the only thing that would be keeping her warm would be the inquisitor's hot pokers.

Fresh morning light woke her, its soft halo laid across the wall. She changed back into her dress, folded Lucas's pajamas with more than a little tenderness, and peeked into the other room.

Lucas lay on the couch, his arm splayed across his eyes to block the sunlight. Her eyes traced his sleeping form, from the slender toes peeking out from under the blanket to the tousled black and gray of his hair. She sighed.

"You know," he said. "It's rude to stare."

She blushed scarlet as he threw his arm off his face with a wry smile.

"You know, it's rude to pretend you're sleeping when you're not," she retorted.

He chuckled, standing and stretching, a bit of flat stomach peeking out beneath his shirt. "You're doing it again," he said.

She crossed her arms and huffed. "I'll be on my way," she said stiffly, heading to the door, mortified at her own obviousness.

"Wren," he said, snagging her arm. "I'm kidding. Would you like some coffee before you go?"

She softened. "It's all right. I should get back."

"Very well," he said. "I'll be working on locating Charger's Estate. I'll let you know when I find it, and if anything comes up, you do the same."

"Thank you," she said, holding his gaze for a moment before slipping out the door.

Maradis was coming to life, its contradiction never more apparent than in these honest morning hours. The yeasty smell of fresh bread and pungent aroma of coffee wafted on the summer breeze while a street sweeper picked up trash and woke the vagrants sleeping in doorways and under eaves.

Wren made it to the Guildhall without complication. The antechamber was empty. No doubt many guildmembers were sleeping late or nursing hangovers, and it seemed the servants were taking advantage of the quiet.

When she made it to her room she slipped through and shut the door, leaning her forehead against it. Thank the Beekeeper that no one had seen her.

"Doesn't someone have a tale to tell?" a deep voice said behind her.

Wren screamed and whirled to face the intruder. "Hale!" she shrieked before sagging in relief.

He was sitting up on her bed, his blond hair tangled around his shoulders, his shirt untucked and half-unbuttoned.

"What are you doing here?" she asked. "You scared the sugar out of me."

He stood. "I could ask you the same question. Or more, what weren't you doing here?"

Her face heated. "That's none of your business."

"I'm wounded, my little egret. I thought we shared everything."

She sighed. "I went to see Lucas to talk about the case, about him vouching for me. We talked late. He slept on the couch. Nothing happened." She shoved down the memory of him rocking her body against the dining room table, his lips hard on hers, his fingers in her hair. Something had happened, though perhaps not the something that Hale assumed.

"Well," Hale said. "The man's a fool then, if you came knocking on his door in that dress and all he wanted to do was talk."

Wren pursed her lips to hold in a secret smile. She wasn't sure why she didn't tell Hale about the kiss with Lucas. Perhaps because she knew he would tease her mercilessly. Or perhaps because he would demand to know what it meant, and she wasn't sure she had an answer. "Speaking of late night door knocking, what are you doing in here?" she asked instead.

"I was worried about you. I looked for you after the gala, but when I couldn't find you, I decided to wait here. I fell asleep."

She softened. "Thank you for your concern. I'm fine. Except I desperately need a bath and a fresh dress. So..."

He didn't move, settling back on the bed. "I'll wait," he said.

"Hale!" she said with a laugh, hauling him up by the hand and shoving him towards the door. "Goodbye. I'll see you at breakfast."

Wren felt like a new woman after bathing and brushing her teeth. She dressed in one of her new dresses, a black skirt with a bodice wrapped in a fabric of light pink with tiny black birds. She cinched it with a wide leather belt and piled her hair onto her head in a wet knot. It would do. She was famished.

The dining room was filled with dark-eyed guild members nursing cups of coffee and piling plates with biscuits topped with rich pork gravy.

She filled her plate with two eggs, two strips of peppercorn bacon, and two biscuits and balanced it with a cup of coffee. Hale was sitting in the far corner at a table with Sable.

As Wren sat down, she stifled a smile. Sable looked worse off than

Wren had ever seen, her normally silky black tresses plaited in a messy braid over one shoulder. She was slumped over a glass of what looked like tomato juice and celery.

"Secret recipe," she croaked when Wren eyed the drink.

Hale chuckled, but the sound was forced. He was watching Sable closely, as if afraid she might fall to pieces before him.

"Celebrate Callidus's appointment a bit too hard, did we?" Wren asked innocently.

"The young don't appreciate their livers," Sable said. "You wait until you're over thirty."

"That doesn't seem to slow Pike down," Hale said with a raised eyebrow.

"That man can drink a horse under the table," Sable grumbled.

"Miss Wren." A servant approached their table.

"Mmm?" Wren asked around a piece of bacon. It was delicious, salty with undertones of maple and pepper.

"There's a message for you." He handed it over and scurried away.

Hale snatched the letter from her and opened it.

"Hey!" Wren protested.

"It's from your honorable Master Oldrick," Hale said. "He found the records about who bought your rose cupcakes."

"Who?" Sable and Wren asked at the same time.

"Mistress Violena," he said with a meaningful look at Sable.

"Mistress Violena," Sable repeated, perking up. "Really?"

"Who is she?" Wren asked. "Do you know her?"

"She's extremely wealthy, a widow, and an old friend... well, benefactor," Sable said. "And she's notorious for..."

"Enjoying the company of handsome men," Hale finished.

"Handsome *younger* men," Sable repeated.

"Too bad we don't have one of those," Wren mused, eyeing Hale sidelong.

Sable cackled. "It looks like I'll be paying my dear Mistress Violena a visit. Hale, you've been going on about wanting to meet her for years now. Here's your chance."

"I'm coming too, right?" Wren said.

Hale and Sable exchanged a glance.

"I'm coming, too, right?" Wren said, more forcefully. "It *is* my neck on the line."

"She lives in Leads, the wealthy enclave across Lake Crima. To the east of Maradis. We'll have to take the ferry and stay the night. It will be a long trip." Sable seemed unconvinced.

"It's not like I have anywhere better to be. I'm going. And that's final."

"That's final, is it?" Sable looked at Hale, as if Wren's mulishness were somehow his doing.

"She learns from the best." Hale chuckled. "Let her come. If we leave her here to her own devices, she'll probably get into trouble. Stay out too late, consort with questionable characters."

Wren narrowed her eyes at Hale over her coffee cup.

He grinned wolfishly.

"Fine, you can come. But we'll have to go tomorrow."

"Why not today?"

"Today, we have the distinct pleasure of suffering through an afternoon-long Guilder's Council meeting. Right now I strongly feel I would rather gouge my own eyes out than attend, but Callidus asked the grandmasters to be there to show support to his new leadership, blah blah blah. Plus, I think it would be good for you to see one. So we suffer."

"Will Guildmaster Chandler be there?"

"Probably. Why?"

Wren looked around and lowered her voice. "We found something."

Wren explained in hushed tones what she and Lucas had learned, including the note they had found in the inside of the whiskey bottle. She kept out the minor fact that she had snuck into Callidus's room, stolen a list, and subsequently had ruled him out as a suspect.

"Charger's Estate. It sounds familiar," Sable said. "Do you know where it is?"

Hale stroked his chin, considering. "I feel like I've been to a party there."

"That doesn't narrow things down. You've been to parties across half the city."

"I won't apologize for being popular," he retorted.

"Lucas is looking into finding it," Wren said. "I think we need to go to the meeting."

"Go to the meeting?" Sable paused over a bite of celery. "Just sneak in and hope there aren't guards, or dogs, or worse? If the person who set this meeting killed Kasper, what makes you think they won't hesitate to kill you?"

"I have to do something," Wren said.

Sable let out a longsuffering sigh. "First, let's find out where it is. Then we'll plan accordingly. We're not doing nothing. Understood?"

"Understood," Wren grumbled.

Sable's dark eyes narrowed. "Wren, I want you to promise me you won't go to that meeting without arriving at a plan with me or Hale." She looked at Hale and revised her assessment. "With me."

"I promise."

"Now, I think I'm awake enough to hold down a biscuit. Excuse me." Sable stood a bit unsteadily and marched to the front of the dining room.

Wren looked at Hale with a spark of amusement. "She's almost motherly when she's hung over."

Hale nodded, as if it were the most obvious thing in the world. "Most people are horrible on the inside but hide it well until the drink brings out their true nature. Sable's the opposite. She does her best to hide what a caring and generous person she is. But sometimes it slips out."

"She's not who I thought she was," Wren admitted.

"Yes, Sable's an enigma that took me years to decipher. It was worth the effort. Stick with us, chickadee. We won't steer you wrong." Hale grinned and stole the last piece of bacon off Wren's plate.

CHAPTER 26

When the hour came for them to leave for the council meeting, Sable was looking much more like her old self. She had bathed and changed into a scarlet dress with a geometric design in black thread marching across the fitted bodice. Her jet-black hair spilled in glossy waves down her back, and her aquiline profile was inscrutable in the light of the afternoon sun.

Wren stood beside her on the stairs of the Guildhall, casting sidelong glances at her sponsor. "Are we going to go?" she finally asked.

"We're waiting for someone else."

"Who?"

"Wren, a word of advice, if I may. I learned a long time ago that you catch more flies with honey than with vinegar."

Wren looked at Sable with a puzzled expression. "Are you telling me… to be nicer? You strike me as someone who gets her way by showing strength, not simpering to those around you."

"Astute observation. But you have to catch a few flies before you make the bees fear you."

"This metaphor… is getting confusing."

Sable turned to Wren. "You're making this wise but obscure mentor bit very challenging. There's a time to be strong and a time to be humble. Learn the difference, if you want to have any hope of succeeding here."

"All right," Wren said. "Why are you telling me this?

The words barely flew from Wren's lips when Callidus thundered through the doors of the Guildhall, uniformed in a black suit and crimson waistcoat.

"What's she doing here?" Callidus asked Sable, speaking of Wren as one might complain of an infestation of weevils in a bag of flour.

Sable shot a pointed look at Wren, and a cold wave of understanding washed over her.

"She is continuing her education. Something that you, as guildmaster, should take an interest in. Seeming as she is the next generation of Gifted in our guild. She and Hale will take over the reins from us some day."

Callidus looked at Wren then, his expression one of calculated appraisal beneath his thicket of ebony hair.

Wren ground her teeth, wanting to smack the pompous look off his face, but Sable's words stilled her anger. That, together with the memory of his delicate fingers dancing across the mandolin strings, bringing forth a song of such sorrow and depth of feeling. There *was* more to this man than he let on, and if she had any hope of making the guild her home, she needed to win him over. And as she considered her options, it chaffed at her, but she knew what she needed to do.

"Guildmaster," Wren said, stepping before him. "I know we got off on the wrong foot. But I want what's in the best interest of this Guild, just as you do. And I don't believe that you think of me as a murderer anymore, though perhaps you once did. So I ask… I hope… that we could start fresh."

Callidus's telltale sneer threatened to creep back on his face, but he held it at bay. "You presume to know me so well?"

"I don't know you," Wren said. "But I'd… like to."

She was surprised to find it was true. Somewhere along the way, a tiny seed had dug into the dry sand of her life and had sprouted a hope. A hope that this could be her home. That she could find a place here. A place where she could be safe.

He nodded once and swept past her down the stairs, striding onto the sidewalk.

Sable took Wren's elbow and pulled her down the stairs after him. "That was very well done," she breathed.

"He might as well have spit on me," Wren grumbled.

"That was progress," Sable said. "I promise."

They hurried to catch up to Callidus, and the three of them walked through the Guild Quarter to Maradis's bustling town center, where the government buildings were housed.

"Have you heard the agenda for today's meeting?" Sable asked Callidus.

"No," Callidus said. "I'm guessing more of the same. The Piscator's Guild will complain about the Centu pirate incursions, the Baker's will moan about the low quality of grain coming out of Tamros, the Distiller's will go on and on about how their well is running dry and it's not fair that we have three of the best... never mind that our forefathers simply negotiated a better treaty than theirs... Oh, and I imagine we will have the pleasure of Pike complaining about the fire in his mercantile. Like that is a problem for the council."

"Have they made any progress in the investigation?" Sable asked.

"They might as well all have their thumbs up their bums over at the inspector's office," Callidus groused, and Wren's eyes widened a fraction. "It's like they don't want to investigate."

"They don't understand why it's so important to us," Sable murmured.

"They're incompetent," Callidus said.

"Why's it so important to us?" Wren asked Sable, her voice low.

"It wasn't just a mercantile..." Sable began, but Callidus cut her off.

"You're telling her?" he said. "Are you going to spill all our secrets?"

"She's one of us, Callidus," Sable said. "The secret has been spilled. There's no reason to keep her in the dark about the details of our situation."

He harrumphed but said nothing more.

Sable turned to Wren. "The mercantile served as a... black market of sorts. For infused merchandise. The Accord requires us to provide all infused goods to the king, but that's always been interpreted… a bit loosely. If an infused confection or wheel of cheese or rack of lamb traded between Gifted, what was the harm? None were the wiser, and we could get what we needed. We did it at the mercantile. With it burned down, this black market is hamstrung. We don't know if it was a coincidence, or someone sending a message."

"A message to the Gifted," Wren said slowly.

"Right."

"A message, kind of like a guildmaster turning up dead?"

"Exactly that kind of message," Callidus said.

"I told you she was quick," Sable said, and Wren blossomed with pride like a starved plant being watered for the first time in weeks.

"That's enough of that talk," Callidus said. "We're here."

The Council Hall was an ornate building of gray-veined marble. It was long and thin, with two rotundas on either end rising like wings from the building's crouched back.

"The Guilder's Council meets in the west end while the Noble's Council is to the east," Sable explained as they summited the broad expanse of marble stairs.

The Council Chamber sat at the end of a hallway clothed with plush burgundy carpets and paintings of guild tradesmen of old. The Chamber itself was a massive circle with tiered rows of wooden benches stretching towards the soaring dome.

Sable and Wren settled into seats near the front by Callidus. Wren grimaced, trying to get comfortable.

"They say they made the seats so hard to discourage council members from pontificating," Sable whispered.

"Does it work?" Wren asked.

"Not in the slightest," Callidus said, keeping his hawk-like gaze straight ahead.

Wren stifled a smile. As more council members filed in, Wren saw a few she recognized from the gala. She tried to pull from her memory the names Olivia had shared with her but eventually gave up. She was terrible with names. She let the parade of humanity wash over her for a time until one face jumped out at her.

"It's Guildmaster Chandler," she said to Sable, nodding with her head. "Right?"

Sable nodded and grabbed Wren's arm in a vise grip as she began to stand. "What do you think you're doing?"

"We need to talk to him, right?" Wren said.

"After." Sable pulled her down. "We'll corner him alone. I don't want other council members thinking we're up to something."

"Why would they think that?"

"The Confectioner's and Distiller's Guilds have always been adversaries. They're the two most powerful aperitive guilds and have vied for power for centuries. It's practically a blood feud at this point. It all started over the crown giving our Guild a better grant of water rights around the city. If it seemed like we were joining forces... the other guilds would get very nervous."

"Ancient enemies? You didn't see fit to tell me this until now?" Wren eyed grandfatherly Chandler with an appraising new eye. "A bottle of whiskey killed Kasper. It doesn't seem like much of a stretch—"

"Keep your voice down," Sable said. "Of course it's crossed my mind. He's one of the most obvious suspects. But... it's almost too obvious. He's no fool. Why would he poison something that could be so quickly linked back to his guild?"

"Sometimes the most obvious explanation is the right one," Wren pointed out.

Sable's answer was drowned out by the council chair calling the meeting to order. Any straggling council members took their seats, and the meeting began.

What followed were four of the longest hours of Wren's life. Wren squirmed and straightened, becoming more and more certain that the benches had been designed as a sadistic torture device by a disgruntled guildmember. Guildmember after guildmember raised a concern, followed by a discussion whereby it seemed that every council member in the room needed to weigh in, enjoying the sound of his or her own voice for five minutes at least without saying anything of substance. This continued for some time until the chair called for a vote. Half the time, the vote wouldn't even occur, and the issue would be "tabled" until the next meeting, which Wren presumed meant that the entire useless circus would occur all over again. She tried to pay attention, tried to glean any piece of information that she could add to the puzzle of her situation. In the end, she gave up, glazing over into daydreams where she stood and ran screaming from the room.

The only interesting part came at the end when the council weighed in on the sentences pronounced by the guilds against offenders caught violating their regulations. "Why does the council have to approve guild sentences?" she whispered to Sable.

"The crown didn't want any one guild to become too powerful, to be able to try and sentence offenders independent of the royal courts. But the royal courts didn't have the capacity to deal with guild offenses. So this was the middle ground that was struck. The guilds have the ability to try their cases and suggest sentences and the council approves or alters them."

It was a strangely macabre line of shuffling offenders they brought in, three in all. A master who couldn't pay his guild fees; a merchant who sold fraudulent merchandise, passing it off as guild-made; and a woman in a tiny southern village who had pretended to be a master seamstress, when she had failed out as a journeyman in Maradis twenty years before. The reach of the guilds was long, and the punishment swift. Wren cringed as the woman was sentenced to losing her two index fingers, so she would never sew again.

Wren looked at Sable with horror when the woman's suggested sentence was approved by the council. "She knew the risk," was all that Sable said.

Wren felt wrung out and bleary-eyed when the council meeting finally came to an end. They walked out, and Wren rubbed her sore back, groaning. "If I never go to another of those meetings, it will be too soon."

"I share your assessment," Sable said. "But I thought it was important for you to see how the guilds are really run. We need people like Callidus and Beckett to look out for the interests of our guilds so we can attend to more interesting work."

Wren nodded, considering this.

"Speaking of…" Sable tilted her head at a cluster of men talking across the hallway. Chandler was gesticulating wildly, his gray hair askew, a playful look on his lined face. Wren began to move towards him, but Sable stopped her. "Not him. *Him.*"

She nodded at a short, weak-chinned man in a brown suit and waistcoat.

"Who's that?"

"The artisan who came with Chandler. Honestly, Wren, you need to pay better attention to details."

"I'm excellent with detail when it comes to chocolates," Wren said. "Just not people."

Chandler's associate was standing a few paces away waiting patiently for Chandler to finish whatever story he was regaling his fellow council members with.

Sable glided towards the artisan, all feline grace and swishing crimson fabric. The man widened his narrow-set eyes and gulped audibly when he realized Sable was headed his way.

Wren quickly followed, stifling a smile. Sable would eat this fellow for breakfast.

"You're with the Distiller's Guild, correct?" Sable practically purred. "An associate of Guildmaster Chandler?"

"Yes, Grandmaster. He's my sponsor. I'm Bastian."

"Wonderful. I don't want to bother him when he's knee deep in a story, but we had a question about a fabulous bottle of whiskey we tried and thought you might be able to help."

"I'll try," the man said, brightening considerably. He clearly knew whiskey and thought he could help.

"It was a private label. Destrier's Reserve. Do you know who makes it?"

"Of course. That's Guildmaster Chandler's own label. He makes it himself—a few dozen bottles a year. He gives them out personally for harvest gifts and such."

"Isn't there any other way to get my hands on a bottle?" Sable winked at the man. "Surely, you know where they're stashed?"

"Any bottles that remain at the guild are locked in the guildmaster's own locker. He's the only one with the key. Trust me, Grandmaster; the only way to get one of those bottles is from Chandler's hands himself."

CHAPTER 27

W ren was as jittery as a grasshopper as she and Sable walked back to the Guildhall.

"He did it," Wren said, angry that it had taken her this long to see it. "Chandler killed Kasper. The guilds hate each other. It fits. By diminishing our Guild, throwing it into chaos, he could raise the stature of his own. Maybe even snag one of our artesian wells he was so desperate for, now that his is running dry. Why are you not excited? We solved it!"

"You're forgetting one very important point," Sable said.

"Oh? What's that."

"The poison had two parts. Until we know that Chandler had access to the cupcake, we've solved nothing."

Wren's excitement fizzled like a fallen soufflé. She had, in fact, forgotten all about the cupcake. She let out a frustrated hiss of breath.

"Don't worry. Tomorrow we will take the ferry to Mistress Violena's in Leads, Hale will charm the guest list out of her, and we'll have our answer. You need to calm down."

"How can I?" Wren moaned. "The king and his hot-poker-happy inquisitor are a week from Maradis. My time is growing short."

"It won't come to that," Sable said, hiking her dress to walk up the Guildhall's huge steps. "Now, have you finished your assignment?"

"What assignment?"

"I believe I assigned you to make me a batch of mint truffles. Where are they?"

Wren bit her lip. "I made the ganache, but with all the excitement of the gala yesterday…"

"I don't want truffles from two-day-old ganache. You're a journeyman of the Confectioner's Guild, not some housewife who doesn't know the difference between tempering and seeding." Sable stood for a moment in the antechamber under the chandelier. "I want macarons. And not those disgusting coconut macaroons. Macarons. Four flavors. Pistachio, ginger, chocolate mocha, and lemon basil."

"Four types of macarons?" Wren exclaimed. "That'll take me all night!"

"You better get working then," Sable replied coolly before gliding into the Guildhall.

Wren heaved a huge sigh and headed towards the teaching kitchen. There was little she could think to do to further the investigation before tomorrow. She had better get cooking.

Wren arrived at the front of the Guildhall the next morning in a lavender frock dress with a neatly-tied box of macarons under her arm. About halfway into the first batch, her raging thoughts had settled into the relaxed, near-meditative state that marked her cooking. Though her heart had panged slightly with thoughts of Lucas as she ground the lavender and the fragrance of the herb escaped into the air, for the most part, her mind was clear.

Sable wore a self-righteous smirk as she and Hale came down the stairs, and Wren knew then what she had suspected—that Sable had known her assignment was exactly the distraction Wren needed.

"Feeling better?" Sable said.

"Much." Wren grinned. "Plus, macarons!" She hefted the box. She had brought a few of each kind for the trip. Four batches had made a heap of cookies, so the rest had stayed behind in the teaching kitchen.

Hale pulled a bottle of sparkling wine out of the bag on his shoulder with the pride of a new parent. "We're going to have an excellent trip!"

The ferry ride from Maradis to Leads was a fairy tale. They were able to stand on the back deck of the sturdy green boat and watch as the skyline of the city grew smaller behind them. Stately buildings of dark stone, soaring towers of tan travertine, and spires of creamy marble stood silhouetted against the pure blue of the sky and the deeper indigo of the lake. To the east, behind the enclave of Leads, the forested peaks of the Cascadian Mountains stretched tall, as if they could touch the heavens themselves. And to the south, graceful and soaring snowcapped Mount Luminis stood sentinel over it all. The scene rendered Wren speechless.

"I almost understand why people say Mount Luminis is the home of the gods," she mused, for once fixing on a sight more beautiful than Hale.

Hale, who was leaning against the railing, the wind tousling fine hairs from his bun, merely nodded in understanding. "Come on," he said. "Let's go collect Sable."

They walked around the front of the ferry, weaving past other passengers enjoying the idyllic scene. Sable was standing at the front railing of the ship's prow like a figurehead, her black tresses and forest green skirt streaming in the wind.

"Sable loves the water," Hale said, his eyes bright, seemingly filled with the vision of her. "She misses it."

"Did she grow up around water?" Wren asked.

Hale nodded. "She's from Magnus, from a remote village out on the ice floes. When Alesia colonized the south, they forcibly removed thousands of native children, bringing them here to be 'civilized.' Sable included. She doesn't talk about it much. Perhaps she'll tell you of it someday."

"I guess we're all orphans in a way," Wren said, sympathy welling in her. Wren's life hadn't been easy, but she couldn't imagine being ripped from everything she had ever known to be raised by strangers in a foreign land.

They went to stand on either side of Sable and watched as Leads came into view, an elegant hillside of brightly-painted lakeside houses and half-timbered warehouses. Wren couldn't help but wonder what secrets this town would reveal.

Mistress Violena's estate sprawled across the green lakeshore south of Leads with abandon. It was the grandest house Wren had ever seen, so large she thought it must have rivaled a small palace. It was set in tiers against the lakeshore, with such expanses of lake-facing windows that it seemed more glass than stone. Sable explained that the inside was decorated in the fashion of the Centu Isles, the seafaring clans who lived on islands to the west of Alesia. Pike was Centu, but somehow none of this seemed like Pike—it was all clean lines and low-slung furniture and glazed vases overflowing with orchids. A servant led them out a set of double doors to the backyard, which was less a backyard and more a sprawling estate of its own, filled with lily-clad ponds, stone footpaths, manicured lawns and draping maples. It was on one of those lawns that Wren got her first glimpse of Mistress Violena.

She was wrapped in a white silk dress, and her pure white hair was cut short—as short as a man's, but styled artfully about her brows. She squealed like a schoolgirl when she saw Sable, giving her a crushing hug despite the crystal glass she held in one hand and the croquet mallet in the other.

"Violena," Sable said, bringing the woman over, their arms still about one another, "this is Hale." Sable's words sounded a bit like an auctioneer advertising her prize colt.

"You *are* hale, aren't you?" Mistress Violena said appreciatively, her sharp eyes sparkling with mirth. Her face was deeply lined and her hands were spotted with age, but her body showed no infirmity as she stood straight and true, appreciating a man perhaps forty years her junior, with all the gravitas of a wolf circling an injured fawn.

Wren found she liked this woman very much. Perhaps she could give Hale a run for his money.

"And this is Wren, my newest journeyman."

"Do you name all your kittens so aptly?" Violena asked, turning her hawk-like scrutiny on Wren.

"I don't name them," Sable said. "It's serendipity."

"Only yourself then?" Violena asked.

Sable clapped her hands, clearly changing the subject. "Croquet, is it? Do you need partners?"

"I am in need of a partner." Mistress Violena cackled. "And I'll be taking this strapping fellow." She poked Hale in the thigh with her croquet mallet.

To his credit, he managed to keep a straight face.

"You know the rules, Sable dear. Get yourselves mallets and drinks and be back out here in five."

"Drinks?" Wren asked when they began walking back towards the house.

"It's how Mistress Violena plays," Sable explained. "You have to have a drink in one hand, a mallet in the other. Otherwise, you're disqualified. I'd suggest starting with something easy, like wine. Maybe water it down a bit, though that's a sacrilege. Start with anything stronger, you'll be passed out before dinner."

Wren gulped and followed them into the cool of the house.

Mistress Violena was a competitive player, but luckily, Hale kept up, hitting his ball expertly through the wire wickets. Unfortunately for Wren, Sable was also competitive, and Wren didn't fare quite so well as a partner. Wren's whacks of the ball became increasingly frustrated and erratic as the game went on. Finally, Mistress Violena approached, counseling her on her form. "It is just a game," the woman whispered conspiratorially, to which Wren had to stifle a huff of frustration.

By the time the game was over, Wren was sweaty, tipsy from wine, and absolutely famished.

"It's time to retire to the sitting room for cocktails," Mistress Violena announced, still fresh as a daisy.

"Hydrate," Sable murmured to the two of them, deathly serious.

Luckily, cocktails were accompanied by appetizers—delicate bacon-stuffed figs, hard crackers piled with tomatoes marinated in olive oil and spices, and a plate of the finest cheeses the Cheesemonger's Guild could produce. Cocktails turned into dinner, and dusk fell over good conversation and even better food—grilled octopus and mint-coated lamb shanks and fresh green salad comprised of arugula and grapefruit. Mistress Violena ate with gusto, and it was leaning back in her chair, stretching out her stomach that she finally turned to Sable and asked why they had come.

"You had a party," Sable said. "Some weeks back. You ordered some cupcakes styled like roses from Master Oldrick's shop in Maradis. We need to know who attended that party."

Mistress Violena eyed Wren appraisingly. "Does this have something to do with your dear guildmaster's premature departure?"

"It does," Sable said.

"And I take this to mean that you do not think your darling Wren here is the culprit?"

"You know about that?" Wren asked with dismay, her face heating.

"I know about everything," Violena said. "For instance, I know that the king and his dog of an inquisitor are sleeping at an estate a day's ride north of the city. They will be back in the palace by mid-afternoon tomorrow."

Wren's stomach lurched.

Hale cursed and banged his fist on the table, rattling the dishes and startling them all.

"Are you sure?" Sable asked, her arching brows narrowed in dismay.

"Sure as the grave."

Wren felt ill. Her stomach was roiling, protesting the rich food and hot sun and sparkling wine. Her hand flew to her mouth. "I'll be right back." She stood and ran from the room, headed for the nearest washroom.

Wren emptied her stomach two times before feeling well enough to stand back up and make her way to the sink. Her complexion looked ashen in the ornate mirror. She felt shaky and uneven, like she was back on the ferry, riding across a rolling sea. There was no way she could prove Chandler was the killer before the inquisitor came for her. Tomorrow or the next day.

She could run. She was already out from Maradis's city walls. Mistress Violena's home was filled with expensive treasures—surely, there'd be jewelry and coin and enough to keep her going for months. But if she ran, what would become of Lucas? He'd be executed—going to the grave thinking she'd betrayed him, that what had passed between them meant nothing to her. She couldn't bear that—to be the one to crush his optimism and send him to the gallows.

And it would only be a reprieve of her sentence, anyway. Perhaps a part of her had known—when she had fled her home six years ago with only a waterskin clutched to her chest and blood under her fingernails— that she would pay for what she had done. She thought she had paid when she had ended up in Brother Brax's orphanage. She thought she had paid when Ansel, the one person who had promised to keep her safe, had betrayed her, leaving her alone and brokenhearted. But it seemed the gods didn't believe she had paid her debt. They had come to collect. Letting Lucas pay it for her wouldn't make it stop; it would only make it worse.

Wren let out a shaky breath and leaned her head against the door. She was wrung out, empty.

A soft knock sounded on the other side of the door. "Wren?" Hale's voice. "Are you all right in there? I brought you some water."

Wren wiped her mouth and opened the door, emerging to find Hale with a soft look on his face. She took the glass gratefully and downed it.

"We're close, Wren," Hale said. "Mistress Violena is certain her butler still has the guest list. We'll prove Chandler is the killer. It'll be fine, you'll see."

Wren nodded, unwilling to let her cynicism dampen the bright lamp of his hope. Its glow was almost enough to banish the darkness. Almost enough for her to believe it would be fine.

CHAPTER 28

Sable and Violena were sitting in the dusky dark of the patio overlooking the cool black expanse of the lake.

"Feeling better?" Violena asked as Wren and Hale took two seats.

Wren nodded, embarrassed. "I'm sorry."

"Don't be." Violena shushed her.

They sat in silence for a while, Sable nursing the dregs of a large glass of whiskey. It was perfectly quiet, but for the chirp of the crickets, and the clink of Mistress Violena's boats against the dock and the ice in Sable's glass. Stars were emerging overhead like winking eyes. Wren's heart twisted painfully in her chest. As a child, she had loved the calm of the forest, the comforting presence of ancient trees holding the world still around her. This was the closest she had gotten to that feeling in years. Despite what might come tomorrow, the quiet of the lake made her glad that tonight she was alive.

A sound broke the silence, sobs as soft as raven feathers. Sable. Sable was crying. Wren looked at Hale in alarm, unsettled to see her sponsor, normally composed with a will of iron, so undone. He wore a look of infinite tenderness on his face. "These stars," Sable said, murmuring to herself, seeming to have forgotten the rest of them were there. "I don't see them. I don't see the great spirits in these stars. Are they gone? Because I abandoned them?"

Wren had absolutely no idea what Sable's words meant, but the twisted sorrow pained her like a physical thing. It was clear that Sable was mourning. And that Sable was very, very drunk.

"You didn't abandon them," Mistress Violena said. "You were taken. And you survived. Your clan lives on because you survived. That's what the spirits would want for you."

Sable shook her head, her black curls coming loose and dangling about her face. "Look at me. This dress." She picked at the fabric disdainfully. "The sea would swallow me whole in this, the whale spirit wouldn't even recognize me as a clan child. I didn't survive. I died. And was reborn as this... unnatural surrogate."

"You adapted," Hale said. "All animals do it. It's a natural process."

"I can't live without the sea and the stars and the ice... I should go back."

"There's nothing to go back to," Violena said gently. "You know that."

Sable hung her head, wrapped in a world of her own misery.

"I think perhaps it's time to get Sable to bed," Violena said. "Hale, could you...?"

"Of course." He stood and wrapped one of Sable's arms around him, but she was as limp as a rag doll. In the end, he swung her up into his arms. "Good night," he said. "I'm going to stay with her, make sure she's all right."

"Thank you, dear," Violena said.

When Hale and Sable had disappeared, Violena leaned back in her chair. "That girl. I doubt she'll ever be able to see far enough past her stubbornness and pride to realize she has a good man who loves her waiting on the other side."

Wren realized her mouth had fallen open and she quickly closed it. Hale and... Sable? Hale was in love with Sable? How could Mistress Violena know such a thing? She hadn't even met Hale before tonight. But... Wren's mind flashed back through her weeks at the Guild. Hale and Sable's easy quips, the light in his eyes when he looked at Sable. How she was the only woman he didn't flirt with, didn't joke with. As if their relationship were too sacred a thing to sully. Even when he talked about her. All that she had accomplished at such a young age, her political prowess. Wren had thought it to be admiration and fondness, but she could see now…

Wren turned back to Mistress Violena with new respect.

"I know people," the woman said. "And their words may lie, but you can always discern the truth. If you know how to recognize it."

Wren shook her head with amazement and moved one chair over so she was sitting next to Violena. She felt like she needed to be this woman's apprentice. "What was Sable so upset about? If you don't mind me asking?"

"She gets like that sometimes—when she drinks. When she's near the water. I should have remembered. It's been so long since she's been upset like that, though."

"It's because she's from Magnus?" Hale had explained a little on the ferry, but Wren wanted to understand this piece of Sable. As best she could.

"Sable's life started out very different from the one you see today. Her clan lived in the far south. They made their living fishing—hunting seals and whales. They were a proud clan. The Alesians had made it that far south in their "humanitarian" efforts around the time Sable was six. They pretended to be there in peace. What they brought was disease. A new rule. Many of the adults in Sable's village fell ill and died. It was a story repeated throughout Magnus. Sable, together with many of the other children, were brought back to Alesia to be raised in crown-sponsored boarding schools."

"The rest of her family died?"

"There's nothing left of her village now. Back then, the king was 'leasing' some of my property in Maradis for one of these schools. Not that he gave me any choice in the matter. Or fair rent. I decided if there were children living on my property, I was going to make sure they weren't mistreated. I visited from time to time, trying to make efforts to improve their situation. I swear to the Sower, every time I visited, Sable was in trouble. She was twelve by then, and she was a terror. Practically feral. I think they switched her so much, they broke the branch they used. But I saw something in her. There was intelligence in those eyes.

So I brought her to live with me."

"She grew up here?"

Violena nodded. "She's like a daughter to me. I helped her to find a way to live in this world while not forgetting her old one. But sometimes, the guilt comes out. Like tonight."

Wren's understanding of Sable opened wide.

"If I were you, I wouldn't mention this to her. Ever. That's best where Sable is concerned."

Wren nodded. "Thank you for sharing this with me."

"Now, in payment, you have to share something with me."

"What?"

Mistress Violena's eyes were sharp in the dark of the evening, her white hair standing out like a halo. She leaned forward, wine glass in hand. "What is it you're not telling Sable?"

Bells of alarm sounded in Wren's mind. "What do you mean?"

"Like I said, girl. Their words may lie, but faces never do. I don't believe that you killed Kasper, but that doesn't mean there's not something off about you. Sable may be too distracted to notice it, but you can't get anything past me. So what is it?" Mistress Violena peered into Wren's face as if her soul were showing.

Wren clasped her hands together, struggling not to squirm under the intense scrutiny. The woman was right, of course. It seemed she had a nose for lies like a pig did for truffles. Wren had to tell her something, but could she dare tell her anything as audacious as… the truth? As soon as the thought surfaced, it filled her. The desire to be told. To share this burden that she had kept buried deep in the earth for six years. The desire for another human being to know—truly know her.

Wren eyed Mistress Violena, her lungs tight, as if she couldn't get enough air. "If there were something… what would you do with the information?"

"I have no desire to throw you out on your ear, if that's what you're worried about. But old habits die hard, and I'm very protective of Sable. I need to know you aren't a danger to her. Or that god-like sculpture of a man she calls her artisan."

"I'm not a danger to her," Wren said. "They've taken me in. I'm grateful to them. I owe them. Isn't that enough?"

"No. Because some secrets want to be told. And this one does. If you don't lay down this burden now, it will rear its head at the most inopportune time."

Wren wilted, her willpower gone. She did want to tell this secret. "If I tell you, will you keep it between us?"

"I will promise to share your secret only if I deem it necessary for Sable's safety."

"That's not really an answer," Wren grumbled. "Fine." She stood, pacing to the railing of the patio, looking down at the waves gently lapping at the lakeshore. She didn't deserve to be here in a place so achingly lovely. She didn't think Mistress Violena would share her secret, her deepest shame, but if she did, what harm was there? The king and his inquisitor had returned, and she had no proof that Guildmaster Chandler had poisoned Kasper. She was likely to be questioned tomorrow, and who knew if she would ever be the same? It was time.

Wren turned and faced Violena, a weariness washing over her. "I didn't kill Kasper. But I did kill someone."

Violena nodded as if this was the most obvious thing in the world. She gestured to the chair next to her. "Tell me what happened."

Wren sank into the chair gratefully, downing a finger of whiskey that Hale had left in his glass. She coughed and spluttered as the liquid slid down her throat, setting fire to her insides. *Good, let me burn.* "I killed my father."

One of Violena's eyebrows did rise onto her wrinkled brow at that. "What happened?"

"We grew up in the foothills of the Cascadian mountains. A little logging town called Needle Falls. My mother died in childbirth—giving birth to me. I guess I killed her too," Wren added with a grunt of irony. "My older brother was my world. Hugo was... everything to me. And I was everything to him. My father had been in a bad logging accident when I was little, and his foot had been crushed. He could work, but barely. He was in pain all the time. So he drank. All the time. When he drank, he got violent. Hugo protected me from him. He took the brunt of it. By the time I was ten, things were bad. We had no money. Whatever my father made, he drank away. We were in debt to the royal mercantile. I was working at the bakery for as many hours as they would give me, paid in burnt loaves and leftover eggs. Hugo was fifteen. He was big, muscular already. Old enough to work. Strong enough to fell trees. Strong enough to die in that forest, his first week on the job."

Wren closed her eyes, but the image of Hugo's broken body would never disappear from her vision, not completely. His broad, easy smile and dimpled chin, crushed beyond recognition, a mangled mess of blood and skin. Hugo, who had made her a crown of aster flowers and called her 'the princess of the birds,' told her stories of where she would fly to one day. Who flew himself too soon.

She sighed. "My father went berserk that night. Full of gin and sadness, he was throwing furniture across the cabin, punching the walls. I tried to keep out of his way, but Hugo wasn't there to protect me anymore. So I couldn't. He got me. I think he broke a few ribs, tore out a chunk of my hair. And I was so... full of sorrow and anger myself... at the unfairness of it. That the gods would take Hugo, not him. You see, I had prayed for my father to die. But the gods were laughing at me, punishing me for wishing my father dead. Hugo paid the price."

"The gods don't work like that," Mistress Violena said gently. "They wouldn't punish a young girl for wanting to be safe in her own home."

"They punish me still," Wren shot back. "Why else did I get wrapped up in this mess? Why else will I be executed for a murder I didn't commit? I tried to stay away from them, but they keep finding me. No matter where I go." She felt herself coming unmoored now, the careful locks and doors and walls she had placed in her mind being thrown open. She had tried not to think about the gods for years, since she had apprenticed to Master Oldrick. But they wouldn't let her be.

"You defended yourself. Self-defense isn't murder, Wren. You have to forgive yourself." Mistress Violena reached out a hand to lay it on Wren's arm, but Wren jerked away.

"You haven't even heard the end. I could have run, could have hid and let him tire himself out and fall asleep. He usually did eventually. But instead I grabbed our cast-iron skillet. I wasn't even strong enough to lift it with one arm normally, but that night I found new strength. I bashed him across the head with it. He fell like a cedar tree, knocking his head against the corner of the coffee table. He was bleeding really bad; blood was everywhere. I should have run for help, for a neighbor, for the doctor. But all I could think about was how he was there when Hugo was gone. How Hugo wouldn't have had to work—wouldn't have died—if he weren't such a worthless excuse for a father. For a human being. And how this was going to be my life from now on, with Hugo gone. So I packed a bag and ran." Wren found herself crying now, tears flowing freely. "It wasn't self-defense. I murdered him. I let him die. I wanted him dead."

Wren fell silent, her head hanging. Tears dripped off her nose onto her dress. She couldn't look up, couldn't face Mistress Violena. She didn't want to see the expression on the other woman's face.

Mistress Violena's hand rested gently on Wren's shoulder, and that simple motion triggered a fresh wave of tears.

"Your father made his bed long before that night. What happened isn't your fault. I'll tell you the same thing I've told Sable many times. And like her, you may have to hear it many times before it sinks in. You deserve a place in this world. A place where you can be safe, and whole, and happy. Never apologize for insisting on it. For fighting for it."

Wren looked up then, and the kindness in Violena's eyes took her breath away. The understanding. Violena's words sparked something within her. Relief. Hope. Fight. She wanted to believe them.

"Tell me that again," Wren said into the moonlight.

CHAPTER 29

Wren fell into a heavy sleep that night, and when she awoke, late in the morning, she felt wrung out—like a twisted piping bag with all its frosting gone. Her head pounded and her throat was scratchy and dry. All in all, she wished she could crawl back into bed and never wake up. But she knew at some point she would have to face the day. So, ever so slowly, she bathed and dressed and made her way to the dining room table.

The long, polished table was empty, but for a single plate topped with a silver cover and a scroll tied with blue ribbon. The scroll had her name on it. Wren let out a breath of relief. Despite how well it had gone last night, she wasn't sure she was ready to face Mistress Violena now that the woman knew all of Wren's secrets. Sharing her story had seemed a grand idea in the magical dark under the illumination of a million stars. Now, in the light of day, it felt too exposing.

Looking about for a servant and finding none, Wren sat down to breakfast, untying the scroll. It was a letter from Sable, and it was clear from the contents that Sable was feeling like her usual self once again.

Wren,

Hale and I have headed back to Maradis on the early ferry. Violena found us the list of those who were present at her party where your cupcake was served, and I think once you see the list, you will understand why we left at once. Stay with Mistress Violena for a few days until Hale and I have proven what we must. This is not a request. It is an order. It is confirmed that King Imbris and his inquisitor have returned to Maradis. It's no longer safe for you at the Guild. We will send word when we can.

Grandmaster Sable

"Stay here?" Wren said out loud, incredulous. She pulled the second piece of parchment to the front and skimmed the list of names from the top.

She didn't recognize these women. Did they mean something to Sable?

And then she froze with a sharp inhale of breath. A name she recognized. Bianca Chandler. The head of the Distiller's Guild's wife.

She re-rolled the letter and shoved it in her pocket, standing. The Beekeeper's own swarm couldn't keep her here.

Wren flew about the house until she located a servant. "Please call a carriage to take me to the ferry. I'm leaving."

"Mistress said you'd be staying here a few days?"

"Change of plans," Wren said. "I must return to Maradis. It's urgent."

"You haven't eaten breakfast?" Mistress Violena emerged from her sitting room, a newspaper and a cup of coffee in hand. She wore a brightly-colored Centu robe of silk wrapped about her thin form. "Well, I suppose it's lunch at this hour. You young people sure do know how to sleep."

"No," Wren said, standing by the door.

Violena saw Wren's flittering movements and understood at once. "Where do you think you're going?"

"Guildmaster Chandler's wife was here at your party."

"Yes, Bianca is a lovely woman."

"Don't you see what this means? She ate my cupcake…" Wren's throat began to burn as her words darted too close to the truth of her Gift and the infusion of the cupcake. She trailed off with a grunt of frustration.

"I don't understand why this flaming cupcake matters so much."

"It means that the head of the Distiller's Guild killed my guildmaster. And is trying to frame me."

"Even if that is true"—Mistress Violena set her coffee down and flourished the front page of the newspaper like a shield before her— "King Imbris is back. And if you return to Maradis before Sable does whatever she needs to do, you'll likely be executed."

Wren ground her teeth, trying not to look at the full-page sketch of King Imbris riding tall on a dark stallion, the falcon crown on his head. How had she not noticed how much he looked like Lucas? That stately profile with his prominent Imbris nose, the thick head of salt-and-pepper hair (mostly salt, for the king), the strong chin that hinted at stubbornness—if a powerful man would ever be called stubborn. The same features that drew her to Lucas, that spoke of vitality and intelligence and steadfastness, in his father looked like cruelty and disdain.

"I'll be careful," Wren finally said. "There's a meeting tonight that I must attend. It will be my only chance to prove who gave Kasper the poison. It's a risk I must take." She wouldn't go anywhere near the

Guildhall, wouldn't get caught. But she couldn't let Lucas down. They were supposed to go to the meeting together. What would he think if she didn't show? What if Sable couldn't find what she needed in time? Would the inquisitor take things out on Lucas in her absence? No, she couldn't stay here in safety and leave him in the wind.

"Sable said to stay here."

"It isn't Sable's choice," Wren snapped. "It isn't Sable's life."

"I hope you're not doing this because you think this is what you deserve," Mistress Violena said quietly. "To die a murderer."

Wren squeezed her eyes shut against the word before leveling her gaze on the older woman. "You said I deserved a place. That I should insist on it. Fight for it."

Violena sighed. "You have to pick your battles, Wren. Let Sable fight this one. I promised her I'd keep you safe."

"Am I your prisoner?" Wren countered stubbornly.

"No."

"Then have the carriage brought around. I'm leaving."

"If you know so well how to go it alone," Mistress Violena said. "Very well." Violena left the room, her robe flapping behind her like a war banner. Wren deflated. She hadn't wanted to be harsh with the woman after her hospitality, but what choice did she have? She couldn't miss the meeting at Charger's Estate. It might be their only chance to catch Chandler in the act.

Wren's harsh words to Mistress Violena needled at her the entire ferry ride across to Maradis. She couldn't enjoy the blue afternoon skies or the fresh breeze off the lake like she had on the way over. She would write a letter of apology to the woman, thanking her for what she had done. She had helped them. She had heard Wren's secret and been kind to her. Understanding. She hadn't deserved such treatment.

Wren had brought the last of the macarons, a solitary ginger cookie. She ate it in one defiant bite, closing her eyes to savor the sharpness of the ginger nipping at her tongue. And then that telltale tingle—the taste of infused magic. *Luck be with me.* She sent up a prayer into the universe.

Wren made her way through the city to Lucas's apartment, trying not to look about furtively for Cedar Guardsmen, or worse, the Black

Guard, the king's personal soldiers. It turned out that trying not to look suspicious made one feel all the more suspicious.

Wren let herself into Lucas's apartment building as another tenant left through the front door, a scruffy dog in tow. She knocked on Lucas's door several times, but finding no answer, she let herself in with a few flicks of her wrist and a pin in the keyhole. She couldn't go back to the Guildhall, not right now. She would wait.

She busied herself for a time going about the rooms, inspecting his things. So much could be determined about a person by their possessions. His desk held a fine nib pen and luscious paper, the kind that one buys only when they think carefully about the words they choose to share. On the wall, there was a framed watercolor of three young boys and a toddling girl in pigtails on a lakeshore. His siblings perhaps? Nestled in the corner of the frame was a feathered fly used for trout fishing, perhaps a relic of some country journey. She brushed her fingers against its tufted end. Each of the items in Lucas's apartment held a feel of him that brought a smile to her lips. To imagine that such a man had sprung from King Imbris's lineage was nearly unfathomable.

She pawed through the stacks of books on the floor, taking in the eclectic mix. Economics. Naval history. Encyclopedia of the Ferwich Clans. *The Art of Confectionery*. That one made her pause. Had he been reading up on her discipline? It was strangely sweet. A cookbook. The man could cook? Animal husbandry. Fiction. Mysteries, mysteries, and more mysteries. It seemed Lucas liked to flex his investigative muscles even in his leisure time. Wren herself had never had much love for reading. If she was being honest with herself, it was because she wasn't very good at it. She had stopped attending school at eight to start working in the bakery, and her attendance before that had been spotty. If it hadn't been for Hugo helping her with her letters, she wouldn't have been able to read at all. Her heart twisted painfully at the thought of Hugo, as it always did, and she tucked the memory away carefully.

She had no idea when Lucas would return, and so Wren picked a novel that looked interesting, *The Enigma of the Odette Isles*, and settled onto the couch to wait. That was how he found her, hours later, curled up in the same spot, engrossed in the story.

When Lucas opened the door, her heart leaped at the sight of him. "Hello," she said loudly, announcing her presence.

Lucas started, nearly dropping his package in shock. "Wren! You gave me a fright."

"Sorry," she said, setting the book down gently. "I needed a place to be before we went to Charger's Estate tonight. I hope you don't mind."

"You shouldn't be here," he said. "The inquisitor is looking for you."

Her heart seized in her chest. Was he going to turn her over? Had she misjudged him? "I'll go then. I shouldn't have come."

He set his bag down. "I didn't mean it like that. I won't turn you in. I just meant Maradis isn't safe."

"I couldn't miss the meeting tonight," she said. She pulled the scroll out of her pocket, unrolling it to show him the name. "Bianca Chandler was at the party with the poisoned cupcake. And Guildmaster Chandler gifted the whiskey with the other half of the poison."

"The handwriting does match the threatening letter," Lucas admitted.

"Our guilds are bitter rivals," Wren explained. "They've been feuding for decades over water rights. Don't you see? I don't know if it's politics, or something more personal, but it's Chandler. Tonight we can prove it. Tell me you found Charger's Estate."

"I found it," Lucas said. "But, you know, we may find nothing there."

"I do," Wren admitted. She had thought as much herself. "If the meeting was only for Chandler and Kasper, then Chandler will have no reason to attend, now that Kasper is dead."

"We could be on a fool's errand."

"We have to try. Perhaps others were invited. Perhaps Chandler will be there anyway, confessing his evil plan to the night sky," she said wryly.

"If only we were so lucky." Lucas chuckled.

She smiled grimly to herself, thinking of the tingling she had felt after eating the macaron. Maybe they *would* be so lucky. "We have to try."

"Agreed. But I don't want you to get your hopes up."

"All I have left are my hopes," Wren said, putting the scroll back in her pocket. "So they will go in whatever direction they please."

Lucas approached her, suddenly awkward, all arms and hands with nowhere to put them. "Your hopes are my hopes," he said, finally tucking a lock of auburn hair behind her ear.

"Because if I die, you die." She said it like a statement but meant it as a question.

"No. Because your life matters to me. I've found it a very precious thing that I'm not interested in going without."

She stepped into his arms and he enveloped her, the heat of his mouth on hers, the taste of peppermint lingering on his breath. His kiss this time was slow and deliberate, full of promise, unlike the frantic press of their last meeting. Like he was memorizing her too.

His lips left hers and he wrapped her in an embrace. "You are without a doubt the sweetest thing the Confectioner's Guild has ever produced," he murmured into her hair.

Her heart melted like warm butter, and she leaned against him, enjoying—for the first time in a long time—not feeling alone.

CHAPTER 30

Charger's Estate was a sprawling property on the Northeastern shore of Lake Viri in the Lyceum Quarter. Through some surreptitious questioning, Lucas had discovered its location and its owner. Guildmaster Chandler.

Wren's mind raced as she and Lucas rode in the carriage that would take them to Nysia Avenue, the main drag of shops and bars and unseemly nightlife that cut through the Lyceum Quarter. From there, they would walk, make their way over the fence, and hopefully find the hermitage.

She fought down tendrils of fear that threatened to wrap around her lungs, squeezing them tight. She tried to focus on her hand, which was currently wrapped securely in Lucas's calloused fingers. On the memory of his butterfly kisses trailing fire down her neck... on the way her body flushed and pulsed at the nearness of him. Lucas was something unexpected. Something new, that she wanted to savor like a dark chocolate peanut butter truffle. Her favorite. But that fear kept squeezing, kept circling her thoughts back to the fact that now that she had found him, she had something more to lose.

The tree-lined street was dark and quiet. They skirted the perimeter of Charger's Estate, keeping a hawkish eye out for a way over the tall wrought-iron fence. From time to time, they'd pass someone—a lone soul out for a walk, a group of lyceum students ruddy with wine and company. Each time, Lucas and Wren would melt into each other, his arm would be around her in a flash, his face buried in her hair, hers on his chest, as if they were two young lovers floating in a universe all their own. When the strangers would pass, they'd pull apart, a little more slowly each time. Lucas's fingers would linger in her hair, her hand on the warm flat plane of his chest.

Focus, she thought.

At last, they found their way in. An ancient elm tree sprawled between sidewalk and fence, its branches hanging over into the grassy estate. A limb hung over the sidewalk and roadway, low enough to clamber onto.

After casting furtive glances about, Wren made quick work of it, taking her sandals off and tucking them into the belt of her dress. With her bare feet, she scrambled up the trunk, stretching for the branch and pulling herself onto it.

Lucas gaped at her from below when she straddled the branch and offered a hand. "That was…"

"A holdover from childhood," she said. "We had a lot of trees. Come on, before anyone comes by."

Between his height and her hand, Lucas was able to make his way up onto the branch, hauling himself over it like a fish flopping onto the bank.

"Graceful," she remarked before making her way to the next branch. The thick network was easy to navigate, and in no time, they were over the fence and silently dropping onto the broad lawn.

Wren put her shoes back on and they set off.

"I found an old building permit in one of the city files," Lucas whispered as they moved down towards the gentle lapping of the lakeshore. "I think the hermitage building is by the edge of the water."

"I don't like how exposed we are," Wren admitted, her nerves jangling with warning. The broad expanse of lawn had trees dotted here and there, but very little cover.

"There it is," he said, pointing to a granite rotunda bounded by arched columns. Light poured from within, illuminating stripes across the lush grass.

"Someone's there!" she said, gratified. She knew it was the right idea to come here.

They gave the hermitage a wide berth, skirting around to crouch behind another massive tree. Thick ivy snaked up the walls, punching through panes of the leaded glass dome that topped the structure.

"We can climb the ivy and look in from above," she whispered.

Lucas took out his pocket watch. "It's fifteen to midnight. Almost time."

Without another word, Wren dashed across the lawn in a half crouch, adrenaline pounding in her veins. Hope beat in her chest like a drum. They were going to figure it out. Clear their name. And then… then she could finally think about the future. Think about becoming a master. Finishing what she and Lucas had started…

She filed away these thoughts as she reached the edge of the building. The only windows were too high for her to see through from the ground. She pulled at the ivy, testing its strength. Between the rough edges of the stones and the gnarled covering of ivy, the building seemed easy enough to scale.

Lucas had crept from the tree next to her and was looking up the side of the hermitage uncertainly.

Voices sounded a ways distant, from the direction of the well-lit manor house. Someone was coming.

"Come on," she hissed, and she began to climb.

She made her way to the domed roof without too much trouble. Finding a comfortable perch was considerably more difficult. The stone edge of the dome had a small lip, but if she sat on it, anyone looking up through the glass would be able to see her. However, the dome was made up of three crisscrossing stone arches, which held up the ornate glasswork. If she shimmied along the rim to one of those stone arches, she would be blocked from sight for the most part but still be able to peer in. The pane of glass next to the closest arch was broken as well. So she could hear.

Lucas had made it up the ivy-covered side of the hermitage and was performing the same mental calculus as she. He began working his way to the left, using the ivy to assist him.

She hissed at him and he froze when they both saw Chandler nearing from the manor house.

Lucas hid his face, sinking into the ivy, letting the thick leaves block him from view.

Then Chandler was inside. Wren and Lucas both let out a breath.

She peeked in through the dome as she began to slowly slide around towards the arch that would be her perch. There were other men inside. One was huge, even larger than Hale. He had a thick, brown beard and forearms like tree trunks.

The other seemed quite ordinary—brown hair, scholarly spectacles, a well-tailored waistcoat and jacket. But when he turned to greet Chandler, Wren saw that the man had only one arm. The sleeve of his jacket was pinned neatly.

"I wasn't sure we were still meeting," the one-armed man said. "Now that Kasper is dead."

Wren continued to inch towards her perch.

"Kasper's death only proves that this group is more important than ever," Chandler said. "In fact, I think this group is the reason Kasper was murdered."

"I thought some jealous guild-girl slipped him poison," the big man rumbled.

Wren narrowed her eyes while she continued to inch. She was almost there.

"If you believe that, you're as dense as you look," Chandler retorted. "The girl is a patsy. Someone to distract us while the real killer slips away unnoticed."

Chandler was defending her? If he murdered Kasper, wouldn't he want the suspicion to stay on her? And what was this group? Who were these men and what had Kasper been doing with them?

"So if you have it all figured out, who murdered Kasper?" the shorter, one-armed man retorted.

"The king," Chandler said.

Wren lost her grip on the edge as a piece of granite crumbled under her hand. She pitched forward, through the hole where a pane of glass had once been. Hands windmilling in panic, she fell down, down, into the empty space below.

The big man broke her fall, though not through any intention of his own. A shriek of fear and horror escaped her lips as she toppled over the edge. The three men looked up with surprise, and it was sheer luck that the brutish man was positioned under her.

They both fell to the hard stones with a crash.

Wren rolled off the top of his barrel chest onto the mosaic tiles of the floor. A groan escaped her lips. Everything hurt—she moved gingerly. Nothing seemed broken.

"What in the Sower's name is this?"

"You're... Wren Confectioner?" Chandler asked incredulously, peering at her as she lay on the floor panting.

She struggled to her feet, her head ringing. She was furious at herself. How could she have let herself fall? She might have ruined her and Lucas's one chance to clear their names. To get to the bottom of Kasper's death.

The big man stood as well, rolling his neck and rubbing his head.

"Sorry," she mumbled, trying to back away towards the entrance. Maybe she could salvage this. If she ran, Lucas could still overhear anything else they might say...

"You aren't going anywhere," the man with one arm said, and the big man positioned himself between her and the door in a flash, his tree-trunk arms crossed over his chest. He was surprisingly fast.

Her eyes darted about, like a wild animal looking for its escape. The tendrils of fear squeezed tighter, like a python around her middle. If Chandler had killed Kasper, he would have no qualms about killing her. It looked like her luck had run out.

"Wren." Chandler's voice was soothing, his hands outstretched. "That is who you are, isn't it? I saw you with Sable at the Council meeting." His posture of gentleness only made her more wary, ready to bolt. One couldn't trust kindness. It was just as often a façade as it was real. "We're not going to hurt you. Tell me what you're doing here."

She looked from one man to another, willing herself not to look up to see if Lucas watched the scene. She couldn't give him away. Even if she died, he didn't have to. What would happen to him if she died before she was tried or convicted? Would his vouching simply go away?

"I… I found a message on the bottle of whiskey you gave Kasper. About this meeting," Wren stammered. She could think of nothing clever to say, no lie to get her out of this.

"Clever girl," Chandler said. "But why did you come here?"

"I'm… trying to clear my name. I needed to follow any lead… no matter how… unusual," she said. Her mind raced. Best not to accuse him outright. Perhaps if he didn't realize she suspected him, he would let her leave. A small chance, but one she had to try to exploit.

"What did you think you would find here?" he asked.

"Well… you. Since the note must have come from you, and this is your estate. Beyond that, I didn't know."

"And what do you think you've found?"

"I… don't know," she whispered. "I won't tell anyone I saw you here. I don't even know what I've seen. Please let me go." She knew it was a faint hope. If they did plan on killing her, perhaps she could get them to confess before it was over. Then, at least Lucas could clear his name.

"This is the girl they've framed for Kasper's murder?" the one-armed man scoffed. "You think they could do better than that."

"Agreed. No one would believe this girl could kill a fly, let alone a guildmaster," the big one said.

Wren bristled inside but said nothing. She knew what they saw when they looked at her. Small and skinny, no connections, no nerve. It was the same thing she saw herself most days.

Chandler was looking at her like a puzzle he couldn't quite solve, stroking his lined chin with a hand. "Maybe fortune has brought us a gift. Maybe we can use her."

"It's too dangerous," the man with one arm said. "This girl looks like she'll faint under a withering gaze. She'll be useless to us."

"She's more than she seems," Chandler said. "She's Gifted."

The two men stilled, their appraisals of her turning thoughtful, calculating. She felt like an injured lamb being circled by three hungry wolves.

"If she's Gifted," the big man said, "how do we know she's not compromised? Perhaps she really did play a hand in the murder."

"She's not compromised," Chandler said. "The king doesn't know about her. Kasper discovered her only weeks ago. Days before he died."

The king? What did the king have to do with this? Again, it took everything she had not to look upwards, not to find Lucas and meet his gaze. If these men had something against the king, the last thing she needed was to deliver a royal prince into their hands.

"And Kasper told you this?" the big man asked.

"He did. Kasper and I had begun to trust each other before his untimely end."

"I don't like the timing. A few days is enough to get to her. With the right motivation, anyone will turn on his guild brothers. Or hers," the one-armed man said.

"It's not her," Chandler said, more forceful now. "I have a feeling about such things."

You know it's not me because you killed him yourself, Wren thought. These other two men were unknown commodities, though. Who were they, and had they had a hand in Kasper's murder? From their fine clothes, they appeared to be wealthy merchants or guild members. But which guild? And why were they here at this secret meeting?

"Pardon me if I don't trust your feelings when it comes to something like this. There's only one way to know for sure." The one-armed man pulled an engraved steel flask out of his pocket.

"Is that ice wine?" the big man asked. "I haven't been able to get any of that since the market burned down."

"A Vintner's Guild member owed me a favor," he said. "You never know when it will come in handy."

"All right," Chandler said. "If you want to use it on her, I suppose."

Wren looked back and forth between the men, who were all but ignoring her as they decided her fate. Ice wine? Something from the Vintner's Guild? She thought of the wine Kasper had made her drink that had burned her throat and sealed the secret of the Gifting to her lips. Her tongue went dry, and whatever slim bit of bravery she had fled her. She bolted for the door.

Once again, the big man was faster. He hooked a hand around her ankle, yanking her feet out from under her. She hit the stones like a ton of bricks, her palms stinging, blood in her mouth from where she'd bit her lip. She groaned as he hauled her up by her upper arms and deposited her on the stone table in the center of the room. "Don't make this harder than it has to be, girlie," he said, leaning perpendicularly over her chest with the bulk of his body, pinning her arms and torso beneath him like a vise, crushing the wind from her lungs. She struggled and squirmed, her legs kicking uselessly, her heels scrambling at the table, but she couldn't move. A tidal wave of terror washed over her.

"Relax, Wren, it won't hurt you," Chandler said. "It's only to ensure that you tell us the truth."

Her eyes rolled wildly as he neared her head until she looked up and caught Lucas's gaze.

He was poised over the domed edge, his face white and furious, his hands clenched into fists. He was going to try to rescue her. He couldn't compromise himself. Whatever happened to her, he couldn't come down here.

She stilled and shook her head slightly, pinning him to his spot with her gaze. *No,* she tried to tell him with the force of her look. *I will not let you risk yourself for me again.*

So she opened her mouth and let the syrupy sweet liquid dribble down her throat.

CHAPTER 31

The big man released her. Wren coughed, swallowing thickly.

Chandler took her hand and helped her sit up.

The big man looked at her with an appraising eye. "She's got more fight in her than I thought."

She glared at him, suppressing a growl.

"Now, we want to ask you some questions," Chandler said. "What is your name?"

"Wren Confectioner," she said. The words felt sweet on her tongue.

"Now, I want you to tell me your name is Melissa," Chandler said.

Wren looked at him, blinking.

"Please, indulge me."

She sighed. "My name is Mel—" As she tried to say the syllables, the flavor on her tongue turned to ash, to a taste of rot and death fouler than she had ever known.

She coughed and staggered off the table, gagging in the corner. Her shoulders heaved as she retched up saliva and bile.

"What guild are you a member of?" he asked. "Quickly now, tell me."

"Confectioner's," she managed with a shudder. As she said the word, the flavor in her mouth transformed back to caramelized sugar with a hint of raspberry.

She panted with relief, standing and wiping her mouth.

Chandler took her by the shoulders and led her back to sit down in a chair by the table. "Now you see what we are dealing with."

She nodded sullenly, shuddering at the memory of the taste in her mouth.

"Why did you really come here?"

She closed her eyes, wondering if she was signing her own death certificate. But they would know if she lied. She couldn't suppress her reaction to that taste. "I came for evidence of Kasper's murder."

"Evidence from who?"

"From you," she said, opening her eyes and meeting his gaze.

He appeared genuinely taken aback. Was he such a proficient actor? He looked to the other two, who came around and stood with Chandler, watching her.

"You think I murdered Kasper?"

"Yes," she said, watching him for a tell, for a sign that his surprise was feigned. She saw none.

"Why?"

"Because of the note I found from you, threatening Kasper."

"What note?" the one-armed man asked, drawing nearer.

"It was... hidden in Kasper's drawer. It was vague but said that Kasper had threatened to reveal guild secrets, and if he did, he wouldn't last much longer."

"How do you know it was from me?" Chandler asked.

"It was signed 'C,' and the handwriting matched yours."

Chandler let out a surprised bark of laughter, turning and pacing across the room. "Well, gentlemen," he said. "We wondered why he didn't try to frame anyone worthwhile, and now we know. He was playing the long game."

"I don't understand," Wren said. The men ignored her.

"If the note was in Kasper's desk, then whoever took over for Kasper would find it and suspect you," the muscled man said to Chandler. "Subtle."

"Tell me"—Chandler turned to Wren—"were there any other clues that made you suspect me?"

She was struggling to keep up. They were acting like Chandler wasn't the murderer. Was it an act for her benefit? But if Chandler had killed Kasper, wouldn't it be easier to just kill her too? Wren's head was spinning.

"Girl," the big man said, "answer the question."

She glared at him. "Your wife was at the party where my cupcakes were served. Only one was eaten at that party. The rest were taken, poisoned, and given to Kasper."

"Bianca?" Chandler blinked. "Genius."

"If the girl took the letter, then Callidus won't be able to discover it and suspect you. Did you remove the letter, girl?" the man with one arm demanded.

"My *name* is Wren," she said through gritted teeth. "And yes, I removed it. Now will someone tell me what in the Sower's name is going on here?" Dare she hope… it didn't seem like these men intended to kill her. And if not, she wanted answers.

Chandler chuckled, pacing more. "We can use her. She can help. Agreed?" He turned to the other two.

The one-armed man glowered but gave a curt nod.

"Agreed," the big man rumbled.

Chandler pulled up a chair across from her. "What I'm about to tell you is of the utmost secrecy. I did not kill Kasper. I had nothing to do with it. That letter was a forgery."

Wren felt herself coming unglued. If it wasn't Chandler, then where did that leave her? Leave Lucas? Back at the beginning. Worse than the beginning. "Take the ice wine, or whatever it's called," she said. "Or I won't believe a word you say."

"Show some respect—" the one-armed man began, but Chandler held up a hand.

"Fair point." He motioned for the other man to hand the bottle to him and took a swallow. "Satisfied?"

Wren crossed her arms before her and nodded.

"Now. The substantial fellow to my left is Guildmaster Bruxius, head of the Butcher's Guild. This fellow to my right is Guildmaster McArt, Head of the Cheesemonger's Guild."

Wren eyed both of them, uncomfortably aware of the amount of power contained in this room. She was definitely out of her league.

"Together with Guildmaster Kasper, we formed a loose coalition of interested guildmembers. We were concerned with the direction Guild relations were taking."

"I don't understand."

"I'm sure your guild has told you that the Gifting is kept absolutely secret."

She nodded, wondering what Lucas was making of all of this. Could she explain it to him if he already knew? Or would her throat turn to fire anyway?

"The king has kept a firm grip on the Gifted and infused foods, using them to cement and grow his power and the power of his followers. Technically, he is supposed to have access and control over all infused products. But there was a bit of an informal agreement, a market of sorts, where the guild members and heads could exchange and trade these goods."

"Right," she said. "The mercantile that burned down."

"So you're not entirely in the dark," Chandler said. Was that a spark of respect in his eyes? "The decline of our informal market didn't start with the fire. It started two years ago with the Red Plague."

Wren shuddered, thinking of the plague that had swept through Maradis and Alesia, taking one in five souls with it. Commerce had shut down for weeks as the plague had ravaged the land, moving on as swiftly as it had come, leaving bodies and wails of sorrow in its wake.

"A member of the Baker's Guild had a cure to this plague. The guildheads petitioned the king to abandon the Accord and disseminate the cure. It would have required us to reveal some truth about the Gifting, but not everything."

"The king refused," McArt said, his words hard.

"So we decided we would do it anyway," Chandler said. "Only the Gifted Baker's Guild member disappeared and was never seen again. Even the guild members couldn't get the cure. Many died. Including my daughter. And grandchildren." The words caught in his throat.

Wren looked between the men, at the sorrow that flashed across their features. Truly, everyone had lost someone in the plague.

"The plague entirely spared the royal family and loyalists. Suspicious, don't you think?" Chandler said.

Wren nodded woodenly. Olivia had mentioned her suspicions about the part Willings had played in the Red Plague. She wasn't surprised to hear that the king had saved his own hide at the expense of his people. That was the reality of life each day in Maradis. But clearly, it had shaken these privileged guild members to the core.

"After the plague, the market between guilds was shut down. We reestablished it somewhere else, and then a few months later, the building was condemned. Our guards were being bought, turned against us as spies. We established runners for a while, but they would disappear for a few days, only to turn up with their throats cut. It's an increasingly tiring game of cat and mouse. The king is determined to control all Gifted and infused goods. This has become unacceptable to us."

"He oversteps and overreaches," McArt added. "He forgets how much he owes the guilds. The Gifted."

"The Accord is up for renegotiation next month. Kasper had made it clear that the terms would be radically different this year. The games had to end. The guilds would accept nothing less than control of their own infused goods. If not, we would expose the truth of the Gifted to everyone. When you're made guildhead, you're released from the binding wine. So the king knew the threat was real."

"And you'd neutralize the king's most powerful weapon," Wren said, realization growing. She set aside the new revelation about the binding wine. That there was a cure. She'd have to worry about that later.

Chandler continued. "But before any of this could occur, Kasper was found murdered."

"And a mysterious threatening letter is found, pointing suspicion to the king's next most outspoken opponent."

"Killing two birds with one stone," Bruxius said.

"So, our dear Wren, can you think of no one besides me who might be behind Kasper's death?"

The realization sank in. "The king," Wren breathed. "The king killed Kasper." Wren kept her eyes averted from Lucas. Would he believe his father capable of such a thing?

"A man as important as the king doesn't do his own dirty work," McArt said. "He had help. Someone on the inside."

"A Confectioner's Guild member?" Wren asked. "I thought for a while it was Callidus, but I don't think so anymore."

"And why would he plant a letter for himself to find?" Chandler said. "It was all but certain that he would take over the guild when Kasper died."

"Someone else." Wren sagged in her chair, faces flashing before her. How well did she really know anyone at the guild? Sable? Hale? What if they had purposely misled her from the beginning, pretending to help her to more successfully frame her? Beckett or Marina? And then there were so many more guild members she didn't even know. Faces she had seen, names on a page. She couldn't start again from scratch after all this time. Time for her and Lucas had run out. "I don't know where to begin," she admitted, despair welling within her. Just an hour ago she had been so certain that it was Chandler, that they were drawing near to the truth. Now there was another layer of the onion to peel. And she was getting awfully sick of onion.

"Would your mistress, Sable, be amenable to our cause?" McArt asked. "We've been hesitant to approach her. But she may have connections that can help us discover the truth."

"I... I think so," Wren said. "I think she can be trusted. But... I can't be sure."

"We'll have to take the risk," Bruxius said.

"If she'll come, bring her here tomorrow night at the same time. We'll share our intelligence openly, and see if we can piece the puzzle together," Chandler said.

"All right," Wren said, standing, sensing that she was being dismissed. That was fine by her. She wanted out of this room, to be away from these men. To be able to breathe and think.

"And Wren," Chandler said. "This time you can come in the front door."

CHAPTER 32

Chandler's men escorted Wren up the long gravel drive and out the front gates. They offered to take her back in a carriage, but she insisted upon walking. Finally, reluctantly, they abandoned her, depositing her on the long tree-lined street.

Wren began walking back towards Guilder's Row, keeping her steps slow.

A man dropped down in front of her onto the sidewalk from a tree branch. Wren gasped and reared back in surprise, clutching her chest. "Lucas," she said. "You scared the sugar out of me!"

"Now you know how I felt when I saw you go tumbling headfirst into the hermitage! Gods, Wren, how reckless could you be?"

"I didn't do it on purpose," she said, sullen at his reproach.

He let out a deep breath and took her face in his hands. His touch was gentle, reverent. "Are you all right?"

"Yes," she said. "I promise. I'm so glad you stayed out of sight."

"I felt like the biggest coward east of the Cerulean Sea, just sitting there and watching them hurt you. They could have poisoned you!"

"But they didn't," she said, taking his hand in hers and beginning to walk again. "And we learned so much. It's a blow, realizing that it's not Chandler, but at least we have new allies in the hunt. We'll figure it out," she said with more certainty than she felt.

"Wait, you aren't telling me that you believe all that business. It's obviously Chandler! He concocted a great story, sure, even with all the nonsense about Gifts and cures and whatever else he was babbling about. But there's no way my father would kill a guild head."

Wren stopped in her tracks, her hand halting Lucas like a tether. "Wait, what? It's not Chandler," she said. "That wine they made me drink..." She felt her throat tightening. Curses! She thought him overhearing about Gifts would loosen her tongue. No such luck, apparently.

"I don't know what they made you drink, except that it made you retch like poison. That doesn't prove him innocent—that he forced some strange substance down your throat."

"He drank it too," she said. "He..." Blooming flaming wine! The words roared within her, on the tip of her tongue. She had to tell him! To make him understand.

"The Gifted..." She doubled over, one hand on her knee, another on her burning throat.

"Wren, you're not well. Let me get you back to the Guildhall. We'll figure out a way to put the case together against Chandler."

"No," she cried, tears prickling in her eyes from the pain of the wine that sealed the truth in her. "It's... your father."

"No?" Lucas said, his hands forming into fists at his sides. "I'm telling you, my father may be obsessed with power and even cruel at times, but he has to be to do his job, to keep the country secure against his challengers. He doesn't resort to political assassination. If you think otherwise for some mad reason, then tell me why I should believe you right now. Tell me what was going on in there. What all of that meant. Gifts and infusions and wine that makes you wretch. Tell me the truth. Or I can't help you."

"Lucas," she croaked, taking a shuddering breath. *Tell him anything! Something!* She tried to skirt the truth, to find the edges of the hold the power had on her, words she could say, clues she could give him. But all she could manage is "I... can't."

His face hardened. "Then I'm done helping you. Because if you can't trust me, Wren, how in the Sower's name can I trust you?"

He whirled on his heel and stalked down the street, leaving her clutching her throat under the dark boughs of an elm tree.

Wren walked back towards the Guild Quarter with only her misery for company. Lucas hated her. His final words—the fury and hurt in his expression—twisted at her gut. She didn't know what was worse, her panicked realization that she had lost one of her few allies when she needed him the most, or the ache in her heart left by his absence.

What chance did she have against a foe like King Imbris? She had never paid much attention to politics, and now, for not the first time, she wished she had. She knew of his brutal colonization of the Magnish Clans in the South—an entire civilization sacrificed for minerals and glory. She knew that he handpicked boys as young as ten to train for his legendary Black Guard, leaving their families with nothing more than conciliatory words of duty and honor. She had heard that his aggressive trade deals with Tamros had weakened its economy and peace-loving people to the point where Aprica saw it was ripe for the picking. The rumors said there hadn't been a day since he had been crowned where there wasn't the head of at least one "enemy" staked by the palace gates. The man was a locust, gobbling up Alesia's plenty with a ceaseless appetite. As far as she could tell, his only redeeming feature was that he had managed to father children as kind as Lucas and Virgil.

Wren's rumbling stomach steered her to a restaurant open all night. After sliding into a wooden booth in the back, she ordered a bowl of lamb stew. The stew was greasy and the crust of bread was hard, but she finished it all and ordered another. She was famished.

The lone waitress took pity on Wren, and after clearing her dishes, left her alone to marinate in her dark thoughts. Wren's body felt heavy and tired, and her eyes scratchy and raw, but she couldn't go back to the Guild and sink into her heavenly bed. A cell and a date with the inquisitor waited for her there. Somehow, she had found herself homeless on the streets of Maradis once again. She had meant what she'd said to Mistress Violena. It seemed the gods were punishing her.

By the time the sky began to lighten in the east, Wren knew what she had to do. She needed to get into the Guild to talk to Sable, to share what she had learned from Chandler and the others. At this early hour, no one should be up. It was a risk, but she didn't know what else to do.

Wren circled around the back of the Guildhall, using the servants' entrance. The hallways were dark and silent, lit only by the watery light coming through the windows. Wren padded up the stone steps, keeping to the shadows as she poked her head around the corner to survey the second floor hallway. It was deserted. She slipped silently to Sable's door, knocking lightly.

No one answered. She couldn't risk knocking any louder. Wren tried the knob and found it unlocked. She opened it, peeking her head inside.

"Sable?" she whispered, peering through the dark open doorway into the shadow of the bedroom. The large four-poster bed was just visible through the doorway. She could see Sable's foot resting on top of the white cotton duvet.

"Sable?" Wren hissed, slipping into the room and silently closing the door behind her. Her mouth had gone dry and her senses were firing with alarm. She tried to dispel the sinking sense of wrongness that crept over her. Sable was sleeping on top of the covers. Nothing unusual about that in the late-August heat.

"Sable!" Wren said, moving to shake the woman awake. She froze, her hand hovering inches from Sable.

Sable was lying on top of the bed, her bare foot and one arm hanging off. Even in the dusky light, Wren could see that the tips of Sable's extremities were tinged a macabre gray. Her skin was pale, and her eyes were open, staring vacantly at the ceiling.

Sable was dead.

CHAPTER 33

Wren flew from the room, her heart thunderous in her chest. She slammed the door shut behind her, sinking back against it once she was safe in the hallway again.

Sable was dead. Dear gods. And from the strange color on her fingers and toes... it didn't look natural. A servant turned into the hallway at the far end, carrying a tray. Wren lurched into action, turning the other way and striding away. She had to tell someone. But if she was the one who'd discovered the body, they might suspect her. They already thought she had murdered one grandmaster. But she couldn't just leave poor Sable there to rot... how long would it be before someone discovered her?

Her mind grasped for a solution and latched upon one with a death grip. *Hale.* He would know what to do. His room was a few doors down the hallway.

She reached his door and pounded on it, trying to hold in the tears that were threatening to spill down her cheeks. "Hale," she cried, her voice choked. She pounded again.

Hale pulled the door open as she was poised to pound a third time. He was shirtless, his hair disheveled. For once, it had no effect on her. She barreled past him, her hands flapping uselessly, feeling the grip of panic pull her wits from her.

"Wren!" he said, capturing her hands in a firm but gentle grip. "What in the gods' name is wrong with you? Why aren't you at Mistress Violena's?"

"Sable." The word ripped from Wren's throat in a keen that sounded half-animal.

He stilled. "What about Sable?"

Wren hitched in a breath, trying to get control of herself. "I went to see… her…" Wren managed. "She was lying there… She's dead…"

"What?" His grip tightened painfully and a black cloud passed across his face. "Are you certain of this?"

"She was… so pale… I think she was poisoned," Wren managed.

Hale stood for a moment, his eyes darting about, a man poised on the edge of a cliff. And then he exploded into action. "Stay here!" he bellowed before tearing from the room, the door slamming behind him.

Wren looked around the room helplessly, tears flowing freely, her breath coming in jerking gasps. She finally collapsed into one of his chairs, drawing her knees up to her chest and burying her face in them. She wished she could sink into the ground, wished that the earth would swallow her up so she didn't have to face the horror of this reality. Kasper had tried to help her, welcome her into the Guild. He had died. Now Sable, her protector—almost her friend—had succumbed to the same fate. The killer had struck again, and Wren had no idea who they were or why they had killed Sable.

"Damn it!" Wren screamed, hurling one of the glasses on the nearby table into the fireplace. She had never felt so impotent, so ignorant. She had thought she was beginning to understand this world, the games they were playing, the puzzle pieces, but she had never had a chance. She would be executed for Kasper's murder, and Lucas too. She was cursed. Everyone who got close to her died. Her mother. Hugo. Her wretched father. Kasper, Sable. And soon, Lucas. She knew she shouldn't have let them in, should have kept them at arm's length. Their names and faces circled in her head, a macabre parade that crowded in, threatening to suffocate her. She squeezed her eyes shut, wishing that the darkness would take her.

Her hysteria had calmed by the time Hale returned. She stood as he closed the door behind him, his chest heaving.

Wren looked at him with misery in her eyes, wondering if she should try to comfort him. "Hale—" she began softly.

"What kind of poison was it?" He looked up, meeting her gaze. His eyes flickered dangerously with barely-restrained malice.

She stepped back involuntarily. "What? I don't know."

"Is there an antidote?" he asked, taking a menacing step towards her. She had always seen his size as an integral part of the cheerful package that was Hale, but now his towering height and solid muscle exuded danger. His face—his face was a thunderstorm she had never seen before. Gone was his golden sunlight, in its place... gray wrath and sharp lightning.

"An antidote?" Wren stuttered, taking another step back. "Wait... she isn't dead?" Hope blossomed in Wren's chest.

"No, she isn't dead. But she's dying. I guess you weren't as thorough as you were with Kasper."

His words froze her where she stood. "Hale," she said. "I had nothing to do with Sable—"

"Then why did they discover a knife with a poisoned blade in your quarters? The servant was removing a tray of dishes and there it was— a dagger where there should be a butter knife! A foreign coloring on the blade!" He advanced on her and she backed away hastily. Her back thunked into the wall.

"That's crazy! I haven't even been to my room," she protested. "Someone must have planted it!"

"Fool me once, Wren," Hale said, towering above her, "shame on you. Fool me twice, shame on me. You really expect me to believe that you happened to be in the wrong place at the wrong time twice? At some point, coincidences stop being coincidental."

"Whoever killed Kasper is trying to frame me, just like they did before!" Wren's mind was whirling. A poisoned knife? In her room? Someone really was trying to frame her!

"How could you, Wren?" Hale's fist hit the wall next to her head, punctuating the ice of his words. "Sable took you in! Trusted you! You were family!"

She cringed beneath the weight of his anger, closing her eyes. And then she was eight again, back in the little bedroom she and Hugo had shared, cowering in the corner. She could smell the stale sweat on her father's skin, the liquor on his breath. She could feel the heat of his anger radiating off him as he shouted at her for hiding his booze. She hadn't hidden his liquor, she'd begged him to believe her, tears and snot streaming down her face. He had just drunk it already and was too drunk to realize it.

Hale's words pulled her back to the present. "If Sable dies, I will kill you myself. Now tell me what poison you used! Give me the antidote!" His eyes were blazing now, feral. His hand closed around her throat.

Her hands clutched around his thick wrist, trying to lever herself so she could draw in a breath. "If I poisoned her, why did I come here? Why didn't I run?" Wren croaked, struggling to stay in the present, to keep herself from shutting down completely. "Think!"

His grip loosened slightly as he seemed to consider this.

A mad idea sprang to her mind, which was quickly darkening due to loss of oxygen. "Guildmaster Pike," she said. "He said he would give me aid. He knows… poisons. Antidote…"

Hale released her and she curled into herself, clutching her neck, pulling in a ragged breath.

"He never gets involved," Hale said.

"For Sable," she wheezed, "he will. He said I could seek him if I needed aid." She prayed it was true. It had been a gallant comment at a fancy ball. Had the man meant it? But he did seem fond of Sable. It would have to be enough. He had to help them. He had to save her.

"We go now," Hale said, wrenching her arm and hauling her to her feet. He spun her to meet him until their noses were inches from each other. "You better hope you can convince Pike to give you an antidote," he growled, "or Sable's fate will seem kind compared to yours."

Hale dragged Wren through the servants' hallways out the back of the guildhall. His grip on her wrist was tight and chaffing, and she tried to keep up with his long strides. The manhandling didn't wound her nearly as much as the thought that Hale was lost to her. That he now saw her as an enemy. He had grown on her until his friendship had become a light in the storm, a constant to count on. Its absence left her situation feeling all the darker.

The Spicer's Guildhall was nestled in the heart of the Port Quarter, rather than on Guilder's Row. Just another way the Spicer's Guild held their guild apart, adding to their air of mystery.

The ambulance carriage for Maradis Hospital had just come to a clattering stop in front of the hall as they scuttled around the corner. Three inspectors galloped to a stop behind it, vaulting off their horses and running inside.

"They can arrest you later," Hale spit. "After we save Sable."

He pinned her against the side of the Guildhall with an outstretched arm while he considered. "I'm taking a horse," he said. "Wait here." He turned, leveling the full force of his baleful gaze on her. "Don't test me."

She shrank against the wall. "I'll wait."

Hale stood and sauntered down the stairs, grabbing the reins of one of the inspectors' horses that was milling about. He swung into the saddle with an easy grace and motioned her to follow.

She looked about and darted down the stairs, praying that no one happened to look out the front doors. She scurried around the far side of the horse and Hale leaned down, hauling her up painfully by her armpit into the saddle behind him.

He kicked the horse into a gallop before she got her seat and she grabbed his waist to keep from falling off. The horse's hooves clattered on the stones, sending pedestrians dodging out of the way.

In a matter of minutes they came to a screeching stop in front of the slate gray monolith of the Spicer's Guildhall. The building loomed above them, its walls colored dark from the rain of a hundred seasons.

Wren leaped down from the horse before Hale could throw her off, stumbling unsteadily after the mad dash of the ride.

Two guards pulled the door open before them, one blanching at the furious expression on Hale's face.

The Spicer's Guildhall couldn't have been more different from the white marble and chocolate brown carpets of the Confectioner's hall. Wren saw it all through a daze of shock and pain and fear. The inside of the Guildhall was dark and moody, red light emanating from elaborately-filigreed lanterns. Tapestries depicting swirling scenes of naval battles and sea monsters adorned the walls.

A guild member met them at the back of the antechamber, a bearded man with a thin silver hoop in one ear. "What business do you have here?" he asked, standing in their path.

"We must see Guildmaster Pike," Wren pleaded. "He said he would help me if I needed it."

"I'm afraid Guildmaster Pike is not taking visitors," the man said, crossing his muscular arms over his chest while sizing them up.

"It's a matter of life or death," Wren said. "It will only take a moment."

"Gave you my answer," the man said.

"Enough of this wasted time," Hale said, lifting the man bodily from the ground by the collar of his shirt. "We will see Guildmaster Pike—" He cut off suddenly and his body stilled.

"Hale!" Wren said before seeing that the guildmember held a wicked curved dagger to Hale's throat. Gods, this place was foreign territory. What had been the strange phrase Pike had mentioned? Swordfish? Fish's spear?

"Please," she said. "Enough, both of you. Grandmaster Pike said if I ever needed him, I should ask for the… marlin's blade!" The memory had blessedly returned.

The guildmember's dark eyes opened a hair's breadth, and he removed the blade from Hale's neck, sheathing it. "Put me down, you brute. I'll take you to see Pike."

Hale complied, and without another word, the man turned on his heel and headed down a corridor to the left. Hale and Wren looked at each other, her mouth dry at the sight of the stranger in her friend's face. They hurried after him.

"Wait here," the man said when they reached a set of double doors engraved with a proud schooner tossed about on a wave. The doors shut in their faces.

"Let me do the talking," Wren hissed. "The last thing we need is you threatening Pike. Men in his position don't take to being bullied."

Hale growled but nodded. Curtly.

The door opened, and Pike's smiling face appeared behind it, his grin as wide as a cat's. "Wren," he said, welcoming her inside. "And… is this the infamous Hale?"

Hale nodded, opening his mouth to say something offensive, no doubt.

Wren cut him off. "Guildmaster, I am sorry for barging in. But Sable has been poisoned. She hangs on the edge of death. Please help us find an antidote."

Pike swore. "Flaming hells. How did this happen?"

"It's not important," Wren hurried. "An antidote? Sable's body was pale and blue-tinged. Her fingers and toes had gray spreading up the tips. Do you know this poison?"

Pike nodded. "I am the Head of the Spicer's Guild. I know every poison. That sounds like the work of sumac poison."

"Is there an antidote?"

"Yes," he said. He crossed the room to a massive armoire and threw open the doors. Inside were drawers and shelves covered in tiny bottles. Wren goggled at the sight.

He skimmed the labels, dancing over them with his fingertips. "Ah-ha!" he finally said, selecting a small red vial. "Give Sable three drops of this, no more, no less."

"I'll take it," Hale said, snatching it from Pike.

"How many drops, boy?" Pike asked, his eyes narrowed.

"Three," Hale said.

"Go save her," Wren said. "I'll make it back myself."

"You're coming with me," Hale growled.

"The hospital's halfway across town," Wren said. "It'll slow you down with both of us. I won't run," she said. *I have nowhere to go,* she thought.

Hale looked from Wren to the vial in his hand before turning and sprinting from the room.

CHAPTER 34

"Can I get you a drink?" Pike asked as Wren heaved a tremendous sigh of relief at the sight of Hale's back disappearing out the door.

She eyed him warily.

"I don't make a habit of poisoning my guests," he said wryly.

"Am I that easy to read?" she asked.

"One doesn't rise to the head of the most ruthless guild without knowing how to read people."

"Once I thought I knew how to read people..." She trailed off, and as the adrenaline of their flight dimmed, the horror of her circumstances crashed in upon her like pounding waves. Sable was gravely ill—perhaps dead already. Lucas hated her. Hale wanted to kill her. And she had no idea who the real killer was. Wren's knees grew weak, and she sank onto one of the colorful pillows that littered the floor.

"Yes, the girl needs a drink," Pike said, retrieving a decanter of amber liquid and joining her on the vibrantly-hued rug.

She observed it all mutely, the riot of color and shapes, carved figurines of fantastic animals, wood-hewn patterns of spiraling mandalas on the walls. The room was a treasure trove of a lifetime of travel and trade. Just a day ago, she would have delighted to behold it, the color so incongruous against the guild's black reputation. Now, she felt numb. Like she would never taste chocolate again—only the bitter dirt of the grave.

Pike handed her a glass patterned in a geometric design of gold that caught and refracted the light of the hanging lanterns. Pike clinked it against the one he held loosely in his fingers.

"Drink it," he said. "It will clear the fog."

Wren complied, letting the liquid slide down her throat. Whiskey. She hadn't developed a taste for it, but she welcomed the burn. The feeling of something raw and angry and real.

"Thank you for helping me." Wren looked at him then. He wore loose, violet trousers and a white shirt half-unbuttoned. The dangerous edge of sword and boots and high-collared coat was missing here, and he seemed like just a man. She saw that sharp edge for what it was now—a carefully-chosen uniform—a front to terrify the world. She felt safer here, in the den of this near-stranger, than at her own Guildhall. "It's hard to know who your friends are in my Guild."

"Make no mistake—I'm not your friend," he said. "Though you are safe here. It's my policy not to have friends. People who owe me things, people whom I owe things to. Those who are loyal, and those who are not. It keeps things simpler."

"I see the value of that approach," she admitted. It had been her approach, too, before she had gotten wrapped up in daydreams of friendship and family. Before she had remembered how nice it felt to have people care for you. Before she had let her guard down.

"It's the only way to survive for people like you and me." The way he said it made her again think that he knew of her Gifting. "Though there are the rare few who are something more. Those who defy categorization. Like Sable." Her name rolled like velvet off Pike's lips. It was clear Hale wasn't the only man holding a torch for Wren's sponsor.

"Will she live?" Wren asked quietly.

He stroked his beard in consideration, his face grave. "It depends on when she was poisoned. How much, how long it's been in her blood. Maybe the poison will spare her. Perhaps she'll get lucky."

Wren let out a dark huff of laughter. Despite her Gift, she didn't feel like she had enjoyed many strokes of luck lately. "You speak of poison as if it's sentient."

"Poison's a funny thing," he said. "Like a woman. Every formula is different. They demand to be known, to be understood. Each has telltale signs. A smell, a taste. A color and viscosity."

"You sound almost… fond of it."

"I suppose I am, in a way. How do you think a son of a Centu pirate secured all of this?" He waved at the room around him before standing and retrieving a tobacco pouch from a desk drawer. He sat back down.

"You poisoned your way to the top?" Wren asked. "I can't believe you'd admit that."

"I never said that," he said, rolling himself a cigarette. "I said I owed it to poison. I'll share a little secret. I managed to secure my first fleet of vessels by trading in the stuff, being willing to procure the deadliest. Some of these poisons"—he lit his cigarette—"fetch a king's ransom."

"You've never used it?"

"Poison is the coward's way to kill. For those who are aren't strong enough to face the truth of their deeds. Real men kill with swords. They look their enemy in the eye when they send them to meet the Huntress."

Wren pondered this as the smoke from Pike's cigarette drifted over her. She wrinkled her nose. It did seem cowardly, the king killing Kasper in secret. Trying to frame Chandler. The king was the most powerful man in Alesia. If he wanted Kasper dead, he should have faced the political consequences and taken on the guilds in the light of day.

And now, Sable.

"Someone planted a knife in my room. With the sumac poison on it," Wren admitted. "Everyone will think I'm a coward."

"Ah," Pike said. "That explains why Hale looked ready to hold you under the surf and never let up. Did he give you those bruises?"

Wren's hands flew to her neck, fingering the tender skin there. The animal rage in Hale's face flashed over her, and she closed her eyes.

"It's plain to see you're far from a coward, Wren Confectioner. As clueless as a greenhorn when it comes to the spiderweb of guild politics, but no coward. I'm confident you have everything you need to get yourself out of this predicament."

"I have nothing." Her voice came out hard and bitter.

"Do you know that I was once sentenced to death, Wren

Confectioner?" Pike blew an expert ring of smoke.

"No. When? For what?"

"Piracy is punishable by death in the Cerulean sea. But it's how I got my start. By the time I was twenty-five, I had a fleet of three ships, loyal crews. I appointed my most deserving two men as captains of the other vessels. I kept the most impressive ship for myself, naturally."

"Naturally," Wren said, taking another burning sip of whiskey. Pike was a good storyteller, full of drama and bravado. She found herself settling into his story.

"I had one crew member, a man full of sulfur and rot named Hancock. He troubled me to no end, but the man was a hell of a sailor and had an uncanny way with the weather. So I let him stay. Hancock wanted one of those other ships and was furious when I didn't name him one of my captains. He fomented rebellion in my ranks, biding his time. Now, in those days, the Spicer's Guild was always chasing us. The guild head had it in for me, felt I was a barnacle on his hull he needed to be rid of. And one day, in the waters off the coast of Nova Navis, he found us. Now, I wasn't worried, their three guild vessels were no match for us—my vessels were armed to the teeth, rigged with armor-plated battering rams and surprises for anyone who drew too near. But in the heat of battle, Hancock mutinied with the scoundrels he had managed to turn to his side. They killed the rest of my crew and steered their iron-clad bow into my beautiful ship, leaving us to flounder with our guts leaking out into the sea. My crew in the other ship defended us as long as they could, but when Hancock turned on them, they ran. I was arrested and brought back to Maradis to be tried for piracy."

Wren's eyes were wide now. "What happened?"

"I was executed for piracy, obviously." Pike laughed, taking a swig of whiskey.

She rolled her eyes. "Come on, tell me."

"I had no more aces up my sleeve. I sat in a cell in the Block, and I swear I could see the Huntress's dark eyes burning though my cell door. The morning of my execution, the guildmaster came into my cell and knocked me across the face with a baton. This was surprising, you see; he was a snively little fellow. But the man was livid, beside himself. 'Where are they?' he asked me. 'Where are you keeping them?' 'Where's who?' I say. 'Don't play coy with me!' the man bellows. 'My wife! My children!'"

"What?"

Pike held up his hand, signaling for silence as he continued. "I went with it. I said 'You'll get 'em back when I get a full pardon for my crimes. Announced publicly. And more than that. I want to be named a master in the guild.' I figure, I'm a doomed man, so I might as well shoot for the moon. 'When I get all that, you get your family back.' The man hits me again with the baton, just for good measure, and storms from the cell. Next thing I know, I'm being cleaned up, trotted before the guilder's council, pardoned, and named a master. I swagger up the dock to my last ship while that guildmaster's family flees the other way, released by my crew."

"Your crew kidnapped them? And held them for ransom? How in the gods' name did you accomplish that from the Block?" Wren was in awe.

"I didn't have the foggiest notion they were doing it! I just played along. Though don't tell anyone that. I've carefully curated my legendary reputation."

Wren huffed in disbelief.

"This is all to say that sometimes, what feels like nothing is really something. You may have more cards in your hand than you realize. You need only play them when the time is right."

Wren looked at him sharply, studying his black eyes, those thick lashes and dark eyebrows. She shook off her despair and fog of moments earlier, finally thinking clearly again. It wasn't over yet. Clearly, he thought she possessed something worthwhile, something that would help her. But what? She didn't have a crew of loyal pirates to spring her from the Block when the inquisitor came for her. She had alienated all of her friends. She had no allies. Yet... here was one of the most powerful men in Maradis sitting in front of her. Could she use him somehow? How could he help her?

"Don't hurt yourself thinking so hard." He was rolling another cigarette.

"No wonder Sable rebuffed you," Wren said weakly. "There's no way she could put up with your bad jokes."

"Words like knives," Pike said, pantomiming a chest wound.

Sable. A ray of clarity burned through her. Wren did have something new. A new clue. Someone had poisoned Sable.

"How did you know what antidote to give Sable?" Wren asked.

"Every poison has its own trademark. Sumac poison tinges the fingertips gray, the skin a shade of pale blue. The body always tells the tale if you know the signs."

"And you sell these poisons as well?"

He nodded.

"Did anyone buy sumac recently?"

"A man of my profession wouldn't get very far if he told those types of secrets. I don't disclose my customers. Not even for Sable. But in this case, there's nothing to hide. No sumac purchases lately."

"Do you sell Gemini? The twin poison?"

"The poison that killed your grandmaster?" he asked.

"Yes." She blushed. Of course he knew that was how Kasper had died. A man this well-connected in the area of poisons would know of such things. "If you did... sell Gemini, would you have records of such things?"

"Again, I am confident that any such records, if they existed, would tell you nothing of use. I'm not the only purveyor in Alesia."

"Of course." She wilted slightly. The man was as slippery as butter. She'd never get any information from him, even if he had it. She tried another tack. "What about... Gemini's signs? You said poisons smell? Taste? What are its distinguishing features?"

"A worthy question. When added to food, it adds an ever-so-slight sweetness, a citrus taste. One half of the twin is colorless, but the other has a blueish tinge. Especially if it comes into contact with sodium chloride."

"Salt?" she asked.

"Salt," he said. "You cannot put it in certain foods because the color will turn. On the tongue, if it comes into contact with salt or salt water, it will turn a bluish shade, almost like ink."

Something niggled at the back of Wren's mind. A bluish tinge. "What if... it was on your skin. If you spilled it. And it came into contact with salt or... sweat. Would it stain the skin?"

"Yes, of course."

Wren's mind strained, sifting through memory after memory, pulling together the threads of something. Someone.

"How long would the skin stay stained?"

"Well, it would fade if not exposed to salt, but a reapplication would reveal it once again. Perhaps a few days. It's powerful stuff."

A few days.

"And would it be a liquid? What would you keep it in?"

"The two halves are liquid; you must keep them separate. It could be in anything. A flask, a bottle. A stoppered vial."

"A perfume bottle," Wren said.

"Yes, I suppose, though you'd have to be careful not to spray it by mistake." He chuckled.

The whiskey glass slipped from Wren's hand, rolling down the mountain of pillows to the tile floor.

Guildmistress Greer with blue-tinged fingers, wiping the tears from her eyes the morning after Kasper had died. Greer snapping at Wren to put down her perfume bottle. Greer who oversaw all food, drink, and gifts coming into the Guildhall. Who could easily have sent food up to Wren's room with a poisoned knife nestled on the tray.

Wren shoved her shaking hand into the pocket of her dress, pulling out the scroll of names Sable had left for her at Mistress Violena's. On it were the names of those who had attended the garden party where her cupcakes had been discovered. Wren hadn't looked any further than Bianca Chandler's name. But Sable had.

Wren unrolled the scroll, her eyes widening as she found the name she had known would be there. The last name on the list. Iris Greer.

CHAPTER 35

Wren stood as if in a dream. Iris Greer. Guildmaster Kasper's own sister. No one had suspected her because it was unthinkable. No one except Sable. Wren looked down at the message clutched in her hand. Sable had known. She must have. And when she'd confronted her, Greer had tried to kill her.

"You have a look about you," Pike said, watching her with a bemused expression on his face.

She shook her head, trying to clear it. "I realized something important."

"Who killed Kasper?" he said.

"Yes. And I know where to find proof."

"Good girl," he said. "Go get her."

"Thank you for the whiskey," she said, pausing at the door. "And the antidote. Two words I never thought I'd say together."

The sound of Pike's laughter followed her down the hall. She was out the front door before she realized what Pike had said. *"Go get her."* He had known.

Wren went over what she knew as she strode back towards the Guildhall. Greer had been at the party at Violena's home where one of Wren's cupcakes had been consumed. Either she or Bianca might have recognized the effects of a Gifted item… Either knew about it. Greer must have taken the cupcakes back with her and poisoned them. Greer was in charge of monitoring and approving packages that came into the Guildhall. No doubt when Guildmaster Chandler had sent Kasper a bottle of his small batch Destrier's Reserve, Greer would have known about it. Perhaps had even taken the gift up to Kasper herself. She could have added the second poison, knowing that no one but Kasper would drink his private stash. But somewhere along the way, she had gotten the poison on her fingertips. And when the lingering Gemini had come in contact with her false tears, it had tinged her fingertips blue. When Sable had discovered the truth of Greer's involvement, Greer had poisoned her—framing Wren a second time. Wren was an easy scapegoat since the suspicion was already on her.

What Wren didn't understand, what she didn't have the first clue about, was why. What possible reason did Greer have to poison her brother? The king's likely involvement meant that money could be a factor—perhaps she had been paid handsomely. But she had a secure position at the Guild and comfortable surroundings. Would an offer of payment truly be enough to turn her against family? Wren thought of the voluminous closet, the rainbow of dresses and shoes and hats. Perhaps her finery reflected more than just nostalgia for her old life. Perhaps she wanted it back.

Wren approached the broad square at the end of Guilder's Row and ducked into the shadow of a building. *Lucas*. Should she go to him, share her theory? He hadn't thought the king could be involved, still believing Chandler guilty of the crime. And he had seemed so angry with her when she wouldn't explain the Gifting. No. Words wouldn't be enough to sway him. Not without proof. She needed to confirm that the Gemini was in Greer's quarters. Once she did, she'd level her accusations at Greer in public before the woman had a chance to hide the evidence or kill again.

Wren ducked between two guildhalls as she neared the end of Guilder's Row. The hall was still crawling with inspectors, no doubt investigating Sable's poisoning. She bit her lip, peering around the corner. How to get inside without being seen? Greer's quarters were on the second floor. She could take the servants' entrance and stairs most of the way there, but she could easily run into the wrong person in the hallway. Entering the Guild at all was a dangerous gamble. What she needed, she realized, was luck.

With a silent prayer, Wren looped around the neighboring Cuisinier's Guildhall into the yard behind her hall. The gravel expanse was blessedly empty. Wren slipped through the door, darting towards the teaching kitchen where she had stashed the rest of the macarons. Sable had asked for four types, so even after cutting the recipes in half, the batches had made extra cookies. Wren thought of the carefree ferry ride across Lake Viri with a pang of regret. How quickly things had changed.

She heard the tap of heels on the tiles of the hall and ducked into a nearby teaching kitchen. She flattened herself against the wall, watching the figure pass by. It was Olivia.

Wren let out a sigh of relief when she disappeared from view. *Poor Olivia,* Wren thought. This would devastate her. She had already lost her parents, her granduncle, and now her grandaunt? Wren shoved down her guilt. Greer should have thought of that before she'd gotten into this whole dirty business. Wren wasn't going to let herself and Lucas be executed to protect Olivia's feelings. Her friend would get over it. In time.

When the coast was clear, Wren turned out of the kitchen and came face-to-face with Marina. Wren inhaled a sharp breath, her heart jumping like a startled rabbit in her chest. "Gods, Marina!" she said.

Marina walked into the kitchen, a smirk wide on her face. "The murderess herself," she said. "Here for another victim?"

"I'm not a murderer," Wren said.

"That's not what they're saying," Marina said, spinning a measuring spoon that had been discarded on the countertop. "And if you're not a murderer, why did you run? The guards saw you and Hale fleeing the building this morning."

"I didn't run," Wren said. "I went to get an antidote. And now I'm back."

"But not really, are you?" Marina said. "Or you wouldn't be skulking about. Perhaps I'll just holler for the closest guards."

"Don't!" Wren hissed, her eyes wide.

"You're a danger and a menace. My father says it served Sable right, getting poisoned. Teach her to take in mongrels like you. You don't belong here."

Another time, Marina's words might have stung her. Wren had wanted desperately to fit in here, to find her place. But her entire universe had narrowed to one focus: Greer. Wren simply didn't have time for this. "I don't care what you think of me, Marina. I didn't kill Kasper and I didn't poison Sable. I'm going to prove it."

"Not from the Block you aren't," Marina said. "I'm sure the Grand Inquisitor will be eager to meet you."

Wren growled, her nerves as tight as a taut bowstring. She wasn't going to let Marina's petty vendetta against her jeopardize her last chance of clearing her name.

In one fluid motion, Wren seized a copper-bottomed pot off the stove and whacked Marina across the head with it. The girl crumpled to the floor, as limp as an empty sack of flour.

Wren's eyes went wide as she regarded Marina's unconscious form. Blood dribbled from a cut on the girl's forehead, and her glasses had skittered across the floor. Horror filled her. Had Wren hit her too hard? Gods, had she killed Marina? Wren knelt down, feeling for Marina's pulse. It was there. Fluttering against her throat, but there. Wren blew out a deep breath. Thank the Beekeeper.

Wren smoothed back Marina's hair and tried to arrange her body in a less awkward angle, sending the girl a silent apology.

Shoving down her trepidation, Wren poked her head into the hallway. It was empty. She darted to the next teaching kitchen and through the door, breathing a sigh of relief. Her macarons sat on the marble counter where she had left them, neatly wrapped in brown paper and twine. She ripped open the package, shoving the first cookie in her mouth—lemon studded with flecks of basil. Tangy and chewy, the macaron's magic glittered on her tongue, a last lifeline in a sinking sea of danger. She grabbed another one—a green pistachio, biting into it before she had fully downed the last. Her life had once been so simple, about the uncomplicated monotony of making confections. Day after day in the kitchens, forming and stirring and drizzling. Now… she didn't know what she had become. Skulking and attacking and falling from roofs and picking locks and wolfing down an entire pack of macarons. She'd thought she had left all of this behind when she had joined the guild. Turned her back on those who had turned their backs on her. But somehow the danger had found her again, in a new and more sophisticated form.

Wren polished off the chocolate mocha now, unsure if she was still eating for comfort or for luck. As she swallowed thickly, she set down the box, knowing she had delayed enough. This luck would have to be enough to get her into Greer's rooms.

She next filled up a little herb pouch with salt from the shaker, tying it off and tucking it in her pocket. She would have to test the contents of the bottles to be sure they contained the Gemini poison.

The hallway was deserted. She backtracked and mounted the servants' stairway to the second floor. Her heart hammered and her palms sweated. This was her one chance. If she was taken by the guards, she'd never have another opportunity to prove Greer's guilt. She couldn't fail.

As she repeated those words in her head like a mantra, Wren rounded the stairs. And came face-to-face with a maid. She drew in a sharp breath. Would she have to leave a trail of unconscious bodies in her wake?

But the maid just bobbed a curtsey, hurrying past her and down the stairs. She didn't seem to know who Wren was or that she was wanted by the entire guild.

Wren breathed a sigh of relief, continuing on her way. She smiled grimly at her luck. Finally, her Gift was coming in handy.

She reached the door to Greer's rooms and paused with her hand poised over the handle. What if the woman was inside? She usually was bustling about the Guildhall during the day, directing servants, taking inventory, working in the office. But what if she wasn't today? With Sable's poisoning and the investigators in the hall... who knew what the woman was up to? Indecision plagued her. She didn't want to confront the woman outright; it would be Wren's word against Greer's. But she had to do something. She was so close.

Her decision was made for her as a set of booted footsteps sounded up the far stairway. Someone was coming. Wren turned the handle and slipped inside, shutting the door quickly.

She surveyed the room and sagged in relief against the door. It was empty and quiet. The room smelled of roses, the myriad vases now filled with tender pink blossoms. They didn't look like the rooms of a murderer. But what had she expected? Vials of blood and torture implements hanging from the wall? Wren knew better than most that people weren't always what they seemed.

In the closet, a dozen ornate glass bottles of colored and clear glass glittered on Greer's vanity. The bottle that Wren had been smelling when Greer snapped at her had been made of lavender glass with a cork stopper.

Wren took it and carried it to the desk. She didn't want the poison to touch her skin, but she didn't know any other way to do this. As long as she didn't ingest it, she should be fine. Plus, the poison had two halves. Hopefully, this half was the same half as she had eaten in the cupcake. Or if the cupcake poison was the other half, perhaps it had worn off. If she didn't find out, she'd be dead anyway. Her luck would have to hold.

Wren took out the stopper and placed the heel of her hand against the opening, turning it over, letting the liquid splash against her skin. She re-stoppered the bottle and took the little pouch of salt out of her pocket. She rubbed a few grains of salt on her hand. Nothing.

She looked at the other bottles, repocketing the salt packet. Had she remembered wrong? Was it one of the other bottles? Or had Greer gotten rid of the poison altogether? The thought chilled Wren. If that was the case, she'd never be able to prove Greer's guilt. No one would believe Wren that she had seen the discoloration on Greer's fingers. Not when she had such a motivation to point the finger at another.

Wren sighed, looking down. Her eyes widened and she let out a gasp of disbelief. There on her palm was a spot of blue.

Even as elation flooded her, a sadness did as well. This meant that Greer actually killed her brother. As much as the pieces had fit together, Wren hadn't wanted to believe that.

"Why did you do it?" Wren asked, looking at the bottle.

"An intriguing question." Greer's voice came from behind her.

CHAPTER 36

Greer stood calm and serene, wreathed by the closet door. She wore a navy blue dress trimmed in eyelet lace, and her flaxen hair was swept back in a twist.

Wren eyed her warily, the bottle gripped tightly in her palm. Her mind raced through her options. She had planned to leave the poison here to be discovered later. If she took it with her, it would be her word against Greer's that she had discovered it in the Guildmistress's rooms.

"Marina will be fine," Greer said, her smooth face impassive. "You should have hit her harder. She scampered off to find me the second she came to."

Wren was silent. She had no words, no plan, no clever retorts.

"Poor Wren," Greer said. "I see you thinking hard, looking for a way out. By now, you've realized that there isn't one. I'm sorry it came to this. You were simply an expedient scapegoat."

"Why?" Wren asked. While she was stalling, she was genuinely curious as well. "Why did you kill your own brother?"

Greer's gaze hardened, and she paced before the doorway, as if choosing her words carefully.

"Kasper was a sentimental fool. He had all the power in the world, power that should have been mine by rights, but he had no ambition. He would have been content to putter around his kitchen making peanut brittle all his life, squandering the Gift the Beekeeper had given him. The only reason he even rose to guildmaster was because I made it so! Not that it ever benefited me in the end. But when I found out that Kasper was going to throw all of his power and influence away by crossing the king and revealing the secret of the Gifted... I couldn't let him be so foolish. Just because some peasants died of plague?"

"Thousands died!" Wren said, shivering at her memories of watching from her little room above Oldrick's shop as carts of bodies passed by.

"The secret of the Gifts are what keep Alesia strong. And what keeps the guilds in power. Showing their hand would make the guilds an enemy of the king and put a target on all of our backs. How long do you think it would take before Aprica invaded? The Ferwich clans? Before the Gifted were assassinated, picked off one by one? Or taken, enslaved to new masters? No, it could not be. I knew Kasper's plan was folly, that he and Chandler had lost their minds over their dream of an egalitarian future where Gifted skipped through the meadows with poor and rich alike. It's a fantasy!"

"So you killed him over a... policy disagreement?" As much as Wren was horrified by what Greer was saying, a small part of her agreed. In the minutes she had known Kasper, she had seen the light in him. The hope and joy and sparkle that didn't fit into this dark world. Optimism was not a quality that lasted long under the crushing weight of reality. The fact that Kasper had held on to his for so long was nothing short of a miracle, but it was a miracle that had blinded him. Blinded him to the gritty, ugly truth of what revealing the Gifts could do. It could be the end of the Gifted, the Guilds. Or worse.

"Kasper and I debated the prospect of revealing the Gifted until we were blue in the face. The man was as stubborn as a mule. So when I was approached about a solution, I knew it was my patriotic duty to assist." Greer idly stroked a jewel-toned scarf hanging on the wall.

"And I'm sure you were handsomely compensated as well." Wren's eyes narrowed.

Greer lifted her chin defiantly. "One doesn't take a risk for no reward.

Kasper didn't understand that. I ran this Guild for the last twenty years. I had the business sense and could have been the most powerful woman in Maradis. If not for the unfortunate circumstances of our births. That should have been *my* Gift," Greer said. "But he took it, and he squandered it. And more than that. He kept me here, practically his prisoner, to serve as guildmistress. Guildmistress! Pah." Greer let out a sharp bark of laughter. "I was a glorified servant. Francis met with kings and diplomats, brokered deals and made fortunes. I decided which tea to serve them."

"What do you mean, practically his prisoner? Couldn't you have left?" Wren furrowed her brow. She needed to extricate herself, but she found herself stalling. She genuinely wanted to understand why this woman had killed her brother.

"You know that in Alesia, women are only allowed to marry if their male guardian allows it?"

Wren nodded.

"Kasper refused to let me marry again. After Carter died..." Her blue eyes went hazy for a moment before hardening. "He said I couldn't be trusted. With a husband. Or children. Or... a family-in-law."

"Why would he...?" Wren trailed off, memories surfacing of her second day at the Guild when the seamstress flitted about her with a measuring tape, telling the tragic story of how Earl Greer's entire family had died shortly after he had, shortly after Iris Greer had lost her baby and been turned out.

"Bad meat... was it?" Wren said slowly, grasping the bottle of poison in her sweaty hand. Dear gods, the woman had poisoned her late husband's whole family?

A predatory smile crossed Greer's face. "They deposited me in a carriage and hustled me down the street before my baby's body was cold. Without a Greer heir in my belly, I was nothing to them. They had never wanted Carter to marry me. I was too lowborn, too uncultured. They deserved what they got." Greer was now winding the scarf between her tight fists in an unconscious gesture.

Wren backed up a step.

"I didn't get what I deserved, though." Greer's voice thundered, hard as iron. "Because I was a lowly woman without an heir, the Greer riches went to some third cousin in Tamros. Francis was so horrified by the whole affair he refused to let me marry again. I lost my chance to have children. To have a life. A place in society. A household to run. All because Kasper was so syrupy-sweet that he couldn't get past what I had done."

"I'm… sorry," was all Wren could think to say.

"But it's not too late for me, you see. Why do you think I take such pains to keep up with fashions, to stay looking young?"

"You plan to marry?"

"I was made me an offer I couldn't refuse. A handsome husband, a position in court, riches beyond any charity Kasper deigned to give me. A guardian who would approve any choice I made. A chance for the life Kasper refused me. Finally." Greer heaved a huge sigh, closing her eyes for a moment, as if telling her tale had unburdened her.

Wren tensed to run, but Greer snapped her eyes open, stepping into the closet doorway.

"Why are you telling me all this?" Wren asked.

"Because no one will believe you," Greer said confidently. "I'd just kill you myself, but the king needs someone to publically take the fall for Kasper's death. Give the people the closure of an execution. I thought you'd appreciate understanding why you were sacrificed in the end. It's for the greater good. If that brings you some comfort."

"*Your* greater good! Don't you think people will wonder why Kasper's sister has suddenly risen in fortune?" Wren asked. "They're not fools."

"They won't wonder after I catch the murderer of the head of the Confectioner's Guild," Greer said, a sly smile crossing her face.

Wren felt like a mouse being eyed by a cat.

"And when Callidus discovers the threat from Guildmaster Chandler, so carefully hidden away in Kasper's desk, they will discover your puppet master. Because everyone knows a simple girl such as yourself couldn't have planned and executed such a daring murder. Once he is linked to you, both of you will meet the headmaster's axe. And that inspector too. The one who tried to cover it all up."

Wren's mouth tightened in anger. Greer may have had tragedy in her past, but she had chosen her own path. To kill. At least the planted letter was gone, and there was no way to link Chandler to her or Lucas. At least Chandler would be spared this vicious charade. Now if only she could save Lucas.

"Lucas has nothing to do with any of this," Wren pleaded. "Leave him out of it." The poison was heavy in Wren's hand—the only real evidence linking Greer to the crime. Her best laid plans were gone, and she had no idea what to do. This woman had boxed her in on all sides.

"I'm sorry. We can't do that. He was foolish enough to vouch for you. He will pay the price."

Wren panicked, adrenaline surging in her. If her time on the streets had taught her anything, it was that when talking and threats and bravado ran dry, there was only one option. Run.

She bolted for the door, rushing past Greer. The woman grabbed her arm with an iron grip, pinning her against the doorway. Wren struggled, trying to pull her arm free. The older woman was surprisingly strong.

Greer's gloating grin was macabre, chilling. It filled Wren with anger, drowning out the fear. She pulled the top off the bottle of Gemini poison and threw it in Greer's face.

The woman recoiled, gasping and sputtering. The opening was all Wren needed. She shouldered Greer aside and sprinted out the door.

The hallway was filled with six armed men in brown uniforms of the Cedar Guard. Wren's momentum bowled her into the first, and he reached up with his gloved hand, took her by the neck, and slammed her against the floor.

Wren slipped into blackness.

CHAPTER 37

She saw her journey to the Block in flickers and glimpses, her head a pounding mess of fog and pain. Her feet knocked against stairs as she was half-carried, half-dragged down to the main floor of the Guildhall. Marina stood by the door, a bloody rag pressed to her forehead and a look of dark satisfaction on her face. Lennon stood next to her, his brown hair mussed, his eyes wide.

She reached out a hand towards him. "Help…" she thought she managed before she was through the door into the blinding sunlight of the morning. And then there was only blackness as she was tossed inside a dark prison carriage, just a hard box on four wheels. When they turned off Guilders' Row onto the cobblestone streets of the Guild Quarter, the thunks of the carriage wheels set her reeling, her teeth clacking together until she tasted blood. There was cold sweat and sharp breaths and then nothing as she lost consciousness once again.

Wren woke on a hard stone bench. She opened her eyes with a groan and revised her assessment. It was the floor. She was in a cell. Forbidding gray stones pressed around her claustrophobically.

Her head pounded as if a herd of wild horses had been set loose inside it. She sat up, holding her temples to keep the room from spinning. It didn't work.

"Easy there," a woman said, reaching out a hand to steady Wren.

Wren jerked away, the sudden movement setting her head rattling once again.

"I won't hurt you," the woman said. "Just another prisoner like yourself."

The cell came into focus as Wren's vision cleared. A huddled shape sat across from her, her eyes shining in the torchlight of the hallway.

"Where are we?" Wren croaked.

"The Block," the woman said. "Women's quarters."

Wren shuddered.

"Want some water?" the woman asked. "That's all I can offer you."

Wren nodded, and the woman lifted a wooden cup from a bucket. The water tasted of stale sawdust, but it helped clear her senses.

"Thank you," Wren said, handing it back. "I thought everyone was thrown together in the Block? Not that I'm complaining," she amended.

"Used to be that way, I hear. The women kept dying. Those they want to keep alive, they put in here. The guards and interrogators still sometimes take advantage, but you can live through it."

Wren shuddered, closing her eyes to the horror of it, and realizing that the horror was inside her own head—as well as all around her. Nowhere was safe. She had to keep it together. Think. Not let her fear paralyze her.

"How long have I been in here?" Wren asked.

"Few hours," the woman said. "Got a pretty hard bump on the head. I'm Penelope," she added.

"Wren. What are you in here for?"

"My husband's fault," Penelope said, the anger in her words palpable.

"Did you kill him?" Wren asked.

Penelope barked a laugh. "No, though if I got my hands on him now, I just might. He tried to play tough in some trade negotiations with

Steward Willings. We own a lead mine in the mountains. Threatened to withhold the product unless our terms were met. I told him that we would never get a fair price from the king, but he's so naive! Took over after his father died last year."

"What happened?" Wren asked. "How did you end up here?"

"That bastard Willings told my husband that they would be withholding his wife until he stopped withholding the lead."

"Your husband didn't give them what they wanted?"

"He did! Of course. I wouldn't have married a man who'd choose lead over me. But that was a month ago. They haven't released me. I've been told I'm being held for 'insurance.'"

Wren shook her head in disgust. "For how long?"

"Don't know," Penelope said glumly.

Wren saw now that under the layer of grime, Penelope's dress had once been fine, a thick damask fabric. She didn't think she'd live long enough for her dress to get that dirty.

"What about you?" Penelope asked.

"I'm being framed for murder," Wren said, resigned. "The worst part is, I finally figured out who did it. But it was done at the king's behest."

Penelope *tsked*. "Can you blame it on someone else? As long as they have someone to take the fall, it doesn't have to be you, right?"

Wren thought of Chandler, his warm smile and grandfatherly affect. She shook her head. "I couldn't do that. I couldn't live with myself."

"Better living with regret than dying without," Penelope said. "Your honor won't keep you warm in the grave."

Wren pulled her knees against her chest and rested her chin on them. "I think it's too late for me," she said. "My fate was set before Kasper even died. I just didn't know it."

"Given up, have you?"

"The worst part is that I'm not the only one who will suffer. If I die, a man… a man I care about is doomed as well."

"Then you better not give up," Penelope said. "Despair suffocates in a place like this."

"I don't know what I can do," Wren said. "I don't think I'll be around long enough for despair to get me. The headsman will be quicker."

As Wren's words echoed through the cell, the door flew open, making them both jump. In the doorway stood a tall, broad man with a bald head that shone in the flickering light. He was finely dressed in the king's emerald colors, but the broadsword at his hip and the dark expression on his face told her all she needed to know. This was the Grand Inquisitor.

"That one." He pointed. "The confectioner. Take her."

Two guards half-marched, half-dragged Wren through the cellblock. She found her legs weren't working very well, her knees weak.

Hands reached through the bars as they passed, coated in grease and grime. Through the bars of other cells came lewd names and threats as the prisoners recognized that there was a woman in their midst.

They turned a corner and entered a room filled with horrors. The torches' flickering shadows fell on a table of wicked blades and screws, along with a long, low table that she could only assume was a rack. The metallic tang of blood mixed with the acid of urine flooded her senses, a potent cocktail that made her stomach roil.

Cold sweat pricked her skin as the guards set her in a chair and fixed her wrists to the arms with leather straps. Then they left, the door swinging closed with an ominous thud behind them. Wren sucked in a deep breath, desperately trying to find a place of calm. She had been hurt before, wounded, beaten. She knew physical pain—the gnawing ache of a belly that hadn't eaten in weeks, the burn of frostbitten toes coming back to life, the sting of a constable's lash. None of it had broken her, she told herself. *But none of those pains,* her inner voice spit right back, *was the artist that Grand Inquisitor Killian is rumored to be.*

The Grand Inquisitor took a leather apron off the wall and pulled it over his head, tying it behind his back. Then he pulled a stool out of the corner and sat upon it. A smile flashed across his face as he regarded her, but it was gone before she was sure it hadn't been her imagination. "Do you know who I am?" he asked.

"You're Killian. The Grand Inquisitor." Her words sounded small, scurrying like mice into the corners of this horrible room.

"And you know why I'm here?"

She looked at him, the easy seat he took, one ankle crossed over his other knee, his back straight. So arrogant and cocksure. "You're here to question me. About the murder of Guildmaster Kasper and the attempted murder of Grandmaster Sable."

"Smart girl," he said, flicking an invisible piece of dust off his apron.

"But that's not exactly right. I'm here to take your confession."

"My confession?" she asked.

"Yes. That is my task. I can take it willingly or by force." He leaned forward, meeting her gaze with his own black eyes. "It is up to you."

She leaned towards him, as far as the restraints would let her. Her heart thundered in her chest. "I didn't kill Kasper, and I didn't try to kill Sable. But I know who did. I can give you the real killer. And proof, too."

"The hard way then," he said, standing.

"Wait!" she said. "I'm telling you the truth. I didn't murder anyone. I'm innocent. It was Iris Greer, Guildmistress of the Confectioner's Guild."

He stood at the table, considering the various implements, running his fingers over them as a piano player might play a scale he knew by heart.

"The Guildmistress?" he said. "And Kasper's sister, if I remember correctly. Surely, you could have picked a more probable murderer to accuse."

"I didn't choose to accuse her," Wren said. "She killed him. Then she tried to kill Sable because Sable found out the truth."

"Did she?" the inquisitor asked, picking up a thin silver pin and holding it up to the torchlight. "And did you discover what possessed the Guildmistress to murder her own flesh and blood?"

"Because Kasper and the other guildmembers were threatening to reveal..." Wren paused, the secret of the Gift about to spill out of her. The wine wasn't reacting. Which meant that this man knew about the Gifted. And if he knew about the Gifted...

Wren's eyes widened as the pieces fit into place. How blind she'd been! If it *was* the king and Steward Willings who had truly conspired with Greer to murder Kasper, surely the inquisitor knew it. He was the king's righthand man, the sword that carved through the flesh of the king's enemies. Her pleading for him to listen to her about the conspiracy was a fool's errand. If it was truly the king, her fate was sealed.

His grin had split wide, revealing straight white teeth.

"You're here to frame me for Guildmaster Kasper's murder," Wren whispered. "And the poisoning of Grandmaster Sable."

A laugh escaped from him, surprisingly warm against the chill of the dark room. "Like I said. I'm here to take your confession."

She felt hollow as the weight of her predicament settled upon her. There was no way out. No hope of convincing this man of the truth, no proving herself innocent. He knew the truth. And he was here to ensure it died with her.

"I admit, I'm a little impressed that you figured it out. I thought we had covered our tracks well. Willings had been working on Greer for two years. She was our secret weapon."

"I'm frequently underestimated," Wren said numbly.

The inquisitor chuckled. "I'm afraid your pluck won't save you, as charming as it may be." He waved the long needle he held over the nearby candle, making its tip glow an angry red. "And so I say again. I'm here for your confession."

"No," she breathed. "You may be able to pin the murders on me, but I won't help you do it. I won't confess."

"I was hoping you'd say that." He crossed the room and clutched her hand in one lithe stride. And then he began to push the needle under her fingernail, and she began to scream.

CHAPTER 38

When the guards deposited Wren back in her cell, she crumpled to the floor, numb with shock. Penelope hurried to her side as the door slammed behind her.

"Can I get you anything?" she asked. "Water…?"

Wren leaned back against the door, closing her eyes as tears leaked down her cheeks.

"Water… would be good," she finally said hoarsely.

She took the cup as Penelope handed it to her, reaching with her good hand. She risked a glance at her fingers on the other hand and quickly looked away, nausea roiling within her. Her fingernails were mangled and bloody, her pinky fingernail hanging on by a thread. Her hand radiated pain like an angry sun, smothering her thoughts with its dull roar. The inquisitor had been about to start on her other hand when he was called away.

"Don't miss me too much," he had said with mock sweetness, his face swimming dangerously close to her own. "I have so much I want to share with you."

"Oh, your nails," Penelope said, her voice full of sympathy. "He often starts with that, I hear."

A sick sense of curiosity came over Wren. "What comes next?" she whispered.

Penelope's face twisted as she bit her lip.

"Never mind," Wren said. "It's probably better not to know."

"I'm sorry," Penelope said. "You seem more... composed than some of the other girls coming out of Killian's chamber, if that makes you feel better."

Wren let out a bitter laugh. "A little, I guess. I told myself that I would be strong, that he wouldn't break me. But who am I kidding? A few more minutes and I would have given him anything. There's no hope."

"Can't you give him what he wants? He likes it when they resist; it excites him."

"He wants me to confess to the murder. But he knows I'm innocent, the bastard." Wren's hands tightened into fists and she hissed as a wave of pain rolled over her.

Penelope's eyes were sympathetic.

"He'll keep torturing me until I yield, won't he?" Wren asked.

She nodded. "No need to put yourself through it, is there? If there's no other way..."

"None that I can think of," Wren said. All of her efforts and schemes, uncovering the truth, it meant nothing in the end. She was completely powerless against the might of these foes. Her only hope of rescue had been Guildmaster Sable and Hale, but who knew if Sable would ever wake up. Maybe she was dead already. Perhaps Grandmaster Chandler—when he realized she never showed up to the meeting? But if the king and his lackeys were trying to frame Chandler, then trying to help her would only damn him further. No, it could not be.

"I'm in this alone," she finally admitted. "Except for poor Lucas, whom I will take down with me."

"Who?" Penelope asked.

"I can't confess," Wren explained. "A friend... he vouched for me. If I confess, I will be dooming him as well." As much as the thought chilled her, it also strengthened her resolve. She could withstand Killian's attentions. Not for herself, but for Lucas.

"He must be some fellow."

"He is," Wren whispered, his face appearing in her mind's eye, the crinkles at the corner of his eyes when he smiled, the way he ruffled his hand over his hair.

Penelope sighed. "Wren... no one defies Killian. Not trained warriors, not hardened criminals. The man is ruthless. He sews rats into people's stomachs and lets them eat their way out."

Wren flinched, her mangled hand inadvertently straying to her stomach.

"Don't put yourself through his machinations needlessly. If he is determined that you confess, you will confess. Unless he accidentally kills you first."

Wren grimaced. "Thanks for the glad tidings, Penelope," she said.

"I'm sorry," Penelope whispered again, her eyes glittering with tears. "I've seen a few girls come in and out of here... just spare yourself the pain."

The cell door opened and torchlight flooded into the cell.

Wren's heart was in her throat, her eyes wide. But the silhouette was not Killian's. A reed-thin youth entered the room bearing a tray. In the flickering light, his face looked no more than sixteen. His eyes were wide, as if he had more to fear from them than they from him.

The other woman rose, keeping the wary distance of a wild animal lured close with the promise of food.

There were two bowls on his tray, and Penelope snatched hers away as he offered it. Oily stew with a heel of hard bread, from the look of it. The last thing Wren's stomach wanted was food, but she needed to eat. As the boy held her bowl out to Wren, he looked her straight in the eye. "This one is for you," he said. "Just you."

Wren froze as he withdrew, disappearing and shutting the door as quickly as he had appeared.

"How odd," Penelope said.

Wren looked down at her bowl. In addition to the soup and bread was a thick slice of white cheese with a shadowed blue rind.

"You got cheese?" Penelope asked around a mouthful of stew.

Just you, he had said.

"I think…" Wren said, suddenly aware of Penelope's interest resting heavily on her and the cheese. "It might be poisoned."

Instantly, the other woman leaned back imperceptibly.

Wren's mind whirled. Poisoned… or something else? Could it be that she wasn't entirely without allies after all? She had met the Head of the Cheesemonger's Guild, after all. A Gifted master.

She thought of the boy's youth and nerves. Had he infiltrated the Block to get her this cheese? For what end? Did she dare think that it was infused with the magic of intelligence and intellect? Or could it be actually poisoned?

Well, she told herself, then she would be rid of Killian, and Lucas would be free. Either way, this was the best option she had.

She took a bite.

The salty tang of the cheese flooded her mouth. Creamy and as smooth as a dream, with a hard rind—the richness of the cheese belonged in a palace, not these macabre surroundings. It was the stuff of kings and monarchs, not condemned confectioners.

"Well?" Penelope asked. "You think it's poisoned? It's a strange thing to poison, cheese. How do they even get it in there?"

Wren shook her head, swallowing, not wanting the perfection of the flavor to leave her. "I don't think it's poisoned," she finally managed.

The next instant the tingles began—an effervescence that spilled from her tongue through her whole body, right down to her mangled fingertips. It swirled through her mind, a whirlwind of texture and awareness, taking her world-weary intellect and shooting it through with a pure bolt of energy. Connections, insights, brilliance dazzled through her, as if her mind had suddenly been welcomed into a vast new library of knowledge. A disbelieving laugh bubbled forth from her. The cheese was truly infused. With a gift of the mind. Perhaps the guildmasters did not have the means to save her. So they did their best to help her save herself. But… that wasn't possible. She was beyond saving. But Lucas…

Her thoughts whirled, faster, faster, computations and calculations and connections firing and tallying. Wren leaped to her feet.

She knew what to do.

Wren pounded on the door, excitement bubbling within her. "Guards!" she shouted. "I want to see the inquisitor!"

"Wren—" Penelope hissed.

The guard peered through the bars at her. "Girl, no one *asks* to see the inquisitor."

"Well, I do," she said. "I'm ready to confess."

The Grand Inquisitor's guards took her back to the room of horrors. Was it the inquisitor's office? Fresh blood gleamed on one of the screws on the table. The new universe of her mind offered her hundreds of possibilities for its use. She shuddered. Sometimes ignorance was preferable.

One of the cheese's side effects was to allow her a blessedly dispassionate evaluation of her circumstances. The verdict was in, the results were unassailable. The chances of she and Lucas both getting out of this mess alive were infinitesimal. But she could save Lucas. If she struck the right bargain.

The inquisitor entered, exuding power and barely-restrained violence. He wore no jacket, and his sleeves were rolled up, revealing muscled forearms. His brocade violet waistcoat hung unbuttoned. She was surprised to see that he was handsome—a chiseled jawline, a finely-wrought mouth, and dark eyebrows that hinted at what color his hair would be if he hadn't shaved it bald. She had been too terrified to notice the last time she had sat in this room.

"Am I to understand you've had a change of heart?" he asked, ushering her to sit in the chair. His manners were as pleasant as a diplomat's.

She sat.

He didn't bother to tie her arms to the chair. Apparently, they were now talking man to man, so to speak, rather than torturer to tortured.

"You've put me in a bit of a bind," she said.

"One of my favorite pastimes," he said, flashing a predatory grin.

She suppressed a shudder of disgust, forcing herself to hold his gaze, forcing her injured hand to lay still on the arm of the chair, rather than curl against her body for protection. "I understand that I will confess, one way or the other. Eventually."

"You've come to terms with it sooner than most," he said. "I admit I'm disappointed."

Her nostrils flared in distaste. However handsome he was, the man was abhorrent. "There is another for me to consider."

A look of confusion crossed his face before realization dawned on him. "Lucas Imbris," he said. "I'd heard the two of you had grown close."

"Yes."

"In over his head, that fool boy. The king was most displeased upon his return. I told him not to let his children galivant around Maradis, playing as priests and scholars and inspectors. But kings think they know better."

"You see the trouble it places me in. I can't confess without dooming him. And whereas I might yield to save myself more pain, I will fight with all I have to spare him." She had thought long and hard about whether the king would truly kill his own son just to spite him. From what she knew of the king's character, about his esteem for his younger children, the answer was *yes*. Or at least, it wasn't a clear *no*. She had to do this.

"What do you propose?" he asked.

"I'll confess. Write it out," she said. "You have your scapegoat. But I want you to spare Lucas. I know the laws are malleable in Alesia. The king can pardon him."

He *tsked*. "You presume that your confession is worth such bargaining power. I'm afraid that's far from the case. I could get it without making any concessions."

"The guilds, the city, they know of your skills, your interrogation... tactics." She twisted the word. "There will always be doubt whether you coerced a false confession from me. But if I give it freely, appear before them whole and unharmed..." *Mostly whole,* she thought.

He stood, seeming to ponder her proposal, pacing twice before the cell door. "I could make you such a deal. But there would be a condition."

"What?" she asked warily.

"You will also confess that your actions were directed by Guildmaster Chandler."

Her breath stilled. Give up Chandler? Why? Even as she thought the word, the connections formed, showing her Killian's aim.

"I see," she said. "All the evidence linking Chandler to the crime is circumstantial. Maybe you can make the case, but it's tenuous. He has powerful friends. It won't look good that the crown is pressing the case against him so hard."

"But if we have an incriminating witness…" Killian said.

"There will be no doubt."

"You choose. Chandler or Lucas."

Either way, her life was forfeit. Could she lie and doom Chandler to this fate? Do damage to the cause of the guilds, help the king? She thought of his kind eyes, of Bianca's, his wife's, gentle smile. They didn't deserve this.

But… her mind buzzed like a hive of honeybees. A new path opened up before her, a desperate, last-ditch fool of a plan that would most likely get all of them killed. Or… it could save them all. She ran through the permutations again, the myriad scenarios playing out in an instant. Yes, it *could* work.

"Agreed," she said. "I'll testify against Chandler. Tell them that he paid me to murder his rival Kasper to increase his guild's influence."

Killian's gaze warmed. "Excellent. Guards," he called, "fetch me paper and ink."

"I have one more condition."

"I don't think you understand how negotiation works, girl," he said. "You need to have leverage to make demands."

"It's a small thing. An indulgence that will help you as well. I want to confess publicly at my execution. And I want Greer there sitting in the front row, so I can look her in the eyes as I die. So she knows I'll be waiting when the Huntress comes for her."

"Impossible," he said. "Give you a platform to spout off accusations? You must think me a fool."

"You forget, you have Lucas's life in your hands. I know it is forfeit if I don't behave. A public confession will be better for the king anyway, an accusation of Chandler that will shock the city, ring through the guilds. Invite the guild heads so they will all be there to witness his downfall. After the performance I put on, there will be no way anyone can accuse you of forcing me to speak the words. All this, before the drama of me losing my head."

He considered. "I cannot agree to a public confession. Can't have your fellow guild members making some last-ditch defense of your innocence. But I can secure Greer's attendance. And the attendance of a few more. A private party of sorts. Witnesses to your final hours. And Chandler's."

Wren nodded curtly, her heart sinking a little lower into the blackness that already surrounded it. Though she didn't know if she had any friends left at the guild, part of her still hoped they cared. That they would take note, perhaps be there at the end. Killian had dashed those hopes, like he had dashed all others.

"Why do you want this? Truly? Not just for revenge with Greer."

She offered him an answer that held a kernel of truth. "I don't want to die alone."

He stroked his chin, as clean shaven as his bald head, before giving a curt nod. "You have a deal."

CHAPTER 39

The inquisitor brushed aside his instruments of pain and cruelty to make room for Wren to write her confession. She took the quill with clumsy fingers still roaring with pain from Killian's earlier attentions. Slowly, she penned her confession, the spiderweb of lies that would seal her fate and perhaps Chandler's. She risked so much... too much? She couldn't know. Though doubts plagued her, the clarity that had come from the infused cheese soothed her fears like a balm. She finally had all the pieces, saw all the angles. It was time for one final gamble.

When she was done, Killian picked up the parchment and read it. "Very eloquent," he praised. "Quite a tale indeed. You could have had a future in the arts of espionage. Together with your Gift... it's really a shame to lose such an asset."

She sighed. She was growing weary of bantering with this horrible man. "Is it sufficient?" she asked.

"Indeed. You have met your terms. Lucas is being released—"

"Lucas!" she exclaimed. "He's here? Why?"

"He *did* vouch for you," Killian explained, as if to a child. "So I was within my rights to arrest him. I brought him here to ensure you were properly... motivated... to confess."

"You're a bastard," Wren hissed, a low anger thrumming in her veins.

"Spare me your righteous indignation. He's being released as we speak. But he *will* be at the execution. To remind you what you have to lose if you get any... wild ideas."

Wren found strange comfort at the thought that Lucas would be at the execution. If her plan went awry, at least there would be one kind face to look on as she left this world.

"When?" she asked simply.

"Tomorrow," he said.

"So soon?" she asked, her stomach dropping.

"The peace treaty with the Apricans failed. They already move on our border. The king has a war to fight; he can't be concerned with petty matters of guild politics."

"Is that what I am?" she said bitterly.

"Don't be morose," he said. "You're giving up your life in the service of your king. Think of yourself as a soldier of sorts. There are far more pointless ways to die."

They walked into the hallway together, side by side, the guards traveling behind them. It was almost like they were equals now. Co-conspirators in the king's grand design. Her mouth twisted in a hard line. The king deserved to pay for playing with their lives as if he were a puppet master. But he wouldn't, she knew. The rich and powerful never paid the price. Always people like her.

She was lost in a downward spiral of despairing thoughts when they almost crashed into another set of guards and a prisoner coming from an adjoining hallway.

"Lucas!" Wren said, her eyes roving over him for signs he had been mistreated. He looked tired and disheveled but unharmed.

"Wren," he breathed, his hand partially reaching for her before falling.

"How lovely." The inquisitor clapped his hands in mock delight. "A final reunion. And farewell."

"They say you confessed," Lucas said. "That you're to be executed tomorrow. I'm being released."

She looked at Killian, biting her lip. "Can we have a moment alone?"

"No." He snorted, crossing his arms and leaning against the wall.

She sighed, looking in Lucas's dark eyes, trying to say with her eyes what she couldn't with her lips. "I did confess," she said. "I deceived you. I did murder Kasper."

"But Chandler..." he said.

"Chandler was my patron in this dark deed," she said. "I'm sorry... for everything. I never wanted to lie to you. What was between us... It was real."

He shook his head, the muscles in his jaw working. She could see he didn't believe her. *Good,* she thought, a desperate relief flooding her. *Please don't believe me.* She didn't want him thinking the worst of her. To see disdain on his face, disgust where there had once been esteem... she thought it would shatter whatever fragments of her heart remained, whatever torn bits of her resolve.

"If you did this for me..." he said. "It's not right, for you to die... for me."

"You risked everything for a girl you had only just met," she said. "Am I not allowed to do the same for a man..." A man that I love, she realized. She wanted to say it. But not here. Not in this place, with the howls of prisoners and Killian's sneer bearing witness. Better it die with her. And so she finished her sentence. "That I respect."

"All right," Killian said, shoving off the wall. "Tearful goodbye time is over. I have places to be, people to torture."

Lucas's guards began pulling him down the hallway, away from her. "Wren!" The word was mangled.

"Thank you for these weeks," she called. "They were an undeserved gift. And Lucas..." she called. "The Destrier, keep him on his estate!"

Killian snorted as they kept walking. "Nice coded message. I hope you take comfort in the fact that Mr. Imbris is powerless in all of this."

"You're an ass," Wren grumbled under her breath. But her thoughts weren't on Killian. They were on Lucas and Chandler. She hoped upon hope that Lucas understood her message. Keep Chandler away. Give him an opportunity to escape, if her confession truly implicated him. If her tenuous plan went wrong.

Killian laughed out loud. "It's really a shame we have to kill you."

They reached a cell and the guard opened the door, shoving her inside.

"This is new," she said, looking around the interior, which boasted a small bed with a shabby straw mattress, a bucket of water, a table, and chairs. It almost looked like a room at an inn.

"I thought you could use a little comfort on your last night on earth."

"You don't want me talking to the other woman and telling her our little arrangement," she quipped.

"Smart girl." He shook his head with a rueful smile. "I could put you in with the men… You wouldn't get much talking done."

"This is fine," she said hastily. "Thank you. And I'd like to make a request for my last meal."

"Your last meal?" He arched an eyebrow. "You've heard about that, have you?"

The Block was notorious for two things. One, the cruel ends prisoners met inside it, and two, the elaborate last meals they earned before they died. Maradis was a city that loved its food, and this macabre little homage reflected that.

"I want puffed pancakes with maple syrup and fresh loganberries, and eggs scrambled with spinach and truffles, and bacon. The thick kind with peppered edges."

"Breakfast for your last meal?" He raised a dark eyebrow.

"Breakfast food is the most delicious," she said. "I never understood why such things were relegated to the morning."

"Very well." He inclined his head slightly. "I will have the guards inform the cuisinier of your order."

And with that, the door clicked closed.

Wren was deep in her own misery when her last supper was delivered hours later. The injured fingernails on her hand burned like fire when she moved, a palpable reminder of her weakness, her helplessness. Had she been a fool to agree to sell out Chandler in exchange for Lucas's life and one last shot at her own? It was bad enough that the king had gotten away with murdering Kasper, but if things went wrong, she'd be ridding them of another guildmaster in the process.

It wasn't *fair*. She had figured it out. She had solved the puzzle, had exposed the real killer. It should have been enough. It should be Greer in this cell, her last meal like ash on her tongue, while Wren was finally, after so many years, free to live her own life.

"Life isn't fair," she said out loud, reminding herself. The powerful have the means to keep their power, and the weak stay weak. She had learned that at a very young age. From her father, from the head of the Sower's orphanage, and then from Ansel and his gang. Just look at the guilds themselves—the Gifting. The entire system was designed to funnel wealth, power, and privilege up to those at the top, and ensure that no one else had access. It would take a revolution to change the way things were—a revolution that may or may not ever come. And she was out of time.

She had come so close. But in the end, close wouldn't matter.

Wren's dinner was getting cold, and so she tore herself from her rumination and dove in. She ate her eggs first, shaking on salt and pepper, enjoying each fluffy bite. Next she slathered the airy rounds of puffed pancake with glistening maple syrup, fresh succulent berries, and powdered sugar. Last, the bacon, thick crisp slices that mingled salty with sweet. She savored the interplay of flavors on her palate, the sensations of chewy and crispy and smooth. Taste and smell and touch—a good meal and a full belly—the sensations of being alive. The honesty of flavor and texture and pride of craft. These were the things she would miss when she was gone. When she was done, she picked up the plate and licked the maple syrup off it with a smile. Might as well enjoy every morsel.

And before she got up, she palmed the salt shaker and went to the little bed, hiding it beneath the pillow.

Sleep didn't come easily. Though the sharp insight the cheese had bestowed upon her lingered, those energies now turned to poking holes in her flimsy plan. So many roads led to death and ruin for her and Chandler, her and Lucas. There was only one thin chance where they all got through it alive. All she had to do was expose Greer in public, in a place where the king or his inquisitor could not deny her role without exposing their own. It was a ghost of a chance.

She thought of Lucas, the look on his face as she had passed him in the hallway. At least he believed she was innocent, despite her confession. He had been surprisingly loyal, from that first reckless moment in the Guildhall. She had never met a person like that before, she realized, a person so selfless. Who did something because it was the right thing to do, not because it benefitted him. And look how he had been repaid.

She grimaced. A hard lesson for him to learn, and she regretted that she had been the one to teach it to him. She regretted much when it came to Lucas. Perhaps it would have been better if he had never vouched for her, if they had executed her that first day after Kasper's death. Perhaps it would have been easier on everyone, herself included. If her foolhardy plan didn't work, she would most certainly be wishing that had occurred.

Perhaps her most poignant regret, though, if things all went south, was her betrayal of Hale and Sable. True, she hadn't actually betrayed them, but it hurt to know Wren might die leaving Hale to think she had. She didn't even know if Sable still lived. And then there was Olivia. All of them had shown true kindness to her. For a brief moment, a span of days, she had felt she belonged. There had been laughter, and fun, and hope. To think she might die a murderer in their eyes… it weighed upon her like a stone.

Eventually, the hallway outside her door grew silent. She sat up, peering out the bars. No guards. Moving quietly in the darkness, she tore a strip off the hem off her dress and filled it with a little pile of salt. With furtive movements, she twisted and tied it, then tucked it into the pocket of her dress. She lay back down. With a grim smile on her face, she drifted off to sleep.

CHAPTER 40

The morning came before she was ready. The clarity and dispassion of yesterday had fled completely, leaving her alone with her fears and worries. When the guard opened the door and revealed Killian as her escort, her stomach roiled with the terror of what this dawn brought with it. This was madness. Why had she so boldly agreed to the executioner's axe?

"Ready to meet the Huntress?" Killian asked, smelling of fresh soap and leather.

"Does anyone answer *yes* to that?" she grumbled.

"A few," he remarked thoughtfully. "Those who walk these halls have burdens a plenty. Some are ready to lay them down."

"I am only burdened by the truth," she said with a strength she did not feel. "But I suppose I'm not the only one to take the truth with me to my grave."

"No." He smirked. "You are not."

The execution was to take place at the municipal court, a brick building that sat in the center of Maradis amongst its government-building brethren. Its graceful bell tower stretched towards the turquoise sky, a hand trying to reach the heavens. As she sat in the carriage drawing her from the horrors of the Block to the horrors that would greet her next, she recalled that she had once seen an execution in the wide square before the court.

The square held stocks and a gallows, stern warnings to those who might think to cross Alesian justice. She had been eleven, she thought, in the height of her years in the Red Wraith gang. When she had happened upon the crowd, she'd figured there were too many pockets to pick to pass it all up. She hadn't realized why the crowd had developed until it was too late.

The suddenness of it had shocked her, the lack of drama and ceremony. Up the steps the man had been shuffled, world-weary with defeat in his eyes. Then the noose had gone around his neck, and then the bottom had dropped out from under him, and he'd hung, shaking and twitching, his face turning as purple as an eggplant. He hadn't died instantly. He had suffered.

Wren had frozen with her hand in a noble's pocket, so shocked by the display of casual brutality, stunning even for she, who had seen death. On the streets, boys and girls, men and women fought and struggled and bled, held on to life with a vise grip that betrayed the hopelessness of their circumstances. To see life snuffed out so quickly and efficiently… had been a surprise.

Well, now, she was glad for it. Glad that it would be over quickly, that Lucas and Greer and the rest of the treacherous nobles wouldn't see her fight and struggle and beg. A quick flash of the axe blade, and it would be done.

Killian was watching her from across the carriage, his dark eyes full of something that might have looked like compassion.

"You don't deserve the gallows," he said. "It's a crude death."

"The axe?" The word stuck in her throat.

"Lethal ingestion," he said. "A fitting end for a poisoner."

Wren blanched. She had never heard of the king executing prisoners via poison.

"Will it hurt?" she whispered.

"No. It makes the hurting finally stop."

Wren, Killian, and their Cedar guardsmen were the first through the courthouse door. The inside was crossed with soaring timbered beams, and the creamy plaster of the walls was adorned with portraits of past magisters in their black robes. The golden scales of justice inlaid in the parquet floor seemed a farce beneath her feet. The king held those scales in Maradis. And he tilted them how he pleased.

Wren's hands were unbound. Killian had not bothered restraining her, knowing the threat he held over Lucas shackled her tighter than any irons. She prayed that Lucas and Chandler would forgive her for her last-ditch plan. Either she would succeed and they would live, or she would fail and doom them all. She kept her hands in her pockets, half to keep them from shaking, and half to reassure herself that the precious little bundle she had squirreled away last night was still there. Yes, it was.

As they entered the chamber that would likely be her last glimpse of this world, Wren let out a bubble of manic laugher. "Where did you find an interior decorator who specializes in beheadings?"

Killian grinned a sly smile.

The room was round, with rows of seating lining the curving walls. Directly across the door was raised-box seating which must have housed the magister, and beside it a smaller box with an iron ring for manacles. For her. But in the middle, the middle was a massive oiled wood block, with a gleaming axe propped decorously on top of it. Channels in the floor began where the chopping block sat and ran between a row of seats and out through a tiny hole in the side of the room.

"The nobles demand things to be tidy. Nothing worse than attending a beheading and getting blood on your brocade slippers. But don't worry, sweet Wren. None of your scarlet blood will fill those marble veins. You'll die quietly in your chair."

She swallowed thickly. He reached out and twirled a lock of her auburn hair in his finger before letting it fall. "It is a shame I have to kill you," he murmured.

She stiffened, suppressing a shudder at his nearness.

"Please go sit. The rest of the attendees will be arriving soon."

The attendees. Like he was hosting a party. She turned to the little wooden box, biting her lip. Its yawning mouth mocked her, as if once she entered, she would be gobbled up forever. But its wooden sides and front would disguise any surreptitious actions she took from the eyes of the crowd. And so with steps of lead, Wren stepped into the box and sat.

Wren fiddled with the ragged hem of her dress as the room filled in, trying to focus on something, anything besides what was about to happen. The magister arrived, a fat beetle of a man with black robes and a shiny bald head. Next Wren caught sight of Guildmaster Pike in a fine crimson coat and polished black boots. He looked relaxed, leaning back in his seat, not meeting her eye. She found herself disappointed, expecting his to be a friendly face.

As more attendees arrived, the chattering voices, vibrant clothes, bursts of laughter, and the fragrant cups of coffee mingled together, threatening to overwhelm her. The reality of this day, this moment, this place, struck home as one figure walked through the door.

Greer. The woman wore an elegant gown of purple trimmed with thread of bronze. Wren recognized the seamstress Elda's masterful hand. Greer's blonde locks were twisted into a fancy knot, her face serene. She carried a lace handkerchief in her hand. The mourning sister, come to witness justice for her brother. She caught Wren's eye briefly, and then looked away at Wren's grim smile. *Good.* At the least the woman felt a kernel of guilt for dooming an innocent guildmember.

Greer sat across the room from her, halfway between the box and her door. Wren's mouth went dry. No, that wasn't right. Greer needed to be close to her for her last-ditch desperate scrap of a plan to work. *No, no, no.*

She flexed her hands to try to work some feeling back into them. Her injured nails screamed in protest, but she embraced the pain, wrapped herself around it, let it focus her. "I don't suppose—" she began.

"That I would spare your life?" Killian asked. "No, that I cannot do."

"Worth a try," she said weakly, her mind racing to think of what she could do.

"Would you mind moving Greer closer to the front?" she asked. "I want... to be able to look her in the eyes as I die, so she knows that I will be waiting for her in hell. You promised me."

"So ruthless," Killian said, a hint of admiration in his voice. "I will find her a spot of honor." Killian crossed the room with a predatory swagger, bowing before Guildmistress Greer. Wren's eyes were pulled from his retreating form with magnetic force when another entered the room across from her. Lucas.

She drank in the sight of him, from those flecks of gray in his dark hair, distinguishing his otherwise youthful appearance, to the sprig of rosemary in his buttonhole to the soles of his wingtip shoes. His mouth was set in a hard line, the muscles of his jaw working, his hands in fists at his side. He was flanked by two Black Guards. King's guards, loyal to a fault. A sad smile ghosted across her lips as they looked at each other from across the room, volumes passing between them, words unsaid, kisses unkissed. The hint of a future that hung only by one tender thread. She mourned him, mourned what they might have had, where this world had brought them. To the edge of the abyss.

But still, there was a chance. As Greer settled into a seat within a stone's throw from Wren, hope bloomed. One final chance.

The magister settled into his seat above her, cracking his gavel on the wooden podium. "Let's get started," he announced in a nasal voice.

Wren wiped her sweaty palms on her dress as the crowd quieted down, slipping her hand in her pocket to confirm, for the hundredth time, that the tiny packet was still there.

"We are here today to hear the confession of one Wren Confectioner, and to witness her execution before the gods. She has been accused of the crime of the unlawful killing of one Francis Kasper, Head and Guildmaster of the Confectioner's Guild, and the attempted killing of Aiyani Sable, grandmaster of the same guild. The Grand Inquisitor has heard her confession, which has been written out and will be read for our edification today. Is this so, Inquisitor?"

"It is." Killian inclined his head, leaning against the little box where Wren sat, a picture of ease. He must have been here a hundred times, ushering terrified criminals and victims alike to their grave. And no doubt he would be here many more times after she was gone.

"Proceed."

Killian handed her parchment confession to Wren, giving her an encouraging smile that didn't touch his eyes.

Wren took the parchment and unrolled it on the wooden bannister before her, her hands shaking. As she cleared her throat to begin to read, she saw a figure slip through the doors across from her and take a seat.

His arrogant smirk pasted across his pockmarked face, his red hair clashing against the rich gold brocade of his tunic. Willings. She narrowed her eyes. Here to see the results of his handiwork, no doubt.

"I, Wren Confectioner..." Her voice was small and thin in the vastness of the room, the vastness of the moment. She coughed, a dry rasp, a tickle deep down that could not be itched.

"Do hereby confess to the unlawful killing of Guildmaster Kasper." She coughed again, longer this time, trying to clear her throat. The crowd shifted in their seats, impatient, the sounds of murmurs and slipping of silk against wooden benches permeating the quiet room as they fidgeted.

She tried to continue. "The murder was premeditated and executed through the use of the Gemini poison..." She coughed again, her body shuddering, as if her lungs were rebelling against her, unable to say the lies.

"Will someone get the girl a glass of water?" Killian said, motioning to a servant with a flick of a hand. The servant disappeared.

Wren tried to continue. "The poison was administered through a..." More coughs. "Cupcake that I baked. The second half of the poison was administered..." She shuddered into another coughing fit.

The servant returned, red-faced, with a sloshing glass of water offered to Killian.

He handed it to Wren, who took it, drinking gratefully. As if this charade weren't bad enough.

She returned to reading with a shuddering hand. This was getting to the bad part, the part she didn't want to read, the part that named Chandler, a man who had seemed smart and savvy and kind. Such a rare package for a powerful man. Like Kasper had been. But she couldn't stop, and so as she continued reading, while her hands moved below the wood bannister of the box surrounding her, retrieving the packet of salt from her pocket, opening it and pouring it into the water with nimble fingers.

"The second half of the poison was administered through a whiskey that was gifted from Guildmaster Chandler, of the Distiller's Guild."

She looked up, surveying the room. Killian was nodding encouragingly, while Willings was leaning forward, a gleam in his eye. Greer was doing her best to look disinterested, but she sat as straight as a board, her body tense.

And Lucas. his face was pained, his body quivering, as if he might stand up at any moment and shout for the atrocity to stop.

"No," she said loudly, looking at the magister. Her voice rang out over the room. "This confession is a lie, forced from my lips at threat of death."

She saw Killian's eyes narrowing, his muscles tensed to spring, as if he could capture the words before they came from her mouth. The time to act was now.

"The truth is, the murderer is in this room. She is among us, and I can prove it."

Wren stood and scrambled over the side of the box, the glass of salt water in her hand.

"Stop her!" the magister cried, and the crowd parted before her, dashing out of her way.

Killian lunged for her, but he was too late.

Wren threw the glass of water in Greer's face, just as she had done with the Gemini poison not twenty-four hours before.

Killian grabbed her around the waist, bearing her to the ground. "Lucas is dead, girl, I swear it," he hissed in her ear. "I'll kill him myself."

Wren looked up from where she sprawled on the ground to see Greer brushing the water from her face. The damage was done. The salt water had revealed the undeniable truth. Greer's face was dyed blue with poison.

CHAPTER 41

"What is the meaning of this?" the magister bellowed. "Order! Restrain that girl!" He banged his gavel before him.

The guards who had accompanied them from the Block moved in, snapping irons on her wrists and hauling her to her feet.

Killian motioned to the door, and they began to march her towards it.

What? No! She couldn't be taken away to some secluded location where they could kill her in private!

"Inquisitor!" the magister called, his voice cracking like a whip. "You aren't going anywhere until this mess is sorted out."

Wren sagged in relief. Bless the fat little man.

Killian turned on the magister, a predatory smile on his face. "The girl is clearly mad. I apologize for wasting the court's time. She must have tried to throw some poison in the face of Guildmistress Greer to try to cast suspicion upon her. We know she is well-versed in such dangerous arts."

"No!" Wren cried. "Guildmistress Greer killed Kasper! And tried to poison Sable. She framed me. Her face is dyed blue because the poison reveals itself when exposed to salt water! The poison that killed Kasper was hidden in her room! I found it there!"

The room erupted into whispers and shocked gasps.

The magister banged his gavel again. "Silence!"

Greer's face was livid under the blue mottles on her flesh. The crowd parted around her with wary looks and shuffling feet. Greer's fists were clenched and she looked as if she would pounce on Wren at any moment.

"That is an outrageous accusation," the magister said. "Inquisitor, did you not receive a confession from this woman?"

"I did." Killian ground his teeth. "It was quite clear."

"He tortured me!" Wren said desperately, struggling against the guards. "I would have confessed to anything."

The magister banged his gavel again, seeming to soften at that. Killian's methods were well known throughout the kingdom. "No more outbursts from the prisoner!" He pointed at her. "Now, give us your account, Confectioner. Briefly."

Wren shook the two guards off her and stood proudly, her chin in the air. "I had never met Guildmaster Kasper until the day he died when I saw him go down before my very eyes. My cupcake was chosen as the vessel for the poison as I am of little consequence and would make a convenient scapegoat. The day after Kasper's death, Greer had been crying, and I noticed a blue stain on her fingertips. I thought nothing of it until I learned that one of the telltale signs of Gemini poison is that it stains the skin blue for a few days after exposure. It can be revealed through salt water. Guildmaster Pike of the Spicer's Guild told me this."

"Is this true, Guildmaster Pike?" the magister asked.

Pike rose slowly to his feet, his handsome face dark. Clearly, he was not pleased with her revealing so publicly one of the secrets of his tradecraft. She met his eyes, pleading with him, shooting silent apologies his way.

"The girl speaks the truth," he finally said, his voice ringing out clear and strong across the room. "Gemini is rare, and this feature of the poison is shared with no other toxin I am aware of. I presume the glass of water you threw contained salt?"

Wren nodded vigorously. "I kept a packet from my last meal and added it to the water."

"The stain on Guildmistress Greer's skin does come from the Gemini poison. That is my professional evaluation." With this, Pike sat down.

Wren continued hurriedly, not wanting to let anyone else cut in before her tale was told. "Guildmistress Greer was in charge of all food items that came in and out of the guild and easily could have slipped the other half of the poison into the whiskey as well. Then, my sponsor, Grandmistress Sable, and I discovered that Greer had been present at a party where my cupcakes had been served. The same ones that Kasper was killed with. She had access to the cupcakes, brought them back to the guild. The day after we discovered this link, Sable was poisoned herself, and the poisoned knife was planted in my room, on a tray from the kitchens. I think Sable confronted Greer, and Greer poisoned her for it, again framing me."

"Isn't the Guildmistress Kasper's twin sister?" The magister looked to Greer.

"I am," she said, her eyes flashing, still managing to hold herself with pride despite the blue staining her face.

"What would possess a woman to murder her own brother?"

"Do families never have such disagreements?" Wren asked. "Do they never become deadly? Greer disliked the direction Kasper was taking the Guild and disliked serving him. She saw her opportunity to raise her influence and took it." Wren wanted to say more, explain that Willings was in on it, and Killian, and the king. But she feared to say too much. She might be able to take down Greer if the woman's allies abandoned her. But she would never be able to take down Killian or the king. It would be suicide. She just needed to convince this man that Greer was to blame. It would be enough to save her, and Lucas, and Chandler.

"These are heavy accusations," the magister said. "What proof do you have?"

"She told me herself," Wren said. "When I found the Gemini in her chambers amongst her perfume. And Guildmistress Sable would be able to confirm it."

"It is her word against mine," Greer said, her voice strong. "And Guildmistress Sable is gravely ill and may never wake."

No thanks to you. Wren glared at the woman.

"Guildmistress, tell us your tale."

"The girl fled after Guildmistress Sable was poisoned, which an innocent party would not do. She then snuck back into the guild, attacked another guild member, made her way to my chambers, and planted the Gemini to frame me. When I found her there, she attacked me, throwing it in my face. I didn't understand why at the time, but now I see. It was to perpetrate this charade on this court, a last desperate attempt to escape the consequences of her murderous actions. To frame me. Kasper was my brother. We have lived and worked together for decades. I am a member of this community, known to many of you." Greer turned slowly around the room, meeting eyes and gazes. "I would ask you to believe me over the word of some nobody guild rat." At the last word, Greer narrowed her eyes at Wren, her eyes filled with venom far stronger than Gemini had ever been.

Wren looked desperately around the room, trying to gauge the tenor of the crowd. Their faces were hostile, unfriendly. To her. She had not convinced them. Not when Greer had so much more credibility in their eyes.

The magister looked thoughtfully between the two of them.

"What say you, Grand Inquisitor?" the magister asked.

"The... *methods* I subjected her to were not inhumane. She did not endure much before her confession. She had a guilty conscience."

Willings stood up in the back. "This would be the pronouncement of the king as well, were he here. I am confident."

"Very well," the magister said. "Wren Confectioner, you have made your confession, and you cannot recant here. It is my pronouncement that you are guilty of the crimes you are charged with, and you will be executed by lethal ingestion." The gavel came down, and Wren's blood seemed to freeze in her veins.

"Proceed with the execution."

Wren went limp as the two guards seized her by the arms and deposited her into her chair. Another came forward with a vial of crystal liquid, innocuous as water.

"No!"

She heard Lucas shout, surging forward from his seat.

"Get him out of here," Killian barked to two more guards, who intercepted Lucas before he made it onto the main floor.

The despair in Lucas's eyes as he was dragged from the room was no doubt mirrored in her own. *No!* she thought, tears leaking from the corner of her eyes. *This wasn't how it was supposed to go.* Everything had gone right. She had proven that Greer had the Gemini, that it had stained her. It should have been enough.

As a guard seized her chin, Wren came back to herself, fighting his grip, her eyes rolling wildly. She struggled and bucked in the chair, her blood roaring in her ears, reason leaving her. The other guard grabbed her by the hair, twisting her head back painfully.

And then Killian was before her, crouching, speaking words that she could barely comprehend through the primal terror that threaten to overwhelm her.

"Don't make me truss you up like a ham. It was a valiant effort, but it failed. You may choose how you leave this world. Kicking and screaming like a child, or with honor."

Some sense of his speech sunk in, and she stilled. The fingers in her hair, the bone-wrenching grip on her chin, loosened slightly. "But I'm innocent," she whispered. But even as she said the word, she knew it wasn't entirely true. She wasn't wholly innocent. She *had* killed her father.

He brushed a tear off her cheek with his rough thumb. "Here," he murmured, "there is no guilt or innocence. There are only the king's allies. Or enemies."

And with that cruel lesson, he stood.

Wren did not want to be trussed up like a ham. Better to die with a little dignity. So she sniffed, straightened, and nodded to Killian. He took the vial of liquid from the third guard and unstoppered it.

She sat trembling like a leaf in a gale and closed her eyes. Closed her eyes to the room, the crowd, this life.

"Open your mouth, Wren," came the inquisitor's sing-song words.

She complied.

"STOP!" a voice shouted from the back of the room as the door banged open. "Stop this at once!"

The entire room seemed to turn in unison to the new voice. Her eyes flew open and her teeth clacked closed.

No… it couldn't be. But… it was. Guildmaster Callidus.

"Guildmaster, the matter is closed," the magister said, his words laced with annoyance. "The girl has been sentenced, and the execution must be carried out."

"I have new evidence. By law, new evidence can be presented before the time of execution, and it must be fairly considered by the court," Callidus said, striding into the room. "Get away from her." He pointed to the guards, who seemed to shrink under the weight of Callidus's thin finger.

Killian slowly stood, re-stoppering the vial with animal grace.

"The girl has confessed." The magister huffed in annoyance.

"A forced confession," Callidus said. "Trust me, you will want to hear this evidence."

He held his hand towards the door, a showman revealing the grand finale. Through the door came Hale, bearing Sable in his arms. Sable's face was pale and gaunt, her fingers still tinged that unnatural gray, but her dark eyes were open and sharp. Hale looked at Wren with silent apology written across his face, his handsome face haggard with worry and exhaustion.

The sight of him filled her with relief, laced with an undercurrent of curling fear. She could still feel his hands around her throat, choking the life from her.

"Grandmaster Sable," Callidus said. "Can you point out for the magister your attempted murderer?"

Sable dramatically swooped a shaking finger across the room, past Wren, to land on Greer. "It was Guildmistress Greer. She nicked me with a poisoned knife and gloated that she would frame the girl. She gloated about poisoning her brother as well."

The room exploded into a din of chatter and shocked noises.

"It's a conspiracy!" Greer said. "The three of them seek to frame me."

"What reason would I have to shield the identity of my attempted poisoner?" Sable sneered at Greer.

"Perhaps the word of a journeyman has no value against the word of a guildmistress," Callidus said to the magister, "but surely two grandmasters have some say. And I tell you, this woman is guilty. It is as plain as the blue on her face."

The magister gave a long-suffering sigh, rubbing the bridge of his nose. "Guards, take Guildmistress Greer into custody. She will be questioned by the Grand Inquisitor."

Wren sat back, too stunned to understand all that was happening. Her mind struggled to process it. Would Willings and Killian abandon their support for Greer now that she had been exposed? Cut their losses?

But Greer made the decision for them. She drew a knife from her belt and bolted towards the door. "It's poisoned," she shrieked, clearing her path as people struggled to avoid the wild swipes of her blade.

It only took one guard to block her path with a powerful blow from the shaft of his spear. She doubled over, the wind knocked out of her, and another guard wrestled the knife from her fingers with a gloved hand.

They locked irons on her wrists as she struggled like a wild animal, her hair falling in disarray around her, the blue stain on her face lending her a bedeviled look.

"It was Willings!" she screamed as they hauled her away. "I was working for the king's steward! My task was official, sanctioned by the king himself. He paid me to do the job!" Greer shouted as the guards tried to haul her from the room.

Steward Willings's face turned as red as his hair, and he tried to slink through the crowd undetected.

The magister seemed to wilt at the chaos around the room, the roiling bodies and shouts.

"Steward Willings, where do you think you're going? You'll have to accompany the Grand Inquisitor until this is all sorted out. Take him into custody as well," the magister said. "Gently!"

The sounds of Greer's shrieked confessions trailed off as she disappeared out the door and down the hallway.

"There is the matter of my journeyman," Callidus said to the magister, who was wiping his brow with the sleeve of his black robe.

"Yes, yes," he said. "Quite an exciting day. Take her irons off, Grand Inquisitor, if you may. In light of Guildmistress Greer's confession and Grandmaster Sable's testimony, Miss Confectioner is cleared of all charges."

CHAPTER 42

Wren reveled in every sensation as the carriage jostled beneath her. The shaft of morning light flickering through the curtains, the sound of the horse's hooves on the cobblestones, the teeth-jarring bumps when carriage-wheels hit a pothole. Even Callidus's grimace as he gazed out the window, steadfastly refusing to meet her gaze. The mundane made miraculous. She should be dead right now. On her next journey to meet the Huntress, or the Piscator, or whatever god came to claim her to gloat at the mess they had made of her life. But here she was. She had been given a second chance.

She found herself grinning, giddy at her narrow escape from death's cold grip, at Callidus's refusal to show he cared, despite so clearly revealing that there was a heart beating within that frigid body.

"You saved me," she said, her smile so wide, her cheeks hurt.

"Yes, well," he said, still looking through the slit in the curtains. "Lennon refused to leave my office, yammering like a dog at a squirrel about them taking you, about Greer calling the guard to secret you out of the hall. Plus, there was the matter of the traitor in our own house who needed to be dealt with."

"You saved me," she said again, refusing to let him excuse his kindness away as self-interest. "You protected me. Thank you."

He finally turned to meet her gaze. "You are a member of my Guild," he said softly. "It is my duty to protect you."

Why had she not noticed how young he was? Perhaps only thirty. She had never truly seen him—looked past his unpleasantness to the man beneath. She wouldn't make that mistake again. There was something there. Something worthwhile.

"How did you know? That it wasn't me?"

"Olivia came to me and confessed that her grandaunt had asked her to take a tray of food up to your room, though you weren't at the Guildhall. She thought little of it, but when they found the knife that poisoned Sable on the tray… the pieces fell together. I don't like being played the fool. Not within my own Guildhall."

She nodded. "You have my gratitude. And my loyalty," she said.

He nodded curtly, his coif of black hair quivering. "You're Gifted. You're too valuable a resource to squander in light of what's coming."

"What's coming?" she asked.

"Our king has declared war on the guilds. Not open war, but war nonetheless."

"Murdering Kasper…" Wren said.

"And framing Chandler. Burning the black market yet again. This was the opening blow. The king has always been a tyrant, make no mistake. But he was a tyrant we could tolerate, content to rule over his kingdom while the guilds ruled theirs. But something has changed. I don't know if it's Aprica sniffing at our flank or the upcoming negotiation of the Accord, but the king is no longer content to let the guilds rule freely. He aims to consolidate all power and wealth in himself. We cannot allow it."

Wren bit back a sharp retort about the guilds only caring about threats to their own power. It wouldn't do to alienate him so soon after he'd rescued her. Callidus wasn't Kasper. "What will happen?" Wren asked.

"The guild heads have much to discuss. We will need to secure another form of government. A new king. Or perhaps not a king. By all accounts, the king's eldest son has the worst parts of his father, with more for good measure. Replacing one Imbris with another will not solve our predicament. The sun must set on the Imbris line."

She swallowed thickly, looking out into the bright sunshine. What would happen to Lucas if the Imbris line was overthrown? She had a sinking feeling that the excitement of the last few weeks was not over.

The carriage came to a stop and Callidus held the door while she stepped down. They walked up the five massive steps and through the Guildhall doors together.

"Guildmaster?" she asked. "What does your Gift do?"

A half-smile. "It's the luck of location. Of being in the right place at the right time." And with that, he nodded his head to her and strode up the stairs.

Wren was left standing in the antechamber, dumbfounded. What was she supposed to do now? She looked around the Guildhall, and then down at herself. A bath then. And a hot meal.

She flagged down a servant and asked for both in her chambers.

Wren walked up the stairs to the second floor slowly, still in a daze. When she turned the corner from the landing, she was nearly bowled into by a uniformed inspector and two Cedar Guardsmen. They were escorting... Olivia. Olivia's cherub cheeks were slick with tears.

"What's going on?" Wren asked the inspector, who held Olivia's arm in a firm grip. "Where are you taking her?"

"Just to the station to give her statement. She's not being arrested."

"I didn't know," Olivia said, a symphony of misery in her voice. "She asked me to bring a tray of food up to you... I didn't know the knife was poisoned! How could I have known? She was my grandaunt."

"It's all right," Wren said and found she meant it. It wouldn't have been an easy choice for Olivia to choose Wren over her last living relative, knowing what it would mean.

"Come on, miss. You'll be able to share everything at the station," the inspector said, not unkindly, beginning to move again and escorting Olivia down the stairs.

"I'm sorry for what she did... that I waited so long to tell the truth," Olivia turned, blonde curls caught in fresh tears. "I could have spared you..."

"What matters is that you did," Wren called. "I will always count you a friend."

The relief was palpable on Olivia's face, and a smile crept through the tears.

Wren watched until they were out the door and gone before continuing towards her room, a weight of sorrow descending on her. It seemed impossible that her and Olivia's friendship would ever be the same carefree thing it had once been. Too much had passed between them. How could Olivia truly forgive Wren for exposing her grandaunt's crimes? The woman would likely be executed. Wren looked at her mangled fingernails, still stinging and raw. Could she truly set aside all resentment at Olivia for the part she'd played, however unwitting, in framing Wren for Sable's poisoning? She didn't know. All she knew was that she was willing to try.

The door to Wren's room stood open on its hinges. She surveyed the inside in dismay. It looked like a hurricane had descended. Someone had ransacked it completely, perhaps the guild servants, perhaps the inspectors looking for more evidence of her guilt. Even the mattress had been ripped apart, the feathered insides decorating the room like soft white snowflakes.

Wren sighed and began picking things up, setting the books back on the shelf, her few dresses back on their hangers. A maid was already running the bathwater in the washroom. Another dropped a tray of hot butternut squash soup and rosemary focaccia bread on her table with a curtsy.

"We can come back with a broom for the feathers," the maid said.

"Tomorrow," Wren said. "Thank you." She wanted to be alone. She *needed* to be alone.

Wren ate greedily as the bathwater finished running, letting the mundaneness of the movements wash over her, keep her from processing, from truly thinking of all that had happened in the last few days.

And when the last bit of fluffy, salty bread had soaked up the last remnant of the nutty soup, she went to the bathing chamber and stripped off her clothes, dirty and bloody from the Block.

Wren sank into the piping hot water, scented with the fragrance of orange blossom, hissing as the wounds under her fingernails hit the heat. She sank under the water, submerging herself until her lungs cried out for air. And when she rose, she was crying in great shuddering gasps, her throat tight with knotted tension. As her tears mingled with the scented water, she let herself sob, let herself mourn. For the pain she had suffered, the exhaustion of holding it together when she'd wanted to do nothing but fall apart. For the fear and terror that had met her at the edge of the grave this morning, for the thought that she would die alone, mourned by no one, her passing marked by nothing. For the anger at a corrupt king who had doomed her without even knowing her name, who held women in cells and doomed families to backbreaking labor without a thought to their humanity.

But mostly, she cried with relief, and hope, and disbelief. Because she was here, alive, when by all accounts she should have been dead. And for the first time since childhood, she had something to live for. More than just another day of work, another day of going through the motions of life. She had people to live for. Unexpected allies who had forced their way into her life and saved her when she couldn't save herself. Chandler and Pike. Lennon and Olivia. And Callidus, the most unexpected of all. A family—Sable and Hale, who had come through for her at the last minute. As complicated and messy as any blood relations, but a family nonetheless. And maybe—love. Her thoughts of Lucas were like vignettes of the best parts of life, fresh coffee and rolled-up shirtsleeves and his body pressed to hers. She had felt more alive in her hours with Lucas than in so many years before. This thing—this beginning—terrified her and exhilarated her in turns. If there was a chance, any chance at all, she wasn't going to shy away. Not this time.

Wren slept through the afternoon and evening and didn't wake until the morning rays kissed her cheeks. She lay curled in the half of her bed that hadn't been ripped apart, reveling in the feeling of safety. No more running. No more ticking clock that counted the hours until her doom. No more murderer lurking in the shadows. She was a journeyman of the Confectioner's Guild, and this was her home.

It was Wren's stomach that forced her out of her lazy decadence, complaining bitterly for attention. She rose and dressed in a rose-gold frock overlaid in white-dotted tulle. It was the last of the dresses she and Olivia had bought her first day in the guild. She ran a brush through her hair and twisted half of it back from her face, pinning it at the crown of her head. When she emerged from the bathroom, a tray sat on her little table bearing a bowl of steel-cut oatmeal with berries and clotted cream, a cup of steaming coffee, and two letters.

The first was from Sable, short and to the point. *"Come see me when you wake,"* it said, signed "S."

The second was from Lucas. Her heart trilled in her chest. She had assumed he had been freed once her innocence had been proven, but it was good to see the proof.

Wren-

I recall promising that when this was all over, I would escort you to Salted Cream, the ice creamery worth killing over. As we both just escaped execution for murder, it seems the best time to undertake such a dangerous mission. I am a man of my word, after all. Meet me there at 2?

-Lucas

Wren couldn't keep the grin from her face. Lucas and ice cream. She could hardly think of a sweeter combination.

CHAPTER 43

Wren headed to the Maradis Hospital first. She stopped at a florist's shop and bought a bouquet of sugar-soft peonies for Sable. She buried her nose in them as she walked, making the rest of the way to the hospital.

Wren found Sable sitting up in bed, her ebony hair hanging like a curtain as she wrote. Around the bed was a sea of flowers—bouquets of every size, shape, and color—cheerful tulips, soft breathy lilacs, exquisite roses.

"Wren!" Sable said, looking up.

"I brought you these." Wren chuckled, looking down at her humble bouquet wrapped in brown paper. "Maybe you can use them to fertilize the rest of these behemoths."

Sable waved a hand dismissively. "Pike chose now of all times to decide he can't live without me. The man is embarrassing himself, truly. Give them here." She grabbed the flowers and inhaled deeply. "Perfect," she breathed, closing her eyes for a moment. "This place smells like sick people and death. I can't wait to get out of here."

"When can you return to the Guildhall?" Wren asked, sitting at the foot of the bed.

"The doctor says a few more days. The poison almost killed me. If you and Hale hadn't gotten the antidote…" She trailed off. "I blame myself, really. When I saw Greer's name on that list, I was sure it was a mistake. I've known her for years, she was so kind to me when I joined the guild… I wanted to give her a chance to explain, to provide an airtight alibi. All I did was give her a chance to kill me."

"You couldn't have known—"

"But I should have known! I got cocky."

"She hid her true nature well. For so long. She fooled everyone, didn't she?"

"But not you," Sable said, her eyes gleaming. "I'm proud of you. You figured it out without me, put the pieces together. And the bit with the salt water at the execution! Masterful!"

"It didn't work," Wren grumbled. "I would have been executed if you and Callidus and Hale hadn't come."

"Yes, well, the deck was stacked against you. That magister is in the king's pocket, as sure as Killian or Willings are."

"It's not right," Wren said darkly, her good mood turning.

"No, it's not. But," Sable said cheerfully, "Willings was arrested too. With all those witnesses, and Greer testifying against him, the king and the inquisitor will have to distance themselves from him, let him take the fall. I'll bet he'll meet the headsman's axe before the month is out."

Wren felt a grim satisfaction. It was fitting that he would suffer the fate he had tried to bring upon her.

"Greer's been sentenced already." Sable's voice was softer.

"Poor Olivia."

"Greer should have thought about that before she turned against us. The guild. She was a traitor to us all," Sable said.

Wren nodded, looking about the room because she couldn't bring herself to look at Sable without tears burning her eyes.

"Hale's not here," Sable said, changing the subject.

Wren raised an eyebrow.

"I sent him away. He told me what happened… what he did to you. And that kind of violence, from someone so close… it takes a woman time." Her voice was sad as she said the words, far away. As if she had felt the sting of intimate betrayal in her own past. "I told him he couldn't see you until you were ready. On your terms."

"Oh," Wren said, her voice small. "I appreciate that." She was torn in two when it came to Hale. Part of her was furious that he had turned on her, that he had believed her capable of harming Sable. And she was wary of the temper and power that had nearly choked the life from her— that had transformed her into her helpless younger self in the blink of an eye. But the other part understood that he had been defending Sable, the one person in the world he cared for more than himself.

"For what it's worth, he was out of his mind over you. As soon as I awoke and confirmed what had happened, he practically drove me back into the grave with his panic over you, over how we would get to you. He felt terrible for how he had treated you. Lucas got us a message that you were to be executed. When Hale heard that... he was the one who convinced Callidus to bring me to the courthouse, to intercede on your behalf. Neither of us would be here if not for him."

Wren nodded, swallowing thickly. To know what he had done for her, it did make a difference. "His betrayal hurt the most, I think. Not... what he did"—Wren rubbed her neck unconsciously—"but the fact that he didn't trust me. My word wasn't good enough. He believed that knife. Over me."

"Tell me something. Did you truly trust Hale? Or me? Before these last few days?"

Wren's face heated. "No."

"You and I are alike in so many ways. And Hale. It's hard for us to trust. To let people in. Look at me. I've known Hale for years, and I still didn't tell him that Greer was on that list. I wanted to handle it myself, to spare her any suspicion or doubt. It's no excuse, but... I guess I just want you to understand."

"That it was as hard for him to trust me as it was for me to trust him?"

Sable nodded. "After so many years of people letting you down, it's hard to believe there's anything else. But there is. With Hale. And me. And you. Just... keep an open mind. I hope you can forgive him in time."

Wren pondered this. Perhaps things between her and Hale would never be the same. But maybe... they could make a new beginning. She thought of his jests and easy laugh, his big arm slung around her shoulders. What would her life be at the Guildhall without Hale? With only distance and estrangement between them?

"Thanks for telling me," Wren finally said. "I… I want to learn to trust him again. I'll try."

"Give him that chance. If anyone deserves it, Hale does. And he will fight to earn that trust." Sable took her hand, squeezing it in a grip of surprising strength. "After all, we're family. We have to look out for each other."

Wren and Sable visited for an hour, comparing notes on the clues that had revealed Greer's treachery, the king's troubling moves, politics, and plans. At last, the doctor bustled Wren out of the room, insisting Sable needed to sleep, and it was time to meet Lucas, anyway.

She found him sitting on a bench outside the shop, looking across the street at the sparkling expanse of Lake Viri, the sun and breeze in his face. Her stomach flipped with excitement and nervousness when she saw him, his checked white shirt with sleeves rolled up and waistcoat unbuttoned, like that first day she had bumped into him on the street. He hopped to his feet at the sight of her, greeting her with a grin and an embrace that enveloped her in warmth and the rosemary-fresh scent of him. He buried his nose in the crook of her neck, not letting go, as if he didn't care who might see them. She ran her hands up his back, feeling the straight arrow of his spine. Finally, reluctantly, he released her, tucking a stray lock of hair behind her ear.

"Lucas," she said, a jangle of nerves and raw emotion. She needed to get this part out of the way first. "What you overheard at Charger's Estate…"

He shook his head. "I made a mistake that night. Not trusting you. I don't mean to make that mistake again. If there's something to tell, and you want to tell me someday… I'd be honored to hear it. And if we never speak of it again, that's fine too. I trust that whatever you did… if you did anything… was for a good reason."

A lump formed in her throat and she nodded. "That means more than you know," she managed.

Lucas clapped his hands. "Now, ready for this mind-blowing experience?"

Wren nodded up at him, her spirit soaring.

A bell tinkled as they passed through into the shop. She closed her eyes for a moment, savoring the smells of sugar and waffle cones filling her nostrils.

It was a patron behind them who disturbed the spell of the moment. "Are you in line?" the woman asked with a hint of annoyance.

Wren started, staring back at her as if she had appeared out of nowhere. "Go ahead. We need a minute."

Wren hadn't even looked at the expansive list of ice cream flavors on the chalkboard behind the counter. And she didn't really want to look at it, to look anywhere but at Lucas's smile. Lucas took her hand, covering it in the warmth of his own. "Someone once told me the strawberry rhubarb is to die for."

"I've heard that, too," Wren said, resuming her memorization of every crinkle by Lucas's eyes, the scrape on his knuckles, the smile he couldn't seem to put away. She wanted to take it all in.

"I never would have forgiven myself, you know," he said. "If you had died for me. I'm still mad about that."

"That I tried to keep you"—she pointed to him—"from dying for *me?*"

"Well, when you put it that way, it does seem unreasonable. But it's supposed to be my job to make gallant sacrifices for the good of... innocents."

"Your job as an inspector?" she asked.

"Right," he said.

"I couldn't let you die for me," she said softly. "Not if I could do something to stop it. And I'm sorry I put you in danger, with the bit with the salt water and Greer. It was too risky. But it was my only play."

"It was just risky enough," he said. "If you hadn't done it, you wouldn't be here. Maybe I wouldn't either. So thank you."

"Is that what this little meeting is for?" she asked. "A thank you?"

"Yes," he said, rubbing the back of his neck awkwardly.

"Okay," she said, disappointment welling within her.

"No," he said, shaking his head.

"No?"

"What can I get you?" The boy behind the counter interrupted whatever Lucas was about to say.

Wren glared at him. He was tall as a beanpole, with dirty blond hair and a storm of brown freckles across his face.

"Two cones with strawberry rhubarb," Lucas said. "Is that okay?"

Wren nodded.

The boy behind the counter folded his lanky frame over the tubs and began scooping.

"You were saying?"

"Where was I?"

"No, this wasn't a thank you," Wren reminded him.

"Well, yes and no," he said. "The truth is, the thought of losing you paralyzed me. It paralyzes me still. I don't want to be… without you." He looked up, his face flushed.

A smile crept onto her face. "Why?" she asked.

"Wow, you're enjoying this, aren't you?" he said, grinning back. "Going to make me spell it out, are you?"

"Four fifty," the boy said in a monotone, setting the cones in a little holder on the counter.

Wren looked daggers at him.

Lucas paid for the cones, handing one to Wren. They left the store and resumed their places on Lucas's bench.

"Continue," she said.

"You were shamelessly forcing me to bare my deepest emotions," Lucas said. "Is that where we left off?" He took a lick of his ice cream, and his eyes widened. "Wow, this is really good."

"Sounds right. I don't think it's such a bad thing, you know, after so many secrets and lies, to be completely honest with each other." Even as she said the words, her smile faltered. There was one truth she wasn't able to tell him, the truth of her Gift, and what it meant to the king. But she would find a way to work around that.

"I agree completely," he said. He grabbed her hand, his solid and warm in her own. "I am falling for you. You're lovely and talented and brave. Incredibly brave. I don't blame you if you'd want nothing to do with me because of what my family has done to you. My father. But if you're willing, I want to give this a try. Us."

The words warmed her even more than the sweetness of the sun on her cheeks. "I want that too. I want… you. But your father… he tried to have me executed. I can't imagine he'd approve."

"I'm a sixth son. My father has never wanted me for his political purposes; my brothers serve that role perfectly. He doesn't care what I do, and if he did, it wouldn't stop me from being with you."

Wren grimaced. "He's the king..."

"I don't care," he said. "I'm nothing to him. He doesn't even have to know. We'll be discreet. Stay out of his way. Give him nothing to concern himself with."

Wren thought of the conversation she'd had with Callidus in the carriage. Somehow, she didn't think that would be possible. A war was coming, and it was coming to their doorstep. But still, the image Lucas painted was so lovely, the earnestness and hope written across his face. They could be discreet. She was tired of playing it safe, of letting her fear paralyze her.

"If my father targets you again, I'll protect you with my life," Lucas said. "I swear it."

That's what I'm afraid of, Wren thought. But caution be damned. She had already made up her mind. Her luck had brought Lucas to her, and now he had woven his way into the tapestry of her life and heart. She wouldn't give that up without a fight.

And so she squeezed Lucas's hand and leaned forward, pressing her lips to his. His kiss tasted of strawberry rhubarb—the silk of ice cream still on his lips. Sensation flooded over her as the sugar-sweetness hit her taste buds. Her eyes flew open and she pulled back, her gaze flying to the shop window. To the bean-pole boy scooping ice cream. Because the effervescence on her tongue was the telltale tingle of someone's Gift. It was the taste of magic.

The End

Don't miss **The Confectioner's Coup**, *Book Two in The Confectioner Chronicles! Available Now*

Read the story of Hale Firena before he joined The Confectioner's Guild in **The Confectioner's Exile.** *Available Now*

FROM THE AUTHOR

Thank you so much for taking the time to read *The Confectioner's Guild!* I hope you've enjoyed reading about Wren's adventures as much as I enjoyed writing them!

Reader reviews are incredibly important to indie authors like me, and so it would mean the world to me if you took a few minutes to leave an honest review wherever you buy books online. It doesn't have to be much; a few words can make the difference in helping a future reader give the book a chance.

If you're interested in receiving updates, giveaways, and advanced copies of upcoming books, sign up for my mailing list at http://claireluana.com. As a thank you for signing up, you will receive a free ebook!

And don't miss *The Confectioner's Coup*, Book Two in the Confectioner Chronicles!
Read on for a Sneak Peek.

THE
CONFECTIONER'S
COUP
CLAIRE LUANA

"Ice cream's not technically a confection, you know," Wren said, her knees bouncing nervously.

"Oh?" Callidus murmured, without pulling his gaze from the ice cream shop. Salted Cream. The ice cream shop where she and Lucas had shared their first date, almost a month ago. The ice cream shop where she had discovered another Gifted confectioner—a boy who could stir magic into food as deftly as spun sugar.

"Master Oldrick always said a confection had to be rich in sugar *and* intricate in detail to qualify," Wren said. She was rambling. Normally, uneasiness turned her quiet. But Callidus's silence seemed to be bringing out the opposite in her.

"Oldrick is an idiot," Callidus said, finally turning and resting the full intensity of his bright blue gaze on her. Tall, windswept ebony hair crowned his narrow pale face. "Confection is a broad definition. Are truffles intricate in detail? No, they're brown lumps. A child could make them. Besides. We want ice cream to fall under our guild's purview."

"Because we want Thom," Wren said, turning back to the shop across the street from them, adjusting on the hard wooden bench.

"Precisely," Callidus replied. There were only four Gifted currently at their Guild, since the old Guildmaster Kasper was murdered. Guildmaster Callidus, sitting beside her, Grandmaster Sable, Wren, and Hale. Wren pushed away the rush of emotions that flooded her at the thought of her blonde god of a colleague. A fifth Gifted would be a valuable addition.

They had been sitting on the banks of sparkling Lake Viri for an hour, as the bright and heat of the September evening slowly leeched away. It was twilight now. They were here for the Gifted boy, whose name, they had discovered, was Thom Percival. They were here to invite him to join them. To share Alesia's most feared and treasured secret—that the cuisiniers and bakers and distillers of Maradis made food infused with magic. But first, Thom's master had to leave the blooming shop.

A cool breeze blew, ruffling Wren's auburn curls. She pulled her cardigan tighter around her narrow waist with a shiver. "What's he doing in there?" Wren complained. "They closed a half-hour ago."

"It's his shop. Tallying the day's sales? Taking inventory? Perhaps you've forgotten what it's like to work for a living. It seems every time I see you around the guild, you and Prince Imbris are wrapped around each other."

Wren's face heated. One time! One time he'd walked in on her and Lucas kissing in the library. Gods, would there be no end to her mortification? It'd probably be etched on her tombstone. *Here lies Wren Confectioner, whose Guildmaster once caught her kissing a boy.* Her thoughts rallied a comeback. "Well perhaps if you didn't cut me and Sable out of Accord negotiations, I'd have something to keep me busy."

Callidus's face darkened, his thick brows furrowing.

Wrong thing to say. Wren winced. The Accord spelled out the terms of the uneasy alliance between the Alesian king, Hadrian Imbris, and the guilds. The Accord was renegotiated every twenty-five years, and negotiations had started a week ago. Callidus's mood had been growing fouler by the day.

"If you would tell us what's going on," Wren said gently, "we could help—"

"You're as bad as Sable," Callidus snapped. "It's guildmaster business. End of story."

Wren stifled her grimace, lapsing back into silence. Grandmaster Sable, her sponsor and one of the most powerful confectioners in the guild, was even more frustrated than Wren about being shut out of what was going on. Wren was confident Sable would find a way to get Callidus to tell them—eventually.

The light inside the shop dimmed and died. "Looks as if they're finished for the night," Callidus said, uncoiling himself from the bench.

Wren stood too, twisting one way then the other until her back gave a satisfying pop. "Why tonight?" she asked. "We've had our eye on him for a few weeks."

"I had a feeling about tonight."

Wren said nothing, contemplating his words. Callidus's magic was one that brought him to the right place at the right time. She was firmly convinced that it had been his Gift that had brought him to the municipal courthouse a month ago just seconds before the Grand Inquisitor executed her for a crime she hadn't committed. It was part of why Callidus had started to grow on her over the past month, despite his unpleasant veneer. Had his Gift brought them here on this night for a reason?

Thom and his master, a small bearded man, emerged from the shop. The master said goodnight to Thom with a little salute and sauntered down the sidewalk, his whistle catching on the breeze. Thom locked up the shop door with a jingle of keys and turned off the two ornamental lanterns that flanked the entrance. Wren studied him in the low light, trying to take his measure. He was the type of tall that seemed to apologize to the world for towering over it by rounding his shoulders. She thought he would be handsome, when he filled out a bit. Right now, his lankiness was almost painful to look at.

Thom turned right and headed up the street, the opposite direction as his master.

"Now's our chance," Callidus said. "Come on."

Wren hurried to keep up with his long steps as Callidus crossed the street, angling to intercept Thom.

But someone beat them to it. As Thom passed an alleyway between two brick buildings, hands reached out and grabbed him, yanking him off the sidewalk. Thom let out a muffled exclamation before he disappeared into the gloom.

Wren stumbled a step, giving her head a little shake. It happened so fast, it could have been a trick of the light—or her imagination. But Thom was gone. "Callidus!" She grabbed his arm. "There's someone in the alley."

They broke into a run. "Cedar Guard!" Callidus bellowed. "Someone call the Cedar Guard!" Despite the cloak of darkness that had fallen, the night was warm, and the walking path around Lake Viri was a popular destination. There were people about. Hopefully someone would run for a guardsman.

They dashed into the mouth of the alley. Three shadows were scuffling against the far wall behind a tilting pile of packing crates.

"Unhand him!" Callidus shouted, running forward.

Wren lagged a step behind, caution tugging at her feet. She had never been good at running towards danger. But she couldn't let another guildmaster get himself killed right in front of her.

One of the two attackers turned to face them, advancing with menacing steps. The man wore all black, and a black mask covered his face and head. What kind of bandits were these? A gleaming knife appeared in one of his hands, and a shudder of fear tore through her.

"Callidus—" she said, but to her shock, Callidus reached under his suit jacket and pulled a little blade from a sheath strapped to his back.

"Stay back, Wren," he said, his voice calm. "Leave the boy," he said to the two men. "The Guard are on their way. You'll find easier prey elsewhere."

Wren looked around desperately for a weapon, wishing she had a blade herself. Not that she was much of a fighter. The teetering pile of packing crates was the only thing she could see that might be remotely helpful.

"We found him first," the man said, his voice low and velvety. In the dim light of the alley, Wren could see little, except his build. He was a tall man, muscular and trim. He looked like he would break Callidus across his knee.

The man dove for Callidus with a wicked slash of his blade. Callidus leaped back to miss the swipe, almost running into Wren. She scrambled out of the way, pressing herself against the rough brick of the wall, her heart hammering in her throat.

Callidus and the man in black exchanged a few more faints and attacks, Callidus miraculously managing to avoid being split open on the man's glinting blade. But Wren could see that it was only a matter of time. Where their attacker's movements were slow and controlled, Callidus's slashes were wild and panicked. The man was toying with him. It was only a matter of time before the tables turned. Deeper into the alley the other man had Thom forced to his knees and was binding his hands behind his back. In a moment, Thom would be dealt with and the other man would be free to join his friend in dispatching her and Callidus. She had to do something. But what?

Letting instinct move her, Wren let out her most blood curdling scream, the sound piercing and shrill. It distracted Callidus's attacker for a split second, and Callidus dove, scoring a cut on the man's bicep. He stumbled back with a curse. Wren grabbed onto the wooden slats of the packing crates and heaved with all her might, the rough wood digging splinters into her fingers. Her effort was enough to tilt the pile, and with a crash, the crates toppled onto the man fighting Callidus. One of the stray crates tumbled into Callidus, knocking him to the ground as well.

"Callidus," Wren cried, running towards him. Oh, gods. Was he all right? She had made it two steps when a rough hand tangled in her hair, yanking her backwards. She gasped at the razor-sharp pain, reeling as the other attacker slammed her against the brick wall, one hand in her hair, the other taking her by the chin and pinning her to the wall.

Her thoughts guttered like a candle as fear and pain overtook her. The man's hooded face loomed in her vision, only his green eyes visible, narrowed and angry. "You'll pay for that," he spat, and a whimper escaped her, the sound pathetic and mewling in her own ears.

Out of nowhere, Thom barreled into the man with a tackle, sending them all crashing to the hard cobblestones in a jumbled pile of limbs and bodies. Wren landed on top of the man with the hood, and scrambled to push off him. As he reached to grab her again, she did the only thing she could think of, kneeing him in the groin with all her strength. He let out a garbled scream of pain, curling in on himself. Wren saw, in that moment, that the man had only four fingers on his right hand—his middle finger was missing completely. The thought fled then as shouts sounded from up the street. Thank the Beekeeper. The Cedar Guard were coming. Wren stumbled to her feet, pulling Thom out from under the man, who was rising with a curse. The man who had faced off with Callidus had crawled out from under the crates, knuckles scraped and bloody.

The two masked men exchanged the briefest of looks before turning and running into the darkness.

"Are you all right?" Wren asked Thom, who was leaning precariously against the wall, his hands still tied behind his back.

He nodded. "You?"

She nodded back. "Callidus," she took a few shaky steps, but he was rising, four Cedar Guardsman silhouetted behind him.

"What's going on?" The first guard asked, the silver buttons on his uniform gleaming.

"They went that way," Callidus pointed. "Two men. Black hoods and masks covering their faces."

The guard motioned two of his men to follow, and the guards drew their swords, dashing into the night.

"Is everyone all right?" the guard asked.

Adrenaline still surged through Wren's body, setting her limbs buzzing like bees. "I think so."

Callidus nodded.

"I wouldn't mind being untied," Thom said.

The Cedar Guardsman—a Lieutenant named Bryson—sat them on the bench across from Salted Cream and questioned them for the better part of half an hour. Wren and Callidus explained how they had been walking along the lake when they had seen Thom yanked off the sidewalk, and had tried to help. No, they didn't know each other. Yes, it was lucky they were there. No, Thom didn't know why anyone would want to attack him. They hadn't even gone for his wallet.

The other guardsmen came back, and reported that they hadn't found a trace of the two men wearing black.

"Well," Bryson said, scratching the back of his neck. "We'll see what we can uncover. We work with the Grand Inspector's office on cases like this. Maybe they'll be able to get to the bottom of this."

"Thank you," Callidus said.

"I'll have a guard escort each of you home," Bryson announced. "Just to make sure you don't see any more excitement tonight."

Callidus pursed his lips, but nodded.

Wren knew why he was upset. They wouldn't have a chance to speak with Thom alone. If anything, the strangeness of the night made it all the more important that they share the secret of the Gifting with Thom, and invite him to join them at the Guildhall where they could protect him. A Gifted confectioner was a valuable commodity. If someone else knew what Thom was—it might explain the attack. Perhaps someone else wanted Thom's Gift for themselves. But who?

Wren racked her brain for a way to secure a meeting with Thom without raising the guards' suspicions. She touched her scalp gingerly where the man had grabbed her. It stung something fierce, but she didn't think he had pulled out any hair. "Join us for dinner tomorrow, Thom," Wren offered, looking sidelong at Callidus. *Come on Callidus, go with it,* she prayed. "As a thank you for saving me."

"I should be thanking you for saving me," Thom said, dipping his head so his unruly mop of blonde hair fell over his eyes.

"Please," Callidus said. "We'll send an invitation with all the details. We insist."

"Okay." Thom nodded, giving them a shy smile.

Wren offered a reassuring smile back, relieved. She ignored the flicker of guilt that accompanied her relief. Thom had no idea what he was getting himself into with the Confectioner's Guild. But, on the other hand, did the guild know what it was getting into with Thom? Because someone had just tried to kidnap him, and they had no idea whom, or why.

ABOUT THE AUTHOR

Claire Luana grew up reading everything she could get her hands on and writing every chance she could. Eventually, adulthood won out, and she turned her writing talents to more scholarly pursuits, going to work as a commercial litigation attorney. While continuing to practice law, Claire decided to return to her roots and try her hand once again at creative writing. She has written and published the Moonburner Cycle and the Confectioner Chronicles and is currently working on several new fantasy series. She lives in Seattle, Washington with her husband and two dogs. In her (little) remaining spare time, she loves to hike, travel, binge-watch CW shows, and of course, fall into a good book.

Connect with Claire Luana online at:
Website & Blog: www.claireluana.com
Facebook: www.facebook.com/claireluana
Twitter: www.twitter.com/clairedeluana
Goodreads:
www.goodreads.com/author/show/15207082.Claire_Luana
Amazon: www.amazon.com/Claire-Luana/e/B01F28F3W4
Instagram: www.instagram.com/claireluana

Check out these other reads by CLAIRE LUANA

The Moonburner Cycle

Moonburner, Book One

Sunburner, Book Two

Starburner, Book Three

Burning Fate, Prequel